UNRAVELED

- A NOVEL -

Gene Miller and Karen Kavner

Manse Street Stories

PUBLISHER'S NOTE

This book is a work of fiction. Names, characters, places, and incidents either are the product of the author's imagination or are used fictitiously, and any resemblance to actual persons, living or dead, is entirely coincidental. While some of the story's actual settings, events, locales and institutions are mentioned, the characters involved in them are imaginary.

Cover illustration and design by Michael Whitehead.

"All men should strive to learn before they die
what they are running from, and to, and why."
--James Thurber

"Baseball is ninety percent mental. The other half is physical."
--Yogi Berra

PART ONE

1

BILLY RUBIN was going insane.

Or, at least, that was what he had come to believe. How else could he explain the events of the past thirty-six hours, as he sat awash in crimson and gold alongside his USC teammates on a hastily erected platform on the outfield grass?

His mind was elsewhere, as the university's marching band high-stepped across Dedeaux Field, stirring the crowd to a fever pitch. A cluster of local dignitaries, including the mayor, and a sprinkling of celebrity alumni were poised to deliver words of pride to the enthusiastic supporters that packed the stands to honor their hometown heroes. Despite the iconic presence on the stage, all eyes remained focused on just one person, as the restless crowd began to chant his name.

But Billy didn't hear them. He barely heard the trumpet's trill. His head was bowed, his eyes unfocused, his thoughts inward and troubled. Why had he yet to remember anything about the final game of the College World Series?

Baseball had been the most important thing in Billy's life for the past four years. He'd worked too long and hard to get here. He'd earned every penny of his baseball scholarship and then some. And yet, if anyone knew what he was thinking at this moment, he was certain his 'Golden Boy' image would quickly turn from hero to psycho.

With the final notes of "All Hail" fading from their ears, Coach Patterson stepped up to the microphone. Patterson's eyes were moist with raw emotion as he thanked his team for giving him his greatest season ever. He could feel the mounting groundswell of anticipation bursting from the stands.

And so, short of inciting a riot, he decided to give them what they were clamoring for, "Faculty members, students, friends and fellow USC Trojan fans, a young man who truly needs no introduction. I give you...

team captain and this year's College World Series MVP..." The remainder of Patterson's words swallowed by the thunderous roar rising from the stands.

"What the fuck you waiting for Rubin?" Mackenzie sputtered, poking Billy in the ribs with his elbow. "Christ himself to show up with an engraved invitation?"

Billy looked up with a start, then turned to the lumbering leftfielder seated alongside him. "Huh?"

"Get your ass up there," Mackenzie snorted, jerking his head toward center stage where Coach Patterson stood waiting. Billy rose to his feet, threw back his shoulders and stepped forward.

"I... I don't really know what to say," he began. His words echoing through the giant speakers like the disembodied voice of God.

"Well that's a first," Patterson quipped, setting off a ripple of laughter and applause.

Don't just stand there like a jerk, said a little voice inside the young athlete's head. *You're Billy Rubin, damn it. You're a hero. Say something!*

He stepped forward and grasped the microphone firmly with both hands. "I'd... I'd like to thank my teammates," he began. "Coach Patterson, the University, and most of all... all of you! Go Trojans! Fight On!"

The fans leapt to their feet, thanking him back with an ear-splitting, standing ovation. Patterson waved his arms in a valiant attempt to quiet the crowd so Billy could continue.

The young athlete stared out into the endless sea of anonymous faces, longing to receive their unconditional love and praise, yearning to erase the years he struggled without it. Yet, somehow knowing it would never be enough to fill the numbing emptiness in his soul that so often left him feeling unbearably cold and alone. He tried to think of something clever or at least humbling to say next. But taking credit for this game weighed heavy on his heart. He felt like an imposter, a poser basking in the glory of game saving heroics he had no memory of.

He frowned, desperate to piece together the past thirty-six hours. The earliest memory of which, was having been rudely awakened at the Omaha Crown Plaza Hotel by a room service waiter pounding on his door. Billy remembered pulling the blanket up over his head hoping to

4

log a few extra hours of sleep before the big game. But the knocking persisted, forcing him to toss back the rumpled bed sheets and swing his long, unsteady legs onto the floor, clumsily making his way to the door, side-stepping half empty Chinese take-out cartons and a dozen or so drained Heinekens strewn across the carpet like a minefield. Although he insisted he hadn't ordered anything from room service, he wasn't about to stand there in his underwear and engage in a heated debate with some gap-toothed hotel employee.

As Billy pushed the service cart off to the side, his eyes took in the headline emblazoned across the front page of the morning paper propped against the black coffee carafe –

'USC WINS COLLEGE WORLD SERIES!'

That was the moment Billy's world began to come apart. His face drained of color; his hands began to tremble as he took in the words…

'TROJANS SQUEAK BY TEXAS, 1-0.'

The article credited his homer in the fourth and miraculous game-saving catch in the ninth with stuffing the Longhorns. Billy stopped reading and slowly lowered the paper. He pressed the inside corners of his eyes with his thumb and forefinger then covered his mouth with his hand and stared off into space.

He grabbed the newspaper again and turned the page. There in brilliant color was a photo of him leaping high in the air, his glove nearly a foot above the wall, the ball snagged in the webbing. The picture unnerved and confused him as he studied it, hoping somehow the image would morph into someone else defying gravity, and making that incredible catch.

But it was undeniably Billy; only he had no recollection of the catch, or the home run, or of even playing in the game.

Back on the field, Coach Patterson finally managed to restore a semblance of order among the wildly excited crowd. He nodded to Billy, prompting his star athlete to continue. Billy opened his mouth to speak, then pursed his lips and slowly shook his head. He hesitated, then unexpectedly returned to his seat beside his teammates. The crowd was baffled. They hungered for more, but none was offered.

As the formal celebration wound down, the fans were invited onto the field to meet and congratulate the players in person. Though his heart wasn't in it, Billy obligingly posed for pictures, shook hands and signed autographs 'til his fingers cramped. Despite the adoring crush of humanity, he began to experience the familiar, disquieting sense of isolation. He tried to shake off the feeling; to mask it beneath the disingenuous façade of 'super jock' he had come to enjoy and the fans had come to expect.

"How 'bout one more autograph, good looking?"

Billy turned in the direction of the tall, slender blonde in an oversized Trojan tee displaying his name and team number on her back. His face brightened, instantly imagining her naked. "Sorry Miss, you know how it is... so many fans... so little time... how 'bout if I just grab your butt instead?"

Julie Hatcher laughed as she threw her arms around his neck, covering his face with kisses. She tasted like chocolate, sweet and familiar. For a moment he felt calm and safe again.

"I didn't think you'd be here today. Didn't you have a job interview or something?" he asked, slipping his arm comfortably around her waist.

"I told them I had the flu and rescheduled. You know I wouldn't miss today for anything. But I have to ask... what was up with that humble, ten second speech?"

Billy tried to dismiss it. "I don't know. Maybe I just got nervous."

"Nervous? You?" she laughed. "Yeah. Right."

"Could we just forget about it, okay?" he said, his fingers squeezing at a sudden stabbing pain in the base of his neck.

She studied his face. "Sure, if you'll tell me what's going on? 'Cause you don't look like someone who just won the College World Series."

"Nothing's going on. I just need to get out of here, that's all."

On the way over to the parking structure, Julie reached inside her purse. "I made a copy of the final game for you. I must have watched it a hundred times. That catch was amazing. I mean... it was un-real!"

"Yeah, great," Billy muttered dismissively, as he dropped it inside his jacket pocket, knowing Julie had no idea just how 'unreal' that catch truly was to him as they took the elevator to level three and headed past the rows of cars sandwiched tightly together. When they didn't spot his car right off they circled back, slowing their gait, searching unsuccessfully for the sight of the familiar dented rear bumper. He scratched his head and thought though unlikely, he might have parked it on a different floor. After checking levels one and two, Billy's heart began to race. Where the hell was it! He was certain the parking stickers were clearly displayed on the rear window, so they couldn't have towed it. He seriously doubted anyone would have taken the trouble to hot-wire his piece of junk car, so it had to be here somewhere. But where?

"What about the roof?" Julie suggested. "We haven't checked up there yet."

Billy shook his head. "It's not on the roof," he insisted. He didn't even know you could park up there. Yet to Billy's surprise, when the elevator doors opened into the blazing sunlight, there it stood in all its battle-scarred glory. He stared in disbelief. He might as well have found it parked on the moon.

He walked with unsteady steps to the edge of the rooftop and peered at the unfamiliar treetops below, certain he had never been up here before. Nothing made sense. First the game, now the car. His fingers tightened around the steel guard railing. He felt like he was drifting through an alternate universe, but he was determined not to share what he was feeling with Julie. At least, not until he could figure out was happening to him.

The air was stale and stifling when they finally arrived at Billy's cramped and untidy sublet in the Valley. But he didn't stop to crack open the windows shuttered tight the whole time he was away in Omaha. All he wanted from the moment they stepped inside was a shot of vodka and to escape into the soft, sensuous curves of Julie's body. He didn't want to talk, or think about anything. He only wanted to dull his confusion and feel her nails dig into his back as he entered her. To hear the pleasured moans that rose from her lips as he explored her willing body. In a fevered attempt to drive the bedeviling memory lapse from his brain, he made love like he played baseball; focused and hard, with driving passion bordering on mania that left their bodies soaked and spent.

In the quiet pre-dawn hours, Billy lay awake staring at the saw tooth-shaped crack in the ceiling left by last year's series of minor tremblers. All he could think about was the game he couldn't remember. Julie's words echoed in his head. *'That catch was amazing. I mean... it was un-real.'*

He stole out of the bedroom as quietly as possible so as not to wake her, took a hard swallow from the open vodka bottle by the couch and slid Julie's copy of the game into the DVD player. If there was even the slightest chance it could jog his memory, it was worth a shot. He muted the sound and stared at the screen. Any time he made a fielding play or came up to bat, he pressed rewind, and watched it over and again. He replayed his fourth inning home run a dozen times with zero recollection. Then came the phenomenal catch that ended the game. His body, fully extended, his glove above the wall, the ball speared in his mitt. He pressed pause. He studied it, trying to will his brain into submission. But still – nothing.

Tears of frustration pooled in his eyes as he tossed the remote aside, collapsed onto the couch, and prayed for a miracle.

2

The following evening, traffic was light in the southbound lane going over Coldwater Canyon into Beverly Hills. Billy felt fortunate given it was rush hour, not to be mired in the snail trail of cars crawling back into the Valley. He checked his watch. He didn't want to be late for his appointment with Dr. Sharon Edwards. It took the better part of the day to track her down, but he had no choice. Losing an important chunk of his memory was driving him crazy, and she was the only shrink he could think of, short of going on-line or thumbing blindly through the yellow pages. Besides, she made a great impression on him when she came to the university to guest lecture in one of his psych classes last semester.

When he called her office, the receptionist flatly informed him, with a touch of heartless condescension far exceeding her level of importance, that an appointment was simply not possible. "We are booked solid for the next four months and we are not accepting new clients at this time."

Billy wasn't about to give up that easily. So he decided to mention how disappointed the head of the psychology department at USC, Professor Harley Groton would be to learn Dr. Edwards wasn't able to accommodate his favorite nephew.

The receptionist put him on hold for what seemed like hours, then came back on, obviously irritated at having her authority usurped. She proceeded to inform him in a voice that would form ice inside a sauna that Dr. Edwards would be happy to stay late and fit him in after her regularly scheduled appointments.

Billy was pulling into an empty parking space when he suddenly remembered he was supposed to meet Julie for dinner in twenty minutes. As he dialed her number, the perfect, plausible-sounding fabrication conveniently popped into his head. He knew she would never stand in the way of his baseball career, so he told her an important sports agent had phoned and said he was leaving town and the only time they could meet was tonight. He could hear the disappointment in her voice, but couldn't see her face as she hung up the phone, uncurled the rollers in her hair, unzipped the pretty blue dress she had just slipped into, and ripped open a fresh bag of Hershey Kisses. It wasn't the first time Billy canceled their plans at the last minute, nor would it likely be the last time she would find herself taking second place to baseball.

He took the steps up to Dr. Edwards' office on the top floor of a turn of the century, three-story walk-up on Little Santa Monica, flanked by a quaint French Bistro on one side, and a trendy, ridiculously over-priced cupcake shop on the other.

When he entered the tiny reception area, he was pleased to discover Dr. Edwards' surly assistant had already left for the day. He was alone with nothing but a variety of neatly stacked magazines from Reader's Digest to National Geographic, none of which held much interest for him. He picked up the 'new patient' form attached to a clipboard hanging by the door, filled it in as best he could and waited impatiently.

Promptly at seven, Dr. Edwards came through the door of her private office and extended her hand. She looked about forty, dressed in a lilac-colored business suit, the skirt a stylish, yet appropriately modest inch above the knee. She was far more attractive than he remembered. In fact, he thought Dr. Edwards looked much too pretty for someone who had just put in a full day's work. He couldn't help but wonder if she might have taken the time to freshen her makeup because he was coming in.

"Nice to see you again, Billy."

He stood up and followed her into her spacious, well-appointed office and took a seat on the soft, black leather couch across from her desk. He followed her with his eyes as she picked up a pad from a nearby table and sat across from him on a matching love seat.

"By the way, Billy… you might be interested to know I happened to speak with Professor Groton earlier today. I've known Harley Groton for years… did you know he was an only child? No siblings… and of course… no nephews. Guess my receptionist misunderstood what you told her."

"I had no choice," he responded, without the slightest trace of any wrong-doing on his part. "She said you were booked for months. I couldn't wait that long."

"Well," she said, with a knowing smile. "Now that you're here, why don't you tell me what was so urgent and how I might be able to help you?"

"Yesterday," he began. "I couldn't find my car."

"I see," Edwards remarked, unimpressed. "And did it eventually turn up?"

"Yes. But it wasn't where I know I left it. And before that... in Omaha, it might sound crazy, but I wound up paying for some room-service food I swear I never ordered. And that wasn't half as crazy as what happened next." Billy leaned forward, driving his fingers through his mane of thick black hair as he studied the swirling patterns in the Persian rug beneath his feet. "I was told... or should I say, I read in the paper that it was my home run and game winning catch that clinched The College World Series." His mouth went dry. He paused and swallowed hard. The ridged roof of his mouth felt like a charred English muffin as the tip of his tongue brushed up against it. He wanted to continue but his train of thought became jumbled by the sonorous ticking of a large cherry wood clock on the wall. His eyes fixated on the ornate second hand as it ticked off the minutes of his session like a metronome. It was already twelve past the hour, which meant he had only thirty-eight minutes left to find out what was happening to him.

Dr. Edwards waited patiently for him to continue. When he didn't, she prompted him gently. "Billy, what exactly did you mean by, you read in the paper that you won the game?"

Billy turned toward her, his eyes wide and searching. "It means... I have no recollection of playing in the final game. I can deal with forgetting where I parked my car or ordering room service -- but an entire game. Never! Nothing big like that has ever happened before and it really freaks me out."

Dr. Edwards leaned over and jotted something down in her notes, then looked up with a reassuring gaze. "I don't doubt that, Billy. Something like that can be very unsettling. But there might also be a relatively simple explanation. First, I need to ask if you had any alcohol or taken any drugs before, during, or after the game?"

Billy was fast losing patience. He came here for answers, not stupid questions. "Look. No offense, but you're on the wrong track. I'm not some falling down drunk. I'm an athlete." He slumped deeper into the couch. "Okay. Fine. I may have had a few beers in the hotel room after the game… I think."

"You think?"

"Like I said, I don't remember much. But Billy Rubin doesn't do drugs. I don't even like taking aspirin. Unless…" Billy paused, "…unless someone managed to slip me something when I wasn't looking."

"And why would someone do that?"

"'Cause you don't get to be as good as I am without making a few enemies along the way. People get jealous. That's just the way it is. But listen, Doc. I haven't slept in days. I got a lot going on right now. I need you to fix this fast."

The doctor stole a glance at her watch. "Unfortunately, that's not how psychology works. I'd like to run a couple of diagnostic tests the next time you come in… and perhaps after that…"

"I told you, this can't wait. My career is about to blow up. I got people to see. Places to go."

"As do I, Mister Rubin," as she rose from the love seat.

Billy jumped up, "Wait. Dr. Edwards, please. I'm sorry. I promise I'll make another appointment. I'll come back and take all the tests you want. But can you meet me halfway? Can you just tell me there's a shot I'm not going crazy?"

"All I can tell you Billy is that it's not uncommon for someone in a situation of profound stress, like playing in an important game, to experience brief bouts of temporary amnesia."

"I want to believe that, but it doesn't seem possible. How could I forget virtually everything I did in the game?"

"Have you ever heard the famous story about Elvis Presley early on in his career? He was in the middle of a show when he spotted one of his personal idols in the audience. Hours later, he was completely unable to recall anything that happened on stage from that point on. He couldn't remember the songs he sang or even leaving the stage following his performance. The next day he awoke to rave reviews. What you experienced could be nothing more than that. But we won't know for sure until I have a chance to administer and evaluate the tests."

As Billy headed for his car, his cell phone rang. The voice on the other end belonged to Scott Erikson, major league baseball's most powerful sports agent. Although Billy had been approached by numerous agents before, he'd continued to hold out, biding his time, waiting for the best-of-the-best, figuring a talent like his deserved nothing less.

When Erikson suggested getting together to chat over a few drinks, Billy couldn't help but smile. How ironically sweet was that – the little fib he told Julie turned out to be true after all.

3

The ball rocketed from the mouth of the black, cylindrical, steel machine at a torrid ninety-five miles an hour. Billy swung and connected with the sweet spot of the bat and drove a sharp liner into the net of the batting cage. His eyes narrowed, zeroing in on the target. His chiseled arms glistened in the midday sun, as he whacked another ball whizzing toward him like a bullet shot from a thirty-eight.

Billy was flying high. Scott Erikson had come to the meeting last night with a rock-solid game plan fully in place. He assured Billy the Kansas City Royals would take him first in next week's major league baseball amateur draft. Of and by itself, this was no big surprise. What was a surprise was that the agent had already pressured The Royals to commit to a three million dollar signing bonus. In typical Erikson style, he made the deal before he even signed the client, which greatly impressed Billy.

As Billy continued his onslaught, a raspy, guttural voice hollered out from behind. The thick Chicago accent knifed through the chain link fence. "Hey stud, take it easy. What'd that poor, defenseless, fucking ball ever do to you?"

There was no mistaking the wild, hot-peppered cadence. Billy didn't have to turn around to know who it belonged to. "Holy shit," he yelled, laughing. "Little Frankie Tortiricci! What rock did you crawl out from under?"

"Hey, Billy Boy... you can drop the 'little Frankie'... we're not in fuckin' Chi town anymore. It's just *Frank* now."

Frankie Tortiricci was the living embodiment of every hopeful wannabe drawn to the promise and glitter of Hollywood. Twenty-four hours after he got off the plane at LAX, he bought a car, a hot dog at Pinks, trendy sunglasses and a copy of the Hollywood Reporter. Though originally from the tough streets of Chicago, he soon came to embrace the L.A. mentality as his own. Over time Frankie managed to scrounge up a modest living as a Hollywood talent agent working for a mid-level agency way out in Chatsworth, far from the Hollywood glamour he coveted. Yet, if anyone asked him, how things were going, even in his darkest hour, he'd always say, 'couldn't be fucking better.'

"What's with the bird's nest, man?" Billy asked with a smirk, referring to the tacky-looking hairpiece perched atop Frankie's pointy little peanut head.

"This?" Frank snorted back easily. "I got tired of throwing away good money on prissy little West Hollywood stylists with big fucking egos and little fucking dicks. A hundred percent natural, straight off the head of some fucking Greek resistance fighter. And, lemme tell ya something, the babes cream over it. If I had a buck for every time I got laid because of this thing, it would'a paid for itself sixty times over."

'Little Frankie' the moniker bestowed in his youth was not merely reflective of his diminutive stature, but due to the fact Frankie had an older sibling named Frank as well.

The Tortiricci family dynamics in general left much to be desired. Their father, Frank Sr. and their mother, Sylvia, were barely speaking by the time their second son was born, making it nearly impossible to come to a collaborative decision on a name for their new, unplanned offspring. So, it just seemed easier to call him Little Frankie.

Despite the mutual parental hostility, Mr. and Mrs. Tortiricci continued to live under the same roof as a matter of financial necessity. Mrs. Tortiricci would send her sons down to the basement, to which Mr. Tortiricci had been banished, whenever she needed some cash or felt the need to remind him what a miserable, whoring, asshole-loser he was.

"Now, Little Frankie," she would say. "Go tell your fucked up father since he didn't leave me any grocery money this week, I'm not cooking for him anymore. He can eat dog food and drop dead!" Then, she would lean over and kiss the five-year old on the mouth, tell him what a good boy he was, and send him down the basement stairs to deliver her message word-for-word.

Growing up, Frankie did his best to fit in, but the neighborhood kids, including Billy, rarely gave him the time of day. Until one sticky summer afternoon, when the three, no-neck, greasy Loubet brothers came gunning for Billy, after word got out that Billy had been spotted making out with their kid sister Lucy in the alley behind the 'L.' The slow-witted, brawny Loubet brothers grabbed Billy, stuffed him into a steamer trunk, dragged him from the alley and up onto the train platform intending to send Billy off to God knows where on the very next train.

After shoving the trunk onto the last car of the 4:35 headed east, the Loubet brothers took off, righteously satisfied that they'd upheld their sister's honor. They were so busy laughing and slapping each other on the back, they failed to notice Little Frankie, out running an errand for his mother, seated in the rear of the train car. As soon as the doors closed and the train pulled away from the platform, Frankie could hear someone yelling to let them out of the trunk. At first Frankie tried to ignore it. The last thing he needed was for the Loubet brothers to find out he'd messed up their plan. But, when he realized it was Billy calling out for help, he decided to risk it and let him out.

Despite Frankie's unheralded act of kindness, not much changed between them as they were growing up. But Frankie figured a day would eventually come when Billy might be persuaded to return the favor.

"So what brings you by the batting cage?" Billy asked, pulling a couple of waters from his gym bag and offering one to Frankie. "As I remember, you couldn't hit a ball if it were tossed by a six-year-old girl."

"Cute, Billy Boy. I'll let that one slide, 'cause we got us a fuckin' history. When I spotted your junk heap parked by the cage, I decided to swing a u-ey." Frank took a mouthful of water and spit it back out on the ground. "I hate L.A. bottled water. Gimme good old Chicago tap anytime over this shit. By the way, did ya know I'm representing Kip Chapman?"

"Who's that?" Billy asked.

"You're kidding, right? Chapman's the starting right fielder for the Cubs 'Triple A' farm team. The guy's unbelievable. A fucking hitting machine. Another year or so, he'll be graduating to the Bigs."

"What happened to all those Hollywood A-list actors I heard you were representing?"

"Fuck 'em! Actors are psychos. You know that. I had to get away from them."

"Still working for the agency?"

"Nah. I'm on my own now. Strictly sports. I got a shit load of hot prospects lining up to sign with me."

No matter how much time had passed since Billy last saw him, Frankie was still the same old Frankie. Always embellishing the truth, always making a situation appear a thousand times better than it was.

"Hey Billy, I got a proposal for you. I happen to know you're without representation… and me and you… we got a history going all the way back to when we was kids. Don't forget who pulled your ass outta the steamer trunk before you ended up a hundred miles outta town." Billy looked up and wiped the sweat from his brow with the back of his sleeve. "Was that you, Frankie?"

"Damn fuckin' straight it was me."

Billy took a long swallow from the water bottle and shrugged his shoulders. "Sorry, Frankie. You're a day late. I met with Scott Erikson last night and I'm thinking of signing with him."

Frankie didn't expect to be side-lined quite so quickly. He took the blow and sprang into action. "Whoa! Tell me you're not thinking of putting your future in Scott Erikson's greedy mitts!"

"Why? What's the problem? Erikson handles the biggest stars in Major League Baseball."

"Exactly," Frankie countered. "Erikson's got too many big shots to give your career the attention it deserves. Look, I feel duty-bound to give it to you straight up. And I'm only telling you this because we got a history. I know a little something about this guy. The majors can be rough on a rookie. Don't expect someone like Erikson to be there to hold your hand. What you need is someone who's always gonna have your back. Someone like me. Look, I hate to be one of those guys that says, I told you so, but right now I'm telling you, I told you so. Again, I'm only telling you this because we got a fucking history."

Billy leaned back, his fingers entwined with the chain link fence as Frank spent the next thirty minutes pounding the hard sell like a country pastor digging for donations, convincing the faithful God only comes to those who contribute. But even Frank knew after the first five minutes his sales pitch was going nowhere. Even he would sign with Erikson given half the chance.

"Hey, I guess you gotta do what you gotta do," Frankie admitted, resignedly, "even if it's the biggest fuckin' mistake of your life."

Billy grabbed his bat and went back to murdering the pitching machine, as Frankie glumly walked back to his car. Both men knew exactly what the other was thinking. Because in the end, as Frankie said, they have a history.

4

A week later, Billy signed with Erikson and was indeed drafted number one by the Kansas City Royals. When he picked up his three million dollar signing bonus, he felt like a kid in a candy store. That very afternoon, he headed directly to Beverly Hills and picked out a brand new Caspian Blue metallic Mercedes Sport convertible. Then, looking for a more appropriate place to park it than the crumbling carport attached to his cramped, one bedroom apartment in the valley, drove out to Malibu and signed a lease on the first house on the beach he could find.

As he sat cross-legged on the living room floor of his old apartment, surrounded by packing boxes, Scott Erikson phoned. The agency was throwing a little party tomorrow evening at The Peninsula Hotel to introduce Billy to the people that mattered. The guest list consisted of the agency's top clients; local sports celebrities, the news media, and representatives from various sporting good companies. Billy's only responsibility was to show up on time.

The next morning, Billy dropped his best suit off at the cleaners, hopped into his brand new wheels and headed for the beach. He spent the afternoon basking in the sun as well as his newfound glory. He had a big night ahead, and rehearsed in his mind how he would charm the pants off everyone gathered to celebrate his success.

As he emerged from the choppy surf, his cell phone rang. It was Dr. Edwards' irritating assistant calling to schedule the battery of psychological tests Dr. Edwards had suggested. It had totally slipped Billy's mind, and seeing as he was on such a high right now, poking around his psyche seemed kind of pointless. The disturbing incident surrounding the College World Series no longer seemed particularly urgent, so he pressed seven and deleted her message.

He checked his watch. As much as he hated leaving the beach so soon, he needed to drive back to the valley and pick up his suit before they closed.

He settled his sand dappled loins into the soft leather bucket seat of his new Mercedes. Breathed in its rich, leather-scented smell and gunned the engine, relishing its raw unbridled power. Despite the fact he was on a schedule, he decided to opt for the scenic route along Mulholland. Then, he'd take his time getting dressed. Maybe even stop and get the car washed before he glided by to pick up Julie. Tonight, despite Erikson's admonition, he would most definitely not be the first to arrive at the gala planned in his honor. Instead, he'd let the momentum build. Let the crowd of big shots mark time waiting expectantly for his grand entrance.

He fiddled with the radio as he headed up into the hills, searching until he came upon a hard, bass-driven heavy metal tune. He cranked up the volume, his body vibrating in sync with the booming rhythms, while taking in the lush, sprawling scenery below. His fingers drummed against the steering column as he negotiated the winding curves and hairpin turns. With no one up ahead, he hit the gas with a heavy foot, coming up out of a turn onto a quarter mile stretch of flat open road. Unexpectedly, the car began to buck and lurch to the right. An adrenalin rush jolted through his body. He grabbed onto the steering wheel with both hands and fought the car back to the center of the lane.

He checked his rear view mirror, relieved his spirited hijinks hadn't been observed by one of L.A.'s finest hiding off-road behind a clump of bushes somewhere. What he didn't need right now was a speeding ticket to spoil his perfect day. Not that he couldn't afford one, thanks to the three million dollar signing bonus. It was just that he had far better plans for that money. His mind turned to happier thoughts, like private jets and World Series rings – one for each finger.

As he gazed down at his hands visualizing how that might look, the steering wheel suddenly slid through his grasp as if coated in axle grease. The auto jerked to the right again. Billy tightened his grip with everything he had, pulling hard to the left, fighting for control.

It felt as though the shiny brand new hunk of steel had a will of its own as it began to accelerate without Billy hitting the gas pedal, like something out of a 'B' horror movie. The music on the radio began to blare tauntingly from the rear speaker system, assaulting his ears as it leapt from station to station, from Mozart - to Hip Hop - to screaming ads for pre-owned cars in Spanish - to the rich dulcet voice of Elvis singing

'Amazing Grace.'

Billy hit the brakes but the car wouldn't slow. The gas pedal froze, locked in position. He tried to kick it up with his foot, to no avail.

His eyes opened wide, afraid if he so much as breathed or blinked he would lose traction on the curves. The speedometer climbed to FIFTY. He tried to break again, but the harder he pushed down, the faster it seemed to go. There was no time to react -- just act.

The needle hit SIXTY. Billy felt like someone had strapped him into a ride at Disneyland. He thought of bailing, but the door locks jammed. He was trapped.

At SEVENTY-FIVE, his fingers grew numb. Someone on the radio was blabbering on about cremation at Forest Lawn. Billy clenched the steering wheel with a vise-like grip, as the tires squealed and jostled along this particular pot-holed stretch of road.

He thought of Julie. And how much he wanted to see her. His heart was racing. His mind became a tangled blur. He tried to visualize her face. In that instant he thought he felt the car slowing down slightly. He took a breath. And then another, slower and deeper than before, as the speedometer gradually inched its way back down toward sixty, then fifty… then forty…

He swallowed hard. His head fell forward in relief. Sweat dripped from his forehead onto his chest. Another breath, long and cleansing.

Then, as the haunting crescendo of Amazing Grace rang out from the speakers, the gas pedal hit the floor.

The Mercedes, on a particularly brutal S-turn zoomed out of control and headed straight for oblivion.

The road beneath Billy was gone – the entire valley opened up as the Benz sailed off the edge towards Encino. With Amazing Grace ringing in his ears – Billy's world turned horribly black.

He found himself lifted upward by a gentle, unknown force. Weightless as an autumn leaf. Spiraling into nothingness. He hovered high above, watching as the blue Mercedes somersaulted down the jagged canyon, ultimately landing upside-down against a tree in a thick, muddy ravine below Mulholland. He could see his body locked behind the wheel, both airbags deployed. His legs trapped beneath the collapsed dashboard and steering column. He could hear sirens screaming somewhere off in the distance growing gradually louder. He watched in quiet awe as the brave rescue workers were carefully lowered into the abyss and used the 'Jaws of Life' to pry his limp torso from the wreckage. He felt totally detached from the activities below – as if watching them unfold on a movie screen. Yet, despite the disturbing images, all Billy could feel was an undeniable sense of euphoria.

And then, "Holy shit," he shrieked. "Hey! Some asshole totaled my new Mercedes!"

He began spiraling downward at a frantic pace, until the surreal moment when he found himself flat on his back, his arms immobile, his legs useless.

His listless body was strapped to a gurney, hoisted out of the canyon and into a waiting ambulance. The blaring sirens echoed through the once peaceful hillside as they made their way back down the winding canyon road. But, Billy heard little to nothing as he drifted in and out of consciousness. His body covered in blood, his face battered and bruised, his left femoral bone protruded through the skin of his leg, his right knee crushed like mashed mango, his foot dangling precariously from his ankle by a few undamaged tendons.

He was rushed to Cedars Sinai, where Julie kept a silent vigil in the hospital chapel. She lit candles and prayed, while a team of elite surgeons worked on Billy for a grueling sixteen hours.

When a grim-faced nurse entered the chapel, Julie fell to her knees by the altar, afraid she had come to tell her something awful. She couldn't bear to think of a life without Billy. "Please God. I'll do anything – just please let Billy be all right," she begged, before finding the courage to face the nurse.

"Mister Rubin is out of surgery."

Julie searched the nurse's unreadable expression. "Is he… is Billy going to be okay?"

"We won't know how successful the surgery was for a few more weeks," the nurse continued, "but he's young and strong and the doctors are hopeful."

Her heart thumped like a shell-shocked kettledrum, as the nurse spoke of the severe damage caused by the crash. And of how the surgeons were able to reconstruct the bones in Billy's leg and shattered right knee by grafting bone fragments from other parts of his body; and why they needed to insert a titanium rod from his hip down to his knee.

Julie's head was spinning. She was grateful Billy was alive, but feared he might not be as grateful as she if he was left unable to play baseball.

The days immediately following surgery were spent in a drug facilitated, semi-conscious stupor. Since Billy had no immediate family, the task of handling hospital paperwork and consulting with doctors and specialists fell to Julie, who never once left Billy's side. She slept when she could, curled up in a chair by the window.

As Billy's waking hours increased, the only thing separating him from gut-wrenching agony was the constant morphine drip positioned like a stoic sentry by the side of his bed. Despite the pain, Billy demanded the doctors wean him off the drip. He didn't like the way it made him feel, clouding his thoughts and slurring his speech. He didn't like feeling anything less than Billy Rubin.

For the next three and a half weeks, the athlete's once agile limbs were encased in rigid braces, held together with wires and pins in a private room at Cedars Sinai's orthopedic wing.

At first, there were the dozens of get well cards arriving daily and a constant stream of well-wishers bearing bright colored flowers, and every manner of sugary confection and balloon bouquet until they over-flowed his room and spilled out into the nearby nurses' station. Scott Erikson stopped by briefly to assure him both he and the Kansas City Royals remained one hundred percent behind him and were certain he would be ready to play by the start of next season, still a full nine months away. Even Frankie, cursed with a longstanding fear of hospitals had enough class to send an elaborate fruit basket, despite the fact Billy hadn't had the good sense to sign with him.

Billy gathered strength from the many cards and emails from his fans who never once allowed for the possibility that he might enjoy anything less than a full and complete recovery. But as the days wore on, the mainstream media began voicing a markedly different take on the young athlete's prognosis; speculating that the Royals' once phenomenal young prospect may never play a day in the majors.

Across the internet, countless blogs and sport sites, including ESPN quickly followed suit, all but writing him off. Despite Julie's efforts to keep Billy insulated from the media's jaundiced speculation, one afternoon while she was in the hall conferring with the nurses, an unseasoned orderly inadvertently dropped off a newspaper along with his afternoon bowl of Jell-O. Billy went into a tailspin. When a nurse raced in to try and settle him down, he became belligerent, violently upturning anything within his reach. The once charming, cocky, Billy Rubin was apparently nowhere to be seen, replaced by a monster lashing out at everyone, including Julie. He was relentless, threatening monumental lawsuits and conjuring up Draconian tortures to punish each and every one he held responsible for putting him behind the wheel of the demonic car that nearly drove him to his death.

When his rage subsided, depression set in with a vengeance. He spent hours lying awake in his hospital bed, staring through the viewless window without uttering a word, rarely expressing interest in anyone or anything around him. As the days wore on, he continued to withdraw further into himself. Julie's concern for his state of mind increased. It began to frighten her. It was so unlike the Billy she knew.

The once constant stream of visitors began to lessen, eventually stopping altogether. Although a few old college teammates and acquaintances continued to express interest in coming by, Billy wanted no part of it. Eventually Julie adjusted to the silence, spending her time devouring articles on the latest rehab techniques she could find on her laptop or in the hospital library. Despite Billy's lousy attitude and occasional raging outbursts, she managed to get through most of the days. But the nights haunted her. Too many painful, sleepless four a.m.'s spent watching Billy, drowning in anger, self-pity, and broken dreams.

One day, he called her to his bedside and reached for her hand. "I'm done, Julie," he said, his eyes welling with unshed tears.

She took his hand and squeezed it firmly. "Nothing is done," she whispered. "Let me help."

"What's wrong with you?!" he suddenly exploded, jerking his hand away. "You can't help me. Nobody can," he screamed, as he sent an empty bedpan flying across the room.

"Fine. If you want to scream or fling bed pans, go right ahead. But, if I were you, I'd save my strength for getting out of here."

Billy turned his face away, his mood growing darker. "I think," he said slowly, "it might be better if you didn't spend so much time here. I'm sure you've got better things to do than sit in a chair and watch me lie in bed all day."

"Then, get out of bed. Please," she urged. "Make some kind of effort. I don't understand why you won't even try using your walker or working with the physical therapist."

"I thought I just asked you to leave." But Julie didn't budge. "God damn it!" he screamed. "What part of get out don't you understand?"

She was shaking, moments from spilling the tears she'd been struggling to hold back. "Fine. I'll leave you alone for a while if that's what you want. But I'm coming back. I'm not giving up. And I'm not going to let you give up either."

Billy laid his head back against the pillows. He was tired. Tired of the constant pain, tired of Julie's Pollyanna encouragement and the pitiful glances from the damn nurses. He just wanted to shut his eyes and let reality fade away for a while. He knew he could always ask for a sleeping pill, or sedative, but that would mean relinquishing whatever shred of personal control he still managed to laud over the enemy, which at this point was everyone out there who could walk on their own.

Then, a rather weak little voice piped up from the hallway. "Hey mister. Are you somebody famous?"

Billy opened his eyes and turned his head to see who was asking, nearly missing the frail, young boy leaning unsteadily in the doorway.

"I said, 'are you someone famous?" The boy repeated.

"Me? No. I used to be, but not anymore. I'm nobody," Billy responded.

With the aid of a metal walker, nearly as tall as him, the boy managed a few awkward steps into Billy's room and looked around.

"I don't believe you," said the boy, standing his ground.

"Do I look like I care?" Billy replied.

"You sure got a lot of flowers and presents for a nobody. And, just so you know, smart ass, my room's right across the hall, so I saw the reporters and all the people who came to see you." As the young patient managed with a great degree of difficulty to reposition his clunky walker back in the direction of the doorway, he shook his head in disgust. "I don't get it. Why would you want to lie to a sick little kid?"

"Who says I'm lying?" Billy answered back.

"Cut the crap, mister. I might be dying but I'm not stupid. But… if that's the way you want it. Cool. I got better things to do."

Billy couldn't help but smile at the young boy's cocky comeback. "Oh yeah. Like what? You going mountain climbing?" Billy waited, anticipating a barbed reply that didn't come. "Hey! Hold up a minute. Sorry. That was a cheap shot," he called out. "So, what's your name?"

"I asked you first," said the boy, pivoting slightly on his good leg, fixing Billy with a defiant stare.

"William Joseph Rubin… but apparently," he said with a wink, "some people prefer to call me *smart ass.*"

The boy grinned slightly and took a careful step back inside the room. "My name is Gene, with a 'G' not a 'J.'"

"Gene, huh? Short for Eugene?" Billy asked.

"Nope," the boy replied. "Just Gene. Not short for anything. It could've been worse. They almost named me Jodi. I think my mom was hoping for a girl. So what did you do to get all this attention?"

"I played baseball."

"Oh. I don't really follow baseball."

"You sure you're not a girl?" Billy quipped.

Gene pursed his lips into a, *oh that's reeeeel funny* kind of smirk. Billy propped himself up against his pillows and motioned for the boy to pull up a chair beside him.

"That's okay. The doctors said it's better for my leg if I stand or walk around on it a little more."

"What happened to your leg?" Billy asked.

"I broke it in three places playing soccer," Gene said rather proudly.

"Ouch!" Billy offered sympathetically. "Triple play, huh? That's rough. But, I've got good news for you, Gene with a G, not a J -- you might miss a couple months on the soccer field but not too many kids die from a broken leg. So what was that baloney you were spouting about dying when you were heading out the door?"

The young boy paused for a moment before responding rather matter-of-factly. "Oh it wasn't baloney. I have Leukemia... and... from the way Mom's always crying after she talks with the doctors... I figure there's a pretty good chance I could die."

Billy remained silent as he looked at the brave young boy who stood before him, deeply humbled by the child's simple assessment of his situation. There was no clever comeback to Leukemia.

"Hey. It's okay. It's not for sure I'm gonna croak. There's always a chance they'll find a cure," Gene said, upbeat. "Which is why, in the meantime, it makes sense that I do what the doctors tell me to do. Like exercising my leg. I could stay in bed and eat ice cream all day and feel sorry for myself but what good would that do? I'd have to be pretty stupid not to try everything I can to help myself get back on the soccer team. Don't you think?"

"These doctors are plenty smart," Billy quickly added in agreement. "They'll find a way to turn things around. You keep doing what they say and you'll be back kicking ass in no time. Believe it."

"I do. But, right now I'm getting kind of tired so I think I better get back to my room," Gene said, as he made his way over to the doorway. "See you around, famous baseball guy."

"See you around, Soccer Man." Billy watched as the courageous young boy disappeared from view, wishing he had the power to miraculously cure him. Or at least, the ability to somehow bottle the kid's boundless positive spirit.

Billy tossed back the Calico cotton covers and stared at his bruised and useless lower limbs with disgust and determination. Reaching for the guardrails surrounding his bed, he pulled himself to an upright position. He slowly and carefully moved his stiff, unyielding legs till they dangled unresponsively off the side of his hospital bed. He extended his arm, caught hold of the metal walker resting by the foot of his bed and drew it closer. He took a breath, grit his teeth, and in one wondrous moment summoned the strength to hoist his body to a standing position.

6

On a warm Thursday afternoon in August, to avoid any prying reporters, Billy ducked out through a side door of Cedars Sinai hobbling on a pair of shiny, new crutches. While he waited for Julie to bring the car around, he smiled up at the sun. Despite the continuing throbbing pain and stiffness in his lower back and legs that caused him to walk with a guarded gait, the shimmering rays filtering through the smog layered Westside made him feel alive again. After being cooped up for so long, he couldn't wait to get his life back on track.

He rolled down the window and breathed in the sweet salt air as they turned onto Pacific Coast Highway. When they pulled up to the entrance of the beach house, Billy spotted a squat little man in a business suit waiting by the front door. Billy's eyes squinted against the sun trying to decide if he was friend or foe. The last thing he needed right now was a tabloid photo of him limping to his door splattered across some lousy rag. This was totally unacceptable. Where the hell was Scott Erickson, he fumed, as he reached for his cell phone. This was definitely not the homecoming he envisioned.

"Mr. Rubin?" The man blurted, as Billy turned his face away and rolled up his window. "I hope you don't mind that I showed up unannounced," he continued, volunteering his business card. "Alonzo Villarosa, State Farm Insurance. I know you were anxious to get the results of our report on the crash." Billy narrowed his eyes and studied the claim agent's calling card pressed up against his window. "I was planning on bringing it to you in the hospital but when I learned you were being released today, I thought I should hurry it right over here to your home."

When Billy didn't react, Julie spoke up, explaining that this might not be the best time to bother Billy with reports and paperwork. He needed his rest and perhaps Mr. Villarosa should come back at another time.

"No. It's okay, Julie." Billy interrupted. "I'm not an invalid. The sooner we find out who's to blame for what happened the better."

Once inside, Villarosa opened his briefcase and confidently placed the official looking, vinyl bound report on the dining room table in front of Billy. "As you know," he began, matter-of-factly, "the L.A.P.D. traffic division found no evidence of oil build-up or any sign of traction slippage along the stretch of road you were driving on. At least nothing serious enough to cause the car to hydroplane as it did. So we had our own automotive experts," he added proudly, tapping his forefinger atop the report for emphasis," go over every inch of the Mercedes looking for mechanical malfunctions but their findings showed the brakes, steering column and the entire hydraulic system were in perfect running order at the time of the accident."

Billy leaned forward and flipped open to the first page of the document, "And?"

Villarosa tread carefully. "And so, given the lack of skid marks, the company's only logical conclusion is that the unfortunate incident was due to driver error."

Villarosa's words hung in the air like the Goodyear Blimp. Billy couldn't believe this moron was sitting in his dining room calmly stating the nightmare Billy barely survived was somehow his own fault.

Billy felt his chest constricting. Somebody had to be fudging the facts, paying off mechanics in an attempt to make him look guilty. "So, let me get this straight -- the insurance company thinks I hung out at the beach, caught a few rays, got in my new Mercedes and then ran it off a cliff on what was supposed to be one of the greatest days of my life?"

"Absolutely not," Villarosa responded, with utmost sincerity. "It was a terrible accident. Accidents happen. You hadn't owned the car very long. You couldn't be expected to be all that familiar with how it handled. You could've been distracted by a tune on the radio..."

"Bullshit!" Billy seethed.

Villarosa didn't flinch, "... or maybe you were on the phone... or texting... things happen. That's why people have insurance," he tried to explain with a placating smile. But Villarosa's smile went unnoticed as Billy turned away attempting to keep a fragile lid on the rage building inside him. He peered out the window at a duo of pink tinged clouds hanging motionless in the otherwise cloudless sky like a freeze frame of

Sumo warriors engaged in mortal combat when a sudden piercing pain blasted through his shattered right knee.

"I don't know what you and your fucking bullshit insurance company are trying to do. But you're not gonna get away with it!"

Julie reached for his arm. "Billy please, calm down. You shouldn't let yourself get so worked up. It's not good for you. Mr. Villarosa is only trying to…"

"Don't tell me what this asshole flunky is trying to do," he sputtered, yanking his arm from her grasp. "Someone is out to get me! Don't you see that!" he screamed, his face flushed fuchsia with mounting fury as he attempted to stand and found that he couldn't.

"Why would anyone be out to get you? That's crazy, Billy," she pleaded.

"Crazy? You weren't the one forced over a cliff at ninety miles an hour. You weren't the one laying in a goddamned hospital bed for months. I know what I'm talking about. Someone is deliberately trying to fuck up my baseball career. And this dirtbag," jabbing an angry finger at Villarosa, "is trying to cover it up!"

Julie was embarrassed by Billy's outburst. "I'm so sorry about this, Mr. Villarosa," she offered, as the claim adjuster squirmed uncomfortably in his chair.

"Don't you dare apologize for me," Billy screamed, smashing his fist so hard against the table, Villarosa's accident report bounced an inch into the air. "Not to him. Not to anyone. I expect you to back me up. Don't ever do that again."

"Billy. Stop. Please. I just think if you can calm down we can discuss this rationally and…"

"I don't want to be rational. I don't want to discuss anything." Billy railed out of control. "If this blood-sucking, pencil-pushing, bastard can't tell me who is out to get me… he can get the hell out of my house!"

Julie's eyes begged Billy to stop, but he was far beyond her reach. Villarosa summoned whatever professional composure he could muster, gathered his papers, rose from the table and turned to Julie. "I think it's best that I leave."

Julie sat alone at the dining room table she had set for two, making lazy swirls from the melting drips of chocolate that formed on the platter beneath the painstakingly perfect dessert she had labored over for hours. She had worked hard to make Billy's first dinner home from the hospital special, putting aside her hurt feelings by his callous words and wild accusations earlier. She glanced at her watch. Billy had taken refuge inside his bedroom. It was obvious he had no intention of joining her for dinner. But she couldn't just leave him to fend for himself right now. He hadn't even eaten since morning. She decided to swallow her pride and make up a tray as a peace offering.

"Oh man, that smells great, baby," Billy said, with surprisingly cheerful animation as he turned down the volume on the TV and sat up in bed, inching his tender legs carefully over to the side. "I'm starving. Guess I got so caught up in the game I forgot how late it was getting. C'mon," he said, pushing back the covers, making room for her to sit beside him. "You know, the only thing I love more than watching the Cubs is your Chicken Marsala."

Julie didn't quite know what to make of the positive shift in his attitude, or what inexplicably happened to bring about the change. But she wasn't about to question it. As they watched the game together, there wasn't a mention of the ugly episode with Villarosa. No talk of revenge or treacherous plots. Instead, as Billy pulled her closer, "I've been thinking. I don't care what those overly cautious docs at Cedars said about taking things slow. I can't wait to put on a uniform and get out there again. I'm gonna have Erikson call the Royals in the morning and have them set up my rehab team immediately." Julie smiled up at him. She loved seeing the old Billy again, excited and happy.

As Julie drifted off to sleep curled tightly in his arms, Billy wasn't thinking of the grueling months of rehab ahead, or even of the amazing three-quarter moon peering down through the huge wall of glass. In his mind he was back on the baseball diamond, smashing homers, fielding fly balls, playing in the major leagues for the Kansas City Royals.

Six days a week a town car picked him up and took him to a private, state-of-the-art training facility in Santa Monica. To protect their investment, Royals upper management flew in both, Ty Hill, the team's strength and conditioning coordinator and Jeff Blum, the team's physical therapist to personally oversee Billy's rehab strategy.

The workouts began slowly at first. A little too slowly in Billy's 'bring it on' estimation. The trainers and their assistants began with basic stretching techniques to restore greater range of movement in his legs and damaged knee. Then, as the weeks went by, graduated to a ramped up, torturous series of exercises in the custom built aqua tank, where Billy pushed against the water's force, often exerting his body beyond the point of pain. Day after day, he spent hours pumping away on a stationary bike, forcing his legs back into shape. Billy fought through each and every agonizing movement, refusing to resort to painkillers. He was determined to rebuild his body no matter what it took. Nothing was going to get in the way of a total recovery.

September rolled around and Billy hobbled down to the beach on his crutches, as the fiery orange sun was about to kiss the top of the ocean for the last time before disappearing into the horizon. He sat down upon the tightly packed, white sand, as Julie snuck up behind him carrying two plastic flutes and a bottle of champagne.

"What are we celebrating?"

"I didn't want to jinx it until I was sure. But I got the job I interviewed for last week."

"What job?"

She dropped to her knees and threw her arms around his neck. "You are about to kiss the new assistant to the associate marketing director for the Bedford Regency Hotel chain. I start first thing Monday."

Before their lips could meet, Billy's cell rang. He checked the caller ID, "Hey Coach. How's it going?" he said, motioning to Julie to give him a second. She leaned back patiently on her haunches and watched as a smile burst across his face. "Yeah… you're kidding me? No way… shit yeah I'll be there… and Coach... thanks man. You just made my day!" For a moment, he forgot how weak his legs still were and tried to get up without the help of his crutches, only to fall back onto the sand, whooping like he won the lottery.

"What Billy? Tell me what's going on?"

"That was Patterson. They're retiring my number. Good ole' thirty-nine. You know how many college players get their number retired?" Julie shook her head. "Well, I don't either," Billy laughed, as he lay back down on the sand. "But I'll tell you this… damn few."

Julie stretched out next to him, her head resting against the crease of his shoulder. "I'm really happy for you, Billy."

He craned his neck to catch a final glimpse of the crimson colors fading into the twilight. "Can you believe it? They even want one of my bats to put in the display case in the athletic center."

"That's really great, Billy," she whispered, not that he heard her.

"Hey, where's that champagne, Julie? Cause *now* we've really got something to celebrate!"

When they'd polished off the last of the champagne, Billy lay back contentedly and closed his eyes, stretching his arms back above his head, feeling the warm grains of sand sift between his fingers. Julie's new job was all but forgotten like the fragile seashells floating out with the tide.

7

Billy had been to the Galen Center at USC many times before, but never for a roast in his honor. Though the luncheon was a tribute to his past achievements, in truth there was a palpable sense of relief among some of the current Trojan players that Billy was no longer on the team. He had always made it seem so easy on the field. Too easy. No matter how hard anyone else worked, their efforts couldn't come close. With Billy's departure, the bar would now be considerably lower.

He dabbed at the corners of his mouth with his napkin as wisecracking, Pat Mackenzie rose from his chair and proceeded to clang his sticky dessert spoon against the rim of his water glass, silencing the din of lively chatter.

"To Billy," he began, lifting his glass, "who craved the limelight so bad, that when all the fuss over hitting a league-leading sixty home runs and being named College World Series MVP finally died down, drove his car off a cliff just to keep his name in the news."

The room fell silent. Few among them found this particular subject appropriate to ridicule, much less laugh about. Mackenzie searched for support, but found none in the frozen faces of the faculty or his teammates.

Then, to his abject relief, came the sound of a raucous laugh. He turned to see Billy pounding the table, carrying on as if his sides ached. A cautious titter emerged as others began to gradually join in. If Billy found Mackenzie's remark something to laugh at, who were they to disagree. Still, humor based on a mangled car and a broken body left many uncomfortable at best. The prevailing sentiment in the room was that Mackenzie should shut up and sit down. But Mackenzie, emboldened by Billy's reaction kept on topic, hammering away. "Billy had a GPS system made especially for him. It only goes *off road*."

When Mackenzie concluded to a smattering of applause, Billy reached for his crutches and excused himself to the men's room. Inside, he was seething. He bent his head forward into the basin and let the cold water run down the back of his neck and trickle across his face. As he lifted his head and toweled off, he stared into the mirror. His eyes were glazed, his skin was taught, his nostrils flared. He barely recognized himself. What he needed was some fresh air.

When he returned to the dining hall, Mackenzie was waiting for him.

"You alright?" Mackenzie asked. "All in good fun. Right? All in good fun."

"All in good fun," Billy answered, slapping Mackenzie on the back.

As the luncheon drew to a close, each member of the team stopped by Billy's table before taking off to personally congratulate him and offer a proper, final goodbye.

Mackenzie saved himself for last, tackling Billy with a giant bear hug. "C'mon, lemme give you a lift home. I'm parked right outside," Mackenzie offered. "Wait till you see my new ride. It's a brand new Vette. Graduation gift, from my folks. So beautiful... when I die, I want to be buried in it. Of course..." he said, with a wink and a tip of his head, "...it doesn't go airborne like your Mercedes did, but hey, I wouldn't trade it for a million dollar signing bonus."

"Actually, it was *three* million... but who's keeping score, right?" Billy grinned slyly. Mackenzie's face fell as Billy stepped in front of him and out through the Galen Center's doors.

As they walked toward the parking lot, a cluster of their teammates were gathered around Mackenzie's Corvette. Mackenzie's jaw dropped. "Motherfucker," he shrieked at the top of his lungs, racing to his car. The tires had been slashed, the headlights smashed, the paint along the doors was gouged down to the metal.

"Oh man. Pat..." Billy offered with heartfelt sympathy, as he worked his way over. "Who could've done such a fucked up thing?"

"Some sick son of a bitch, that's who!"

8

As the months went by, crutches gave way to a walking stick. When Billy wasn't at the rehab center, he could be found at the local batting cage. Although he could once again connect with an eighty-five mile an hour fastball, the pain in his legs would still rear its ugly head whenever he tried to torque, or put weight on the knee.

The daily grind of rehab began to take a toll. Especially during the winter holidays. He continued to curse the cruel, twist of fate that unfairly robbed him of everything he felt entitled to. He was looking forward to Christmas and the chance to distract himself by spending more time with Julie. Unfortunately, during the holidays, she had to work a double shift at the hotel. It was difficult enough to wrap his mind around the possibility she didn't actually object to working such crazy hours. But, how could she not see how much easier it would be for both of them if she quit the stupid hotel job, at least until he fully recovered and left for spring training.

He stepped off the escalator on the first floor of the Beverly Center, careful not to get jostled by the onslaught of last minute Christmas shoppers spilling into the mall. He was confident the delicate gold bangle bracelet he purchased at Le Cadeau would convince Julie to call in sick for at least a day or two over the holidays.

He balanced against his cane as he tapped her number on his cell, cupping his free ear with his palm to block the mall's piped-in, holly-jolly, background music. He was getting ready to head to the Grove on Third and Fairfax next, and wanted Julie to meet him there for dinner. Regrettably, Julie was overwhelmed with paperwork, stressed beyond her limit and barely able to find time to turn down his last minute invitation.

Suddenly, Billy was no longer feeling the holiday spirit. Nor did his mood improve by the time he made his way in a cab through the heavy cross-town traffic.

If possible, there were even more people packed into the Grove's outdoor shopping complex than there were at the Beverly Center. Hundreds of tourists and locals scurrying down the cobblestones that led to the absurdly gigantic, oddly fake-looking tree constructed of pre-cut, natural branches, spray-painted and screwed into place. A symbol of Christmas that would ironically tower over the largely devout Hasidic neighborhood for weeks to come.

Billy headed for the nearest bar. Around his fourth Boilermaker, a slightly chubby, yet attractive young woman in a Santa hat, bandana top and jeans cut off mid-thigh, slid into the empty seat alongside him at the bar. She was from Beaver Creek, Ohio, population thirty-eight thousand, staying at the Farmer's Daughter motel across the street and had never heard of Billy Rubin or his illustrious college baseball career. Billy offered to buy the next three rounds of drinks.

She was nervous, so was he, but for different reasons as they closed the door to her motel room. She was inexperienced; he was concerned she might not take the same care to avoid injuring his legs as Julie did when they made love. Then again, what they were about to do wasn't exactly *love*.

She emerged from the bathroom naked, except for the Santa hat, and quickly turned off the light. Even in the dark she could feel his eyes taking in her less-than-perfect figure. A sudden surge of modesty made her rush to cover her small round breasts with her hands. Billy was gentle as he led her over to the bed. His strong hands pressed against the curve of her spine as he drew her close to him. He circled her nipples, flicking them lightly with his tongue, then sucked hard as they stiffened between his lips. He kissed the inside curve of her neck while guiding her hand towards the zipper of his jeans.

Her full lips parted as he slid his fingers between her thighs. Her knees buckled slightly as he stroked her, coaxing her body to respond. She wasn't Julie. Not even close. But right now, he wanted her just the same.

When he was inside her, there was no need for conversation, just the sound of unfamiliar bodies bouncing together atop the scratchy, starched gingham comforter.

When he was done, he dressed as quickly as the alcohol in his system and his injured legs would allow.

He stepped back out onto Fairfax and hailed a cab as it pulled out of the Grove after dropping off a fare. He leaned back in the taxi and closed his eyes. He didn't open them again until the cab pulled up in front of his beach house.

His back hurt. His legs hurt. His head throbbed incessantly. He was cold and sweating at the same time as he reached inside his pocket and took out his wallet to pay the driver.

As the cab disappeared into the fog, he felt around for his house key and was startled to discover Julie's bracelet was missing. He was sure he had placed it securely inside the back pocket of his jeans when he left the jeweler. He checked through each and every pocket. It was gone and by now, so was the cab. Billy rifled through his wallet for the receipt then tried to reach the jeweler on his cell. But it was nearly midnight and the shop was closed. He could hear his house phone ringing. By time he fumbled with his front door key and got inside, it had already gone to voicemail. It was Julie, once more apologizing for not being able to meet him at the Grove for dinner and hoping he had a fun time without her anyway.

"Love you like crazy," he heard her sweet voice say.

9

Come February, although an MRI still showed some swelling in the knee, Billy managed to convince the Royals' team doctor he was ready for spring training.

Julie couldn't believe the time had come for Billy to leave as she lovingly helped pack his suitcase, spread open at the foot of the bed. Her emotions were all over the place, but she did her best to keep up a brave front. Despite how much she knew she would miss him, she couldn't help but smile at his child-like anticipation. "Heads up," he shouted with a spirited laugh, as he lobbed the last of his socks her way from the dresser.

From the moment he awoke this morning, he was like a magnificent bull kicking at the dirt, ready to charge the red-caped matador, continually checking his watch, peering out the bedroom window to see if the airport taxi had pulled up yet. He was totally psyched to get to Phoenix and set the baseball world on its ear.

His heart raced with excitement as the plane gently set down on the glistening tarmac at Sky Harbor airport. His confidence soared. He was pumped as he made his way through the terminal. He could almost smell the ballpark outfield grass, the vendors in the stands hawking their hotdogs, dripping with spicy brown mustard and dark green relish. And of course -- the fans. The fanatic multitudes, generously bestowing their loyalty and devotion to their heroes on the field who could do what the fans could only dream of doing.

He picked up his bags and headed for the waiting transport van that would deliver him to Surprise Stadium, the Royals spring training facility. The moment he stepped from the air-conditioned terminal, it was like walking into a sweat lodge. The fiery Phoenix sun baked his neck and drenched his shirt until it clung, crinkled and puckered to his body like lizard skin.

While the driver heaved his luggage into the back of the van, Billy hopped up onto the van's running board and winced in pain, having put a little too much pressure on the knee. He snuck a glance to ensure the driver hadn't noticed. He couldn't let anyone think he was anything less than ready to play.

Thanks to the arrival of their talented, young rookie, the beaten-down ball club had reason to believe anything was possible. With the start of exhibition season, Billy did everything he could to mask the sharp, stabbing pain he felt as he raced around the bases, patrolled his patch of grass in right, or torqued his knee while smashing the stitches off the ball with every violent swing. To minimize the swelling, after every game, alone in his room, Billy would grit his teeth and lower his body into a tub of ice that shimmered like a frozen sea of diamonds.

The Royals blazed from the gate, taking seven out of eight to open the exhibition season. Then, they packed their bags and went on the road. That's when the team's winning ways began to go south.

Cleanup hitter, Jason Duckworth accused right-handed fireballer, Brad Morris of screwing his estranged wife, Dolores. While Dolores was nothing special to look at, she did have one peculiarity that drove every member of the team, including Emanuel the towel boy, wild.

From time-to-time when the team was on the road, Dolores would show up at the hotel, a bottle of Chivas Regal in one hand, an Entenmann's apple pie in the other. It had to be Entenmann's, Duckworth's favorite. After a few moments of idle chitchat in the lobby, Duckworth and Dolores would head up to his room. Even though they were currently separated, Dolores had agreed to continue having sex with Duckworth, and only Duckworth, until their divorce was finalized. In exchange for these connubial visits, Dolores would get custody of their pet Labrador, Sweet Pea.

The minute Duckworth locked the door to his room, Brad Morris and the rest of the team would secretly set up folding chairs outside his door. The passionate encounter lasted exactly eighteen minutes. For the first fifteen, as they peeled off their clothes and traveled from the door – to the couch - to the floor - to the bed, Dolores would bark out orders like a drill sergeant, carefully instructing her husband in the art of pleasuring her. *Higher... lower... faster... harder!* Simple enough to follow, even for Duckworth. And titillating enough to satisfy even the horniest ball player seated in the cheap seats out in the hall.

For the next three minutes, as Dolores's voice became more frantic, she would move on to chanting an inscrutable phrase, "You... You know... You know." It began pianissimo, whispered between the sound of the bed and Duckworth pounding rhythmically on top of her, then gradually escalated to full on crescendo – YOOO! YOOO KNOW! YOOOOO KNOW! It ululated from deep within her loins, than shot out through the outer tips of her vocal chords.

Three minutes of, "YOOOO KNOW," usually sent most of those assembled racing back to their rooms to quell their stimulated libidos in private.

After a few more eavesdropping encounters, Morris became frustrated. Since he couldn't very well ask Duckworth about it, he believed the only way to learn the meaning of 'you know' would be through first-hand knowledge. He needed an inside man. Toward that end, he decided to initiate a contest with the rest of the team. The first one to bed Delores and report back would win five hundred bucks.

When Duckworth caught wind of Morris' little contest, and had reason to believe Morris had reaped both the physical and financial bragging rights that went along with it, he went after him with a vengeance the minute he stepped off the field and into the clubhouse. Had it not been for the intervention of half the team, Duckworth might have killed him.

When Royals' manager, Archie Lockwood, flat out asked Morris if he lured Dolores to his room for a sexual tryst, Morris vehemently denied it, swearing he never 'did' Dolores.

But Duckworth wasn't buying it. He knew his wife was a borderline nymphomaniac and in a weak moment, might even screw a degenerate like Morris.

Duckworth was ready to explode again and Lockwood could sense it. But the manager had been in situations with ballplayers far dicier than this. He asked Duckworth, what made him think Morris had sexual relations with his estranged wife?

Duckworth, embarrassed, took a moment, then replied, "I heard a woman's screams coming from Morris' room," he said, blushing through his anger.

"A lot of women scream during sex. Why are you so damn sure it was Dolores?"

Duckworth shook his head, staring down at the floor before responding. "Because no one else screams, *you... you know.*"

Stifled laughter could be heard among his teammates, except for Morris, who never once changed expression. The manager was confused. "What the hell does 'you know,' mean?"

The team shot straight up at attention. They too were still dying to find out. The air was thick with anticipation. Even Billy raised an eyebrow.

And then, Duckworth, mortified, replied, "I don't know what it means. I never asked." His embarrassment quickly changed to fury, "But Morris is still a fucking liar! It was *my* Dolores, screaming, *'you know'* inside *his* room last night!"

As the irate, muscle bound power hitter raised his fists, Morris took a step back. "Listen, Ducky, I swear it wasn't me. I wasn't even in my room last night. I went and bunked with Martinez. I couldn't get any rest the way the new kid yells in his sleep all night."

All eyes turned to Billy who looked as surprised as anyone at being accused of not only talking loudly in his sleep, but of screwing a teammate's wife.

"Don't look at me. I never even met the lady."

Duckworth scowled, his eyebrows knit tightly together, his squinting, furious eyes ablaze. But what was he to do with all this rage? Without Dolores' admission, he had no proof if it was the rookie or Morris. But, his money was on Morris. He swiveled around, tackled the pitcher and threw him to the ground with a crashing thud. Morris grabbed the nearest chair and smashed it across Duckworth's massive frame. The corner of the chair splintered, hitting Lockwood across the forehead. Beads of blood trickled down his cheek. When Duckworth and Morris were finally pulled apart, the manager was furious. He immediately slapped both men with fines for fighting and threatened to fine the entire team if somebody didn't step forward and own up.

As the team filed out of the clubhouse, most of them were wondering if Billy had actually bagged Dolores or not. And if he did, why wouldn't he man up? Even more, why wouldn't he share the secret of 'You Know' with them?

Martinez lingered behind. "Look, man. I didn't want to embarrass you in front of the team, but I know for a fact, Morris crashed in my room last night. So if you're holding out, it's not gonna do nobody any fucking good."

"Back off, Martinez. I'm not going to admit to something I didn't do."

The following day, Billy leaned against the dugout railing, a pariah among a good portion of his teammates. Duckworth was still pissed at Morris. Morris was still nursing a sore shoulder and by the bottom of the eighth the Royals were down, four-nothing, en route to a loss.

Half the team sided with Billy – the other half with Morris. Duckworth despised everyone, including Dolores and her stupid dog, Sweet Pea. Conversation in the dugout and on the bus back to the hotel was kept to a bare minimum. Dissention among the players escalated and the downhill slide continued. The Royals lost eleven out of their last nineteen games to close out the exhibition season.

Finally, opening day of the regular season arrived. Billy was determined to turn things around. The Royals were in the Big Apple for a three game set against the Yankees. Billy swelled with pride from the dugout bench as his face appeared on the Jumbotron and he heard his name announced over the PA. *'Batting third, number thirty-nine, right fielder, Billy Rubin.'*

He stepped from the dugout and searched the crowd until his eyes found Julie, who had flown in for his first regular season game.

Matt McNeely led off, but was soon disposed of on a ground out to short. Luis Martinez followed as Billy grabbed a bat and stepped into the on deck circle. He focused on the Yankee pitcher to see what he was throwing Martinez. But there wasn't much time to focus as Martinez was quickly called out on strikes by a wicked, split finger fastball. Billy banged the donut off his bat then swaggered to the plate like a veteran All Star. The sold-out New York crowd began to boo. But their audacious and colorful catcalls were music to Billy's ears. He dug in. His eyes narrowed as he zoned in on the pitcher.

Suddenly, *'This isn't college anymore,'* echoed in his head. He stood paralyzed in the batter's box, his bat frozen on his shoulder. The first pitch blazed down the middle of the plate at a blistering ninety-eight miles an hour. Billy called time and backed out of the box. His heart was racing. He lifted his cap and ran his fingers through his hair, surprised to find it matted with sweat, yet his body was shivering. He took a deep breath and stepped back in. Relax, he told himself. You're as good as any one of them. Billy cocked the bat, refocusing on the pitcher. Then, a voice said; *maybe you're not.*

The bat began to tremble in his grip. He didn't like hearing words of self-doubt. It made him angry. The pitcher went into his windup and threw. A split-finger fastball on the outside part of the plate. Billy was late on the swing and missed it badly. The New York crowd roared as they rose to their feet clapping and stomping in unison, anticipating a strikeout.

Don't show them weakness. Show them who's in charge! Billy glared up at the stands in defiance. The pitcher peered in for a sign. Billy widened his stance and grit his teeth, his upper lip snaked into a snarl as he awaited the next pitch.

Curveball, low and inside.

WHAM!

Billy mashed the ball with everything he had. He watched it disappear into the night. The Yankee center fielder sped toward the deepest part of the park. The ball ricocheted off the top of the wall and headed along the warning track toward right field.

Billy raced past first. Miraculously, he felt no pain in his legs. It could have been an adrenaline rush, but whatever the case, his legs felt stronger than ever.

He rounded second and headed for third as the right fielder picked up the ball and relayed it to the second baseman. The third base coach threw up his hands and gave Billy the stop sign. But the voice in Billy's head was screaming, *keep going.* He rounded third and zoomed toward the plate. The catcher slammed his mitt with his fist, his body blocking the plate as the second baseman gunned the ball home. It was a bang-bang play.

The ball squirted loose from the catcher's mitt, as both men crashed to the ground. Billy Joseph Rubin had an inside the park home run in his first major league at bat.

His teammates raced out to congratulate him. But Billy wasn't getting up any time soon. He lay there, clutching his knee, the muscles in his face contorted in agony. The stadium grew silent. One of the players frantically waved for a stretcher. Julie watched helplessly from the stands.

The prognosis wasn't encouraging. Billy had dislocated his kneecap when he collided with the catcher's shin guard, damaging much of the surrounding tissue. The graft used from his first knee surgery had ruptured and he had re-torn the anterior cruciate and medial collateral ligaments. The grim-faced doctors informed Julie, on a scale of one-to-five, the knee was a seven.

For Billy, the season was lost. He was sent back to LA and back into rehab for a solid seven months. But this time the knee just wouldn't respond. On November first, Scott Erikson called to inform him the Royals had cut him loose.

10

"Cut the crap!" Billy exploded into the phone. "We both know he's not still in some fucking meeting! This is the tenth time I've called today."

Billy hounded Erikson's beleaguered assistants day and night. Nothing could shake his belief there had to be at least one other pro team out there willing to take a chance on him. After all, he was Billy Rubin. The rules of recovery don't apply to someone like him. The hell with what the small-minded Kansas City Royals thought. His baseball career isn't over until he says it is. His college record alone had to command the respect of any baseball owner with an IQ above seven. And if Erikson has even half the balls he claims to have, he'll make them see it.

A few days later, after not being able to get the agent on the phone, Billy burst into Erikson's office demanding a meeting. But Erikson wasn't in. Billy refused to leave, planting himself behind the agent's desk. Security was called, and Billy, fighting tooth and nail was carried from the office and escorted out of the building.

Eventually Erikson's pasty-faced, third assistant, barely one-step-above an intern, phoned Billy to convey the agent's heartfelt admission that he had tried to shop him everywhere, but, quoting the elusive Erikson, 'It ain't gonna happen.' Because, and only because Mr. Erikson wished the very best for Billy, he had come to believe Billy's interests would be better served by finding representation elsewhere.

As of 6:04 that evening, Billy no longer had an agent.

He grabbed a beer, jumped into his car, and tore out of the driveway heading for the batting cage in West L.A. As he merged onto the San Diego Freeway, traffic came to a dead stop as it often did. Having driven this route a zillion times before, he knew it was just four short exits to Venice Boulevard, no more than a five minute drive from his present location. He threw the car in neutral, then pounded on the dashboard with a resounding blow, causing the glove compartment to fly open with a thud. "Shit," he yelled, as he reached over and slammed it shut. He rolled down his window and leaned his head out. "What the fuck is the hold up!" But no one had a clue.

Another tortuous fifteen minutes passed. He knew the batting cage was closing soon. His eyes took in the ocean of stranded motorists trapped inside their vehicles expressing their frustration in a rising cacophony of honking horns. He decided to contribute to the orchestration, slamming the fat part of his palm long and hard against his horn. But, it failed to lessen his growing rage or get the cars moving again.

Billy turned off his engine and stuck his head out the window. He spotted a motorcycle cop weaving in and around the traffic heading his way. "Hey, Officer, what's the deal?"

"Six car pile-up two exits down. Expect about an hour delay."

"An hour? No f-ing way," Billy groaned, as he flopped his head back against the headrest and wondered what it would cost to leave the car here on the freeway and walk away. After all, it was just a piece-of-shit rental his former agent had leased for him ever since the Mercedes took a nosedive off the cliff. A four hundred dollar towing charge? Hell, they'd probably send the bill to that prick Erikson anyway.

As soon as the officer was far enough away, Billy limped across four lanes of traffic, and made off for the batting cage.

He grabbed a bat and stepped in, defying the ninety-mile an hour machine to fire away. Billy swung and connected, blasting a screaming liner into the net. A searing pain shot through his knee and continued up his thigh. He yelped in agony, then used the bat as a crutch to keep from falling. His furor escalated. He cursed the machine and bashed it repeatedly until the bat splintered and smashed. He grabbed another stick and whacked it harder, by now, his face the color of steamed tomatoes. His hands blistered and swelled. Surrounded by a sea of shattered bats, he fell against the fence, releasing a floodgate of angry tears.

11

Julie stood at the kitchen window watching Billy jog along the damp sand by the water's edge, leaving a trail of angry footprints in his wake. The past few days, he'd made little attempt to conceal the bitterness he felt toward the world.

She shuddered when the front door ripped open and slammed shut with a thunderous crack. He barely acknowledged her presence as he opened the fridge and grabbed a cold draft. He held it to his temples before twisting it open to address his thirst with a long hard swallow.

"What are you doing here?" he asked, less than pleased to find her there. "Did we have plans or something?" As he attempted to set the bottle on the counter, it slipped from his sweaty grip. The honey-brown liquid splattered across the tiled floor like rivulets of amber sea foam. He reached down to pick up the shards of broken glass, cutting his hand in the process.

"Shit!" he yelled, as the blood trailed down his palm. "God damn waste of a good Heineken!" Billy stormed over to the sink to wash off the blood, as Julie grabbed a paper towel and started sopping up the sticky mess on the floor.

"I tried calling, but you didn't pick up."

Billy pulled off his shirt and wrapped it tightly around the open cut. "I was down at the beach."

Julie got up and reached for his injured hand. "Let me see how bad it is."

Billy yanked back his hand. "It's nothing."

She knew all too well when he got like this there wasn't much she could do but leave him be. "I was just wondering if you're still planning on going to the party at my hotel tonight."

Billy reached into the fridge for another beer. "The last thing I need is to hang out with those geeks you work with. I'm not up to fielding a bunch of dumb questions about why I was cut by the Royals. If you're hungry, we could order something in."

"I don't think so," she said, carefully drying her hands on a kitchen towel.

"Why not?"

"Because. Today is my birthday. If that means anything to you."

With little more than a shrug, Billy took another swig, then wiped his mouth with the back of his arm. "What's the big deal? You'll have another one next year."

His eyes were dark and hard. What hurt most was she knew it wasn't the beer talking. It was Billy. Intentionally trying to hurt her. His callous indifference made her feel like screaming. But instead, she looked away, unwilling to give him the satisfaction of seeing how hurt she was. She didn't want to cry. Especially not on her birthday.

"Well, I'm going to my birthday party -- with or without you. Show up. Don't show up. I don't give a damn anymore," was all she said, as she picked up her purse and walked out.

Two six-packs later, Billy swaggered into the Bedford Regency with three-dozen peonies clasped in a hastily bandaged hand and a bottle of Kristal tucked under his arm. As he wobbled through the lobby, he checked his watch and was shocked to discover how late it was. He rang for the elevator, then nearly dropped the champagne when he felt a red-hot stabbing sensation, like someone knocking at the gates of Hell, behind his left eye. He winced and tried to catch his breath. It could be nothing, he hoped. Or it could be the start of another one of those lousy headaches plaguing him lately. When the doors slid open, Billy tumbled inside, making a grab for the rail to keep from toppling over. He pawed at the panel of buttons trying to find Julie's floor.

When the elevator doors re-opened, he stepped out. His footsteps were the only sound he heard. The offices were deserted as it was well past midnight by now. A low, gravelly voice caught him by surprise.

"Are you lookin' for someone or just lost your way, young man? Most everyone's gone home by now, 'cept for me and the rest of the cleaning crew that is."

Billy turned with a start and stared into the kind brown eyes of a lanky, elderly man, with skin the color of velvety Hershey syrup. Billy tried his best to appear soberly focused, not wishing to get tossed out on his ear. Not before he found Julie and apologized. The name Nelson was embroidered in blue above the breast pocket of the kind stranger's crisp uniform. "Mister Nelson," he managed to mumble. "I'm just looking for the birthday party. It's got to be here somewhere."

"Whose party might that be?" Nelson inquired politely.

"Julie's. She works right over there," Billy slurred, pointing down the corridor.

"Julie? Oh, you must mean Miss Hatcher. What a fine, lovely woman. I wish I had known today was her birthday," Nelson sighed, then suggested Billy try one of the private party rooms on the lower floors. Nelson rang for the elevator and offered to ride back down with him.

When they arrived at their destination, Billy stepped out into the hall. "Thanks for your... " Billy stopped in mid-sentence as he turned back, "... help." But Nelson was gone. And so, gratefully, was Billy's headache.

The door to one of the party rooms was propped open with a cleaning cart. The guests had long since departed. The only traces of tonight's festivities were some empty wine bottles, crumpled gift-wrap, a table of dirty dishes, and two young chambermaids giggling and whispering in Spanish as they swept what remained of Julie's birthday into giant black trash bags.

Billy spotted a dessert plate at the head of the center table smeared with small, swirling circles of pink icing. He knew it had to be Julie's. Whenever she was upset, she had this unconscious habit of doing exactly that with her spoon. She must have been pretty steamed when he didn't show up for her party. He felt like a total shit. He thought of calling, but figured she was probably asleep by now.

"Why don't you go on home now, son," a gentle voice spoke up. "Do yourself a favor and go sleep it off." Billy turned. It was Nelson.

But Billy didn't go home. He went back up to Julie's office and left the champagne and flowers on her desk along with an apology of sorts. His brief mea culpa was scripted on a post-it. She found it stuck to her desk phone when she came into work the next day.

Julie -- I messed up. Somehow I lost track of how late it was. I must've conked out after running the beach... Let me make it up to you tonight. Call me.

She glanced at the wilting flowers and warm champagne. While they hardly made up for his hurtful behavior yesterday, the important thing was, he did say he was sorry. Or at least that's what she thought he was trying to say, while conveniently leaving out how totally shit-faced he was.

Although it was only a few minutes into the workday, she helped herself to a handful of M&Ms she kept in a glass bowl atop her desk. Chocolate kept her sane, and more importantly – calm. Despite how disappointed she was that Billy showed up too late for her party, she kind of got how hard it was for him to hang out with her new work friends. Most of whom were considerably older women, few of which had any interest whatsoever in sports. And maybe, just maybe, after everything Billy's had to deal with lately, she should just let it go. She dipped back into the candy bowl, and as the M&Ms danced around her tongue, decided it was too hard to stay mad at Billy for long.

When she arrived at the beach house that evening, there was an envelope marked, *For Julie*, taped to the front door. Inside, a spare house key and the words, *Happy Birthday.* Her heart quickened. She couldn't imagine a more wonderful birthday present than Billy officially asking her to move in. "Billy…" she called, flush with excitement, as she let herself in.

"Up here. On the patio," he answered back.

Lit by slivers of moonlight shimmering through the windows, Julie hurried up the spiral staircase. When she reached the rooftop patio, she couldn't believe her eyes. It was ablaze with hundreds of twinkling tea-light candles. There were balloons of every shape, size and color. Fresh pink peonies adorned the elegantly set, candle-lit table. Billy had gone to great lengths to assemble a belated birthday dinner of all her favorite dishes. Including, perhaps her greatest weakness, an indecently indulgent, Viktor Benes Black Forest cake.

"Happy birthday, baby," he whispered, as he reached for her hand. He pressed each slender finger to his lips, sending tiny shivers through her body. "Say you forgive me for last night." She didn't need to say a word. Forgiveness was already there in her eyes as she melted into his outstretched arms.

He filled two large goblets with wine and downed his quickly after toasting her birthday. His lips found her bare shoulders and the soft, milk-white skin between her neck and collarbone as they danced without music across the rooftop watching the waves below shimmer in the blackened waters of the Pacific. She felt complete and adored as they made love beneath the stars.

"Hungry?" he asked, as they leaned against the rail when they were done feasting on one another.

"Starving. I don't suppose we could start with the chocolate cake and work our way backwards?"

"No way," he grinned, as he led her to the table and held out the chair for her. "I have prepared a very special menu for madam's birthday dinner."

"I feel like a princess. You're going to spoil me rotten with all this attention."

"That's the plan. Besides," he said, as he refilled her glass with wine and his with a double shot of bourbon. "Tonight is a very special night."

"For sure," she smiled, thinking of the silver house key in her purse. And what it meant. Daydreaming how amazing their idyllic co-habitation would be. No more nagging doubts about him seeing other women when he wasn't with her. No more flak from her mother over Billy's lack of commitment. Everything she dreamed of for so long was finally coming true.

Billy tossed back the bourbon, smacked his lips and emptied what was left of the bottle into his glass. "Now. Close your eyes and don't peek," he warned, as he reached into the picnic hamper. "I want you to take your time. Tonight's main course is strictly gourmet and much too expensive to rush. You need to savor the exotic aroma before you dig in."

Julie laughed, delighted by Billy's overly dramatic presentation. His face flushed with color, his eyes glinting in the moonlight as he lifted the dinner plate closer. She wrinkled her nose trying to discern exactly what it was.

"Ummm. Chicken Cordon Blue? Fillet Mignon? Beluga caviar?

"Nope"

"Lobster Thermidor? Oysters Rockefeller?"

"Nope."

"I give up," she whimpered playfully. "What is it?"

"God you're bad at this. Okay. Take a bite."

"Oh my God," she managed to get out while trying to swallow and catch the oil dripping from the corners of her mouth. "I can't believe you bought me Po' Boys from Little Dom's! I hope you'll continue to spoil me like this after I've officially moved in."

Billy grew quiet. His eyes, glassy and distant as they followed the gentle slosh of the bourbon swaying back and forth in his glass. Then he stood and quietly walked it over to the railing and took a hard swallow. His head bent forward, his shoulders hunched up near his ears. He shivered and shook as the alcohol raced through him.

"Billy... are you okay?"

When he didn't respond she grew concerned and followed him over to the rail. "What's happening? Are you having one of your headaches again?" When she reached up to rub the back of his neck, he grabbed her hands and forcibly pushed them away.

"Stop it! Don't touch me. I know what you're trying to do!"

"I... I was only trying to help."

"Don't. You're not fooling anyone." She stared back, bewildered and a little unsettled by the harshness in his voice. "Why are you still here?" he glowered.

"Be... because you asked me to. If we're going to live together, you can't shut me out like this."

"Live together? Are you out of your fucking mind? Who said anything about living together?"

"But, Billy..."

"Billy Rubin lives alone. Always did. Always will.

"Then what was this for?" she asked, pulling the key from her purse.

Billy stared back. "What was that doing in your purse?"

"I... I thought you wanted me to keep it. I thought you wanted us to..."

"To what?"

At first, she couldn't speak. Embarrassed beyond words. How could she have so completely misread his intentions? Then her anger at her own stupidity turned toward Billy. He must've left the key outside so he wouldn't have to bother coming all the way down just to let her in. How like him. How totally self-absorbed and self-serving. She couldn't stand to be in his company for one more second. "Thank you for ruining my birthday for the second time! Thank you for ruining my life!" She slammed the key on the table and raced down the spiral staircase.

He heard the front door slam. He refilled his glass and listened for the sound of her car charging from the driveway. What he couldn't hear was the sound of Julie's heart breaking as she drove away.

In the morning, Billy woke up on the roof with an empty bourbon bottle tucked under his chin. He didn't feel much like clearing off the table. He felt like calling Julie. Which he did. Seven times, but she never picked up.

When he showed up unexpectedly at her office, she was on the phone. He waved, but she didn't wave back. In fact, she didn't seem too pleased to see him there at all. That wasn't like Julie, he thought. One of the things he loved most about her was how her face always lit up with a smile whenever she saw him.

He stood at the edge of her desk, and helped himself to some candy while he waited for her to get off the phone.

"What are you doing here, Billy?"

"I was worried when you didn't call me back. I wanted to make sure you got home okay last night."

"You were worried about how I got home? That's unbelievable! You really have some nerve showing up here today," she pounced, while checking to see if any of her co-workers were watching. "Like you actually give a damn about me."

"What are you talking about? You know I care about you. C'mon," he said, absently shoveling another handful of M&M's into his mouth. "How about we go grab a cup of coffee and a bagel or something. I haven't eaten since last night. What do you say?"

"What do I say?!" She asked, dumbfounded by his outrageous suggestion that she should care more about his empty stomach than the humiliation he caused her last night. "I say, you need to leave. I say, I never want to see you again."

"Whoa. Where's all this coming from?"

"If you don't know, or if you can't remember because you were too damn drunk to remember, you're in worse shape than I thought."

"What?! First of all, I wasn't drunk. And second, didn't we have fun last night?"

"If that was your idea of a good time, you need to see a shrink. Or get yourself into AA. I don't care which. You know what?" she added, keeping her voice as low as possible. "I'm tired of this, Billy. I'm tired of not knowing what is going to set you off. You may think the world owes Billy Rubin a big fat standing O, but as far as I'm concerned the only thing you deserve is the back of my middle finger."

"You think I care!" he screamed. "I don't need you. I don't need anyone."

Her face flushed, as by now everyone in the office was staring. When her desk phone rang, she turned away to answer it. To her relief, when she turned back, he was gone.

12

Life changed for Billy from that day forward. His growing sense of isolation and abandonment grew with each passing hour. His career as a pro ballplayer was gone and now so was Julie. Billy's world became a silent, meaningless prison. The once daily morning jogs across the sand and occasional trips to the batting cage were replaced by hours spent watching mind-numbing television with vacant eyes. More often than not it was the disheartening afternoon judge shows. Judge Lois, Judge Joe, Judge Alex or whoever else had sacrificed their professional integrity for a seven-figure paycheck to pass judgment on the lowest of the low in front of millions of avid viewers. And when the bombardment of courtroom drama became too much to bear, he would sit silently in the dark. He felt increasingly powerless to change the direction his life had taken.

And then, for some reason, his thoughts turned to Nelson, the clean-up man from Julie's hotel. Oddly enough, on more than one occasion recently, Nelson had started showing up in some of his dreams. Even given his current state of depression, Billy had to admit, it was pretty bizarre. He barely met the man and yet, there was Nelson, a few steps ahead, leading Billy through endless darkened tunnels towards a soft, glowing light.

In one of his more lucid moments, Billy wondered if it was less about Nelson and more about Julie.

But Billy didn't want to think about Julie, or Nelson, or even baseball. He didn't want to think about anything. He picked up the remote on the nightstand. There had to be something on this magic little screen to lull him back into a comfortable stupor.

It was nearly seven p.m., too early for prime time, too late to escape into the world of the droning chatter of afternoon talk shows. This time of the evening, Billy knew the only thing on would be endless syndicated re-runs of tired old sit-coms.

He was about to turn off the set when a commercial for a sleep aid came on. There before his eyes was a weary looking soul, desperate for a good night's sleep. This he could identify with. The ad promised verdant green meadows, fluffy white clouds and eight solid hours of rest. It all sounded pretty good to Billy. Particularly, since he had no immediate plans of operating heavy machinery any time soon.

He went into the bathroom and slid open the medicine cabinet. There, aligned like tiny toy soldiers, stood the assembled troops of last resort. Thanks to all the medical procedures Billy had gone through in the recent past, he possessed a virtual arsenal of colorful pills designed to take away any and all of one's pain. Over the years, Billy had never been much of a fan of prescription medication. Given the scathing spotlight shone on athletes who had chosen to enhance their skills through chemistry, he had always avoided putting anything that could possibly be considered remotely suspicious into his body. But those days were behind him now. No one out there gave a damn if he was stoically sober or high as a kite. So why the hell not, he thought. It might be nice to crawl back into bed and sleep in for as long as he'd like. Hours, days, weeks, sounded reasonable. After all, it was his bed. His house. Who was there to stop him? Certainly not Julie. In fact, he wondered, if one pill could temporarily take away his misery, what might three or four do?

Ultimately, Billy concluded, three Xanax tablets should more than meet his expectations for tonight. He thought about whether or not to eat something before pulling up the covers, then remembered he hadn't ordered any groceries since Tuesday and the leftover burrito molting in the fridge held little appeal. So he simply got into bed and closed his eyes, grateful for the end to another day of nothing.

He awoke at four a.m. His head throbbed, but without the familiar migraine-like searing bolts of pain. This was different. This was as if someone had wrapped a thousand pound cobra around his head. He twinged in agony as it squeezed and pressed against his brain. He attempted to sit up but quickly found his arms and legs unresponsive to his mental urgings. His limbs felt swollen and ponderously heavy. The pills he swallowed had indeed knocked him into the arms of Morpheus beyond his wildest expectations, but at a price he no longer wished to pay. He felt trapped inside his body; the same body that once lifted him to dizzying heights on the playing fields, now threatened to betray him.

Had it not been for the incessant urgings of his bursting bladder, he might have remained in bed like that for hours. Somehow he found the resolve to slide off the bed and crawl into the bathroom.

He caught a glimpse of himself kneeling beside the toilet in the full-length mirror and wondered how much worse things could possibly get? He thought about the past few hours and how, in retrospect, blessedly peaceful they had been. He had no conscious memory of any tortured dreams this time, nor of hours spent staring at the ceiling unable to fall asleep. The pills weren't bad. It was the waking up that was the problem.

Billy lingered on the bathroom floor, debating the merits of crawling back into bed, continuing full-speed into a depressive spiral or ending it all, right here, right now in the bathroom. Why not? All the pills he could possibly need were a mere four feet above his head. How hard could it be?

Then something in the recesses of his mottled brain called out to him. *No. Not now. Not here.* He managed to find the strength to rise to his feet and hobble downstairs to the kitchen. He pulled out a narrow drawer by the sink and started searching through the contents haphazardly scattered within. There amongst the rubber bands, matchbooks, paperclips, and assorted odd receipts, he found what he was looking for: Dr. Sharon Edwards' business card.

Dr. Edwards' service picked up. She was out of town at a symposium until next week. And no, they could not put him through to her, nor would they tell him where the symposium was being held. They would however, try to see if they could fit him in when Dr. Edwards returned or they'd be happy to refer him to the on-call psychiatrist.

Billy didn't bother to respond. He simply hung up. There was no way he would put this decision off until next week. He had always let himself be guided by his instincts in the past. He saw no reason to change now.

He calmly walked over to the pantry and took out a large Ziploc bag. Then opened the cabinet and selected a sparkling, elaborately carved, crystal goblet. It was one of a matching set of four, a gift from Julie's mother, who insisted Billy's ceramic USC mugs weren't good enough for her daughter to drink from. He smiled. It seemed only fitting to use the old witch's goblet for one final glass of hemlock. He headed upstairs to the bedroom, pausing only to pick up a bottle of his best vodka.

It was around eight-thirty a.m., still too early for the judge shows to begin, but that didn't matter, because now... it was time for 'The Billy Show.' No laugh track. No commercials, just Billy Rubin, laid out across the bed, some pills, some excellent liquid refreshment, and a plastic bag. He decided to change into a clean terry robe since he didn't really want to be found clad only in the soiled underwear he had dragged himself across the floor in earlier. And then it hit him. He was really going to do this. And he felt at peace.

On impulse he decided to put on his baseball cleats. Just in case there was anything to this afterlife stuff. Who knows, having his custom fit cleats with him might give him an advantage up there.

Not wanting to lose his nerve, Billy decided to take all the pills at once. He washed them down quickly with eight ounces of the vodka, then reached for the Ziploc. He placed it snuggly over his head, then lay back on the pillow and waited for welcome relief from his unbearable existence.

13

Frank Tortiricci knew a good thing when he saw it. And he was determined to make the most of it as he pulled up in front of Billy's house. He didn't give a damn that the Royals and that dickhead Scott Erikson cut Billy loose. Erikson's shortsightedness was going to be Frankie's good fortune.

He heard all the scuttlebutt surrounding Billy's latest injury and how popular opinion held that the once gifted right fielder would never recover enough to get back in the game. But Frankie rarely listened to popular opinion. He went with his gut. Besides, no one else knew Billy the way Frank did. He knew if there was even the remotest of possibilities Billy could fight his way back to full strength, he'd pull it off. And Frankie wanted to make sure he was the agent of record when he did.

He banged on the front door and waited. When no one answered he went around to the side of the house and looked in through the kitchen window. Piles of unread mail and used paper plates containing food that had long since turned, lined the counter tops. Empty liquor bottles were left stacked in the sink and on the kitchen table, a week's worth of newspapers piled high next to an open bottle of ketchup.

He turned to leave, then out of curiosity, turned back around and tried the door. To his surprise it wasn't locked. He took a few steps into the house. "Hey Billy," he shouted. "It's Frankie. You in here?" Frankie looked around. The living room was a mess as well. "What did ya do..." he muttered to himself, as he meandered over to the staircase, "... fire the fuckin' maid? Hey!" he called out. "You up there, Billy?"

He started up the stairs, then hesitated. He didn't feel totally comfortable being in someone's house uninvited, let alone going into their bedroom. Despite that, he continued to slowly climb to the top of the stairs, then stopped again. The door to Billy's bedroom was ajar. He could see the bottom of Billy's cleats hanging off the bed.

"What the… hey, didn't anybody teach ya to take your shoes off before you climb into bed," he chortled, continuing down the hall.

"Holy-mother-of-God," he shrieked, after easing open the bedroom door. He pressed the back of his hand to his mouth struggling to keep down a violent wave of nausea, as he stared at Billy's lifeless open eyes inside the Ziploc bag.

He stumbled to the phone, hit 9-1-1, and screamed, "I need a fucking ambulance! I need a fucking ambulance!"

14

Dr. Sharon Edward's heels clicked swiftly down the hallway of Daniel Freeman's Psychiatric Unit. The police had found her business card on Billy's kitchen table and tracked her down. All she was told was that Billy was in an unresponsive state when he was brought in. When they pumped his stomach they found enough painkillers, alcohol and antidepressants to take down a bear. She didn't wait for further updates on his condition before deciding to drive back to Los Angeles.

When she entered Billy's room she found him hooked up to an IV, his skin gray and pasty, his eyes tightly shut. How different he appeared – so silent, frail and vulnerable. Not at all the boastful, fidgety, controlling young man who had marched into her office demanding a quick fix. She walked to the foot of his bed and addressed him softly.

"Billy, it's Dr. Edwards. Can you hear me?"

Billy gradually opened his eyes and tried to focus. His voice was hoarse and dry. "Dr. Edwards? What are you doing here?"

"The police asked me to come."

"The police? Why?" The IV line tightened as he twisted to sit up. "What the hell am I doing in a hospital?"

"The police brought you here after you swallowed a large amount of pills and pulled a plastic bag over your head. If the doctors hadn't pumped your stomach when they did, you wouldn't be here at all."

Billy started to respond, then violently jerked his head backward. His hands flew up, gripping the back of his neck.

"Are you alright, Billy? Should I get the nurse?"

He took several deep breaths as the throbbing in his head subsided. "No. I'm okay." His eyes darted around the room, taking in his surroundings. "It's fine. Everything's fine."

"It's important that you get back into therapy as soon as you're physically up to it. I'd be happy to work with you."

Billy shook his head, "Look," he said gruffly, clearly annoyed.

"You don't see the big picture." He leaned forward, as if to take her into his confidence. "What if this shit got leaked to the Press? You think anybody's gonna be willing to give Billy Rubin another shot to play ball if it gets around that Billy Rubin's some kind of whack job?"

Sharon Edwards studied his face. His pupils were dilated, his chin jutted forward sharply. "I can't force you to accept therapy, Billy, but I'd like to come back tomorrow and maybe we can talk about it some more."

"Look, Doc... I appreciate your concern, but let me reassure you, the only thing that needs to happen is for me to get out of Los Angeles for a while. There's nothing here for me anymore."

When she asked where he would go, he grew silent for a moment then responded -- Chicago. He liked Chicago. It's where he grew up. It was home and a place someone like him could get lost in for a time without making the six o'clock news.

"And, I'll tell you something else – people in Chicago are straight with you. They don't tell you they're a hundred percent behind you then stab you in the back. They don't tell you they're crazy in love with you one minute, then throw your fucking keys in your face and walk out the door." His voice began to crack. He reached for the water pitcher and slopped some into the plastic cup on the hospital nightstand. His hand trembled as he raised it to his lips. "God damn it!" he yelled, as the water leapt from the cup onto his hospital gown.

"Let me get you a towel."

As Dr. Edwards turned, Billy grabbed her by the wrist. "If you really want to help, you can start by getting the hell out of here," he growled, releasing his grip before rolling onto his side.

"I don't wish to upset you. I'll leave if you'd like."

He turned back and reached for her arm, "No. I – I don't want you to leave. Please don't go," he sobbed.

She moved to the side of the bed and gently placed her hand on his shoulder. It was painful to watch the once, high-spirited young man all but disappear inside the confused and deeply troubled person she now saw before her. "What is it, Billy?

"I'm afraid."

"What are you afraid of?"

"Everything." His eyes filled with truthful tears. "I'm afraid it's gonna happen again."

PART TWO

15

A gust of frigid wind swooped down and lashed wickedly against Billy's back. He tugged on the collar flaps of his lightweight jacket, pressing them tightly to his ears, as he headed for the entrance to the stately, limestone building across the street. One thing was certain... coming home to Chicago after all these years would definitely require a major wardrobe adjustment.

He squared his shoulders and darted inside the lobby. As he rode the elevator up, he shoved his hands deep inside his pockets. His raw, frozen fingers curled around the warm, plastic bottle of little yellow pills the doctors at Cedars prescribed upon his discharge. He could take one every four hours if he began to experience any negative thoughts he couldn't control. So far he had taken only one as he sat on the tarmac at LAX waiting for the plane to take off.

When he stepped out of the elevator, he glanced at his watch. He was ten minutes early for his appointment. Before he lost his nerve, he headed swiftly down the hall to Marvin Rasher's office, only to find it was locked. He was just about to knock when he heard a loud burst of metallic squeaks coming from inside. He waited for it to stop, but the squeaking grew more furious. There was a small, oval-shaped window a little down the corridor. The blinds were drawn and lowered, but didn't quite reach the top of the sill, leaving just enough room for Billy to make out a middle-aged man in shirt and tie, sans trousers, with a somewhat chunky, middle-aged woman straddled on top of him. Seven inches of manhood pounding the perky brunette for all she's worth... a gasping leather chair beneath them creaking in tune with their ardor.

For a moment Billy wondered if he'd gotten off on the wrong floor. He checked the address Dr. Edwards had written down. Nope. Right building. Right floor. If the man inside was indeed the esteemed Dr. Marvin Rasher, he had to admit the psychiatrist had an interesting way of passing time between patients.

Billy needed this to work. He had to get his life back. So he elected to wait silently in the hall until the sordid sounds inside subsided. When it did, he knocked. The door opened slightly and the man poked his head out.

"Doctor Rasher?" Billy inquired.

"Yes?"

"I'm Billy Rubin. Dr. Edwards called you from Los Angeles and set up an appointment for me today. I'm a little early I know."

"No. No. That's fine, Billy. But I wonder if you wouldn't mind giving me a minute or so." Dr. Rasher closed the door, slicked back his hair and hurriedly tucked his shirt inside his pants, then opened the door and ushered Billy inside. To his surprise, the Rubenesque brunette had vanished. Billy scratched his head. He could have sworn there was a half-naked woman there a second ago. In fact, he could still detect the scent of her perfume, heady and sweet.

"Have a seat, Billy," Rasher offered, casually plucking a dainty silk scarf wedged into a fold of the battered leather chair.

Billy surmised the office undoubtedly had a back door – most likely the portal through which the doctor's amorous companion had made her speedy get-away. As he settled his rear into the well-creased leather, all he could think of was the doctor's sweaty bottom bouncing up and down moments earlier.

But now, fully clothed, stiff-backed in the chair across from him, it was almost comical how Marvin Rasher looked every inch a stereotypical shrink. Mid-forties, graying beard and tousled hair, though Billy was pretty sure how it got tousled.

"Perhaps, Billy, we might start with you telling me about the day you decided life wasn't worth living."

Billy squirmed in his seat, trying to reconstruct the time leading up to the horrific event. "I remember feeling kind of lost and tired. I didn't get much sleep the night before. Or the night before that as well."

"Were you drinking?"

"No. At least not when I first got up... I remember turning on the TV. But I don't remember what was on. Then my head started hurting again. I think I went into the bathroom... maybe for an aspirin or something... and then, the next thing I remember is waking up in the hospital and my stomach feeling like someone turned it inside out."

Billy's voice cracked slightly. "When they told me… you know… what I did…" Billy stared down at the floor, finding it difficult to continue. "I didn't believe them."

"Have you ever had suicidal thoughts before?"

"Hell no," he was quick to respond, as he raised his eyes to meet Rasher's. "I swear. If I was in my right mind, I'd never do something like that. I don't know how it happened."

"That's what we are here to try and figure out."

The young athlete looked up hopefully. "I'm willing to try anything. Electric shock, hypnosis… anything. I can't deal with the headaches, and the blackouts… or not knowing if one day I might do something stupid… like try to kill myself again. I've said things, done things… some of which I know I did, and some I can't remember. Or don't want to remember. I totally fucked up all my relationships. I've hurt people. People I care about. Maybe you could just cut my head open and re-wire my brain somehow."

"Unfortunately, Billy, psychological issues can't readily be fixed with a scalpel. Even if a surgeon physically looked inside your brain, we couldn't tell specifically what is causing your anxiety disorder and depression, or what triggered your regrettable anti-social behavior."

"So that's it. I'm gonna stay screwed up forever. There's no way out of this?"

"I didn't say that." Rasher leaned forward in his chair. "Is there a family history of suicide?"

Billy shook his head. "Not that I know of. Both my parents died when I was kid – but they were killed by a drunk driver."

"Were you in the car at the time?"

"No. We were at my Aunt's house in Lake Geneva when it happened."

"We?"

"Me and my sister, Diane. We used to go there in June sometimes. No. Maybe it was July. You know, when school was out. I think. It was a long time ago."

"To lose one's parents at such an early age can be quite traumatic. Can you tell me a little more about it?"

Billy looked up and sighed. "I was a kid. It's not like anyone filled me in on many details. Mostly I remember my sister and all the grownups crying."

"And you?"

Billy just shrugged. "I don't remember if I cried or not."

"Tell me about your sister. Are the two of you close?"

"Not really. Not anymore. Diane just up and left, first chance she got. One day she got it into her head to disappear, and did. No explanation. Nothing. Didn't bother to leave a note, or even say goodbye."

"How did that make you feel?"

"Pretty shitty. But I got over it quick enough, as I recall."

"How much of your childhood do you actually remember, Billy?"

"Enough, I suppose, like everyone else. There were good times and not so good times. Y'know how it goes."

"Tell me about one of the good times?"

Billy thought for a moment, then lifted his head with a crooked half-smile. "I remember the first time I ever whacked a baseball way over the dumpsters."

"How did that make you feel?"

"It felt great. I was ten. I felt special. Like I could finally do something better than everybody else." Billy was starting to warm up to Rasher. Whatever reservations he may have had when he first walked in, no longer seemed to be an issue. At the conclusion of their first session, Billy committed to seeing Dr. Rasher on a daily basis.

Over the course of the next few weeks they talked about life and love and baseball, and the extreme pressure heaped upon young athletes hoping to make it in today's highly competitive sports world.

Though Billy rarely missed a therapy appointment, his mood and level of willingness to participate began to vacillate greatly from session to session. There were days he seemed more in control, deeply thoughtful, at times, even quite disarming and clever. Some days he complained about not sleeping well the night before and appeared restless, more agitated, and almost hostile towards Rasher. Despite Rasher's repeated probing, Billy doggedly continued to stick to his belief that he suffered no ill effects from having been raised by an assortment of distant relatives and caring foster parents. As far as Billy knew, there were no raging lunatics locking him in closets, or wicked babysitters molesting him when no one was home. He continued to blame his separation from baseball, and his last fight with Julie for his out-of-control temper, the blackouts and the depression that drove him to attempt suicide.

Rasher began to suspect his patient's mental state was more complex than social anxiety disorder and clinical depression. Conventional therapy alone might not be enough to properly treat his young client. Which was why, with a little gentle prodding on Rasher's part, he got Billy to agree to venture into Highwater.

16

Highwater Acres was a world unto itself. It sat cloistered amid soaring, welcoming green arbors, perched high atop a formidable hillside, safely sequestered from the higher functioning inhabitants dwelling blissfully unaware below.

Billy followed the warm and cheery-faced, Miss Duncan down a cheery painted hallway into a small equally cheerful room where eight men sat in a circle on straight-back chairs, taking in eight sports sections of the morning paper. Miss Duncan placed a reassuring hand on his shoulder, smiled generously, and told him once again how truly glad they were that he had chosen to join them at Highwater. She assured him, "We are all here to help you, Billy. Each and every one of us."

She closed the door sharply behind her and the men politely snapped their papers shut giving her their full attention. When Billy was introduced, he found himself staring into sixteen unwavering eyes, each set belonging to a distinct and decidedly different personality.

"Shall we begin?" Miss Duncan asked, looking around the circle. But none of those gathered seemed particularly eager to join in. They stared straight ahead, quite content not saying anything. "Alright then, perhaps we should continue where we left off last time." She turned to include their newest arrival. "We were discussing the importance of trust," then turned back to address the group as a whole. "As I recall, Barney expressed a growing concern that he no longer felt he could trust the other members of our group."

"That's true, Miss Duncan," Barney interjected, carefully screening the faces of those assembled.

"Perhaps you can give us an example, so we can better understand why you feel this way."

Barney swiveled uncomfortably in his chair, his thick chubby fingers tightly clutching the underside of his thighs. "There are lots of things people are doing to me," Barney confided in a hushed voice. "Last week, on Thursday, I couldn't find my catcher's mitt. I looked everywhere. The next day, Friday, the door to Benish's room was open, and I saw my mitt hidden under his bed."

"Benish, is this true?" Duncan asked, looking in his direction. "Was Barney's catcher's mitt hidden under your bed?"

The man with the apple pie face and the goofy grin spoke up, "Yes… and no, Miss Duncan. Yes, the mitt was under my bed, but no, I didn't hide it there. Much as I'd like to take credit for screwing with Barney's head, I have no idea how it got there."

Duncan spoke slowly and precisely. "I see. And you wouldn't be lying again, Benish, would you? Because you know how I feel about lying."

"Yes, ma'am. And no, I'm not lying."

Billy eyeballed Benish, looking for a 'tell,' certain he had spotted a quickening of activity around his Adam's apple and a hard swallow or two when he answered. He made a mental note not to buy anything this guy's peddling.

Miss Duncan seemed the soul of patience as she returned her gaze to Barney. "Is it possible you could have left it there at another time and it accidentally got kicked under his bed?"

Barney emphatically shook his head. "I never ever was in his room. He always closes his door every time he sees me coming down the hall. I know Benish took it."

"That's a crock and you know it, Butt-face," was the immediate response from the ebony chiseled, powerfully built man seated directly to Billy's left. The man leaned forward and raised an accusatory finger at Barney. "The truth is you don't trust anybody, including yourself. Never did and probably never will, you screwed-up son of a bitch."

"Why would you say that, Henry?" Duncan asked, calmly.

"Because, Miss D, Barney's not happy unless he's convinced somebody's out to get him. The simple truth is, more than likely, nobody here gives enough of a shit about him to bother doing him wrong. I know I don't. If I did, I would have strangled the little weasel months ago."

At this point, Billy made a mental note to steer clear of Henry as well.

Miss Duncan's soft mackerel orbs looked deeply into Henry's searching for a meaningful connection before she spoke. "Did Barney do something that caused you to feel this way? Some specific incident?"

Henry leaned back deep in his chair before replying. "Nah. He makes my skin crawl, that's all. His fat, whiny ass always accusing people of talking about him."

Okay, thought Billy. Might as well add weird, whiny Barney to the list.

"If he wasn't the only one who could catch Popwell's knuckleball," Henry added, "I wouldn't give him the time of day."

Duncan focused her gaze back onto the group. "Do you all feel this way about Barney?"

Concerned his worst fears were indeed true, poor Barney shifted in his seat unable to look directly at anyone other than Duncan. Billy studied the faces of the men seated in the circle, wishing he were somewhere else right now. What was Rasher thinking sending him here?

"Anyone?" Duncan repeated. "Huff? What about you?"

Huff crossed, then uncrossed his legs, cupping his chin with the squishy part of his palm, thoughtfully stroking the day's worth of stubble shadowing his firm set jaw line, while stealing a sideways glance at the man seated directly across from him. He lowered his eyes, parted his lips as if to speak, then changed his mind, opting to remain silent after all. The covert exchange between the two did not go unnoticed by Billy, or O'Malley, the long and lanky man, with flushed red cheeks and bloodshot eyes seated alongside Miss Duncan. O'Malley immediately proceeded to vigorously pursue a series of nonexistent lint threads to avoid being caught in the glare of Duncan's inquisition. Billy wondered as he looked around, if Miss Duncan had noticed as he did, the subtle way each of the men appeared to look to one person in particular before they spoke. A man named Popwell. It was almost as if they were waiting for a sign from him before deigning to respond to Duncan's questions.

The awkward silence was finally broken by the hesitant voice of a wiry, fair-haired young man with a stubborn cowlick at the top of his head that shot straight up like a haystack. He raised his hand meekly before responding. "I... um, kind of like Barney."

"Really?" Barney sighed, his lips forming a lop-sided, crooked, half smile.

"Good. Thank you, Scooter," Miss Duncan continued. "I'm very happy to hear that." Although no one else was forthcoming with any additional endorsements or rejections, she decided to plough ahead in a conciliatory manner. "I think it's very important to remember we all share a common goal. That of becoming happy and healthy. And the best way to achieve that goal is to strive to understand one another's feelings and try to work through our differences. Wouldn't you agree, Billy?"

Billy bolted upright in his seat, painfully aware that the spotlight had abruptly shifted onto him. Not that Billy was a stranger to taking center stage. But right now, surrounded by a gaggle of somewhat strange strangers, he found himself at a loss for words.

"Yeah. I suppose, but... I really don't know what you want me to say. This whole 'group' thing is still kind of new to me and..." his voice trailing off to a whisper.

"It's really quite simple," Miss Duncan continued. "We need to encourage our individual strengths and work to minimize our collective weaknesses if we have any hope to succeed in the world outside Highwater. And..." she concluded, "that is as true in group as it is when you're out on the baseball field."

Billy's ears perked up. Baseball field? Catcher's mitts? Knuckleballs? Was Miss D simply making a clever analogy or were these collective loony tunes a bunch of frizzed out ballplayers? Was Highwater some kind of happy farm for athletes with mental meltdowns? This was definitely not what Billy had expected.

17

Wafer-like clouds floated like cotton candy above the manicured field behind Highwater's back doors. To Billy's surprise, the rag-tag gang from the morning's group therapy session looked like a well-oiled machine, as Barney hit fungo, grounding to Scooter, who rifled to Huff, back to Henry. Crisp and clean, the perfect double play. Billy scratched his head, wondering how a bunch of random guys in a mental facility could be this good.

After twenty minutes of watching them work their infield magic, Huff trotted over to Billy carrying a bat. "Hey, uh, Billy, or whatever your name is, feel like hitting a few?" Huff extended the bat a couple of inches from his hand.

Billy looked down at the dusty piece of lumber with the hungry eyes of a recovering addict eyeballing a gram of coke, but resisted nonetheless. "Nah. That's okay."

"C'mon, it'll be fun," Huff coaxed, the bat almost touching Billy's fingers.

"I don't play baseball anymore," Billy said.

Huff lowered the bat and brought it down to his side but wasn't about to give up.

"Why not?"

"Long story. Look, why don't you just play your little game and let me sit up here by myself."

"C'mon, take a few swings," Huff said, with a grin. "What have you got to lose? It's just O'Malley out there and even when he's sober he throws like a girl. It's not like I'm asking you to go up against Popwell. The man's a legend. Nobody hits him." Billy snickered with derision, amused by Huff's obvious exaggeration. "You know what I think?" Huff continued. "I think you probably never picked up a bat in your life."

"If you say so," Billy said, trying to end the exchange, shifting his gaze in another direction. But Huff merely tried a new tactic.

"Look. Forget what I said. I bet you're a hell of a player, and... well... me and the guys here got ourselves a little team called The Bellevederes, and the truth is we could use another body. What do you say?"

Billy turned back. "You're not gonna let up, are you?"

Huff smiled. "What position do you play?"

"Right field," Billy answered.

Huff's face brightened. "Oh, yeah? What a coincidence! It just so happens we're in desperate need of a right fielder. One who can hit, that is."

"I don't think so." Billy started back toward the main building, but was stopped as Huff took the handle of the bat and poked it firmly into Billy's sternum.

"What's the big deal? You got something better to do? Why not try being productive while you're here? Be part of the group. Show us what you got."

Billy glared at the bat boring a hole in his chest. "Fine. You want to see some hitting," he sputtered, wrenching the stick from Huff's grip.

Billy stepped into the batters box. O'Malley wound up and threw. Billy swung and connected, driving the ball into the next zip code. O'Malley was caught off-guard, as were the rest of the team, when Billy cranked the next two pitches way out of the yard, rocketing over the trees.

Huff stood in awe. Speechless. They all were. Billy grinned, satisfied not a one of these misfits had ever witnessed the power of a true major leaguer before. He stood in for another round of swats. His Technicolor eyes sharply focused, waiting on each new delivery. Another fastball -- CRASH, a screaming liner off the fence in deep left center field. This time he tossed the bat away with a thud and decided to race around the bases backwards, ala the late, great Jimmy Piersall, a former major leaguer who had clocked a little time in a loony bin or two in his day.

When Billy rounded third and headed for home, he saw Scooter grab the ball, and cock his arm back. Halfway toward the plate, Billy quickly turned as Scooter rifled a strike into Barney's chest protector. Billy slid hard and beat the tag. Inside the park home run. Exhilaration. He remained on the ground, savoring the moment.

All at once, the sunlight seemed to darken as if a thundercloud emerged from the heavens. It was B. J. Popwell, standing over him, larger than life. Everything stopped. Billy was no longer the focus of anyone's attention. His six sensational dingers were but a distant memory.

The players watched in silence as Popwell strode to the mound, a sight to behold in a gray baseball jersey with buttons missing down the front. He was as magical as any major leaguer from the 1920's, clad in faded pin striped flannel pants, high socks, and mud stained spikes so worn, they should have long been retired to a display case.

He was tall and lean, with angular features, and powerful hands with long, bony fingers. He dug a little hole in the dirt with what was left of the metal nub in his spikes as Barney obediently raced to squat behind the plate. Popwell started with slow, easy tosses. But everything he threw was slow and easy. Knuckleball after knuckleball, the slowest pitch Billy had ever seen.

Billy studied his delivery. The lack of rotation seemed to make the ball grow larger, as if he was pitching with a honeydew melon. Billy's juices were flowing. He couldn't wait to step in and crank one all the way to the south side.

"Let's see what you can do now, Mister Billy Baseball," Benish taunted.

Billy stepped into the batter's box and took a few practice swings. Huff's earlier statement returned to haunt him. He couldn't help but wonder if this Popwell was some kind of legend after all. But hey, he was Billy Rubin. He could hit anyone.

Billy kicked some pebbles aside with the tip of his shoe, as Popwell nodded to Barney and reared back with a high leg kick that touched the treetops. It was a lazy knuckleball that seemed to take an entire baseball season to cross the plate. Way over-anxious, Billy swung and missed with such force he nearly hit the ground. He could hear the derisive snickering coming from the infield.

He waited on the next pitch, trying to time it perfectly. He noticed as the ball arrived, it didn't behave like a normal knuckleball. It took a nasty dip and the bottom fell out. He made contact, but just barely, squibbing the ball foul, just a few feet up the first base line. Billy realized if he had a shot, he had to nail the ball right before the dip. Every fiber of his being at the ready waiting for the next ugly pitch to arrive so he could club it into next Tuesday and put the Popwell myth to bed forever.

Popwell came set and threw. The pitch started out low and inside and ended up high and outside. It defied the laws of physics. Billy swung so late and off balance, the bat flew from his hands landing yards past third, eventually coming to a stop in short left field. He was dumbfounded.

As Benish ran Billy's bat back from the outfield, all Billy could do was stare at Popwell whose expression remained irritatingly unchanged.

Billy continued taking cuts without success. The best he could muster was a slow nubber up the third base line and an occasional pop up to the shallow part of the outfield.

The Bellevederes were loving it. They laughed and jeered at every swing and miss, every foul tip off Billy's bat. His anger began to surface. He could feel himself losing control. "What the fuck you morons laughing at? Do you even know who I am?!" he shouted. "Fucking Billy Joseph Rubin. The greatest college player ever!"

And then, he swung and missed. The Bellevederes could hardly contain themselves. Billy began to seriously lose it. He vented his frustration, cursing and kicking at the dirt, while one by one, the members of the team began leaving the field.

"Where the fuck you going?" Billy called after them. "C'mon back here. I'm not done 'til I say I'm done! Do you hear me?" he screamed, punch drunk with exhaustion.

"I hear you," Popwell said in a quiet monotone. Billy swiveled on his heels, his tired eyes burning into Popwell's.

The mighty pitcher reared back and threw – Billy swung and missed, then fell to his knees. He repeatedly slammed his bat against the plate continuing his tantrum. A moment later, he looked around only to discover he was screaming at nobody. Just like a real crazy person.

Later in his room, reeling from his pathetic performance at the hands of B.J. Popwell, Billy reached beneath his bed and slid out a brown leather suitcase containing memorabilia from his playing days at USC. There were newspaper articles, some of which had yellowed, old game programs and photographs, all attesting to his greatness, and a monogrammed, silver flask presented by his teammates the day they retired his number, which Billy had forgotten he packed after promising Rasher to abstain while at Highwater. As Billy leafed through his illustrious achievements, they all seemed a lifetime ago. Until he came upon the photo from the College World Series. Of the catch he still had no memory of. The catch that was the start of several unexplained blackouts. Blackouts that may have led to his near fatal accident; to the end of a promising baseball career and the beginning of his life at Highwater.

He felt humiliated by Popwell. That the great Billy Rubin had been reduced to a 'has been,' a 'once was,' a 'could have been.' His hands shook as he picked up the silver flask and uncapped it. The hell with his promise to Rasher. He lifted it to his lips. It was empty. Someone must have found it and poured out the contents he so dearly craved right now. He railed at the world, as he fired the suitcase against the wall, savagely spraying the contents about the room.

18

Huff, hunched over the lunchroom table, sank his teeth deep into the fat, juicy, charbroiled chicken breast sandwich, as splatters of mayonnaise slopped onto the sports section of his afternoon paper. "Hey, you guys seen this?" Five heads tilted upward from their noonday fare. "The new owner of the Cubs wants to knock down Wrigley," Huff stammered, with a look of panic. "He wants luxury boxes."

"Fuck that!" Henry chimed in. "They don't need luxury boxes. What they need is a solid fifth starter and a couple more power hitters."

"I've never even been to Wrigley," Barney lamented, dredging a fistful of fries through a puddle of ketchup.

"Come to think of it, neither have I," said Huff. "What about the rest of you guys?"

"Yeah. Sure. I've been so many times one of the concession stands named a sandwich after me. The Benish Beefball Hero."

"You lying fool," chided Henry, playfully swatting him across the back of his head. "You never been within a hundred blocks of Wrigley."

"Hey! Ow! And what makes you think I'm lying?"

"'Cause your lips are moving," Henry laughed, before diving back into his lunch.

"I almost got to go," Barney said, pounding his fist on the table. "It was a fifth grade field trip. But when I showed up in the schoolyard, I found out the bus had left without me. The teacher said I got the time wrong, but I know they left me behind on purpose. They were all in on it!"

Henry rolled his eyes, picked up his sandwich and slid his chair a few inches further away from Barney. Suddenly, Scooter raised a timid index finger in the air. "I've been to Wrigley. Me and two friends wanted to go real bad, but none of us ever had much spending money. So, we dug through those big green trash bins in the alleys and cashed in all the cans and soda bottles we could find."

"Dumpster diving. Finally, a sport Scooter might even be good at," Benish chortled.

Scooter lowered his head.

"Give it a rest, Benish. Let the kid tell his story," Henry broke in. "Go on Scooter. What happened?"

"It was on a Tuesday... we hadn't figured on the garbage men carting off most of the trash Monday afternoon. We only found enough for one ticket. So, we decided each of us would get to watch the game for three innings, then we'd come out and pass the ticket to the next guy, so he could go in. I got the last three -- seventh, eighth and ninth. It was the greatest day of my life. Even if I only got to see two batters."

"Two batters?" Henry piped in. "Sounds like your pals might've pulled a fast one. My guess is they didn't let you in till the bottom of the ninth, my friend."

"They tricked you," Barney snorted, righteously. "You thought they were your friends, but they weren't. You can't trust anything anyone says to you – ever."

"There you go again, Barney," Huff intoned. "Always thinking people are plotting and planning."

"It wasn't like that," Scooter said. "As soon as I sat down, it started to rain. At first nobody cared. We were all too busy watching the game. The Cubs led 3-1. Then it really started coming down. Coming down in buckets, and lots of people got up to leave. When it didn't let up, they called the game. But the Cubs won anyway so I didn't mind much at all. It was so cool watching the players run across the grass heading for the dugout. I waved as they ran past but I don't think they saw me, 'cause nobody waved back. I stayed in my seat 'til I was the last person left in the stands. Until one of the security guards told me I had to go home. I didn't care how wet I got. I swear, I never even saw the lightning, or heard the thunder crashing up above. Yup," he said, sighing deeply. "That was definitely one of the best days of my life."

Henry, Barney, and Huff nodded in agreement, like a trio of Bobblehead dolls. Each wishing it had been them sitting out there in the rain that day.

The Bellevederes looked up as Billy appeared, balancing a manila folder and a plate of meatballs and spaghetti. He nodded a terse hello, but opted to sit alone a few tables away. A few nodded back then resumed their conversation.

Before Billy had a chance to so much as twirl his fork, two rather serious looking residents approached him. He knew they were residents because they weren't dressed like any of the staff. Armand was the first to speak. His soft, full face framed by a thicket of blue-black hair, slicked back behind his donkey-shaped ears. He was eager to introduce himself and his cohort, Sven, a man of few words and even fewer independent thoughts. The two men slid into seats across from Billy, and wasted little time letting him know how excited they were to have him show up at Highwater. It seems they somehow knew all about Billy's past athletic accomplishments. Apparently, Popwell and the Bellevederes weren't the only ones at Highwater with a baseball team. Armand's team was called The Titans.

The Titans' prime objective was to intercept and conscript any potential Bellevedere. Toward that end, Armand unabashedly flattered and stroked Billy's ego. He told him how honored they were to meet someone who actually played in the Bigs.

"We're not all that different, Billy. I played a little college ball myself, once upon a time. And, not to brag, but I was pretty damn good."

"Really?" Billy queried curiously. "Who'd you play for?"

"Couple a different schools. You know how it is. I kept looking for the right fit. Besides, that's besides the point. The point, my friend, is that I could've gone pro if I wanted to. But shit happens. You know how that is."

"It's true. Nobody can hit a ball like Armand," Sven jumped in. "He's the best. If it wasn't for Popwell's stupid knuckleball, the Titans would win every game." Sven looked up and caught a glimpse of Henry watching them put the moves on Billy. With a quick jerk of his head, he let the leader of the Titans know they were being watched. Armand suggested they take their conversation to the Music Room and out of earshot of the Bellevederes. Before Billy could protest, Armand placed a rather insistent arm beneath Billy's elbow and escorted him swiftly from the cafeteria.

Once assured they had Billy safely to themselves, they decided to take him into their confidence. Armand was convinced, with Billy on the side of the Titans, they could beat the Bellevederes in a take no prisoners, grudge match. A game, Armand had been waiting a long time for. Up until now, it's been all trash talk, but Armand was intent on making it a reality.

Billy wasn't quite so sure. Although he had no idea how good Armand's team was, he certainly knew first-hand how unhittable Popwell seemed to be. Armand assured him that wouldn't be a problem much longer. He had a plan already in place and adding Billy to their team was the final piece of the puzzle. While Billy had to admit the prospect of knocking Popwell off his pedestal was tempting, he still wasn't sure he wanted to be on anyone's team right now. Armand suggested he give it some serious consideration.

"Good afternoon, gentlemen," Miss Duncan began. "I think today, rather than my suggesting a topic, I'd like to offer each of you the opportunity to discuss whatever you'd like. Is there someone who would like to start us off?" When no one volunteered, Billy reached for the folder he had placed beneath his chair.

"There is something I'd like to clear up," he said. "A certain misconception as to what I can do on a baseball field."

Though no one appeared the least bit interested, Billy opened his folder and pressed on. "These are articles by legitimate sportswriters and photos documenting just some of what I did in college. Not to mention my inside the park home run my first time at bat for the Kansas City Royals. I can't believe none of you ever heard of me."

Duncan slowly shook her head in disappointment. "Billy, here at Highwater we try not to trade on our past accomplishments, especially in group. It's very important everyone feel as though they are on a level playing field, so to speak. I think it would be far more productive to focus on what caused you to come here. Your feelings, your actions. The very purpose of our being here is to listen to one another and try to help."

Billy fell silent as Duncan continued. "If you're not ready to talk about it just yet... well, that's fine too. Huff, we haven't heard from you in a while."

Huff turned from Duncan to Billy, daggers launching from the recesses of his bright, hazel eyes. "I hope you enjoyed your lunch, Billy Rubin," Huff said snidely, leaving no room for any doubt at the implication.

Henry rose from his chair. His thousand-watt smile burst brightly from the blackness of his face. But his eyes bespoke a different tale. Unlike his smile, anger spewed like lava from his mud colored orbs. "We saw you cozying up to the Titans. You got no business being in here with us anymore."

Billy was transfixed by Henry's massive, menacing fists. He looked to Miss Duncan for reassurance Highwater would certainly not condone this kind of threatening behavior. But Duncan remained neutral.

Just when Billy thought the entire circumference of his neck was about to be enveloped by a large, meaty, hand angrily choking the blood flow from entering his carotid artery, Popwell raised an arm above his head. Henry immediately backed off, and returned to his seat.

Billy felt a surge of relief flow though his body. At the same time sickened by the influence Popwell apparently wielded over every man in the room. He was resolutely determined never to fall under Popwell's spell.

Billy looked around the circle of faces. "What's wrong with all of you?" Billy demanded. "Don't you have minds of your own? You're never gonna get out of here if you can't think for yourselves. It's pathetic how you let this guy run the show. Don't you see how he's holding you back."

"Hey, new guy," an angry voice yelled out. Billy spun around to find Popwell glaring back at him. "No one asked for your opinion. Somebody needs to clue you in as to who's in charge around here. So shut your mouth or I'll shut it for you. You got it?"

"You shut up," Billy countered. "You might be able to bully them, but you're not in charge of me."

"What's the matter, little girl?" Popwell growled. "You upset 'cause Duncan won't let you show off your little clippings! Still think you're hot shit in the baseball world? Think again. Fuck your photos. You're nobody in here. You better learn your place or get the hell out before I cut you to ribbons!"

Popwell's mouth twisted into a nasty sneer. He bared his teeth, a rabid animal about to pounce. Then, to Billy's horror, he whipped out a small switchblade from his hip pocket and actually started to hiss.

Duncan quickly stepped in between them. "Put the knife away, Charley," her voice firm and calm. Then demanded sternly, "I need you to leave at once! This is Popwell's session, not yours."

"Fuck off, Duncan. Anyone who talks to Popwell like that deserves to get his ass kicked."

It was bizarre, like nothing Billy had ever seen before. *And who the hell was Charley?*

"C'mon, pussy," Popwell baited Billy. Billy stood his ground as Popwell shoved Miss Duncan aside and lunged forward, nicking Billy's wrist with the tip of the blade. They danced around for a moment until Popwell swiped at him again, this time slicing Billy's forearm. Billy watched the thick red liquid splatter back onto his shirt and snapped. He went for Popwell's throat, sending him tumbling over a chair. It was a free-for-all, as everyone jumped into the melee.

"Popwell, please make Charley stop!" Miss Duncan cried, to no avail, as chairs flew wildly in all directions. Duncan raced to the door to summon help.

Billy fought back, thrashing and brawling, until the door flew open and Duncan returned with two of Highwater's security guards, Watermain and Big Gunther.

Watermain quickly tossed Popwell off Billy. Billy leapt to his feet, adrenalin pumping, and charged after Popwell like a mad dog. Big Gunther slammed him in the back with a massive forearm, knocking him to the ground. The last thing Billy remembered was someone readying the syringe and driving the needle home.

19

When he opened his eyes, his wrist and forearm were swathed in bandages. His hands felt cold and numb against the crisp cotton bed linen. He sat up with difficulty and wiggled his fingers, making sure all ten digits remained accountable. Two large welts hung below his eyes like saddlebags off the mount of a donkey. He wasn't sure how long he'd been out of it. It could have been four hours or four weeks. Maybe four years for all he knew.

Try as he might, each time he attempted to rise above his stupor, he fell back onto the sheets, his legs not yet finding the strength to fully support his body. His throat felt parched. He recalled seeing a water fountain back by the stairwell. He braced his hands on the edge of the nightstand and hoisted himself to a standing position. Moving from the nightstand to the chair, to the door, he slowly made his way out into the hall. He inched along the corridor, maintaining his tenuous balance by grasping the doorknobs of each room he passed, like a loopy Tarzan making his way through the jungle one vine at a time.

As the fountain came into view, he heard what sounded like the faint roar of an animal coming from behind a solid steel door. The noises emanating from deep within the room were definitely anything but human. As he drew closer, the feral wailing grew louder, wilder, more strident. He stood a few inches in front of the door, and peered through the small wire-mesh glass window, terrified by what he saw.

He stiffened like a toe-tagged corpse. He desperately wanted to flee, but found he couldn't move a muscle. He stared through the glass, so focused he could count the number of squares the wires made as they spider-webbed through the pane. Maybe, he prayed, he was merely hallucinating.

Then, a hand crept up and touched him on the shoulder. He jumped and fell backwards, knocking himself to the ground. Watermain loomed over him, curious as to what Billy was doing out in the hall alone at this late hour. Much as Billy would've loved to respond, his facial muscles remained locked in place, unable to speak. Watermain simply tossed him over his shoulder like a sack of rice and brought him back to bed.

In the morning, Watermain returned. The doorknob turned in his hand, but the door wouldn't budge. He pressed the meaty part of his shoulder against the door to no avail. He banged and called Billy's name.

Billy tensed. "Who's out there?" he shouted.

"It's Watermain. What the hell's wrong with the door?" He pressed his ear against it, listening as Billy's feet shuffled closer. Billy carefully removed the chair he had wedged tightly beneath the door handle and let Watermain in.

"It must've gotten jammed," Billy offered, as Watermain entered, scratching his head.

"Guess I'll have Nelson come by and take a look at it," Watermain responded. "In the meantime, you got about fifteen minutes to get yourself over to Dr. Rasher's." The guard eyed Billy's bandaged arm, and sighed. "If I were you," he offered, "I wouldn't be giving the Doc too many details. It might only make things worse for you around here."

20

"I'd like to talk about Highwater," Rasher began.

Billy wasn't thinking about what happened in Group as he sat in the chair in Rasher's office. All he could think about was what he saw behind the steel door last night. He thought of telling Rasher about it, but what was there to tell? It was too horrible to be real. He decided the less he talked about it; the less it could frighten him.

"What do you want to know?"

"How you cut your arm might be a good place to start."

Billy thought about Watermain's words of caution. "It was an accident. It's nothing."

Rasher peered over the brim of his reading glasses, "I can't help you if you're not honest with me."

Billy winced, embarrassed and irritated that someone must have told him about the fight before he had the chance to present his side. For a moment, he wondered if it was Miss Duncan. It bothered him that the kind-faced woman might've been the one who ratted him out. "I don't know what you've heard but none of it was my fault. They're a group of ignorant suck-ups who let themselves be led around by the nose by a violent psycho, who's only claim to fame is an ability to throw a knuckleball." Billy got up and began to pace. "Maybe this was a mistake. Maybe I never should've gone into Highwater."

"Why do you feel that way?"

"Isn't it obvious? I don't fit in. I'm not one of them. And, I wouldn't want to be." Billy walked to the window and peered into the hall through the partially opened blinds, registering how different things look when you're inside looking out. He snapped the blinds shut then turned to Rasher. "It's really fucked up. They wouldn't even look when I tried to show them my clippings. I'm a hundred times better than this Popwell. I deserve their respect."

"Give them a chance, Billy. Instead of showing off your clippings, let them get to know you better. Try getting to know them."

Billy sat down, lowered his head and cradled his bandaged arm in his lap. As far as he could tell, Rasher's therapeutic approach made no sense at all. It certainly wasn't working, as evidenced by the gash in his arm and the pain in his head. Bring on the inkblots and electric prods and try zapping him back to normal. He was ready for anything. Anything but having to sit and listen to Rasher yammer on about linking arms and making nice to a bunch of misfits?

"Would you like to tell me how your arm really got cut?"

Billy raised his head. Rasher leaned forward, his long fingers steepled before him.

Billy paused. "Okay. Fine. One minute I'm trying to talk some sense into these ... Bellevederes... trying to help them... you understand?" Rasher nodded with a 'go on' tilt of his head. "The next thing I know, Popwell jumps out of his chair, comes cursing at me with a knife, and Miss Duncan starts yelling at him to tell some guy named Charley to go away."

"Was that the first time you met Charley?"

"You mean there really is a Charley?" Billy asked surprised. "I just thought Duncan was losing it in all the excitement. I thought she called him Charley by mistake."

"Charley serves as Popwell's protector. He surfaces from time to time, when he feels Popwell is being threatened. He's an alter, which makes him a part of the group. So you need to learn how to deal with him as well."

Billy eyed the shrink with curiosity. "An alter? What do you mean? Like Popwell's alter ego, or an evil twin?"

Rasher treaded cautiously. "More like a multiple."

A multiple? Billy took a minute to process. That's pretty out there, he thought, almost as crazy as what he thought he saw in the locked room behind the steel door.

21

The hallway was insanely quiet. Not a sound. Not a cough. Not a whisper. And certainly not a beastly roar, as Billy headed down the corridor to his room. Yet something possessed him to check out the window of the steel door at the far end of the hall again. If for no reason other than to reassure himself there was nothing to be afraid of.

He crept up to the door and inched closer to the web-wired glass. He peered inside. A bolt of norepinephrine shot through his body. Inside, chained and shackled to the wall was a sleeping, bearded behemoth. The very monster he had convinced himself existed only in his nightmares. He felt like a deer in a hunter's crosshairs, as the frightening creature snapped opened his eyes, sensing someone watching him. The beast turned toward him. An evil inner flame of madness shot through the slits of his eyes.

Billy spun on his heels and ran. Ran back down the hall. Ran down the stairwell. Searching for Watermain, Miss Duncan, or just someone a little more human. He pushed open the stairwell door and headed down another hallway, his footsteps echoing off the empty corridor walls.

Billy entered the Day Room. It was quiet, save for a solitary resident named Rochester seated at a table playing Bingo by himself.

"G-55," Rochester shouted enthusiastically, to no one in particular. Then let out a groan upon discovering G-55 was not a number he needed. Billy inched closer. "B-12," Rochester called out, systematically scouring the empty numbered squares before him with great intensity. "B-12," he repeated, smiling broadly. "A truly fascinating vitamin and... the final number I need for ... *B...I...N...G...O*," he screamed. "Bingo! Bingo! Bingo!"

"Congratulations," Billy offered by way of polite conversation. "What's the prize for winning?"

"Prize?" Rochester responded, haughtily. "There is no prize. Victory is its own reward. Not everyone needs to hear the cheers of anonymous crowds ringing in their ears."

Billy decided it was time to put a little space between the two of them, and ventured over to the doorway to see if anyone else was out in the hall. Rochester scurried up alongside him with a devilish grin. "I hear there's a rumor going around the Bellevederes think you're a bench jockey with a burnt-out bazooka."

Billy stopped in his tracks. "What'd you say?" he demanded.

Rochester suddenly excused himself, saying he'd return anon. When he next appeared, he was dressed in a rather formal, three-piece suit, a bold yellow tulip graced the buttonhole of his lapel. Without missing a beat, Rochester launched back in. "Henry thinks you're an asshole. Benish said you're a loser and a bad sport. Things don't go your way you pull a tantrum like a sniveling, spoiled brat. And Huff thinks you might as well take up knitting while you're here, 'cause you're never gonna get a hit off Popwell no matter how hard you try."

Billy felt his head exploding. "They're a sick bunch of motherfuckers," he screamed.

"Hmm," Rochester pondered, touching a manicured fingertip lightly to his lips. "Perhaps Benish wasn't so far afield in describing that nasty temper of yours."

"Fuck you and the mental disorder you rode in on, Rochester!"

Rochester loved drama. By now, he was rubbing his hands with glee; ecstatic he had pushed the right buttons to fire up Billy's engines. "Hey, why slay the messenger? C'mon, let's go out to the field and put those nasty accusations to rest."

"Not so fast. First, I want to know what else they said about me."

But, before he would impart any more dirt, Rochester excused himself once more and swore he'd be right back. Billy fumed as he waited impatiently. This time Rochester returned clad in bright floral, cabana wear suitable for an ocean cruise. His sartorial changes without reason were beginning to infuriate Billy.

"Why the hell do you keep changing outfits?"

"Because I can. Because I am the master of my earthly realm and will never surrender to mass conformity. Because freedom of expression is all we have left in this cruel, controlling world."

Billy sighed, wishing he had the last two minutes of his life back. "C'mon, Rochester, concentrate. What else did they say about me?"

"What else did who say about who?" Rochester replied, innocently.

"The Bellevederes. What else did they say about me?"

Rochester shrugged. "I have no idea what you're talking about."

Billy had enough. In frustration, he swept his arm angrily across the table sending Rochester's Bingo cards and brightly-colored chips sailing, then charged from the Day Room and out onto the field.

Popwell was warming up. Miss Duncan sat on the first row of the bleachers carefully observing, hoping a little fresh air might help restore harmony and reason following the other day's bloody fracas. Her heart was in her throat as Billy swept across the grass and grabbed a bat leaning against the fence, then marched to the plate and locked eyes with Popwell. Miss Duncan shuddered, fearing he might be planning to use it to bash in Popwell's skull.

"C'mon, B.J., or Popwell, or Charley, or whoever you are at the moment," he challenged loudly. "Throw me some of that crap you call a knuckleball."

Barney didn't know whether to push Billy out of the way or lower his husky frame to a crouch, pound his mitt and get ready to receive the pitch. As always, he deferred to Popwell, who responded with the familiar nod of his head.

Popwell peered through the shadows from under the long brim of his cap. Then, as he came set, Miss Duncan spoke up. "Please, Billy. Put down the bat. It's much too soon to play. Your arm needs to fully heal."

Billy glared back, tore off his soiled bandages and fired them into the dirt. "My arm's fine. I'm tired of people telling me whether or not I'm ready to play!"

"I'm just trying to help, Billy. We all are."

"I don't need your kind of help," he spit out. "C'mon, Popwell, it's getting dark."

Popwell reared back and delivered one of the ugliest knuckleballs Billy had ever seen.

Billy waited… and waited… and waited. And then, it finally arrived – CRACK! A streaming liner over the fence in left center field. Popwell wound up and threw again… and again… and again… CRACK! CRACK! CRACK! Three more gigantic blasts. Going, going, gone. Each one clearing the center field fence with room to spare.

Billy smiled broadly, his fingers finding the raw, crusted surface of his wounds. The Bellevederes were stupefied, standing silent like a collection of chiseled Terra Cotta Warriors.

Billy flung his bat against the fence, then glanced back over his shoulder long enough to soak up one last satisfied look at the stunned faces of the Bellevederes. His eyes darted to Popwell, who held his gaze, then without saying a word, offered Billy an unexpected tip of his cap.

Billy strode off the field with a buoyant gait. There at the back entrance to Highwater, Armand stood watching.

22

"Unfuckingbelievable!" Armand stated, whistling through his teeth. "You're even better than I thought."

"Thanks. But that was nothing. You don't get drafted number one if you haven't got the goods."

"Hey. You don't have to sell me," Armand agreed. "I never doubted how great you were. It just took a little longer to prove it to those psycho losers out there. Not that the great Billy Rubin should ever have to prove how talented he is to anyone. Am I right?"

"Well..." Billy began modestly enough.

"Of course I'm right," Armand briskly interjected, landing a hero's pat on Billy's shoulder. "C'mon," Armand continued, leading him down the hall to the Music Room.

Highwater's Music Room was a maelstrom of activity. The only thing missing was music. Lyle, the Titans' power hitting, first baseman, was straddled over a table, grunting and moaning, engaged in a friendly arm wrestling contest. His formidable opponent, starting pitcher, Grizzybowski, was a sloppy-looking Nordic-type, whose flaxen, shoulder length hair flopped back and forth like a sheepdog, alternately strained and grinned, confident his strong pitching arm would soon prevail. A couple of Titans were gathered round shouting words of encouragement, backing one or the other.

Armand's side-kick, Sven, was down to his last chip in a hot game of poker in the center of the room. But when he spotted Armand, he dropped his pair of queens and scurried right over.

"C'mon, Billy," Armand said, "Let me introduce you to the guys." Armand strode past Sven without a word, marched directly to the upright in the corner, and pounded his knuckles against the ivories, garnering everyone's attention.

"Fellow Titans... this is Billy Rubin," he proclaimed, with a generous wave of his arm. The Titans looked up warily at first. "I just watched Billy murder every lazy-ass pitch Popwell threw at him. I want him treated with the utmost respect." A disbelieving silence spread from face-to-face. "I am not shitting you. Popwell has met his match. C'mon boys. Get up and give the man his due."

As if on cue the Titans rose to their feet and broke into spirited applause. It felt a bit strange. But, hey… a standing ovation is a standing ovation, no matter the source. So Billy tipped his cap, and smiled appreciatively.

Content Billy's ego had been sufficiently stroked, Armand steered him toward a table in the back of the room for a more private discussion, then, lowered his voice and leaned in. Armand's eyes were wild, his tongue flicked back and forth like a rattlesnake, as he dug his nails deep into Billy's wrist. "The way I see it, we join forces and Popwell and his team goes down in flames."

Billy leaned back in his chair and looked around the room. Not a one of those assembled looked particularly athletic, let alone capable of crushing the Bellevederes in a bona fide game. Besides, who knew what dark and disturbing psychoses raced through their troubled minds? Ovations and praise aside, cozying up with a crazy like Armand didn't seem to offer much of an upside.

"Look, Armand. I'm flattered. But Popwell's got a pretty strong team. I don't want to burst your bubble, but, good as I am, it still takes nine men to make a winning team."

Armand scraped his chair closer bringing his face within a hair of Billy's ear. Billy could feel the heat of his fetid breath against his neck. "Don't underestimate the Titans," Armand said, grabbing Billy's arm. "Plus, we've got a secret weapon," he imparted, with a devilish grin. "Diablo," he whispered. His black lacquered eyebrows lifted knowingly like a pair of McDonald's arches.

Billy looked around the room. "Which one's Diablo?"

"He's not here. At the moment, he's temporarily confined to quarters on the third floor. Heavily sedated. Can't have visitors right now. But… you'll meet him soon enough."

Billy grew quiet. Third floor? Confined to quarters? Armand couldn't possibly be talking about the half-human cretin chained to the wall.

Armand's eyes flashed with excitement. His nasty little heart drummed like a snare. With Billy Rubin's arrival, everything was falling into place. No more demoralizing defeat at the hands of B.J. Popwell. No more taking second place in the Highwater hierarchy. The Titans stood poised to wipe The Bellevederes off the map, and when they did, Armand as their self-anointed leader would finally take his deserved place as the rightful King of Highwater.

Now all he had to do was concentrate on getting Diablo released.

23

At the next group session, the Bellevederes remained doggedly intractable, refusing to speak or participate while Billy sat among them.

"I've reached a decision, gentlemen," Miss Duncan began. "One I'm sure none of you will like. But I honestly see no other way for us to move forward." Benish yawned. Barney shuffled his feet, as Billy continued to glare at all of them defiantly. "We simply have to make a better effort to interact in a healthy manner with one another. And so, as of today, Billy is to be included in all your practice sessions and games…"

"What?" Henry shouted, rising to his feet in disbelief. "No way!"

"… or there will be no baseball. You either play together or no one plays. You've left me no choice," Duncan responded firmly.

"But we got a big game against the Titans coming up. Can't it wait till after that?" Huff pleaded.

"I'm sorry. But no. I'm sure we can all agree, your mental health is far more important than a baseball game."

"What if I don't want to play on their team?" Billy tossed out.

"Well," Miss Duncan squared her delicate shoulders, "I suppose you are free to leave Highwater and abandon any hope of functioning successfully in the outside world again. It's your decision, Billy."

Billy hadn't expected to be put in this position. And from the faces around the circle neither had any of them.

Miss Duncan turned her gaze to Popwell. "As captain, I hope you will accept the opportunity this represents and welcome Billy onto the team."

All eyes, including Billy's turned in Popwell's direction. Popwell rose slowly from his chair without the slightest hint as to what he was thinking.

"Are you going somewhere, Popwell?" Duncan inquired.

"We got practice," was all he said as he left the room.

24

Marvin Rasher slammed the phone down in frustration. He deeply resented being made to waste precious time battling with health insurance companies just to get paid in a timely fashion. He hated having to engage in debates with flunkies, barely out of high school, incapable of conducting intelligent, grammatically correct conversations. They weren't like him. What lofty purpose did they serve society?

Marvin Rasher devoted twenty-two years to building his practice and his professional reputation. And he was deservedly proud of both. Too bad he didn't have a pit bull like Charley to go after the insurance companies for him.

What he did have, aside from work, was his beautiful wife, Connie. He glanced up at the somewhat staid photo of her, displayed on the shelf above the bookcase. Then, let his eyes drift to a certain snapshot of Connie in little more than a lacey black, peek-a-boo teddy and patent leather thigh-high boots he kept hidden inside a locked desk drawer.

Rasher's need for his wife bordered on compulsion. He knew it, yet was powerless to resist. He was in fact, completely addicted to the sweet scent of her skin, and to each and every soft, sensuous curve of her body. He simply had to possess her... body, mind, and soul. Not that there was that much to her mind or her soul for that matter.

His attempts at occasional, meaningless dalliances with other women, like the accommodating Miss Dixie Duquette, who made herself available for an office quickie from time-to-time, only served to reaffirm what he already knew -- he hungered for the raw lasciviousness only Connie could deliver. Her perfect features. Her full, luscious lips, her pert little chin, her impossibly enticing breasts, most of which he was still making payments on from her last round of cosmetic surgery.

Despite his present surroundings, he felt his body responding, swelling against the zipper of his crisply pressed slacks. He looked at his watch, and thought about closing up shop early and heading home to

Connie. As he considered his options, the office door burst open with a rude, intrusive crash. Charley stormed in, red-faced and looking for trouble.

"What the hell were you thinking sending Billy Rubin into Highwater?"

The bulge in Rasher's pants deflated. "It's late, Charley, and either you control your temper or I'll have to ask you to leave." Charley slammed the door shut with a force that nearly sent Connie's saintly, framed photo tumbling off the shelf. "I mean it, Charley. I can't allow you to burst in here uninvited any time you feel like it."

"What gives you the right to send that hopped-up jerk into Highwater to challenge Popwell's position? Nobody shows up Popwell. Things were going just fine without this Rubin guy. Popwell was fine. The team was happy. And I was happy!"

"Were you really happy with the way things were?"

"Damn right I was. And now, that battle-axe, Duncan went and screwed everything up by putting him on Popwell's team. Rubin's a threat to the natural order of things. And I don't like it."

"I understand, but I'd like to hear what Popwell thinks."

"If you think he's gonna tell you something different, you're wrong!" Charley crossed his muscular arms against his chest. "Fine. Talk to Popwell... but, if you press him too hard, you're gonna have to answer to me." With that, Charley closed his eyes and shuddered. His head dropped to one side as he leaned back against the wall, then opened his eyes.

"Popwell?" Rasher inquired softly. Popwell nodded slightly. "Did you hear what Charley just said?"

"Charley doesn't speak for me."

"Is it true? Do you feel threatened by Billy's presence at Highwater?"

"I don't feel anything about Billy Rubin."

"You know he was a professional ballplayer before he came here. This could be good for the team."

"Rubin won't fit in."

"Why would you think that?"

"He thinks he's too good to play anywhere but the majors."

"Does that bother you... that Billy has actually played in the majors?"

Popwell stood up and walked to the rear window that opened onto a courtyard. He gazed at the treetops and said nothing more.

Connie ran out to greet Marvin as he pulled his car into the garage later that evening. She was far too excited to wait for him to come inside. She threw her arms around his neck and playfully nibbled on his ear lobes, all of which made Marvin feel like the luckiest man alive.

She literally bounced up and down, her breasts jiggling wildly with every excited hop, despite being weighed down with 1,200 cc's of silicon. "I still can't believe I was able to get him to fit me in so soon."

"That's great, baby," Marvin crooned. His hands encircled her breasts, squeezing gently as if choosing a melon. The left breast was definitely his favorite. Ripe and slightly fuller. His fingers toyed with the thin straps of her chemise, attempting to slide them down off her silky shoulders.

"What are you doing, Marvin?" she protested mildly, as he pushed up her bra and began nibbling her pretty pink nipples. "Pay attention. I'm trying to talk to you."

"I missed you," he gushed unabashedly, slurping, as he briefly came up for air.

"That's great, honey, but we need to discuss a few minor details first."

Marvin wasn't listening as he hoisted her up onto the hood of the Toyota, spread her thighs apart then leaned in lustily, pressing his eager tongue against the satiny crotch of her silk panties.

"Stop! This is important, Marvin. I need you to write a check for the deposit, a.s.a.p."

Marvin leaned back to unbuckle his belt, drop his pants and reveal undeniable physical proof of just how much he craved his wife right now. Connie raised her leg and placed the heel of her foot firmly against the bulge beneath his zipper.

"First write the check."

Being denied her sexually was like cutting off Marvin's air supply. It made him testy.

"For what?" he questioned, apparently hearing her for the first time, in so much as his penis had absolutely no idea what she had been prattling on about.

"For Dr. Kingston – only *the* most sought after plastic surgeon in all of Chicago. Absolutely everyone who's anyone is dying to have him do them. I've been calling his office for weeks, but they couldn't even squeeze me in for a consult. Then something wonderful happened. A slot opened up and he agreed to do me! Somebody died, I think," she threw out casually. "It was like a miracle," she squealed, barely able to contain her joy. "An answer to my prayers!"

Once more, Marvin's mighty manhood shrank as he stuffed his shirt back inside his pants. "Why now, Connie?"

"Why not?"

"Because you're already beautiful. Because I just spent fifty grand last year for cosmetic surgery."

"The best doesn't come cheap, Marvin. Besides, Dr. Kingston is brilliant. Dr. Kingston is a *real* doctor, providing an important, vital service."

"Unlike me," he bristled, knowing his wife didn't regard his chosen profession anywhere near as worthy as a man who sucked, chopped and tightened sagging skin.

"I'm afraid it's going to have to wait, Connie."

"How long?" she pouted.

"Some of my client's insurance companies are dragging their feet. There's a lot of back billing in arrears."

"How long?" she demanded again, sliding off the hood of the car and slipping back into her chemise.

"I honestly don't know."

"Well, Marvin," she bristled. "Then I honestly don't know how long it'll be before you get your next taste of this!" Connie flipped up the bottom of her dress revealing her prize.

Marvin Rasher was a doomed man.

25

Armand strode down the hall to Rasher's office thoroughly convinced he could achieve his objective. All he needed was the empirical evidence neatly tucked under his arm in a brown accordion folder, and a few minutes of Rasher's time. In the past, Popwell had often proved a worthy opponent, but Rasher... well, Dr. Rasher was the kind of easily fooled, bleeding heart do-gooder Armand used to eat for breakfast outside Highwater. This would be cake.

Rasher was on the phone when Armand popped his head through the partially open door. "Excuse me, Dr. Rasher..." he began. "It's Armand. I was wondering if I might have a word with you?"

Rasher held up his hand. Armand waited in the doorway, while the doctor continued his conversation. "The ticket came this morning. That's why I'm calling," he said, silently waving Armand in. Armand took a seat on the couch. "Thanks a million, Ted. I love the Bulls. See you and the guys on Wednesday."

As soon as Rasher hung up, Armand sprung to his feet. "I trust you know, I wouldn't have come here without an appointment if it wasn't a matter of great urgency."

"Of course, Armand. What's on your mind?"

"It's about Diablo, sir," Armand said, approaching Rasher's desk, "and the disturbing effect his physical restraint and prolonged isolation is having on the men."

"Disturbing? In what way?" Rasher asked.

"Most of the residents are starting to view his incarceration as... well... perhaps a little excessive. He's been in there a pretty long time now and there's an over-riding fear that if any of us should fall out of favor with the staff or even with you, that we could suffer the same fate."

Rasher leaned back in his chair. "I don't see that happening. Do you?"

"I never questioned why he was locked away, but I do believe some recent information has come to light that might change the opinion of his current mental state. All the facts you need are right here in this folder."

Armand moved quickly, dropping the folder on top of Rasher's desk. "I believe I can prove beyond a doubt Diablo's mental state is seasonal. Temporary. And, that he and all of us might benefit greatly by his being put back among us. You yourself have repeatedly stressed the importance of showing compassion for the problems of others."

Rasher leaned forward, "I'm curious. What did you mean when you said Diablo's mental state was seasonal?"

Armand reached across the desk pointing to the folder. "The Spring Equinox."

"And what does the Spring Equinox have to do with releasing Diablo?" Rasher queried.

Armand sighed, irked his scholarly presentation wasn't sufficient enough to sway the good doctor. "Okay. Let me try to see if I can help you to understand. The Spring, or Vernal Equinox, is when the equator is in direct path of the sun. It's a time of rebirth, an awakening of the earth, a time for seeding. The energies are very high eight days before and eight days after the peak." Armand paused briefly, his sharp eyes scrutinizing the psychiatrist. "Let me know if I'm going too fast for you," he offered, with a hint of genuine concern.

"That's okay, Armand. So far, so good."

"Okay. Now, these days signify the eight holy days of celebration. A rich and fertile time in our earth's evolution. At this time of year, Diablo suffers from an out of control libidinous madness. He rages against the world. And, therefore, of course should be restrained. But, once that time has passed, so has his madness. And the time has passed. Ergo, Diablo should be released."

With that, Armand took a seat. He folded his arms and smiled smugly waiting for Rasher's response, satisfied he had made his point.

Dr. Rasher tried to sound supportive. "I have to admit it's a very interesting theory. Quite frankly one that never occurred to me before. I'll tell you what, Armand, why don't you leave your papers here with me. It'll give me a chance to look them over and we can discuss it again at our next session."

Armand jumped up. "This can't wait for my next session. How can a man of your intelligence refuse to accept the undeniable, documented proof right in front of you. Every minute you delay releasing him could be doing all of us irreparable damage." Armand leaned in across Rasher's desk to play his final trump card. "I can't help wonder what The American Board of Psychiatry would think if they found out you had all this information and yet failed to act on it in a timely fashion?"

Dr. Rasher sat back in his chair and reflected. "Are you threatening me, Armand?"

"Absolutely not," Armand replied, backing off. "I have nothing but the utmost respect for you. I'm merely disappointed you have obviously misinterpreted my sincere efforts to improve the situation at Highwater as a threat to you."

Rasher took a moment to collect his thoughts, and then slowly rose from his chair.

"I think Armand... what has not been misinterpreted is your continued belief that using intimidation and manipulation is a healthy way to achieve what you want. It's not productive and it's not acceptable behavior. It's obvious we still have a lot of work to do." Rasher glanced at his watch. "Unfortunately however, I have a previous appointment."

Rasher walked over and opened the door, indicating it was time for Armand to leave.

"I haven't given up on you, Armand. I want you to remember that when you leave here. But, while you are under my care, you are going to have to accept my authority. My decisions are based on protecting everyone at Highwater. Which is why Diablo won't be released any time soon."

Armand glared back, as he stomped off into the hall, not about to let his best opportunity to destroy Popwell's dominance slip away.

Rasher walked back to his desk and opened Armand's folder.

Inside, every sheet was blank.

26

Early the next morning, Barney stepped into the hallway in full catcher's gear, pulling the door tightly closed behind him. He waited to hear the reassuring click of the lock tumblers falling into place as he twisted his key securely to the left. Slowly, he turned his head to the right, then left, then right again until he was absolutely certain no one was watching him leave. He took a few steps down the hall, then stopped, turned around and walked back to his room. He reinserted his key, unlocked the door, then yanked it shut once more. This time with a firmer hand. He grabbed the knob and jiggled it to make sure it hadn't somehow come loose since last he checked. Satisfied, he turned his key in the lock again. It was time consuming, this he knew, but it had to be done. Though tempted to repeat the process one last time, he worried it might make him late for practice and he didn't want to give Popwell or any of the Bellevederes reason to blame him for losing any of their allotted field time.

He took a shortcut through the Day Room on his way to the baseball diamond. As he entered, Rochester, clad in a flowing silk, magenta robe, looked up from his half-finished crossword puzzle.

"I need your help with something, Barney. What's a six letter word for divertissement that starts with an *E*?"

"I… I don't know, Rochester," he sputtered.

"Well think about it," he said, extending a shimmering sleeve and grabbing Barney by the arm. "It's important. Knowledge is power."

Barney attempted to squirm free. "I don't have time for this. It's just a stupid crossword puzzle."

Rochester released his grip, but stood up to block Barney's way. "It may look like an ordinary puzzle to someone simple like you, but it isn't. It's an example of inter-communication with the outside world. It's also a way in which I can learn things. All kinds of interesting things."

There was something decidedly sinister in Rochester's tone that unnerved Barney. Something that kept him riveted to the spot. "What... what kind of things?"

"Things for me to know... and for you to find out," Rochester taunted.

"Things about me?" Barney paled.

"Maybe," he hinted.

Barney grew increasingly agitated. A thousand paranoid scenarios tumbled through his brain like an overstuffed clothes dryer. He slid into a chair across from Rochester, demanding to know what he meant by 'maybe.'

Rochester struck the tabletop with a grating, rap-tap-tap of his pen; declaring, nothing more would be revealed until the puzzle was completed to his satisfaction. Barney was frustrated; he didn't know the meaning of divertissement, let alone a six-letter word for it.

"Okay, my friend. Let me see if I can teach you something here. A divertissement," Rochester elucidated, "is a diversion. Possibly amusing. Something employed to divert one's attention from a particular course of action, or thought." Rochester leaned in closer. "Or, what someone might do... if say... someone were to be conspiring against you, Barney?"

Barney sprang to his feet. He threatened to go tell Miss Duncan that Rochester was plotting against him. Rochester pulled him back into his chair, insisting he has no reason to plot against him. He is merely in a position to pick up information from time-to-time, and to point out the obvious to those who need to know. "For example," Rochester continued. "Why are you wearing your baseball uniform?"

"Because," Barney responded impatiently, "I have practice."

Rochester looked down at his puzzle, picked up his pen, scribbled in a few letters, then, surreptitiously covered his crossword within the curve of his hand. "Are you sure the Bellevederes still want you on the team?" Rochester inquired, insinuating he might know differently.

Barney swallowed hard. He stood, bracing himself with the back of his chair. His eyelids twitching with a syncopated fury. He reached for his tormentor's hand and begged him to tell him what he knew, what he had heard about him.

Rochester sighed, then, relishing the moment, quietly told him he had reason to believe Barney's position on the team was tenuous at best since Billy Rubin became a Bellevedere. One little slip up, one minuscule fall from grace and... *WHAM...* the rotund little catcher would be history!

"Face it. Henry doesn't like you. Huff, Benish and O'Malley barely tolerate you. Scooter's opinion counts for very little on any given day. Billy Rubin thinks you're a flaming nut case. Which just leaves Popwell, and we all know Popwell has no personal loyalty to anyone. If he doesn't need you... you are gone, my friend."

Rochester motioned for Barney to step closer, and have a look at what he had written in his puzzle. Within the boxes, he had inked the six-letter word. *Escape.*

Barney's face drained of color as quickly as an ocean wave recedes from shore. He raced from the Day Room and out onto the field.

As the Bellevederes assembled, Barney kept his distance. He sat alone and watched as the others warmed up. He was pretty sure they were whispering secrets about him. Even sweet, gentle, Scooter seemed to be keeping his distance.

When Popwell signaled he was ready to throw, Barney slid the wire frame of his catcher's mask down over his face, picked up his mitt and slowly made his way to the plate. His neck was prickly and hot, his fingers felt too large for the mitt, as he struggled to stuff them into the leather. He considered the possibility someone snuck into his room and switched mitts on him, just to make him look bad.

He crouched down, squinted into the sun, and waited for Popwell's first warm up pitch. He could see Popwell's lips moving, but he couldn't hear what he was saying – that is, unless Popwell was just pretending to be saying something to throw off his concentration.

Popwell went into his wind up. His right arm cocked back behind his head, then came forward releasing the knuckleball toward Barney as he had countless times before. Only this time, the ball Barney snagged so effortlessly in the past, was impossible to catch. It ricocheted off his mitt and rolled onto the dirt alongside the fence.

As he scrambled to retrieve it, he thought he heard them snickering. Mocking him, laughing at his expense. But, still he said nothing. It'll pass. Let this one go. Rochester is a liar, he thought. He took a deep breath and tossed the ball back to Popwell.

But the next two pitches got by him as well. *Sloppy, sloppy,* he thought, stretching his stiff, beefy arms, regretting, thanks to Rochester, he didn't have time to loosen up.

"Hey, Butt-head," Benish yelled from the infield, while playing pepper with O'Malley. "In case it slipped your mind… you're actually supposed to catch the ball."

Barney snuck a peek at Henry, who had stopped what he was doing and stood watching him with cold, condemning eyes. Popwell threw, Barney missed. This time even Huff and Scooter turned to watch. Barney swallowed hard and closed his eyes. When he opened them, the ball was headed his way. He made a wild grab for it, but the ball hit the base of his mitt and took off, bouncing up alongside the bleachers.

By now he felt all their eyes upon him, scrutinizing every dropped ball. No one said a word. They didn't have to. Barney rose from a crouch and ran from the field, hurt, angry and confused, just like the day the school bus left for Wrigley without him.

He locked himself in his room and refused to come out. He refused to take meals in the cafeteria. He refused to attend Group. And soon, his playing days with The Bellevederes were all but over.

27

Huff crouched behind the plate and prayed for a miracle. Beads of sweat dotted his furrowed brow as he waited on Popwell's next pitch. By now, six slow and easy knuckleballs had caromed off his mitt, burrowing in the grass like gophers. Scooter waited off to the side, absently kicking at the dried dirt with the heel of his cleat, nervously anticipating his turn behind the plate.

Huff swallowed hard as number seven came floating toward him. It was a joke to think anyone but Barney could handle Popwell's knuckleball. After another dozen failed attempts, Popwell waved him off. Huff's frustration showed as he fired the waffle-sized mitt into the dirt.

One by one, each of the Bellevederes took their turn attempting to fill the void created by Barney's recent departure. It was fruitless, like trying to lasso a dime with a boxing glove. Their artless attempts were comical, but no one dare laugh, since it was obvious Popwell didn't find this exercise in futility amusing in the least.

When the midday shadows crisscrossed the outfield, the only one left to give it a shot was Billy, sitting alone in the bottom rung of the bleachers. He reached down, scooped up a few pebbles and rattled them in his hand. He could feel The Bellevederes' mistrusting eyes upon him. He tossed the pebbles aside, stood up and donned the mask and chest protector.

"I know we desperately need a catcher, but I hope he gets hit in the nuts," voiced O'Malley.

"Shut up, O'Malley," Huff cautioned. "This guy is our last hope. If he fails, we might as well forfeit to those clowns."

When Billy fared no better than the rest, Popwell walked off the mound, then off the field. Huff began to pace, his hands clasped behind his back. He paused, looking up to the dreary heavens. "Well, now what? It's not like any of us are gonna drag Barney's butt back out to the field any time soon. How's Popwell supposed to pitch if nobody can catch him? Huh?" Huff searched his teammates for answers. Billy appeared indifferent. Henry and Scooter mute, while Benish, seated a few rows up in the bleachers, flipped through the paper's comic section, chuckling when the spirit moved him.

"What if I pitch?" O'Malley offered. "Straight stuff. Fastball. Curveball. Slider." All eyes turned to O'Malley as if he lost his mind.

"Yeah? And who's going to tell Popwell he's not pitching?" Huff asked. "You?"

O'Malley shrugged his cowardly shoulders and took a seat, his proposal summarily squashed.

As Billy removed his shin guards and tossed them into the equipment bag, Henry bristled past, bumping Billy with his shoulder. "Way to go, All American," he jeered, before heading back into Highwater with the rest of the team.

Billy stormed back to his room convinced his attempt to fit in at Highwater was a total waste of time. The hell with Duncan and Rasher. He certainly didn't intend to hang around unappreciated by the likes of Popwell and his motley crew. He didn't know where he was going exactly, but there had to be someplace better than here. Someplace where people would appreciate his extraordinary talents.

He grabbed his suitcase from the closet, yanked open his dresser drawers and started throwing his clothes inside. Hidden beneath his socks was a photo of Julie. He had purposely buried it so as not to feel the empty, crushing sensation in his chest quite so often. Seeing her sweet, trusting face stopped him in his tracks. He knew, if she were here, she wouldn't want him to leave. She'd expect him to tough it out.

It had been awhile since he'd made any attempt to contact her. Maybe, he hoped, she had forgiven him by now for a stupid fight and a string of angry, misunderstood words.

For the next few hours, it was all he could think of. He knew if he could just talk to her. If he could make everything right between them again, he could get through anything.

He glanced at his watch and figured about now she was probably hunched over her laptop, working on some brilliant new proposal to revolutionize the hotel industry in one of those oversized USC T-shirts she liked to wear. A diet soft drink and an open bag of Hershey Kisses within reach. He really hated how much he missed her right now.

He picked up his phone and stared at her number on his contact list, then dropped the phone onto the bed. He paced the floor like an unrehearsed thespian about to step onto the stage. He needed to make sure he had reasonable answers for any questions she might ask. Perhaps the biggest being what was he doing in Chicago, at Highwater, no less. Of course, if he handled the call correctly, kept the focus in another direction, he might not have to mention Highwater at all. He didn't want to lie, but he also didn't want to frighten her off. It was driving him nuts. This was Julie, for God sake! He could always manage to steer the conversation before. But this wasn't before. This was now. What if he let something slip about his suicide attempt or Highwater? He'd have to choose his words carefully. The last thing he wanted was her pity. Maybe he wasn't ready yet. But the urge to reconnect was too strong to stuff back into a drawer like her photo. The need to hear her voice again was overwhelming. Unless… she didn't want to talk to him? What if she had met someone new? What if she wasn't alone? What if someone was lying next to her in bed when he called?

He slumped back on the bed and closed his eyes, but the ugly images streaming through his brain didn't help. He sat up, opened his eyes and grabbed his phone again. *Come on now,* he thought, pumping himself up, you're *Billy Rubin… you have nothing to worry about.* But, just in case, he decided to call on her home phone, the one without caller I.D. Her phone rang once. Then twice. Then a third time before she picked up and said, hello. Billy stood mute, his heart racing as he listened to the music of her voice.

"Hello? Hellooo… who is this?" she repeated, her tone tinged with annoyance.

He heard her sigh just once before severing the fragile connection between them. Calling was definitely a mistake. There had to be another way. Maybe he could try email. Not that he fancied himself much of a writer. Dr. Rasher had asked him to keep a diary, to commit his feelings to paper. So far, Billy had managed to fill less than a page with some tripe about the food and the uncomfortable bed sheets. Still, email seemed less risky than trying to call her again.

It was a little past one a.m. when Billy completed his task. He wrote he was in Chicago and that he missed her. Which was true. He inquired about her job, hoping she'd be happy he remembered as many details about it as he could. He tried to sound supportive and encouraging, telling her the hotel chain was lucky to have her and that he was certain she would do well there. He told her he left L.A. to work out some personal problems. He mentioned he was still playing a little baseball now and then, which was kind of true, in a way, and finally, that he still cared about her and hoped if she felt the same, she might consider writing back.

Satisfied with the finished product, he hit send and turned off the laptop. He was exhausted and exhilarated at the same time. He knew he wouldn't be able to fall asleep just yet, so he decided to head outside.

Just the act of writing to Julie made him feel better, as he looked up at the blue-black velvet sky sprinkled with stars that shimmered above like sequins. He must have been crazy to cut himself off from her. But he was pretty certain she'd take him back. She had to still love him.

When he approached the outfield grass, his tired eyes focused on a solitary figure standing by the bleachers, half swallowed in darkness. It was Popwell, in full baseball uniform, despite the lateness of the hour. He thought about turning around and ducking back inside before Popwell could spot him, but he refused to be intimidated. After all, he had as much right to walk around Highwater's grounds as Popwell did.

"Nice night, huh," Billy offered. Popwell raised a single finger to his lips. Billy sensed, despite Popwell's arrogant silence, he was being asked to follow as Popwell strode from the bleachers.

He led him down an unfamiliar, unlit, cobblestone path; overgrown with weeds and prickly briars. The cobblestone soon gave way to a rough-hewn wooden staircase that led to a dirt road below. As they descended through the blackness, a biting chill pierced Billy's thin cotton shirt like an ice pick. He stopped to glance back over his shoulder at Highwater's rooftops now towering in the distance above their heads.

"This way," Popwell called. Billy snapped back to attention. Apparently, they had arrived at their destination -- a cavernous structure, fronted with eight over-sized garage doors. Popwell grabbed onto one of the door handles with both arms. With one mighty yank, the door began creaking open like a mummy's tomb.

"Holy crap!" Billy whispered, as his eyes adjusted to the darkness. Inside, the building was the size of half a football field. Popwell walked up to the wall and flipped a switch. The interior instantly flooded with light as bright as the midday sun. Two large buses, several utilitarian mini vans and pick-ups were parked at the far end of the otherwise empty garage.

What the fuck am I doing here? Billy wondered, as Popwell lowered the garage door, sealing them inside. *What if this isn't Popwell? What if he's turned back into Charley again? What if he lured me down here to slash my throat and finish me off?*

Popwell turned toward him and reached down into a duffle. Billy took a step back, only to have his fears put to rest as Popwell tossed him a catcher's mitt. Apparently, Popwell had decided, despite Billy's disastrous performance earlier in the day, he was the best shot at becoming Barney's heir apparent.

For the next few hours, Popwell pitched his knuckler, over and over like a tireless machine. Though Billy did his best, the results were much the same as before. Billy grew weary as time wore on, eventually becoming too bleary-eyed to even lob the dropped balls back to him. Finally, he threw up his hands. "Look, I'm just not a catcher. Let alone a knuckleball catcher." He waited for Popwell to say something. But he didn't. Instead, Popwell strode past him, hoisted up one of the garage doors and stepped outside.

Now what? Billy wondered, letting his head drop to his chest. *What other form of torture is he planning?* Whatever it was, Billy had enough. Though he hadn't thought to drop breadcrumbs on the way down, he was fairly certain he could find his way back alone even in the dark. He lifted his head as Popwell returned.

"If you're as good as you say you are," Popwell chided, "you can do this. The problem is you don't understand the knuckleball. You don't understand it here," he said, pointing to his head. "And you don't feel it here," pointing to his heart. "Plus, your stance is all wrong."

Popwell patiently explained the dynamics behind the pitch, then moved on to describe how a knuckleball catcher needs to squat at an angle, with one knee pointed toward first base, to give his receiving hand a better range of motion, depending which way the ball knuckles.

Billy picked up the mitt and decided to give it another shot. After all, it wasn't brain surgery. It was a damn knuckleball. Slowly but surely, he began to see the hypnotic pitch in a whole new way. Before long he found he could almost anticipate the weird twists and turns it would take en route to his glove. His natural instincts took over. Fewer and fewer of Popwell's pitches got by him.

As dawn began to seep in through the dormer windows, not one ball hit the ground. For the first time he and Popwell were truly in sync. He let loose with a free and easy laugh that echoed off the barren walls. He glanced at Popwell to gauge his reaction. Surely, the stone-faced pitcher must have felt it too. In fact, he could almost swear, in one unguarded moment, he thought he spied the corners of Popwell's mouth slightly tilt upward. But couldn't be sure.

Shortly thereafter, Popwell announced it was time to head back before anyone discovered they were here. He turned off the lights, pushed up the door and stepped outside.

Before leaving, Billy stopped to scoop up a baseball left behind lying on the floor, and triumphantly flung it all the way down to the far wall, ultimately coming to a stop beneath one of the buses. A moment later, to his surprise, the ball rolled directly back out to him. He scratched his head and looked around, then shrugged his shoulders and headed out after Popwell.

As the garage door cranked to a close, landing with a solid thump as it hit the ground, Rochester slithered out from behind the bus, picked up the baseball, and placed it inside his velveteen knapsack.

28

Over the next several nights, the pitcher and his newly ordained battery mate continued their private sessions in Highwater's garage. To Billy's surprise, he began to look forward to them. He'd sneak out from the main building to meet Popwell down below long after everyone else had turned in for the night. Popwell insisted their pre-dawn practice drills remain secret, even from the Bellevederes. Despite Billy's resentment of B. J. Popwell's obsessive need to maintain control over everything, he couldn't help but admire the pitcher's work ethic, extraordinary skills and devotion to the game. Aside from himself, there surely was no one else at Highwater that lived to play baseball the way Popwell did.

On the day before the big game, Gunther showed up at Billy's room to let him know a package arrived this morning addressed to him. Billy was surprised that anyone other than his doctors even knew he was at Highwater.

"Did you see who it was from?"

"Nope. What do I look like... the FBI?" Gunther chuckled. "But... judging from the fancy handwriting on the label, I'm guessing it could've come from a lady friend. Guess a player like you had his share of pretty dolls sniffing at your heels before you showed up here. Isn't that right, you lucky bastard, you?"

"No one is supposed to know I'm here, Gunther."

"Well someone does, 'cause it's wrapped up nice and pretty downstairs in the guard's locker room waiting for you to come pick it up."

Billy's curiosity grew as he followed Gunther deep into the bowels of Highwater. They walked through dimly lit hallways painted gunmetal gray, beneath a zigzag of corroded steel pipes above their heads. When they entered the locker room, Billy thought it odd that Gunther locked the door behind them. Then, out from behind the wall of rusted, kelp colored lockers emerged two shadowy figures. Billy quickly realized there wasn't any package waiting for him – just Armand and his strong-armed henchman, Sven.

Gunther had set him up. He was about to be ambushed. Obviously Duncan's decision to put Billy on the Bellevederes had thrown a monkey wrench into Armand's maniacal plot to topple Popwell in tomorrow's game.

Armand stepped forward, his eyes fixed on Billy with a frozen, killer stare. Billy waited for the first fist to fly. He was sure the demented duo were about to break his ribs, or both his thumbs, or worse. His heart lodged in his throat.

Armand savagely grabbed Billy's face and kissed him hard on the mouth. For a second, Billy couldn't breathe. W*as this some sick Titan ritual – first they kiss you then they kill you?*

"You're a fucking genius," Armand announced.

Gunther grinned, content as an overfed lap cat. He liked it when the residents got along. It made his job much easier. As the guard headed out to patrol the grounds, he tossed Armand his key ring, reminding him to lock up when they left.

As soon as Gunther left the room, Armand turned back to Billy. "I knew I was right about you, Billy Boy. First you finesse your way onto Popwell's team, and then, when Barney's gray matter goes AWOL, you step up and let Popwell think the Bellevederes are right back in business. It's beautiful. No. It's diabolical! No way he'd suspect you'd ever turn against him now. So, in tomorrow's game, if the score is close in the late innings, suddenly Barney's replacement comes down with a bad case of fumblitis. It's positively brilliant! I don't know why I didn't come up with it myself." Armand was drunk with the promise of power. "We'll humiliate him in front of everyone. Strip him of his mythic power. Strip him of baseball!" Armand shoved his hand toward Billy as a gesture of their sinister, scheming solidarity. "Thanks to you, it's going to be a great game!"

Billy held back, convinced Armand had gone completely mad by now. He flinched as Armand grabbed his hand and pulled him closer. So close Billy feared he might try to kiss him again. Billy's hand was cold and moist in Armand's grip.

Armand searched his eyes wondering if Billy was truly on board. "I said... it's going to be a great game. Isn't that right, Billy?"

29

An unsettling chill snaked its way through the towering halls of Highwater as Billy donned his uniform and laced up his cleats. He stole a glance at Julie's photo, now propped against the lamp on his nightstand. She had yet to respond to his email, but he tried to remain hopeful.

He spent half the night lying awake ruminating over what Armand wanted him to do. It made him sick. Throwing a game was not in his nature. He had more integrity than that. He decided to march down to the Music Room and let Armand know he wasn't taking part in his plan. But he never made it that far. As he grabbed his mitt and opened the door, there was Armand standing in the doorway unannounced, looking as sinister as ever.

"A word, my friend," Armand intruded, striding past Billy to the metal folding chair leaning against the wall. He swung it around to face him, put his foot up on the seat and leaned his body forward, resting his elbow on his knee. "With regard to today's game..."

"I'm not going to do what you asked, Armand. I'm not going to throw the game."

Armand lowered his head, staring down at the floor before looking back up at Billy. "I can't believe you just said that. You must've read my mind. Don't get me wrong. I still want to knock Popwell off of his pedestal. But, I too realized cheating isn't the way to go. How could I live with myself knowing I didn't play the game fair and square? What consolation would it bring me? Whoever coined the phrase, 'cheaters never win' knew what they were talking about." Billy heaved a sigh of relief that Armand had finally came to his senses. "I told you we're a lot alike, Billy. So let's just have a good, clean game out there today." Armand extended his hand which Billy graciously shook, and turned to leave. Then, almost as if it had slipped his mind, turned back to Billy. "Oh, by the way," Armand uttered, as he held up what looked suspiciously like Gunther's key ring, delighting in the mellifluous jingle-jangle it produced as he shook it back and forth. "I thought it might be useful to make another set before giving the originals back to Gunther."

"Useful? How?"

"You're gonna need them to break Diablo out."

Billy swallowed hard. It never occurred to him Armand might still be planning to somehow bring that freak of nature into the mix. But he held his ground, refusing to knuckle under to Armand's demands.

"You're crazy, you know that. There's no way I'm going anywhere near that room, let alone free that beast."

"Oh, you will, Billy. You definitely will." Armand spotted Julie's photo on the nightstand and picked it up. "Pretty girl. It's funny, don't you think... your lady-friend hasn't come by for a visit... not even once in all this time. Now, why is that, I wonder?"

"She's in L.A."

"That's too bad," Armand sighed. "Or... could it be she doesn't even know you're in here. That your shaky mental status is one big dirty little secret you've managed to keep from her. Funny thing about secrets, Billy. They have an ugly way of coming out when you least expect them. I hate to think how she'd feel if someone suddenly decided to bring her up to speed." Armand dropped the keys onto the bed. Then, before turning to leave, "Oh, and for what it's worth, whether or not your ego can handle it, Popwell let you hit those homers off of him. God's honest truth," he said, raising his right palm in the air as if standing before a judge and jury.

"Fuck you, Armand."

"I knew you'd be pissed. I would be too, after the way Popwell exploited you... letting you think he considered you an equal. A valued teammate if you will. When the truth is, he's been screwing with your mind since the day you got here. Impeding your therapeutic progress. Belittling you. Shamelessly using you to serve his own selfish needs. Just like he does to everyone."

Armand grinned smugly. "Like I said -- it's gonna be a great game!"

30

Popwell walked onto the field as usual, making eye contact with no one. But as usual, all eyes followed his every step. His destination, a small patch of dirt up along the third base line. He loosened the caked soil with the heel of his spike, slowly and gently smoothing the surface with a tenderness often reserved for a baby's cheek. If the outcome of tonight's game held any particular significance for him, you couldn't tell by his actions. He was simply here to play ball as he had done a thousand times before, nothing more, nothing less.

He pulled a scuffed-up ball from his back pocket and rolled it around in his hand. It centered him; this little white sphere that fit so perfectly inside his grip. Clutching it tightly, feeling its weight and texture against his skin helped prevent any buried emotions from bubbling to the surface. Despite what Duncan and Rasher believed, emotions were a waste of time and energy. He was far more comfortable feeling nothing.

Off to the side, Scooter was warming up with Benish, fielding grounders as he'd done so many times before. But today, his stomach was in knots as he valiantly struggled to push away the negative thoughts that kept creeping inside his head. *What if he messes up in the game? What if he's the one who makes the error that causes the Bellevederes to lose?* One muffed attempt after another left him wishing he could somehow dematerialize.

Winning wasn't everything to Scooter. He didn't have the fire in his belly like the rest of them. He much preferred quietly fading into the background. Like he tried to do each year on his birthday. He'd pretend to be sick so he wouldn't have to stand in front of a cake while everyone sang and stared at him. To this day, the scent of birthday candles made him queasy. All Scooter ever wanted was for everyone to get along. He especially wanted everybody to like him. But, after today – most likely – no one would. He thought of telling Popwell he didn't feel well, suggesting maybe he should sit out the game, but he was far too timid to speak up.

The Bellevederes looked around to see who would emerge as Popwell's choice to replace Barney. They didn't have long to wait, as Billy made his way onto the field, still dogged by Armand's ridiculous assertions about his implied lack of mastery at the plate. Was it possible that Popwell had been conning him all this time? Had he really risen to the challenge of the pitcher's hypnotic knuckleball as he let himself believe, or had Popwell merely played him for a fool? He tried to read Popwell's expression, but there was little there to gauge, as he grabbed the catcher's mitt from the canvas equipment bag and took his place behind the plate. The Bellevederes watched in awe as Billy masterfully corralled each and every warm-up pitch.

From a respectful distance across the field, the Titans kept a curious eye on the unfolding events as well. The only one noticeably absent was Sven.

Each time Billy crouched down the key ring burned inside the pocket of his uniform, pressing uncomfortably against his flesh, serving as a constant reminder of his expected participation in the unthinkable plot to release Diablo.

As the clock ticked closer to game time, Billy sensed Armand's growing impatience. He knew he was watching, waiting for him to follow through. Could he trust that Armand hadn't already tried to contact Julie? Billy couldn't take that chance.

He stood up and jogged over to Popwell and told him he forgot something up in his room. The unexpected delay didn't exactly meet with Popwell's approval. Not that Billy gave a damn what Popwell thought at present as he headed back into Highwater without making eye contact with Armand or anyone else.

He made his way through the building, walking with a slow, even cadence, half-hoping something or someone would stop him before it was too late to turn around. But the hallways were oddly deserted. Absent were the bustling aides, nurses and guards. Occasionally, as he turned a corner, a resident or two would pass him by without so much as a nod. Each one more intent on getting where they were going, than paying him any mind.

When he arrived on Diablo's floor, his heart began pounding wildly.

Beads of sweat dripped from his brow. Everything inside him was screaming, telling him to cut and run. But to his regret, the message failed to travel from his brain to his feet. Each step drew him closer to the terrifying room at the end of the hall. The steel door separating man from beast became more ominous, as if pulsing in lockstep with Billy's heartbeat. He could barely breathe. He looked around. He was alone. *How was that possible? Where were the guards? Where was anybody?*

He turned at the sound of approaching footsteps rapidly heading in his direction, hoping it was Watermain or Gunther returning to their post, giving Billy an ironclad excuse to abort Armand's insane plan. Unfortunately, the steps belonged to Rochester, clip-clopping down the hall in crushed black velvet from head to toe. A large silver cross dangling from a chain, swung back and forth like an echo bouncing off the walls of a cave as he hurried past.

Billy called after him as he sped by. "Hey! What's going on? Where are all the guards? Where'd everyone go?"

Without slowing down, Rochester yelled back. "Out front. Crazy Sven is threatening to jump off the roof. Hurry or you'll miss the great splat!"

In that instant, Billy knew Armand had indeed found a way to summon every guard, every staff member from their post to leave the coast clear for Billy to set Diablo free.

Out by the tree-lined entrance to Highwater Acres, a crowd was growing. Residents, nurses and guards held their collective breath. Their eyes were on Armand's loyal soldier some sixty-two feet above their heads, teetering dangerously close to the edge of the red gabled roof. A half dozen guards were positioned on the rooftop along with a visibly distressed Miss Duncan. She tried valiantly to dissuade Sven from what she believed were the actions of a desperate man. Sven, however, stood his ground.

In an effort to maintain his balance, and to blot out the distracting cries from the crowd below, he began to rhythmically chant.

"Blinka lilla stjarna dar, hur jag undrar var du ar!"

Duncan inched closer. But his words made no sense. When she reached out her hand, Sven lurched backward, nearly losing his footing, so Duncan retreated and Sven sang out louder.

"Fjarran lockar dun min syn, likt en diamant I skyn.

Blinka lilla stjarna dar,

Hur jag undrar var du ar!"

Sven smiled. The little Swedish nursery song from somewhere in his childhood would certainly help get him through the next hour or so. He was determined to fulfill his role in Armand's master plan, even if he had to actually jump to do it.

Inside Highwater, the floor beneath Billy's feet began to rumble. At first it was little more than a slight vibration cushioned by the polyurethane midsole in his cleats. Then the trembling rose steadily from his ankles to his shins. *What the hell was going on?*

A guttural, fear-inspiring cry bellowed forth from beyond the thick, metal door. The horrifying scream thundered off the walls, escalating with each successive wail that followed. The floor tiles jumped up to meet his instep. Billy's blood ran cold as he faced his fate. He peered through the plate glass window at the monster within ripping wildly at his chains.

Billy reached inside his pocket and slowly pulled out the keys. There were at least a dozen in every shape and size, yet Billy intuitively selected the very one that slid effortlessly inside the lock, as if he had been heading for this moment from the day he arrived at Highwater. He turned the key, pulled back on the latch and heaved open the door.

Diablo lifted his head as Billy entered. His cheetah-like eyes followed Billy's every move. Predator and prey. Billy took a small step closer, then stopped. As he stared transfixed by the demon-like presence, something other than fear began to course through his body. A sudden, pressing need to know -- who is this repugnant mound of human flesh coiled in the corner like a wounded animal?

He locked eyes with Diablo, then, as if in a trance, knelt beside the beast and jammed a key in the lock that secured the heavy iron chains tightly bound around Diablo's wrists and ankles. When it didn't open, he tried another. Diablo watched calmly, with curiosity, as Billy's frustration grew. One key after another refused to break the bonds.

Billy twisted harder, with greater force. Until... snap. The key broke off in the lock. Billy's nostrils filled with the stench of urine and sweat, oddly entangled with the sweet scent of lilac.

A vision of huge, leathery hands with snake-like fingers surging toward him flashed through his mind. His throat constricted as he tried

119

to cry for help. He thought he was screaming, but he couldn't hear the sound of his own screams. All there was within the paralyzing silence were muffled, whispered words of comfort swirling through his brain and the faint faraway lilt of a lullaby.

A frightening reality overtook him as Diablo rose to his feet with a monstrous growl. Billy jumped back. His entire body shook violently, beyond his control. *What had he almost done?*

Diablo lurched towards him. His massive hands slashing the air between them. Billy stumbled from the room in panic, slamming the thick, steel door with a thunderous clang. He raced down the corridor, down the endless flights of stairs without once looking back, tears streaking from his burning eyes.

Highwater's back doors flew open, and Billy emerged breathless, his uniform damp and clinging to his body. He wiped the sweat and tears from his face with the edge of his sleeve, hungrily drinking in its familiar linen scent. He desperately struggled to blot out the terror and chaos and lose himself in the symmetry and perfection of a baseball game. He loped back toward the infield, refusing to let anyone see just how close to losing it he had come.

He grabbed his mitt and took his position behind home plate. He could feel the laser-like sting of Armand's eyes demanding to know why he returned to the field alone. But Billy somehow managed to keep his focus, refusing to look in Armand's direction.

Popwell surveyed the infield, studying the players. Something didn't feel right. So he gathered the troops to the mound.

"I'm moving Scooter to center," he said, rather matter-of-factly.

Scooter panicked. The rest of the team seemed surprised, but no one dared question Popwell's decision. Until Henry spoke up.

"I don't get it. Scooter's a shortstop, not a center fielder."

"Tonight he plays center field," was all Popwell offered, making it clear his decision was final. O'Malley jogged in from center and proceeded to smooth out the dirt between second and third. Scooter's heart was racing. He had never played the outfield before. He could only pray no balls would come his way.

Popwell toed the rubber and nodded, as the game between the Bellevederes and the Titans finally got under way.

Kirby led off for the Titans. Three pitches later, he was out on strikes. The next batter stepped in, trembling with the knowledge he never stood a chance against Popwell. He was right. Three pitches, three whiffs of the bat.

Then Armand stepped in. Popwell leaned forward, bearing down, taking his time before he threw, studying Armand, making him wait to throw off his rhythm.

Popwell knew Charley disliked Armand more than anyone at Highwater. And if Armand and his team were to somehow win today, Charley might do something horrible. So, he thought it best to do what he could to make sure that doesn't happen.

The outcome of today's game meant everything to Armand. He knew how it felt to be ignored, to have to watch from the sidelines while someone else got the attention and love he craved and deserved. Most of all, he was sick and tired of everyone bowing and scraping to a buttoned up jerk like Popwell. It ate at him. After all, Armand had talent of his own worthy of the spotlight. He also had the smarts, and style a true leader needs. All he had to do was defeat the mighty Popwell and from now on it would be Armand's show.

He readied his bat, clutching it so tight, he feared it might break in two. As the knuckleball sailed towards him, Armand lunged with a mighty swing, not coming close to putting wood on the ball. Popwell wasted little time delivering the next pitch. It was slower and uglier than the first. Armand laid off, but the pitch was called a strike. With two strikes on him, he dug in his heels.

"Where's Diablo?" he hissed between clenched teeth.

Billy looked straight ahead and pounded his mitt, sending Armand's words drifting by like acrid smoke from the tip of a Turkish cigarette. Armand cocked his bat, but the next pitch was high and outside.

"Where is he?" Armand demanded again.

Popwell rubbed up the ball giving Billy a moment to respond. "Your plan sucked," Billy replied, through the steel, cage of his catcher's mask. "The piece of crap key you made broke off in the lock." Armand lost concentration, his eyes darting briefly in Billy's direction. "Relax, Armand. Keep your eyes on the pitch. You don't need Diablo. I got it covered."

The knuckleball arrived. Armand swung. The inning was over.

Armand tossed his bat to the ground before departing the batter's box, while taking comfort believing Billy had his back. As for Billy, he walked off the field after only ten pitches with a strong sense nothing would ever be quite the same at Highwater once the game was over.

On the other side of Highwater, Sven was becoming increasingly weary maintaining his one-man show. He wasn't all that bright. He was starting to run out of ideas to keep himself amused and Miss Duncan and the guards at bay. How he wished he could somehow crawl to the far side of the roof and catch a glimpse of the game below.

Despite his allegiance to Armand, Sven was sorely tempted to come down off the roof when Duncan looked as if she was about to cry. He really hated when a woman teared up. Something about their quivering lower lip. He had to turn away. He had to think about pleasing Armand so he would never leave him behind. Miss D just worked at Highwater, but Armand was his friend and protector for life. He knew where his loyalties lay.

Rochester grew impatient standing on the front lawn waiting for the evening's entertainment to unfold. Staring up at the rooftop, watching a grown man sing off-key was becoming one huge yawn. He yelled up to the guards, "Either drag him down or push him over already!" But, that wasn't how they did things at Highwater. Disgusted, Rochester decided to head for greener pastures, namely the Titans/Bellevederes game out back.

By the end of the third inning, the score remained 0 – 0. Popwell had yet to give up a hit. With one out in the top of the fourth, Armand sauntered into the batter's box again.

"C'mon, Armand, let's stop pussy-playing these guys. Show 'em how it's fucking done," Lyle shouted, urging him on. For the next ten minutes, Armand fouled off twenty-three pitches giving Popwell quite a workout. Yet, the knuckleball pitcher routinely rubbed up another ball and remained expressionless. It was impossible to assess if Armand's strategy had begun to tax his arm or if Popwell was just getting started.

Popwell focused in on Armand, went into his wind up and threw. This time Armand connected with the meat part of the bat, getting it all. A towering fly ball to deep center field. Scooter's heart began to thump as he raced back to the fence, then with previously untested, almost super-human agility, soared upward and reached high above the chain links before crashing to the ground, face down in the dirt. A hush fell over the field as he lay motionless. Armand tore around the bases at breakneck speed, crossing the plate in triumph.

The Titans were over the moon, until everyone noticed Scooter had yet to get up. Both teams ran out to center field and stood quietly looking down at Scooter who remained deathly still. They felt helpless. No one dared make a move. No one except Armand, that is. Despite its obvious inappropriateness, Armand's thoughts were not focused on Scooter's wellbeing, but on the possible impact the young ballplayer's heroic exploits may have on the outcome of the game.

His gaze was riveted to the glove still attached to Scooter's hand, palm down in the dirt. Armand stepped forward to peek inside the black, weather worn mitt to see for himself if he had actually caught the ball or if Armand had in fact put the Titans ahead. As he crouched down, Huff grabbed hold of his arm.

"What the fuck you think you're doing? Can't you see the kid's unconscious."

"I'm not going to move him, I'm just going to peek inside his glove," Armand reassured him. And before anyone else could stop him, Armand reached down and opened the glove on Scooter's left hand. It was empty. Not wanting to appear as the uncaring prick that he is, Armand did his best to mask his satisfied smile.

"We're up, one – nothing," he said, with confidence.

Billy all but ignored him, returning his attention to his fallen teammate. He bent down and carefully rolled Scooter's limp body onto its side, then gently lifted his eyelid, checking for some flicker of recognition. His prayers were answered as the young player's eyes fluttered open, his lungs coughing up a fine mist of dust that had collected in his throat when he hit the ground.

Suddenly, Billy's jaw dropped. "Holy shit," he said, in disbelief.

All eyes followed his gaze to Scooter's bare right hand. There clutched tightly was the ball. It was sheer magic, one of those blissful moments when the impossible becomes possible. Billy knew those moments well, yet still scratched his head in wonder. *How the hell did Popwell know to put Scooter in the outfield?* The astonished Bellevederes could barely believe their eyes.

Billy and Huff reached down to carry Scooter back inside Highwater, but Scooter shook them off, insisting he felt fine. The fall may have briefly knocked the wind out of him, but he assured them he never felt better and couldn't wait to get back in the game. With a little help from Billy, Scooter rose to his feet, proudly waving the ball back and forth in the air, a sweet goofy grin plastered across his face. For the first time ever, Scooter discovered it wasn't so bad standing out from the crowd. It didn't make him nervous. It was actually... kind of... okay. Armand angrily drop-kicked his glove into the air, as both teams headed back toward the infield.

The game remained 0 – 0. With two out in the bottom of the sixth, Scooter legged out a bouncer to third, diving head first into the bag.

Benish came up and lined a double to left center. Scooter came all the way around to score, but luckily for the Titans, the ball skipped through a hole in the fence and Scooter had to return to third. So with runners on second and third, and two outs, Billy Rubin came up to the plate.

He peered over to the nearly deserted metal bleachers. Aside from a few bizarre remarks shouted by Rochester, perched atop the last row, now sporting silk parachute pants, this was the quietest game he had ever played in. The only sounds he heard were his own unspoken thoughts carefully orchestrating the final outcome.

He glanced at the Bellevederes watching from the dugout – united as one, pulling for Billy to bring it home. Armand barked to his pitcher as he pounded his glove and readied himself in case the ball was hit his way. "C'mon, Grizzy. This guy's got nothing. Right over the plate."

But Grizzybowski's control went south and he wound up walking Billy on four pitches. Armand was furious. The bases were loaded and Henry was making his way to the plate. There was a lot riding on Henry's shoulders. He griped the bat between his two strong hands, swung at the first pitch and hit a slow, bouncing ball right towards Armand at short. Henry hung his head and sighed, frustrated he missed his chance to bring the runners home as he motored as hard as he could towards first.

Armand licked his chops, waiting for the routine grounder to arrive. But then, inches from Armand's mitt, the ball took a funny hop, glancing off a pebble, hitting Armand in the throat, knocking him to the ground. Scooter came in to score and the Bellevederes led, 1-0. A joyful roar rose up. Scooter stood taller than he had in years and Henry slapped his knee and grinned from ear to ear. Armand was livid.

Huff came up to bat, hoping to add to their lead. But Grizzy struck him out.

The score remained 1-0 going into the top of the ninth. The Titans last chance. In a matter of minutes, Popwell disposed of the first two batters. It was all up to Armand now, who stood off to the side knocking the dirt from his cleats with the meat part of the bat, then stepped into the batter's box, and whispered to Billy. "Time to turn this thing around."

Popwell's first two pitches were strikes. But Armand appeared unfazed. On the next pitch, Armand threw caution to wind and laid down a bunt that died in the dirt a few feet in front of home plate. Billy tossed away his mask and pounced on the ball like a starving alley cat. He picked it up, and with all the time in the world, threw wild and in the dirt. Henry lunged after it, but couldn't make a play. Armand was on. Henry lobbed the ball back to Popwell who eyed Billy curiously. Billy crouched behind the plate, business as usual.

Lyle stepped up to try and keep the rally alive. As Popwell delivered his first pitch, Armand took off for second. The slow, fat knuckleball was right over the plate. Billy jumped up to make a snap throw to O'Malley at second, but the ball slipped from his hand. Armand slid safely into the bag. The cheers from the Titans were deafening. Billy picked up the ball, and kicked at the dirt. He looked to Popwell and shrugged. The rest of the infield was bewildered by Billy's sloppy play.

"My fault," he admitted, leaving no one to doubt it was little more than lousy luck, as he fired the ball back to Popwell.

Popwell came set, checked Armand at second and threw. Lyle connected and hit a blazing liner right at Benish. The ball burned a hole in Benish's glove and took off a short distance down the third base line. Benish raced after it as Armand, without breaking stride, rounded third and sped toward home.

By now, the Titans' jubilant screams could be heard as far away as the rooftop. Sven couldn't restrain himself any longer. He could hear the excited voices of his teammates cheering Armand home. He had to see it for himself. He knew a straight run across the roof would most likely be intercepted by Miss D and the guards. So there really was only one option left. Carefully placing one foot in front of the other, with eagle-like arms spread wide for balance, he inched his way across the narrow parapet towards the rear of the building. Miss Duncan nearly fainted as she watched helplessly. The guards inched cautiously closer in swarm formation, hoping to position themselves to take him down.

On the field below, Benish picked up the ball, reared back and fired it home. Billy waited, pounding his mitt, blocking the plate. As Armand's gloating face raced toward him, Billy clearly saw him for what he was; someone who would do anything to anyone to win; someone who could watch an innocent like Scooter lay motionless and be thinking about whether or not Scooter caught the ball. And worst of all, someone who could send Billy into a locked room with an animal like Diablo.

But Popwell didn't seem to be much better – a cold, self-serving, control freak who used everyone to remain dominant. Screw both of them. He decided to let the chips fall where they may.

The ball rocketed towards Billy. There was a loud, deafening pop, as the ball hit smack into the center of his mitt. Armand crashed head on into Billy in a wicked collision, both bodies landing in opposite directions in the dirt. Everyone waited for the dust to clear to see if Billy had held onto the ball.

"*You're out!*" yelled the ump, raising his thumb high in the air.

The Bellevederes went wild in victorious celebration.

"No!" Sven screamed in agony from on high. But his anguished cry was lost in the din of the noise below.

"You set me up you son of a bitch!" Armand blistered.

"You set yourself up, Armand. You loaded the gun. All I did was pull the trigger."

Armand's face flushed like a fierce Hawaiian sunset. "You think you're still the great Billy Rubin, college MVP!" he snarled. "You're a nobody here! A zero. I wish Diablo would have finished you off."

By now the Titans began drifting towards home plate. Emboldened by their advancing presence, Armand stepped closer, positioning himself inches from Billy's face.

"You're a fucking dead man, Rubin."

Billy's heart began to quicken. As the Titans advanced, Billy stumbled backward, nearly ploughing into Henry, standing squarely behind him, tall and resolute. Billy spun around, startled to find not only Henry, but the entire team, standing shoulder-to-shoulder.

"You threatening a member of my team?" Popwell asked,

positioning himself between Armand and Billy. Billy couldn't believe Popwell actually had his back.

"Because if you are, Armand," Henry warned, "be prepared to take us all on."

The leader of the Titans was too pumped with rage and a growing sense of entitlement to respond. He glowered at Billy with unbridled venom. "Kill these motherfuckers!" Armand screamed to his team. "Show them who's got the real muscle around here!"

Billy could feel something was changing as The Bellevederes stepped forward, an advancing army, nine men strong. A silence fell over the playing field, the air so still you could hear the plastic beads on Rochester's pointy shoes clang together as he wiggled his feet with glee.

Armand spun around to face his teammates. "What are you waiting for?" he yelled.

The Titans silently stood their ground, until Lyle broke from the pack and stepped forward. "This is your fight Armand. I got no reason to mess with any of the Bellevederes. We came to play ball and we did. We lost fair and square."

Grizzybowski came forward and extended his hand to Henry. "Good game, man."

Henry held back for a moment, then took it. "Yeah. Good game, Grizzy."

Billy couldn't believe what was happening. One by one, members of the opposing teams stepped up in an unexpected show of sportsmanship. Rochester sighed, deeply disappointed. He gathered up his things and started to head back into the building.

Armand, staggered back from the crowd. There was no longer a place for him at Highwater. He yanked off his uniform and threw it to the ground, then stomped half-naked from the field.

Sven leaned over the rooftop, his eyes frantically followed him as he shouted, "Wait for me, Armand! Don't leave without me."

With Sven distracted by the events below, Watermain seized the moment to signal Gunther. But, Sven heard them approaching and panicked.

Rochester looked up just in time to see Sven's flailing body slip from the rooftop. Within moments, both teams, residents and staff gathered around. Armand was nowhere to be seen.

Miss Duncan raced to Sven's side and knelt beside him on the grass, cradling his bruised and battered body, rocking him gently in her arms. Tears stained her color-drained cheeks. No one at Highwater had ever seen Miss Duncan weep before. Her sadness was overwhelming.

31

Alone in his den, Marvin Rasher's churning stomach scorched a path from his esophagus to his neck like the trail of a lit fuse of dynamite. It wasn't from the steak tartar and spicy Caesar salad with extra anchovies he ordered. It was the result of his own deluded desperation.

The evening started off well enough, as he rode the private elevator to the penthouse level at The United Center. He was looking forward to watching a Bulls' game from the comfort of a private suite over-looking the floor with some colleagues. Adding to his buoyant mood was the possibility that by the final buzzer, thanks to a last minute, sizable wager placed with a bookie, through a friend-of-a-friend, he would find himself closer to footing the bill for another round of Connie's needless cosmetic surgeries.

Though gambling was an activity Marvin rarely engaged in, he had to try something to find his way back into Connie's good graces. His higher brain considered the risks, given his current financial circumstances, but his lower brain between his legs screamed to return posthaste to Connie's pleasure path, like a pig rooting for truffles.

It had been almost a week now since Connie so much as let him touch her. The closest he'd come to skin-against-skin was when she accidentally clocked him with the back of her hand, smack-knuckle hard against his forehead while she was sleeping. Though, to be perfectly honest, Marvin couldn't swear it was by accident or even that Connie was really asleep.

Unfortunately, most of the evening at the United Center was spent in agony, watching the Bulls inexplicably stink up the court big time. When he could watch no more, he rested his elbows on the courtesy bar's gleaming granite altar, and silently swore to a long neglected God he would never gamble again if somehow he could just pull this one out. By the final buzzer, he knew God had better things to worry about than whether Marvin now owed some skuzzy bookie a considerable sum or if

Connie would end up with perkier bosoms.

The only bright spot of the night came when his patient, Billy Rubin, unexpectedly phoned a little before midnight. Marvin had just pulled into the garage, tiptoed into his bedroom and was about to crawl into a cold, unwelcome bed when his cell rang. Connie rolled onto her side, flipped up the corner of her pink satin eye mask, and fixed him with an icy glare. Marvin hastily retreated to the kitchen to take the call.

Billy had phoned to share his feelings on the outcome of the game between the Bellevederes and the Titans. He sounded upbeat yet confused by the unanticipated support and unity exhibited by both teams. Marvin was very encouraged. Though Billy might not have recognized the importance of the event, Rasher knew it represented a positive sign of Billy's progress. A door had been opened. Perhaps just a crack, but it was a definite step in the right direction. And certainly a sterling example of just how brilliant Rasher's psychoanalytic insights truly were.

Which is why, as he sat in his office the following day, he still couldn't fathom how he let himself act so irrationally by gambling away a small fortune the night before.

How could he have possibly believed gambling would be the solution to anything? What more proof did he need than to look across the room at his client, David Wagner, one of his most celebrated success stories, stretched out on the leather recliner?

It took months of intense therapy, working with the legendary third baseman to rid him of his insidious gambling addiction, a condition that nearly cost the one-time superstar everything.

When Wagner first came to Rasher's office, his gambling compulsion threatened to permanently taint the memory of a spectacular baseball career that included three World Series championships, five Gold Glove awards and the distinction of having been voted, 'Most Valuable Player,' four times. He was a shining star until he was found guilty of gambling on baseball and, even more heinous, of occasionally wagering against his very own team. Though Wagner fervently denied it, he was banished from the league, and denied entrance into the Baseball Hall of Fame. He became a pariah, lucky to land an occasional low-level autograph signing. Gone were the lucrative endorsements and high-priced speaking engagements.

Then, in an unbelievable turn of events, Wagner decided to come clean. He sat down with the Commissioner and admitted he'd bet on baseball, but never against his own team. He agreed to seek professional help, which was when Marvin entered the picture. With Marvin Rasher's help, Wagner was gradually able to understand how to control his destructive behavior and turn his life around. He wrote a three hundred page, mea culpa, apologizing for his sins and embarked on a twenty-eight-city book signing tour, cautioning young fans and future ballplayers to learn from his mistakes. The book not only raked in the dough, selling five million copies, but managed to soften the hearts and minds of those who once worshiped him. Public sentiment rose up to embrace him. The Baseball Commission was pressured to lift the ban and Wagner was inducted into the Baseball Hall of Fame. From there he went on to manage the Iowa Cubbies, a triple A farm team in the Chicago Cubs organization.

Dr. Rasher felt confident Wagner no longer needed therapy to manage his addiction. Today was simply one of the twenty-four mandated follow-up sessions that had been ordered as part of the conditional pardon he received from the Baseball Commission.

Over time, the doctor had come to look forward to their sessions. And, while it wasn't often the case with other patients, he couldn't help but secretly enjoy being on a first name basis with someone as famous as David Wagner.

On several occasions, Wagner had even invited Marvin and Connie to join him at high profile sporting events, not the least of which had been his induction into the Hall. Connie absolutely delighted in basking in Wagner's reflected glory, making sure the Press managed to find her bobbing blonde curls in as many photo ops as possible that day. It was also one of the rare times in recent memory, Rasher could recall, when Connie was actually thrilled to be Mrs. Marvin Rasher. She was so giddy, so turned on by all the surrounding glitterati that she willingly gave herself to her husband in the back seat of the chauffeured Lincoln Town car on the ride home. Yes, both men had good reasons to be grateful Wagner's therapy turned out as well as it did.

As today's session drew to a close, the conversation turned, as it always did to sports. Wagner was quite animated about his latest crop of young players. In particular, Kip Chapman. "We should definitely sweep Tacoma this weekend," he said, with the utmost confidence. "If I was still a betting man," he added, with a twinkle in his eye, "but thanks to you I'm not, I'd drop a bundle on it. It's a no-brainer."

Despite his earlier resolve, there was something in Wagner's enthusiasm that fed directly into Rasher's desperate plight. The therapist feigned a sigh of relief, slapping Wagner playfully on the back, as he quickly ushered him toward the door so he could call the bookie and lay some cash on Wagner's team to chip away at last night's loss before his next appointment arrived.

Unfortunately, as the office door swung open, there stood Billy Rubin, anxiously pacing in the hall. Billy stopped in mid-stride, startled to discover David Wagner standing in Rasher's doorway.

Dr. Rasher considered it highly inappropriate to have clients cross paths in his office. For a brief moment there was an awkward silence, until Wagner, who obviously could not have cared less about the accidental encounter, spoke up.

"Hey kid. Aren't you Billy Rubin?"

Billy was beyond flattered a man of Wagner's stature had recognized him. "Yes sir, Mr. Wagner, I am," Billy admitted, with a surprising degree of humility.

"Too bad about the knees, kid," Wagner said, before turning back to Rasher. "Thanks again, Doc. See you next month." Billy's eyes followed Wagner as he headed off jauntily down the corridor and disappeared into a waiting elevator.

Billy could barely contain his excitement. "You're the shrink... the one Wagner wrote about in his book. You're Dr. X. The one he credits with reviving his reputation."

Doctor/patient confidentiality would normally preclude the psychiatrist from discussing any patient, particularly celebrity clients with anyone. In this case however, there was hardly anything left to disclose following the publication of Wagner's tell-all bestseller. Not since Wagner had already chosen to publish most of their therapy sessions verbatim, including several references to Marvin's appearance and personal mannerisms. Yet still, he felt obligated to stand by his professional ethics. "You know I can't discuss that with you, Billy."

"No. Of course you can't. I get it." Billy's mind was reeling. The fact that he and Wagner shared the same shrink was mind-blowing. The realization that Marvin Rasher helped Wagner return to baseball, gave

Billy new hope. "Dr. Rasher, can I ask you something? How would you feel about talking to Wagner about giving me a look. I know I could do triple A in my sleep!"

Billy waited as the therapist removed the reading glasses from the bridge of his nose and set them down on the table next to him. "I'm sure you could, Billy. And when the time is right, when we both feel you're ready, I'll be happy to discuss it. But, it's my professional opinion that we aren't there yet."

"But, I'm making progress. You said so yourself last night. I swear I haven't had a drink or a blackout in weeks."

"That's all true. You have the potential for a brilliant career in the majors and I want to help you get there, but I want to make sure you can hold onto it once you get it. If you try to go back before you're emotionally ready, it could prove disastrous."

"You think I might try to kill myself again?" Billy asked, hesitantly.

"I'm not saying that at all. I just feel you may not be ready to handle the pressures of playing in the pros again just yet. I have every confidence that day will come, and I'll be right there doing everything I can to make that happen."

Billy nodded. Much as he hated to admit it, maybe Rasher was right. He certainly didn't want to blow what might be his last best chance by rushing in too soon.

"Now, would you like to continue our discussion about the game between the Bellevederes and the Titans?"

Billy took a seat across from him. "Actually there's something else that's come up I need to talk to you about first." Billy swallowed hard. "Do you remember when I told you about the email I sent my girlfriend a while back?" Billy paused, correcting himself with a frown. "Or maybe I should say, former girlfriend. Anyway, Julie wrote back this morning and said she's gonna be in Chicago on business soon and would like to meet for lunch." His tone was less than enthusiastic.

"That's good news, isn't it, Billy?"

Billy stared down at his feet, embarrassed to discover he was still wearing his bedroom slippers. "Not exactly. I'm pretty sure Julie has no idea what's really been going on. You know… about the suicide and Highwater, and all the shit in between."

"Maybe it's time she did."

"But, if I say the wrong thing, I could lose her forever. How do you put a good spin on crazy?"

"You're not crazy, Billy."

"I don't think I could get that across over lunch in some noisy restaurant."

"You're welcome to meet in my office, if you'd like."

Billy stood up and walked to the window overlooking the courtyard. He placed the warm palm of his hand against the cool glass, and exhaled.

32

No one was more surprised than Billy when Dr. Rasher proposed an outing to Wrigley, believing some time away from Highwater's routine might help calm Billy's jangled nerves over Julie's anticipated arrival.

He slowed his pace, lagging slightly behind Dr. Rasher, as they headed past the old Fullerton 'L' train station with its brick and terra cotta trimmed stone. It had been a while since Billy last laid eyes on the seemingly ancient edifice, inspired by the work of the great 16th century Italian Renaissance architect, Andrew Palladio. So much of this part of town had been lost to gentrification since he grew up here. Gone was the long standing Chicago eatery, Demon Dogs, which used to nestle beneath the towering, rusty steel girders that hold up the venerable 'L.' For a moment, he could almost still see the faded photos of the band Chicago plastered on its walls, and almost smell the faint aroma of the perfectly steamed hot dogs he enjoyed as a child.

Billy picked up his gait, not wanting to fall too far behind as they headed up the wooden stairs that led to the dual island platforms. Being out among ordinary people in the everyday world again was both exhilarating and a little unsettling.

As they waited for the Red Line train that would take them to Wrigley, Dr. Rasher's cell rang. He cupped his hand, cradling the phone tightly against his ear, but the caller's voice was undecipherable as a departing Brown Line train rumbled out of the station on the outside track. He motioned to Billy that he was going to step back down into the stairwell for a moment to take the call.

Billy watched the doctor disappear into the crowd of people rushing in and out on their way to their destinations. He envied their freedom as they went about their business unfettered by fear and delusions. And yet, here in the sunshine, Billy was starting to believe, as Rasher had suggested, he was getting better.

A bracing whoosh of air followed by a thunderous *clang, clang,*

clang rang out, as the Red Line train to Addison announced its arrival, screeching to a halt in the center of the station. Billy looked around for Dr. Rasher, but he was still nowhere to be seen. No need for concern. He knew if they missed this train another would arrive in short order.

Billy craned his neck trying to find Rasher's face among the crowd. Instead, a horrible, familiar visage stared back from the far end of the platform. It was the monstrous face of Diablo. Billy's heart almost flatlined. The contents of his stomach swirled up into the back of his throat. His mind began to race. This can't be happening. He could feel his life's blood drain from his body. He darted behind a cold concrete pillar and leaned back fighting to force air back into his painfully deflated lungs. He tried to remain calm knowing Rasher wasn't far away.

He stepped out from behind his pillared sanctuary and looked around. Diablo had disappeared from sight. Billy exhaled slowly. The train to Wrigley was still in the station. He had every reason to believe Dr. Rasher would return any second; and when he did, they would board the train together and spend a wonderful afternoon enjoying a ballgame.

Keeping one eye on the stairwell and one on the train, Billy began to wonder whether he had even actually seen Diablo or not. Maybe he just conjured him up in his mind, or perhaps he had only seen someone who looked like Diablo. Now there was a sobering thought.

As the doors to the train began to close, a deafening roar crackled through the air assaulting Billy's ears. He turned, paralyzed with fear as Diablo's grotesque face suddenly appeared inches from his own.

Billy leapt inside the train just as the doors slammed shut, sealing him safely inside as it pulled out of Fullerton Station and onto the winding tracks beyond Diablo's grasp.

He slumped back against the door, trying to compose himself. He could get off at the next stop and double back to Fullerton, but Diablo might still be waiting for him there. Or, he could continue on to Wrigley with the hope that Dr. Rasher would eventually follow. *Yes*, he thought, *it's always better to move forward than back. Rasher would definitely approve.* Now all he had to do was let the doctor know where he was and where he was heading.

Billy took out his cell and punched Rasher's number, but speeding past the back alleys that flanked the tracks of the 'L' failed to produce a viable signal. His phone was useless. Why, he wondered, could people in the wilds of Kilimanjaro manage to signal for help on cell phones, yet he couldn't successfully transmit a simple call to someone a few hundred yards away?

The train made its way towards the Belmont Station as Billy meandered through several adjoining cars in search of a seat. His legs still weak, the tension in his back and shoulders, though less pronounced, needed a little time to return to normal. As he pushed open the next set of connecting doors, he stared in disbelief. There was Diablo making his way slowly and deliberately toward him. Billy pushed his way back into the crowded train trying to put as much distance as possible between them -- hoping they would pull into Belmont before Diablo could reach him.

In an instant, he felt the massive, snake-like fingers grip his throat. Billy fell to his knees as the monster forced him to the ground.

A man seated nearby drew back his feet from the aisle where Billy landed, quickly raising his newspaper to cover his face. A frightened, wide-eyed little girl pointed, until her mother pulled her onto her lap and told her it was not polite to stare. Why, his brain screamed, wasn't anyone coming to his rescue? How could everyone stand idly by while Diablo choked the very life out of him?

Billy managed to shove the monster off him and scramble to his feet. He raced through the train shoving people aside as he fled, until he found himself trapped in the very last car. His feet rooted to the floor as Diablo came toward him.

There was no escape. Then he looked up. His eyes found the emergency cord dangling above his head. He reached up and pulled hard. The train lurched to a screeching stop. Screaming passengers tossed about like rag dolls, their bodies tumbling from their seats. Billy's head slammed into the plate glass door, his body ricocheted to the floor. And then... silence.

33

The sidewalk was cold and gravelly beneath Billy's neck. His eyes fluttered open slowly. A woman with a large squinting head inched closer to his face, blocking the sun. Her rouge-red flabby cheeks sagged forward by age and gravity as she bent over him. The fringe of her bright yellow scarf dangled a scant millimeter or two from the tip of his nostrils. It reeked of fried onions and lavender soap. Billy's eyes snapped shut.

"Jeeze. C'mon," she hollered, swiping her arms like a windmill at the cluster of curious passersby inching forward to gawk. "Give the poor guy some room, will ya," the woman demanded, getting the crowd to back up.

When and how Billy had gotten off the train and made his way back onto Fullerton Street was unclear. But he found himself out on the sidewalk, flat on his back. He opened his eyes once more as the woman reached out a helping hand, decorated by island-shaped liver spots and a bracelet made of beads and painted Cheerios.

A few shaky minutes later he was perched on the edge of the curb. His wobbly chin rested atop his knees pressed tightly against his chest. The woman was gone. He rubbed his eyes with the back of his hand. When he looked up, he found himself staring at a freshly pressed pair of dark navy blue pants belonging to one of Chicago's finest.

The policeman's two-way buzzed and crackled. Officer Haggerty scrutinized the caked rivulet of blood that had traveled from a small cut above Billy's left eyebrow to right above his ear. Upon closer inspection, the officer determined Billy's injuries were superficial at most, certainly not necessitating immediate transport to the ER. Besides, calling for a van would mean waiting on the street until it arrived, not to mention volumes of tiresome, follow-up paperwork. What the beat cop really wanted, was to get over to the Addison Street station. That's where the real action was. Some joker pulled the emergency cord and there were bodies bounced and bruised everywhere. Nonetheless, protocol required he offer medical transport to the vic. To his relief, Billy refused treatment. The last place Billy wanted to go right now was to another hospital.

As Officer Haggerty helped Billy to his feet, Dr. Rasher came tearing down the steps of the 'L,' two at a time. Damn Connie, he thought, damn her for bending his ear with her nonsense. He never should have left his patient alone on the platform to take her stupid call. To his relief, he soon spotted Billy. "Officer, I'm Dr. Marvin Rasher," he said, offering his card. "This man is a patient of mine. I'd be happy to see that he gets home safely, if it's okay with you?"

Officer Haggerty assessed the doctor's credibility, and his own official responsibility in the matter. "That okay with you, fella?" he asked. Billy nodded absently.

"Try to relax," Rasher intoned reassuringly. But Billy was having no part of it as the memory of his disturbing ordeal continued to haunt him. His palms were sweaty, his legs twitched as if still trying to escape his tormentor.

Rasher had given him a mild sedative once they were settled into the back of the cab, but the effect seemed to have worn off more rapidly than the doctor expected. Billy sat up on Rasher's couch with a start, his panicky eyes searching his surroundings.

"Is he still out there?"

Dr. Rasher pulled his chair in closer. "Is who out there, Billy?"

"Diablo. Someone let him out. He was at the train station."

"Diablo is locked in his room at Highwater, Billy. Let me reassure you, he will remain that way until it's safe for him to be released. "

Billy was confused. "Then what did I see? Who was that? What was that?"

"Sometimes the things we fear most have a way of forcing us to confront them whether we want to or not. It's part of the therapeutic process. But Diablo may not be the problem. It may be your continued resistance to confront an unknown fear."

There was nothing reassuring in the doctor's words. Therapy was supposed to help him learn to cope, to make him feel better. The thought there could be something buried in his subconscious more frightening than being stalked by Diablo rattled Billy to his very core.

34

Over the next few nights, believing Diablo remained shackled to the wall in his room, Billy slept better than he had in some time. Deep, dreamless nights, brought about by productive therapy sessions, exercise, and an occasional mild sleeping pill. But tonight, he tried to shut his eyes and drift off at least a dozen times without success; rolling, sweating, tossing, assuming every imaginable position. Exhausted, he lifted his head and glanced at the bright, red digital display on the cheesy, plastic alarm clock by his bed. It was 12:02 a.m. He flopped his head back onto the pillow and stared up at the ceiling, wrestling with an anxiety no pill could lessen. Julie would be arriving in Chicago in a few short hours.

By 10:02 p.m. Pacific Coast Time, Julie had managed to work herself into a healthy dither as well, packing and re-packing. Stressing and obsessing over each and every article she folded into the sturdy garment bag. She hated taking the red-eye, but it was the only way she could get into Chicago in time to see Billy before the hotel conference began.

She glared at her suitcases, pissed by her lack of options. There were so many annoying airport security regulations that had to be dealt with nowadays. And, despite the fact she knew her hotel chain provided shampoo and various toiletries nestled in a pretty wicker basket, she still felt she couldn't take the chance that there might be something she couldn't possibly do without. She placed the last of her miniature-size clear bottles and tiny tube of toothpaste neatly in a quart-size plastic bag and crammed them into her carry-on, along with a copy of Billy's email.

By now it was 5:45 a.m., and as Billy peered through the window, he could see a glowing prism of sunlight poking its way up out of the darkness, ushering the start of a glorious new day. Why then on this glorious day, did his thoughts keep returning to the Ziploc bag that nearly ended his life? How could he have hidden away in Highwater all this time without a word of explanation to Julie and still expect her to care about him? Was he deluded enough to believe everything he left behind would miraculously remain in a state of suspended animation until he got his head together?

Any plans Julie may have had about getting some sleep on the plane vanished as she sat in her window seat, head propped against the cold thick glass, watching the glittering lights of cities inch slowly by some thirty thousand feet below. How many times, she wondered, had she rehearsed in her head what she would say when she saw him again. Her thoughts and emotions were all over the map. One minute she couldn't bear the thought of living without him, and the next, she took great pleasure imagining him drowning in shark-infested waters. There were only two things that remained clear – she hated Billy Rubin's guts, and she still loved him beyond all reason.

She must still love me, Billy mused, trying to bolster his confidence. Why else would she want to see me? Unless, he feared, Armand had gotten to her and she was coming to tell him they were done forever, and there was nothing he could do to change her mind.

It was nearly 7:00 a.m. as the wheels on Julie's luggage bumped and rattled their way through the terminal at O'Hare. She quickened her pace, desperately searching for a ladies room. When she found one, she could hardly believe there was a long, winding line to use the bathroom at this hour of the morning. As she waited impatiently, cursing the fact she hadn't thought to go before deplaning, she caught a glimpse of her reflection in the ladies' room mirror. God, she looked awful. She was pale and swollen, not at all, the pretty young thing that used to hang on the arm of the best-looking jock at USC.

She felt old, tired and yes, even queasy. Damn you, Billy Rubin. This is all your fault! She could no longer summon the energy to stave off her bursting bladder. She dropped her luggage to the floor with a thud, and pushed past the dozen or so women and fidgety, whining children waiting in line ahead of her. She nearly knocked down some poor elderly woman emerging from a stall to dart inside before anyone could stop her. She bent over the bowl and heaved up everything she had consumed in the last twenty-four hours, flushed, then sank down onto the toilet seat. She was totally drained. Literally and figuratively. Julie looked at the collar of her jacket, now dappled in splattered, yellow puke. It was disgusting. She felt disgusting. She lowered her face into her hands and wept.

By 7:22, Billy emerged from the shower, summoned his resolve and looked over the contents of his closet. He ultimately decided on something he hoped would convey a sense of 'a man on the road to wellness who sincerely regrets any pain his failed attempt at suicide may have caused you,' kind of look.

Having little to no appetite, he skipped breakfast, opting instead for half a dozen antacids. He stared at the clock. The time couldn't go slow enough. He wanted to wind it back like a crooked auto mechanic rolling back an odometer. He began to perspire. Then, a sharp pain engulfed his entire chest cavity. It was suffocating. He knew exactly what was happening.

Julie waited inside the bathroom stall until she was certain that anyone on line with her earlier was most likely gone. She retrieved her carry-on, which had been moved out of the way against the wall, undoubtedly by some well-meaning patron, or perhaps by an airline employee. She was grateful it hadn't been removed to the lost luggage office, or worse, stolen. As she stared in the mirror, she thought she looked like death warmed over. She sighed, then splashed cold tap water on her face and neck. She did the best she could to tidy up the damage left behind from vomiting and crying. One last look was all it took before the realization hit that this was probably the best she could expect to look under the circumstances. After all, she was three months pregnant.

35

Dr. Rasher eagerly searched through the sports section of the morning paper, unable to find what he was looking for. He went over them again, more slowly this time, page-by-page, and wondered if the Tribune even listed minor league baseball scores. He sat behind his desk, painstakingly squinting through each and every stat until he struck gold. Page fourteen, lower right hand corner, in the smallest print imaginable: IOWA CUBS 5, TACOMA TOM CATS 0.

"Yes," he shouted, pumping his tightly coiled fist enthusiastically.

In hindsight, he regretted having only wagered two hundred, but never having bet on minor league baseball before, he had to be cautious. But now, with Wagner's unwitting assistance, he might actually be able to chip away at his losses and end up back in the plus column.

As he checked the odds on tonight's games, Billy burst through the door, and crumpled to his knees in front of Rasher's desk. "I'm having a heart attack. Call 911."

The doctor pushed the sports section aside, rose to his feet and assessed the situation. "Take it easy, Billy," he said, securing a small paper bag from a desk drawer. "Put this over your mouth and breathe in and out slowly."

Billy shoved his face inside the bag and breathed deep, although it wasn't the cutting edge medical approach he had hoped for. After a few moments he pulled the bag away.

"How do you feel now?" Rasher asked, calmly.

"Like I'm having a heart attack," Billy gasped, his face contorted with pain. "Like my heart's gonna jump out of my chest."

"It's important you to try to relax." Rasher grabbed a hand towel from the bathroom, ran it under the cold water and applied a compress to Billy's forehead. "Does that feel any better?"

"It's not my head. It's my heart. It feels like it's going to explode. Call the paramedics."

"You're having an anxiety attack," Rasher assured him. "Lower your head between your legs and stay calm. It'll pass."

Billy did as instructed, and slowly the pain in his chest began to subside. "Maybe we shouldn't take any chances," Billy stated nervously. "Maybe we should go to the hospital? You know, just as a precaution."

"Might this have something to do with Julie?"

The second he heard her name, a searing pain pierced the top of his solar plexus, knifing clear through to the other side of his torso. "Oh shit!" he moaned.

Rasher handed him a cup of water which Billy grabbed and quickly emptied, then clutched his chest once again. His histrionics did little to change Rasher's opinion. He knew exactly what was going on. It was a classic example of traumatic stress syndrome. Even though the pain felt real to Billy, it was nothing more than a desperate attempt to avoid grappling with the uncertainty associated with Julie's imminent arrival.

Billy grabbed Rasher's shirtsleeve, pulling him down beside him. "I can't go through with it. She'll leave me. I can't let that happen."

Rasher patted his shoulder reassuringly. "It's going to be just fine. I believe you're strong enough to handle whatever happens."

Billy wasn't so sure. He desperately wanted to bolt. But it was too late. There she was -- standing in the open doorway.

He pulled himself together and rose to meet her gaze as she set her luggage on the tiled floor with barely a sound. He wanted to grab her hand, run from Rasher's office and make the past several weeks fade into nothing more than a bad dream. But he knew he couldn't. He just stood there, frozen in place. As did Julie, until Rasher spoke up, extending a hand, with a warm, friendly smile.

"You must be Julie," he said. "Dr. Marvin Rasher. So nice to meet you. Welcome to Chicago. Hope you had a pleasant flight."

Julie took his hand and smiled back, grateful someone had attempted to ease the awkwardness of the moment. "Thank you. Yes," she said politely, hoping the doctor hadn't noticed how clammy her hands were as she fought to remain calm and focused.

"Okay then," Rasher smiled, reaching for his jacket, hanging on a peg behind the door. "I'm sure you two have lots to talk about." Both Julie and Billy had much to say to one another, but Julie still hadn't decided if she would tell Billy about the baby -- at least not yet. And Billy still couldn't decide if he would tell Julie about Highwater – at least, not now. "There's a fresh pot of tea in the back room. Feel free to help yourself," Rasher offered, as he closed the door softly behind him.

Julie lingered by the door, uncertain if she should commit to stepping further into the room. Just about everyone, especially her mother, had told her to put Billy in her past and move on. Which is why she told no one, except Frank Tortiricci, she planned on seeing him this week. She was certain they all would've tried to talk her out of it, except Frankie, who seemed to have a soft spot where Billy was concerned.

"I hope this isn't making you uncomfortable... meeting in my shrink's office. I'm not really crazy, you know. Things just got a little out of hand – and I kind of lost it for a while. God, you look great!"

"So do you. Really... really... good..." Julie responded awkwardly, grasping for words. "I mean... considering what happened."

"How did you find out?" he asked, fearing the worst.

"Frank Tortiricci. But he made me swear on a stack of baseballs I'd never breathe a word of it to anyone. When he told me what happened I tried to get in touch with you, but you just disappeared."

"I'm sorry."

Julie sighed deeply before she spoke again. "I'm just glad you're getting help. Your... your therapist seems very nice."

"Yeah, Rasher's an okay guy. But I didn't pick him for his personality. He's way up there on the 'who's who' of shrinks. The guy's got almost as many diplomas as I've got trophies." Billy hated how that came out. He didn't want to come off sounding like an asshole anymore. Nor did he have to remind Julie, of all people, of his past accomplishments. She deserved better from him. "Can I get you some tea?"

"I'm fine," she said, draping her coat across the back of a chair, while glancing briefly at her watch, which Billy noticed. "Well, maybe some tea would be nice. Thanks."

As Billy went into the back, Julie sank into one of Rasher's leather chairs and looked around the room. How did she and Billy ever arrive at this time and place? How could she not have known what was happening to him all along?

Billy returned, balancing two steaming mugs and a few jelly donuts he found stashed in the cupboard. Julie clasped the mug with both hands and took a sip. Its gentle warmth returning the blood flow to her icy fingers.

Billy walked to the door and cracked it open -- just wide enough to survey the hallway. He had to make sure no one from Highwater was lurking about. It was way too soon for Julie to meet any of them.

"Sorry I couldn't find anything chocolate back there," he said, as he locked the door. "But..." with a hopeful smile, "... the donuts looked pretty fresh."

There was no way Billy could have known for the past few weeks of her pregnancy she couldn't even look at a piece of chocolate without it turning her stomach.

"Did I tell you how really great you look?" Billy offered again.

Julie nodded, and smiled patiently. "Yes. About five minutes ago, I think."

Billy grinned sheepishly, dropped his head, and scrambled his fingers through his hair, hoping to fire up a few sharper synaptic exchanges between his brain and lips before saying something stupid again.

For Julie, there was something endearing about finding the usually confident, quick-witted, never at a loss for words, Billy Rubin, at a genuine loss for words. It was a side of him she hadn't seen in a long, long time, if ever. And, she liked it. When he popped his head back up, there was a kind of irresistible vulnerability to his face. In the past, she would have found it difficult to keep from wrapping her arms around him. But not today.

"Oh, by the way, Frankie asked me to say hello."

"Really? Next time you see him, make sure you tell him I said, 'fucking' hello back."

Julie's smile widened. She knew immediately what Billy meant. How many times did she laugh until her sides ached while Billy told her one crazy story after another about Frankie? Nobody could make her laugh the way Billy could.

"I'll be happy to 'fucking' do it," she said, giggling to cover her embarrassment over using the F word so nonchalantly. To her surprise, it suddenly seemed so easy being with Billy again. Easy to remember what it felt like once upon a time in Los Angeles, when they were a couple.

"There's so much I want to tell you," Billy began. "You don't know how much I regret screwing up the way I did. But, I need you to understand I was a whole other person back then. I've learned a lot about myself since I've been here. All I need is a chance to make things right with us again."

Julie became flustered, uncertain how to respond. "I… I didn't think there was an 'us' anymore. I just thought… since I had to be in Chicago anyway, on company business… I just figured…" Julie twisted her wrist and stole another furtive glance at her watch.

"It's okay, Julie. I don't mean to put you on the spot or rush you in any way. Besides, I'd much rather hear about you and your new job. Oh, and speaking about your job… is Nelson still prowling the halls?" When Julie looked confused, Billy continued. "Nelson. You know… I gotta tell you, without that old guy I never would have found my way around the hotel the night of your birthday party." Julie furrowed her brow, not quite following. "Never mind. You mentioned something about coming to Chicago for a meeting or a… a conference in your email."

Julie nodded, happy to change the course of the conversation. "It's the hotel chain's international conference. Believe it or not, I'm scheduled to address a group of sixty-two managers about improving guest relations."

Billy sat back in his chair. "Sounds important. But then, I always knew you'd do well at anything you set your mind to."

"Thank you. This job means a lot to me. There's a real opportunity for advancement and incentives."

Billy leaned forward to make a point. "I know exactly what you mean. When I signed my contract with the Royals, Erikson made sure I had a big fat bonus waiting for me if I hit over thirty homers. This hotel chain you're working for… The Bedford Regency, right? I hope they're paying you what you're worth?"

"It's not about money. The truth is, I'd work there for free. I really love what I do."

"Absolutely. You've got to love what you do. I mean, look at me. I love playing baseball. I honestly don't know if I could do anything else." Julie took a sip of tea. "What exactly is it you do for them again?" Billy asked, diving into his donut.

"I'm the assistant to the Vice President of Marketing and Public Relations."

For the next ten minutes, Billy simply let Julie ramble on about her work. From time to time, he'd nod or contribute to the conversation with an occasional, uh huh or really? But he was finding it increasingly difficult to concentrate on what she was saying. Every time he thought he heard the sound of approaching footsteps in the hall, he had to fight the urge to get up and check that the office door was really locked. The thought of someone like Rochester walking in sent shivers down his spine. But he didn't want to appear overly anxious, or worse, paranoid like Barney. So he kept his eyes keenly focused on Julie, who could barely believe Billy was this interested in hearing her drone on about work.

"How's your mother?" Billy asked.

Julie did a double take – amazed to hear those words coming from Billy's lips without gagging. It was no secret he liked her mother about as much as he liked getting plunked in the head by a ninety-mile-an-hour fastball.

"Mother's... she's... well, you know.... still Mother. No one can make my life as miserable as she can."

"I'm sure she only does it because she cares so much. Make sure you give her my best when you see her."

Julie nodded, wondering what medication they had him on. When their conversation was interrupted by her cell phone, she glanced at the caller I.D. It was her boss. But she let it go to voice mail.

"I'm sorry, Billy. I really do need to check in at the hotel. I'm already running late."

"Can I see you later today? Or, maybe tomorrow?"

"I'll call you."

"Can I at least go get you a cab?" he asked.

"Sure. That'd be great. But, first I need to use the rest room for a sec."

Rasher's guest bathroom was cheery and bright, decorated in happy, yet soothing colors. The walls were decorated with upbeat, framed homilies, intended no doubt to inspire his patients to think positively, even while they sat on the pot. On the wall above the sink was a small, somewhat tasteful print of Raphael's, 'Madonna and Child.' Julie had always loved that painting. The tenderness and hope it represented, especially now.

When she first found out she was pregnant, she felt angry, very much alone and frightened. She felt no maternal connection to the life inside her. She was about to start an exciting new career. She had her entire future ahead of her. Billy was no longer supposed to be part of that future. She even considered terminating the pregnancy. She went so far as to make an appointment with a counselor at a woman's clinic in Costa Mesa. On the day of her appointment, Billy's email arrived. She took it as a sign, and cancelled.

She still wasn't sure if she did the right thing. Not about keeping the baby -- of that she was certain. But of keeping Billy in the dark. Could she take on raising their child alone... should she even try? Billy seemed so different now, so caring and attentive. She wrestled with her conscience over whether to go back out and tell him about the baby. Her instincts said yes. But, what she desperately needed first was tangible proof – something – anything to allow her to believe this change in Billy was real and permanent. That he could honestly love someone as much as he loved himself.

She stood before the full-length mirror on the back of the door and smoothed the soft curve of her belly with the palm of her hand. She wasn't showing at all yet, but there was a life stirring inside her nonetheless. Oh, the hell with proof! Billy had every right to know he was going to be a dad.

As she came back out into Rasher's office, Scooter was seated behind the doctor's desk, nervously fiddling with a string of entwined paper clips. "Billy had to leave," he said, without looking up.

"Excuse me?"

"I think he went to find you a cab or something. He doesn't know I'm here but, I thought I could, um... keep you company 'til he came back. If that's alright. I'm Scooter." His eyes sparkled and danced. "I couldn't wait to meet you. In fact, all of us wanted to meet you. But, I got here first," he said proudly.

"All of you?"

"Yeah. There's Huff and Henry, Grizzy and Lyle... oh, and Benish, and pretty much all the Bellevederes. Except for Popwell. He's the team captain. But, he's never been interested in meeting new people." Scooter swiveled back and forth in the chair, then stopped. "I don't think you'd want to meet Charley. He's kind of scary."

"What are you talking about?"

"All the guys at Highwater?"

"Highwater?" she asked.

"You know. The mental facility."

"Mental facility," Julie sputtered. "Dear God, stop it! That's not funny." Scooter didn't know what to do. He was afraid he may have divulged a little too much, or worse, offended Billy's girlfriend in some way. He sure didn't want Billy to be mad at him, so before making things any worse, he ran out the door.

36

Julie headed for the taxi waiting in front of the building. The driver hopped out to put her luggage in the trunk. She darted inside and quickly slammed the door behind her, just as Billy tapped on the window, but she turned away.

"Julie, what's wrong?"

At Julie's urging, the driver sped away from the curb. Billy dashed into the street, zigzagging through traffic until he caught up with them. As the cab slowed to round a corner, Billy yanked open the rear door and hurled himself inside.

She held up her hand. "Get out, Billy. Please. I can't do this now." She banged on the glass partition, "Driver, stop the car." The cabbie veered across three lanes of traffic and pulled over by a bus stop.

"Julie, what's going on?"

"If you won't leave, I will," she sputtered, as she shoved open the door and got out, then turned back briefly, asking the driver to wait.

Bewildered, Billy followed her out. "I don't get it. What did I do?"

"When I got your email, I thought you finally wanted to be open and honest with me. That things would be different now. But nothing's changed. You're still lying to me. You're still screwing with my head."

"I'm not."

"Then what's the deal with Scooter? And Highwater?"

At the mention of Highwater, the color drained from Billy's face as he tried to collect his thoughts. "I was always going to tell you about Highwater. I swear."

She took a step back, and stared in wide-eyed disbelief. "You mean it's true?"

"Not the way you think."

"I don't know what to think anymore. I feel like such a fool," she cried, as her legs began to cave beneath her. She felt light-headed and horribly nauseous. Fearing she might pass out, she grabbed Billy's arm to steady herself, then let him lead her to a nearby bench.

"Can I get you anything?" he asked, consumed with guilt.

"No. I just need a minute. I'll be fine."

"Julie, look, this… situation… is not forever. I swear. Highwater is just… temporary. Just please, don't go back to Los Angeles without hearing me out."

"You should have told me about this in your email."

"Would you have come if I had?

"That's not fair. I'm still trying to wrap my mind around the suicide - - and now this. Why did you send me that email? What do you want from me?"

"All I want is a chance to explain. If the things I said or did back in L.A. hurt you, I'm sorry. If I could take them back I would. When I got cut from the Royals, I was so angry and confused… half the time I didn't know what I was saying."

By now, she was so confused she didn't know how to respond. The cabbie reached across the passenger seat and rolled down the window. "Hey, miss, the meter's running. You still going to the hotel or not?"

"Give us a minute. Okay?" Billy shouted, his eyes never leaving Julie. "I swear, I've made a lot of progress since I came here. I've learned to control my mood swings, my anger, my depression, the destructive thoughts inside my head. Dr. Rasher thinks I could go back to playing pro ball pretty soon. But even that wouldn't mean anything without you."

Julie softened, listening with her heart more than her head. As crazy as this all was, Billy seemed to be making sense. He seemed perfectly normal right now, but she couldn't be sure. "I have questions, Billy. Lots of questions."

"And I promise I'll try and answer all of them," he said, taking her hand.

The cabbie beeped his horn, growing impatient.

"I can't do this now. I have to get to the hotel. I can't blow off the conference."

As she rose from the bench and started for the cab, Billy noticed a trickle of blood running down her leg. "Julie, you're bleeding."

She looked down and gasped, frightened by what she saw.

*   *   *

Billy slid back the curtain separating Julie's cubical from the others, and stepped in next to her bed. She seemed considerably calmer than she was seated in the back of the cab, protectively cradling her stomach. Not a word had been spoken on the breakneck drive to the hospital. No talk of Highwater or Billy's psychological issues -- just a tense and disquieting silence.

Julie looked up at Billy. "The doctors said I'm fine. But, I guess I should call my boss and let him know I won't be making any speeches today." Billy didn't react. "Are you okay?" she asked. Billy nodded, though he was anything but. His world shattered the moment he overheard the doctors discussing Julie's pregnancy. How could he have been such an idiot to think she'd been sitting home alone, faithfully waiting for his return? "Billy? Did you hear what I said? It's nothing serious. I'm perfectly healthy."

"And so is your baby," he added quietly.

"I was going to tell you, but…"

"I'm sorry for stressing you out like that. This is all my fault."

"Well, maybe not all your fault. I think I had a little something to do with it."

"I can't believe you let me yammer on about us getting back together when…"

"When I should have told you about the baby sooner," she interrupted.

"I just didn't know you were seeing someone else. And…well… I…"

Julie stared up at him. "What?"

"I just want you to know, I hope he makes you happy."

"He who? Whose baby do you think this is?"

Billy's jaw slackened. This was a question he hadn't anticipated. "Well… I… really don't…" his voice trailing off to a whisper. He looked so completely miserable Julie couldn't take much more.

"It's yours, you big dumb jock!"

37

The Bellevederes and several Titans were hanging out in the bleachers as Billy cut across Highwater's grassy field, lost in thought. Julie was having his baby. It was a lot to process. The definite upside was, now, no matter how badly he may have messed things up in the past, or might screw things up in the future, having a baby together meant Julie would be in his life, one way or another -- forever. It also meant he was going to become a dad and all that that implied. He didn't quite know what to do with that revelation. It wasn't as if he hadn't had a sprinkling of male role models growing up – some of whom were kind of like a dad he surmised. But none of whom truly fulfilled Billy's fantasy of what growing up with his real father would have been like. Someone who shared his DNA. Someone to play catch with. Someone who'd show up at all his games like he would with his own son.

"Well, well," Benish yowled. "Look who decided to show his pretty face."

"Hey man, where you been? You're two hours late for practice," Henry chimed in. "Almost sent the dogs out after your ass."

A shit-kickin' grin stretched across Billy's face as he corralled Henry in a massive bear hug that nearly knocked the strapping athlete off his feet.

"What the… " Henry managed to mutter, before Billy planted a big wet one, smack on his forehead.

Henry mopped his brow as he wrested free from Billy's grasp. "Get off a me! You one crazy white boy, you know that!" He turned back to the bleachers, "Didn't I tell you guys I had my doubts about this boy straight off!"

"Now, hold up, Henry. I've seen that look before," Benish said, slowly circling Billy with long, lazy steps. "I think Billy skipped practice 'cause he was too busy screwing that hot little girlfriend of his?"

"Watch your mouth, Benish. That's no way to talk about the mother of my child."

"Holy Shit!" Henry responded, with admiration.

"Wow. A little slugger, huh?" Lyle said warmly, as everyone clustered around, slapping Billy on the back, offering congratulations. Everyone, that is, except Popwell, who sat quietly off to the side, and Scooter who looked on awkwardly.

"So, what do you think, Uncle Scooter?

Scooter smiled sheepishly. "Can I really be an uncle, Billy?" he asked earnestly.

"No, you jerk," Benish jumped in, bopping Scooter on the head with his mitt. "You can't be an 'Uncle Billy,' moron -- you'd be an Uncle Scooter!" Everyone groaned at Benish's lame attempt at humor although Benish maintained it was simply brilliant.

"You bet, Scooter," Billy offered. "Why not? The whole lot of you can be uncles if you want. Only, Scooter, you gotta promise, you won't pop in on Julie again without checking with me first. Okay?"

Scooter dropped his head, his chin nearly touching his chest in penance, then nodded, and ran off happily to spread the word. Billy turned to the rest of the team. "I need you all to agree to that as well. Julie's been under a lot of pressure lately between her job and the pregnancy."

"So does this mean you'll be leaving Highwater?" Huff asked, with concern.

"Not just yet, but one day soon I hope." Billy responded.

Billy walked over to Popwell, wondering why he hadn't as yet reacted to his good news. "What do you say, B.J.? Can I add you to the list of honorary uncles?"

Popwell bent down, picked up his gear and to Billy's surprise, started walking off the field. He took a few steps, then stopped, and turned around. "Sure your ego can handle second place?" Billy stared back quizzically. "Babies have a way of changing everything. And not always for the better."

38

The ER doctor suggested they monitor Julie overnight. So Billy kept a vigil by her bedside, barely closing his eyes for more than moments at a time.

Come morning, Julie insisted on being released. She had already missed the first day of the conference and didn't want to miss any more. She promised to see her own physician the minute she returned to L.A. But the doctors advised against waiting that long and arranged for her to be seen by Dr. Sarah Constantine, an OB/GYN affiliated with the hospital.

Doctor Constantine was efficient, no nonsense and yet at the same time invitingly approachable. Billy could easily see why Julie warmed to her right from the start. There was something very reassuring about the comforting sound of her voice. He couldn't help but think if he were a fetus struggling his way out of a womb, he would feel far more motivated knowing someone like Dr. Constantine was waiting for him on the other side.

The good doctor patiently addressed all their concerns, explaining in laymen's terms how the first trimester bleeding Julie experienced was far more common than she and Billy had feared. She explained, bleeding doesn't always indicate miscarriage. In Julie's case, it appears to have been caused by something far less frightening – cervicitis – an inflammation due to a yeast infection. A simple prescription should clear it up.

Dr. Constantine turned on the ultrasound monitor and assembled the tools of her trade on a small silver tray table. "I'm really glad you were able to come in with Julie today, Mr. Rubin."

"Please, call me Billy. Under the circumstances... I mean... with you about to show us the first picture of baseball's future MVP."

Doctor Constantine smiled, as she squeezed a tube of icy gel onto Julie's stomach. "You mean this isn't a future Nobel Prize Laureate, or the scientist who finds the cure for the common cold?"

"Baseball pays better."

"You're right about that. Who knows… twenty years from now, your child may be the one to break the curse and finally bring us long-suffering Cub fans a World Series title again."

Sarah Constantine glided her wand-like instrument across Julie's abdomen. Billy's eyes were glued to the monitor as a grainy collection of black and white shapes captured a rather alien looking image of Billy's unborn All-Star. She proceeded to lead them through a crash course in basic fetal anatomy; patiently pointing out the head, arms, legs, hands and feet. "The baby looks perfectly healthy," Sarah Constantine assured them. "Ten little fingers and ten strong little toes. I think we're off to a good start. See if you can spot a little white cloud. That's the baby exhaling. Isn't that amazing?"

Billy honestly had no idea what the doctor and Julie were looking at, but he nodded in agreement. To him, the image on the screen looked more like a gerbil caught in one of those tortuous exercise wheels.

Dr. Constantine continued her gestational play-by-play. "Now this over here is the femur, the longest bone in the body. The length right now gives us a clear indication that the baby's size is normal."

"So that's the femur, huh?" Billy asked, sounding a bit disappointed. "For a moment there I thought it was the little slugger's manhood."

Sarah flashed a knowing smile and asked if they wanted to know the sex of the child.

Julie turned toward Billy. "I do if you do," she said. "It will be much easier to make plans once we know if it's a boy or a girl."

To be honest, until now, Billy had never even entertained the possibility of anything but a son. "Let's go for it, Doc."

Dr. Constantine swiveled from the screen. "Actually, I've known since I turned on the monitor. Congratulations. You're having a beautiful, healthy little girl."

Julie burst into tears. Then began to laugh. Then sat up and hugged Sarah Constantine with pure, unfettered joy. Billy on the other hand remained speechless, slowly taking it in.

A girl? he thought. A little girl. And in an instant, he could not imagine it any other way.

39

The grand ballroom of the Chicago Bedford Regency was filled to capacity. Everyone from hotel managers to corporate VIPs were on hand, exploring ways to increase the bottom line and boost productivity quotas. Julie's head was spinning. She had met so many people over the past few days she could barely keep their names and faces straight. Not to mention the names of all the people that made up Billy's world at Highwater. She tried to accept the fact whatever therapeutic technique he was following, Billy believed he was improving. And maybe he was.

As much as she wanted to believe as Billy did that they might yet have a future, the present demanded she continue to look after herself and her career. She had worked very hard on her presentation for the seminar, and it was extremely well received.

When it concluded, she was approached and courted by a half-dozen branch vice presidents from as far away as Hawaii and Mozambique, all brazenly intent on poaching her from her present job in Los Angeles.

She was flattered, and had she not been pregnant, might have jumped at the opportunity to advance her career by spending the next year or two in exotic locales. But she was pregnant, as evidenced by her swollen, throbbing feet. She'd been standing for the last three hours, and her classy little four-inch pumps were beginning to feel at least two sizes too small.

When the next speaker took to the stage, she decided to sneak out of the ballroom, sink into the soft, cushy couch in the adjoining alcove and slip off her shoes in private. She closed her eyes and wiggled her angry toes.

"Regency Health Spa, ninth floor. Make sure you ask for Gracie. Best foot massage in Chicago. She'll have you back on your toes in no time flat."

Julie smiled, as she struggled back into her shoes. "Ninth floor, huh? Don't think I could make it that far. But thanks. And by the way, you never saw me padding around barefoot."

"Secret's safe with me," he grinned, extending his hand. "Howard Caldwell, Assistant Manager, Bradford Regency, Chicago."

"Julie Hatcher, Barefoot Contessa, Los Angeles."

"Nice to meet you, Countess. By the way, your presentation… super impressive."

"Thanks."

"Apparently, I'm not the only one who thought so. I caught the small army of heavy hitters buzzing around you. If you're looking to make a move, you might give Chicago some thought."

"Chicago, huh? Twelve foot snow drifts and sub-zero temperatures… thanks, but I think I'll stick with L.A.'s warm winters and congested freeways."

"If it's traffic you want, we've got that too. Seriously, Chicago's a great place to live. In fact, if you're free later, maybe I could show you around."

"Thanks, but I don't think I'll have time this trip." Her cell began to ring. It was Dr. Rasher. She had almost forgotten she had left a message with his office earlier, asking if she could run a few things by him. She knew it might sound foolish, or worse, callous, but she had uneasy concerns about the likelihood of their daughter inheriting Billy's psychological disorder down the road. She hadn't wanted to broach the subject with Billy, despite the fact each time they'd gotten together, in the hospital, and at Dr. Constantine's, he seemed so normal, it was easy to forget not so long ago he tried to take his life.

"I'm sorry. It was nice meeting you, Howard. But I need to take this call."

"Sure. I understand," he replied, offering his business card. "But, should you change your mind…"

She took the card with a smile then hit answer on her phone as he walked off. "Thank you for returning my call, doctor."

Rasher suggested rather than have this discussion on the phone, she might prefer to drop by his office later.

But when she showed up, the doctor was in session. "Oops. Sorry, Dr. Rasher. The door wasn't locked and… I… sorry."

"That's alright, Julie. I'm always forgetting to lock that door."

"I'll just… wait out here," she gestured, not wishing to interrupt.

Henry leaned forward on the couch and turned around. "Are you Billy Rubin's Julie?" Her eyes went from Henry to Rasher and back again. It was an awkward moment to say the least. And it gave her pause. Was she still Billy's Julie? Right now she couldn't be sure of anything.

"Julie," Rasher quickly interjected. "This is Henry. One of Billy's teammates at Highwater."

"Hen... Henry... from Highwater? Like Scooter?"

Henry rose from the couch. He could sense she felt uneasy in his presence. "I know Billy asked us to give you two some privacy so you could try to work things out, but I don't think he'd mind if I just said hello. Do you?"

"I'm sure Billy wouldn't mind, Henry," Rasher stated reassuringly.

Henry took a few strides closer, displaying his most dazzling smile. Julie felt the hairs on the back of her neck bristle. She stood frozen in place as he drew nearer.

"I'll say one thing for Billy, he sure knows how to pick 'em. Ain't that right, doc?"

"Henry's paying you a compliment, Julie," Rasher whispered softly.

"Th... thank you, Henry."

"You're welcome."

Julie bit her lower lip. "Maybe I should come back later, Dr. Rasher."

"No," Henry hurriedly offered. "Stay. I need to get back to Highwater anyway. I promised to help Huff and Grizzy work out the new field practice times. I gotta say things are a lot better for everyone at Highwater since Billy arrived. And now that you've come to be with him in Chicago, things are gonna be a lot better for Billy too. I can feel it."

Julie nervously cleared her throat and looked back to Henry. "I... I never said I was staying in Chicago. I'm going back to Los Angeles tomorrow."

Henry seemed surprised. "That's not right! You can't do that to Billy. Tell her Doc. Tell her she's got to stay."

"I'm afraid I can't do that Henry. While that might be helpful, it's not my decision to make. Only Julie and Billy can decide what's in their best interest."

40

Frankie entered Jerry's Deli sporting a lightweight, three-piece summer suit. Sweat drizzled down his forehead like someone caught in a sudden downpour. Only, this was Studio City, California, on the fringe of the San Fernando Valley, and it hadn't rained in two hundred and seventy-five days.

Julie looked up as he made his way across the black and white checkered floor to her booth in the far corner of the crowded restaurant. "Thanks for coming, Frankie."

"You said it was important, so I got here as soon as I could. Out of concern for you and my history with Billy. But..." he added, in a trumpet-like voice designed to be overheard by everyone within a five block radius. "I can't stay long. My phone's been ringing off the hook with scouts begging for a shot at some of my A list clients. I tell ya, this keeps up, I won't have time to take a fuckin' leak." Frankie mopped his sweaty palms against the sides of his pant legs, as he slipped inside the circular red leather booth.

An out of work actor moonlighting for the past six years as a waiter, scurried over and dropped two Rhode Island phone book size menus onto their table. "Hey, Mr. Tortiricci, it's great to see you again. I don't know if you remember me, but..."

Frankie brusquely dispensed with polite conversation. "Forget it, kid. I'm done representing actors. Just bring us some fresh fucking crunchy pickles, okay? I'll let you know when we're ready to order."

While Jerry's diverse lineup offered everything from traditional deli to pizza and fajitas, what Julie wanted wasn't on the menu. She had an important decision to make and she was getting nowhere attempting to make it on her own. Billy's current emotional state wasn't something she felt comfortable discussing with her girlfriends, and certainly not with her out-spoken mother. She needed a sounding board, someone a little detached, yet someone who knew Billy well enough to help cut through her indecision.

"I take it this is about our boy Billy, right, and why he's been fucking hiding out in Chicago?" Julie leaned back and nodded weakly. "So... how's he doing? Still in shape? Maybe thinking of giving pro ball another shot? 'Cause if he is...'" Frankie stopped mid-sentence, as he couldn't help but notice how tense she seemed.

Though she swore she wouldn't break down, Julie's eyes welled with the onset of tears. "Billy's been seeing a psychiatrist the past few months."

Frankie leaned in and lowered his voice. "He's not still... you know, trying to...'" he paused, motioning as if pulling a plastic bag over his head, concluding his macabre performance with a ghastly death rattle.

Julie sat straight up. "Oh God, no, Frankie. I don't think there's any risk of that. Not while he's under a doctor's care."

"Glad to hear it. I still believe Billy's got a few good years of earning potential in him with the right representation."

"He's... he's not quite there yet," she said with difficulty. "He's still battling demons."

"So, who the fuck isn't? We all got demons. Yesterday, some douche bag cut me off on the freeway. I followed him for thirty-three miles just to give him the finger. With the cost of gas, if that isn't crazy, I dunno what is." Despite her serious intent, Julie couldn't help but smile. Frankie spotted their waiter coming out of the kitchen, and waved him over. "Hey, Deniro! What's the soup of the day?"

"Mexican Chicken Tortilla."

"What about Navy Bean?"

"That's tomorrow."

Frankie shook his head and sighed. "Lemme ask you something. Do you know what day it is in China right now?" The waiter shrugged. "It's tomorrow," Frankie continued. "So go bring me the Navy Bean."

"But... but...'" the poor befuddled waiter stammered.

"But nothing. You don't have any here, go down the block to fucking Ralphs and pick up a few cans. How you gonna get an agent if you can't think on your feet?"

"Frankie, c'mon. Give him a break."

"Fine," he relented. "I'm nothing if not flexible. I'll have the Matzo Ball. Just make sure it's hot, with extra noodles or I'm sending it back."

"And you, miss?" the waiter asked, grateful for her intervention.

"Just an iced tea. Decaf, please."

When the waiter walked off, Frankie reached across the table and patted Julie's hand reassuringly. "Look, Billy will get it together. You just gotta have some fucking faith."

Julie met Frankie's eyes, her voice wavering slightly. "I've been thinking of putting in for a transfer to Chicago. I think Billy was hoping my visit wasn't a one-time thing. And his therapist feels it would be helpful to have someone there Billy feels close to."

"So what's the problem?"

"It's complicated," Julie said, absently poking at the pickle dish with her fork. "I'm pregnant."

"Holy Jeeze! That's great. I mean, it is... right?" Julie nodded. Frankie looked around, "Where the hell's that waiter? Pregnant woman," he shouted. "We need more pickles here!"

"I don't need pickles. I need someone to tell me I'm not out of my mind to think my place is still with Billy."

"You still love the guy?"

"It wouldn't be so hard if I didn't. I just don't know if picking up and leaving L.A. right now is the right thing to do. It's making me crazy. Before he wrote, before I went to Chicago, things were a lot simpler. I was determined never to let him hurt me again. For a time, I even convinced myself I didn't care about him anymore."

"What turned you around?"

"He was so different, so supportive, so excited about the baby, so sure we could work things out. If I don't at least try, how will I ever know what could've been?"

"If you want my fucking opinion, here it is. Sounds like you need Billy as much as he needs you. Look, he's always been a little different... a little difficult. We all just chalked it up to how fucking talented he is. You gotta believe he can get his act together. Only for his sake, I wouldn't tell anyone else about the shrink stuff. Go to Chicago. Hide the Ziplocs and give it a shot. See what happens."

"It's not just about me, Frankie. There's the baby to think about."

"Listen, Julie. I know Billy since junior high. On his worst day he'll make a better father than my old man was. And look," he said with a grin, spreading his arms wide. "Look how fucking good I turned out."

41

Julie phoned Howard Caldwell in Chicago to test the waters; to see if there was a position available. Three days later the V.P. of Marketing called with a generous offer.

When she announced her decision to relocate, her friends were convinced she was making the biggest mistake of her life. There were late night calls and tearful entreaties insisting she at least wait for Billy to get a decent job, or put a ring on her finger. But even a last ditch, 'Hail Mary' plea from her mother, who threatened to disinherit her for leaving California before the birth of her first and only grandchild, didn't deter her.

On her first day in Chicago, there were flowers from Billy and a fruit basket with a guest pass to Gracie's foot massage from Howard, waiting in her new office.

She had just gotten off the phone with Billy when Howard poked his head in the open doorway, his jaw firmly set, his brow deeply furrowed, "Got a minute, Julie?"

"Sure. C'mon in. This about the sales meeting?"

Howard shook his head. "Far more important, you're not one of those die-hard L. A. Dodger fans, are you?"

"Huh?"

"Because as a co-worker, I feel it's my duty to warn you, if you want to fit in around here, you're going to have to shift loyalties to either the Cubs or the White Sox. I don't think we even let Dodger fans use our subways."

Julie laughed, not having given much thought to team loyalty since the day Billy was cut by the Royals. "Who do you like?" she asked, leaning back in her chair.

"Oh, Cubs all the way. Family tradition. My father loves the Cubs. My Grandfather loves the Cubs and there's a rumor my great-grandfather was actually in attendance the last time they won the World Series."

Howard slid gingerly into the wingback across from her desk. "But don't let me influence you. You need to see the Cubs in action before you decide."

"Okay. I promise. Let me know next time they play and I'll set my DVR."

Howard leaned forward, going for the coup de grace. "Forget watching them on T.V," he said, pulling two tickets from his pocket. "They're playing the Pirates on Sunday. My dad can't make it, and we just put Gramps in a nursing home, so... what do you say? Interested?"

She surveyed him curiously. "Are you asking me on a date, Howard?"

"A date? No way," he said, backpedaling rapidly. "I'd never date someone I work with. Bad karma."

"Because, I should tell you... I'm sort of... seeing someone ..."

"Oh. Right. Of course you are. I think I knew that. Sure," he covered, masking his disappointment. "Does he like baseball?"

"You could say that."

"Then here," he said, dropping the tickets on her desk. "Why don't the two of you go as my guests?" It'll be worth it if you come back to work Monday a born again Cub fan."

Julie glanced at the tickets, then back up at Howard. "Thank you, but I wouldn't feel right using your family tickets." Julie could see her abrupt turn down may have left Howard in an awkward position, and she felt badly. "You know, maybe another time... it's not that I don't appreciate your generous offer, it's just that Billy and I already made plans for Sunday. I don't think I could change them at the last minute."

"Yeah. Sure. Some other time. No sweat."

In reality, Julie's big Sunday plans with Billy were nothing more than an afternoon picnic at a local park, then perhaps, take in a movie or go out for a quiet dinner. They were still in the process of re-establishing their relationship. While Sunday's little field trip had received Dr. Rasher's blessing, the thought of accepting Howard's tickets, of subjecting Billy to noisy, crowded public events he might not yet be able to handle, made her uneasy. If this was going to work, she knew Billy needed time, and she was prepared to give him all the time he needed.

They arranged to meet near the entrance to Oz Park on North

Burling, a little past four. Though she arrived early, Billy was already waiting by the statue of The Tin Man. He looked good, like the old Billy, in his stonewashed jeans and bright maroon polo shirt. His smile brightened, as did hers, as they caught sight of one another.

Billy found a shady spot among the brightly colored shrubs, not far from Dorothy's Playlot, spread the blanket beneath a towering tree, then helped Julie unpack the picnic basket. It was nothing lavish, simple fare; turkey on sourdough, and some fruit and pastries, mostly appropriated from the hotel dining room. Billy didn't care what they ate so long as they were together.

While they lunched in the late afternoon sun, the conversation meandered through a sea of basic, non-confrontational topics. Julie told him about her day, her new apartment over-looking the lake, and the miserable cross-town traffic.

Billy spoke about Rasher and Duncan. He mentioned the diary he had started without much success. Julie seemed intrigued, so he elaborated further. He told her how sometimes late at night, he'd try to find something meaningful to write about, but rarely did anything important come to mind. But, just to please Rasher, before he fell asleep, he'd try to scribble down some random thoughts. It always seemed to surprise him in the morning light, that he had even had those thoughts inside his head the night before.

Julie encouraged him to keep trying, that she believed in Dr. Rasher's therapy and she believed in Billy's future. She leaned back on her elbows, content to listen to the sound of children's voices drifting from the nearby playground.

When Julie went off in search of a restroom, Billy stretched out on the blanket, closed his eyes and tried to relax. A moment later, he felt the rustle of the blanket beneath him. He opened his eyes, startled to find a young boy no more than six or seven standing before him tightly clutching the hand of a little girl with fresh tears streaming down her face.

"What... where'd you come from?"

The boy seemed frightened. He gripped the little girl's tiny fingers harder, causing her to wince in pain. "I don't know," the boy replied.

Billy sat up, "Are you lost? Where's your mother?"

Tears welled inside the boy's eyes. "We have no mother."

As Billy rose to his knees, the boy and his sister cowered backward, but the young boy's eyes continued to stare into Billy's, as if furtively searching for his help. Billy stood up and looked around. There had to be someone out looking for these two by now. Billy felt awkward and helpless. "It's... it's going to be alright. Don't cry. I'll... I'll think of something. C'mon. We'll go find Julie. She'll know what to do. Just give me a minute."

Billy bent down to quickly gather up the remnants of their picnic lunch spread out across the blanket. When he turned back, the children had vanished from sight. He tore off toward the playground; the contents of the hastily packed wicker hamper jostling and spilling as he raced across the grass.

A park ranger leaned casually against the jungle gym, chatting with a young woman holding a fussy infant in her arms.

"Did you see them?" Billy yelled, as he ran up to them.

"See who?"

Billy dropped the basket to the ground. "The little boy, about so high," he said, frantically indicating with his hand. "And the little girl, his sister I think... they're lost. They were right over there a minute ago. Someone had to see them."

Billy described what they were wearing as best he could remember. As the ranger took off on his bicycle to search the grounds, Julie came out of the restroom and spotted Billy running up to every child bearing even the slightest resemblance to the lost boy and his sister. He looked tormented, desperate.

Twilight began to paint the park in shades of soft blueberry and plum, by the time the ranger returned to the playground. Billy raced over. The ranger met Billy's worried eyes with concerns of his own. "No luck so far. But don't worry. I've got Parks Department people out checking as many of the trails as we can cover before we lose the light."

The ranger's gunmetal gray, walkie-talkie holstered to his hip crackled and spit. "Yeah, Kirk, whatcha got? Okay. Well, keep looking."

"Maybe we should call in the police?" Billy suggested. "Have them search the streets around the park? They could be anywhere by now."

And then, he saw them. The boy and his sister were heading for the swings, smiling as they clung to the arms of a tall, sandy haired man.

"That's them," Billy shouted relieved, as he ran towards them. Julie and the ranger not far behind.

The man seemed confused, as did his wide-eyed children, watching the winded trio approach. "I assure you my kids have not been out of my sight the entire time we've been here."

"That's not true," Billy stammered. "I... I spoke to them. They were crying. They were lost." Billy took a step closer to the boy. "Go on, don't be afraid. Tell the ranger and your dad what happened."

"What are you talking about?" the man questioned, as the suddenly shy little boy took a step behind his dad's khaki clad legs to avoid Billy's probing glare.

"I wanna go on the swings, Daddy," the little girl whined, tugging her father's arm impatiently.

"In a minute, honey," he promised, then turned back to Billy and the ranger. "Look. I don't know what to tell you, other than you're mistaken."

"I guess... sorry to have bothered you," the ranger responded. "But, you know how it is nowadays, you can't be too careful when there are young children involved." The father nodded his head as the ranger smiled down at the little girl. "You kids go have fun now, and mind your dad. Okay?"

The girl half-smiled before grabbing her brother's hand and scampering off toward the swings. Julie watched Billy's eyes follow the family until they disappeared from sight, swallowed within the leafy shadows cast along the playground path.

"Well, I guess we can all relax now," said the ranger, turning off his walkie-talkie. "Glad it was only a false alarm."

Billy turned to Julie, as the park ranger swung his leg over the mid-bar of his bike and took off. "I know what I saw."

"I know you do, Billy," she offered, as she slipped her arm inside his. "But the important thing is that the kids are safe. Right?"

Billy nodded absently as Julie stopped to retrieve the picnic basket, then fished through her purse for her car keys. "C'mon, it's getting late. We should go."

42

A brightly marbled peregrine falcon pumped its powerful wings; its talons deftly gripping Julie's terrace railing high on the twenty-seventh floor. Billy watched in awe as it took flight, ascending toward the neighboring rooftops. He marveled at its strength and beauty, soaring higher and higher into the night sky in a spectacular display of aerial acrobatics, until it disappeared beyond the moon.

For a few fleeting moments, the majestic bird managed to keep him from dwelling on the incident in the park. But, he couldn't erase it entirely. It lingered. There was something intensely disturbing about the look on the young boy's face when he peeked out from behind his father's legs; something Billy couldn't let go of, as if he and the boy now shared a secret neither dare tell anyone else.

Billy turned and caught a glimpse of Julie through the terrace door as she headed for the kitchen. She insisted she planned on cooking something special for his first visit to her apartment. At least that was what she told him as they drove away from the park -- what she wanted him to believe when he waited in the car while she dashed into a market to pick up a few little items on the menu she claimed to have forgotten, only to return with four bags of groceries. Billy knew there had been no special dinner planned before he carried on like a lunatic in the park. It pained him to think she was afraid he might do something weird again if they went out in public.

How he wished they could go back to the way things were before. But now, so much had changed. Lurking in the shadows was a mysterious cache of secrets Billy chose to keep buried deep inside. Secrets he couldn't share with her. And more than a few places, people and events that seemed to persist as secrets, even from himself.

He hated putting Julie through any of this. Hated that he still didn't know if he was truly crazy or not, or if Rasher's therapy could ever restore a semblance of normalcy to his life again. And right now, it couldn't happen soon enough. Like the falcon, he wanted to spread his wings and soar. He wanted his life back.

He slid open the terrace door, and let the sweet familiar scent of Julie's perfume, mingled with the aroma of something wonderful cooking in the kitchen feed his appetite and nourish his soul.

During dinner Julie encouraged Billy to share his tales of Highwater. By evening's end, though Highwater's odd inhabitants kept their promise not to intrude in Billy and Julie's private life, she began to feel as if she was beginning to know and understand them better. Diablo was never spoken of. There was no point, Billy reasoned. Diablo was beyond anyone's understanding, even his. Besides, it was too soon, too unsettling. Too frightening for her to know about now, or perhaps, ever.

The hour grew late. Julie grew tired. With the TV droning softly in the background, she laid her head back on the couch, closed her eyes and slowly drifted off. Billy knew he should go, but couldn't yet bring himself to leave.

On the floor by the couch was a leather bound album Julie had brought with her from L.A., filled with pictures of holidays past, of college graduation and page after page of photos of Billy in his USC baseball uniform; in the batting cage, out in right field, from every home game she attended, and a few from nearby road trips out of town. Even a glossy team photo taken shortly after he began his brief stint as a Kansas City Royal. How hopeful and promising he looked that day. The desire to play pro ball again became almost too much to bear.

Julie stirred beside him, rubbed her eyes and sat up. "I can't believe I nodded off. What time is it?"

"Around one, I think."

Julie moved closer to see what Billy was looking at so intently. "Turn the page. There's a new picture you haven't seen yet."

The image on the very last page nearly brought the young ballplayer to tears as he stared at the ultrasound of his daughter.

"She's really beautiful, isn't she?"

"Uh huh," he answered. "Just like her mother."

Julie smiled and rose from the couch. "It's really late. You're welcome to stay on the couch tonight, if you'd like."

In the morning, Billy woke early, and dressed without a sound. Hints of sunlight escaped between the window slats, flickering and dancing across Julie's face as she slept. It was difficult to resist the urge to kiss her, but he didn't have the heart to wake her. He decided, as he tip-toed from the apartment, to phone her in a little while and explain the decision he had made late last night.

Out on the sidewalk, he found himself uncomfortably distracted. There were far too many people rushing by. Too many cars, trucks and buses bottlenecked in the street. He found it hard to concentrate. Then, church bells began to peal. Rich and echoing through the treetops, reaching Billy's ears, as they sang out the hours. He recalled a stately, old stucco church he had spotted on high from Julie's terrace last night; how its bright white bell tower glistened in the moonlight. He knew it couldn't be all that far from where he now stood.

The church grounds were reverently still, save for the stubborn sweep of a bristle broom in the wizened hands of a nun with fine wisps of silver straying beneath her pious headband and veil. She worked stubbornly at her task, poking at any and all traces of dust, debris and un-named sin that may have found its way to God's front door. No more than one or two cars were in the parking lot, undoubtedly the blessed result of having satisfactorily saved enough mortal souls on Sunday not to require many absolutions on Monday.

This was the place of silent contemplation Billy was seeking. He wanted to trust his instincts, but with Julie in Chicago now and a baby on the way, he had to plan for their future. He nodded and smiled as he approached the sister, who briefly paused in her duties to return a perfunctory tilt of her head before he stepped inside.

The light filtered through the stained-glass windows casting an amber glow upon the time-worn, alabaster crucifix on the western wall and the gilded inscription beneath;

"LET GOD'S LOVE SHOW YOU THE WAY"

He sat in the back and waited, listening for the sound of his own thoughts, rather than the word of God. It was quiet inside the empty place of worship and even quieter inside his head at the moment. He glanced down at his legs, the legs that recently helped carry him to victory at Highwater, and remembered the long, painful months of rehab he endured to get them back to where they were. Hadn't he earned the right to play major league baseball again? Damn right he had!

He pulled a crumpled bill from his pocket and stuffed it into the poor box as penance for having cursed inside the church, believing God had likely heard him, though the words were only in his head.

The sister had left her post by the time he stepped back out into the courtyard. He grabbed his elbow with his opposite hand, raised it up and across his body until he could feel the stretch in his triceps and shoulders. He checked his watch. It was time.

Billy took off running. He ran for miles. Hard and fast like the old days, the bottom of his shoes barely touching the steamy pavement beneath, no longer observant of traffic, faces, or the shops and buildings streaming past. He didn't stop until he found himself in front of Rasher's office. He bent forward and took a moment to catch his breath, grabbing his knees with his sweaty palms. As the seconds forged on he could feel his heart rate slowing.

Perched on the edge of Rasher's couch, Billy began, "I'm tired of sitting around doing nothing but probing my psyche... trying to remember stuff like what happened on my third birthday. In a few short months Julie won't be able to work for a while. We can't live forever on what's left of my signing bonus. I need to go out and earn a living. I need to provide for my daughter."

Rasher nodded, "I certainly understand, Billy."

"So... you're not going to fight me on this? Try to talk me out of it?"

Marvin Rasher seemed surprised by Billy's suggestion. "To the contrary, self-worth and satisfaction from an honest day's work is very important. Most of my clients continue to work while in therapy. The two aren't mutually exclusive. If seeing a therapist disqualified someone from working, half of Chicago would be unemployed. For that matter, so would I."

Billy let out a sigh of relief and leaned back against the cushions. "I was hoping you'd see it that way."

"Have you given any thought to the kind of work you might want to do?"

Now it was Billy's turn to look surprised. "Baseball, of course. It's what I do best."

"True, but it's not the only thing you could do."

"Forget it. My future's in baseball. I can handle it now. I haven't had a drink, or a blackout, or… or anything in months. So if you'd just give David Wagner a call…"

Rasher's voice was measured and even. "We've talked about that before…"

Billy leaned forward in an impassioned plea. "C'mon, doc, quit jerking me around. I've done my part. I never missed a session. I made nice with everybody at Highwater. It's time for me to get back in the game. Can't you see that?" When Rasher didn't immediately respond, Billy glared with mounting resentment. "Know what I think? I think you never had any intention of speaking to Wagner on my behalf. I think you'd like to see me trapped in Highwater forever."

"You're wrong, Billy," Rasher offered in his defense.

"Oh, yeah," Billy growled, his mood bordering on dark and angry as he charged from the couch, and grabbed the phone on Rasher's desk, waving it defiantly in the air. "Then make the damn call."

Rasher's hands remained patiently folded in his lap. He could see Billy was agitated and determined to provoke him. "I told you I can't do that," he said quietly, then stood and took the phone from Billy and placed it gently back on the desk. "You can't expect me to put you in a position that would undermine your progress when I still feel you're not ready."

"Then make me ready," Billy demanded. "You want me to figure out why I'm the only one at Highwater who gets freaked by the thought of Diablo running loose?

"That would be an important step. Yes."

"Then tell me what you know. You must have written something down on him by now. Let's take a look!" Billy spun round and began to yank open drawer after drawer in the doctor's file cabinet.

"I'm going to have to ask you to stop doing that, Billy," Rasher said, calmly.

"I'll tell you what I'm going to stop doing," he exploded, slamming the cabinet shut. "Coming here. I'm done. We're done."

"I'm sorry you feel that way. I want to help you, Billy. But, I can't force you to continue in therapy."

"Damn right you can't," Billy said, stomping his way to the door. "See how you like it when you don't get what you want."

43

Billy hot-footed aimlessly through the city streets, blowing off steam. He considered the possibility of contacting Wagner on his own, but it seemed pointless. Most likely he would just wind up calling Rasher, who would undoubtedly put the kibosh on Billy's attempted end run.

As his foot left the curb, he failed to see the fast approaching bus shooting around the corner, heading straight at him.

"Hey, buddy!" someone shouted. "Head's up!"

Billy jumped back onto the sidewalk just as the bus barreled past belching gray plumes of diesel smoke in its wake, blurring the sooty, 'Go Cubs Go' banner plastered above its rear brake lights.

As Billy swiped the dirt from the corner of his eye, a small ray of hope began to flicker. Scott Erikson had once mentioned that Jim Farley, the Cubs general manager, attempted to negotiate a trade for Billy shortly after his deal with the Royals had closed. At the time the Royals had no intention of letting Billy slip away. Maybe Farley was still interested? What did he have to lose? He was already in Chicago, a short hop from Farley's office at Wrigley -- why not give it a shot?

Billy stepped up to the old-fashioned box office window and pulled out his wallet. A bushy-haired, mustachioed gent behind the glass looked up from his dog-eared copy of Jim Bouton's paperback, 'Ball Four.'

"What can I do you for, sir?"

"One," Billy said. "I don't care where."

The ticket seller's eyeballs glanced upward. "Can't you read?" he said, jerking his thumb to the sold out sign above the ticket window. "The game's been sold out for weeks."

Billy jammed his wallet back inside his pants pocket. There was no point trying to deal with some bottom-feeder scalpers when all he had on him at the moment was thirty-four dollars in cash.

He shoved his hands deep inside his pockets and headed down

Addison, watching the streams of excited ticketed fans rush past. As he wandered by the player's parking lot, someone yelled, "Billy? Hey, Billy Rubin... over here!"

Billy spun round, spotting a short, balding man in a madras plaid, short sleeve shirt and tie, with a press pass dangling from his neck. "Hey," he called again, as Billy pointed a hesitant finger to himself. The reporter nodded, and waved him over to the chain-link fence. "You're Billy Rubin. Right?"

"Yeah, that's me," he said, without a flicker of recognition.

"Paul. Paul Middleman... from the Sun Times. I used to cover the Trojans when I was working out in L.A."

Billy stared at the stranger's face, eyebrows knit in concentration, trying hard to place him. "You probably don't remember me. Then again," he said wistfully, "I had a little more hair on top back then."

Billy's recollection began to take shape. "Son of a gun. Paul Middleman! You used to wear those big horn-rimmed glasses, right?"

The reporter bobbed his head. "Lasik, six months ago."

"How the hell are you, Paul?" Billy grinned, offering his hand, which Middleman shook enthusiastically.

"Great. I couldn't believe my eyes when I saw you over there. It's been a long time. What are you doing at Wrigley?"

Billy took less than a second before the words spilled glibly from his lips. "In town visiting old friends. I grew up around Wrigleyville. Tried to get in to catch the game at the last minute. Couldn't get a ticket. Too bad, I'd give anything to see them murder the Red Sox."

"Wanna catch it from the Press room?" Middleman offered, pulling another press pass from his pocket.

Billy brightened. "That'd be great! But I wouldn't want to get you in any trouble."

"Forget about it," Middleman said. "Nobody checks these too closely anyway. I got a dozen of them. Lemme tell you something, when the other college jocks were too busy guzzling beer and looking up cheerleaders' skirts, you always took the time to talk to me. I never forgot that. I got my first byline thanks to some of your memorable quotes. I figure I owe you."

No sooner had they settled into the bustling, no-frills, Wrigley Press room, than a new plan began to form in Billy's head.

"Hey, Paul. Why don't I go grab us something to eat. It's the least I can do."

Middleman shrugged. "Sure. Why not? How about a hot dog. Easy on the onions, stomach's a little on the grouchy side today."

"Easy on the onions. Got it," Billy echoed, as he wriggled his way through the long row of chairs jutting into the aisles, then bounded down the narrow hallway to the metal staircase, each step pumping up his determination. It was now or never, he thought, and 'never' was not part of the plan.

When Billy arrived at the concourse level, he stopped the first uniformed stadium attendant he could find, flashed Middleman's press pass and asked where he could find the General Manager's office. To his surprise, it wasn't far from where he stood, sandwiched between a string of concession stands. A simple unmarked, white metal door lost amid the light painted cinderblock. Not very imposing, Billy thought, for the office of a man responsible for a hundred and eighteen million dollar plus payroll.

The door however was secured by a coded keypad. The customer service window was a few feet away. Billy went over and asked the woman behind the glass if she might buzz him through so he could speak with Mr. Farley.

"Do you have an appointment?" she asked.

"Mr. Farley knows who I am," Billy spoke confidently.

"I'm sorry, but Mr. Farley isn't in his office. If you like, you could leave him a message. I'll be happy to see he gets it when he returns."

"Thanks, but... maybe I'll just stop back later."

The opening strains of the National Anthem blared through the concourse speakers as Billy balanced the food tray on the lip of the condiment counter. He was slopping equal dollops of ketchup and mustard, careful not to get too many onions on Middleman's dogs, when he spotted the General Manager himself, walking briskly down the concourse toward his office. Billy hurriedly wiped the grease from his hands with a wad of napkins, left the food on the counter, and caught up with Farley just before his hopes and dreams, along with the GM could disappear behind the metal door.

"Mr. Farley," Billy said, as he approached. "I'm not sure if you remember me... Billy Rubin? You spoke to Scott Erikson about buying the rights to my contract with the Royals a little while back."

"Billy Rubin. Of course I remember you. You were a heck of a ballplayer back then."

"I was wondering if you had a minute."

"Gee. I'm really sorry Billy, but I'm on kind of a tight schedule this afternoon. Why don't you give my assistant a call, and see if we could set something up for some other time."

Some other time didn't work for Billy. It had to be now, as he quickly concocted a freshly conceived fabrication. "David Wagner thought you might be interested in what I have to say."

"How do you know Wagner?"

"We have a mutual friend." Billy decided not to elaborate further, hoping Farley wouldn't follow up by checking with the I-Cubs manager.

Farley looked at his watch. "Okay, ten minutes. C'mon up."

As he took a seat across from Farley's massive rosewood desk, the GM's gaze shifted to the Press pass dangling from Billy's neck. "What are you doing with Middleman's Press pass?"

"It's a long story... Paul's a friend... look, it's not important, but what I need to speak with you about is."

Farley eyed him curiously. "Okay, son. What's on your mind?"

Billy shifted in his seat. "Look. I know this isn't the usual way to go about this... without going through proper channels and all that bullshit protocol. But, I'm in the best shape of my life. The knee is completely healed, both legs, stronger than ever."

"Glad to hear it."

"I want to tryout for the Cubs."

Farley rocked back in his chair. The silence that followed was agonizing for Billy. Farley stroked his chin and leaned in over his desk. "I'm curious, when was the last time you picked up a bat?"

"This morning, in the batting cage," Billy lied.

"I mean against major league pitching?"

Billy clasped his hands together staring at the floor, knowing an honest response would show him in a less than favorable light, but also knowing Farley was no fool. "With the Royals... against the Yankees," he admitted, reluctantly. Farley furrowed his brow. They both knew that was a while ago.

"You're putting me in an awkward situation. You're right, this isn't the way I usually go about recruiting players."

Then, with a surge of re-born arrogance, Billy spread his arms wide and declared, "Then again, Billy Rubin is not your usual ballplayer. You said so yourself. I was one heck of a ballplayer. Still am."

Farley eyed the cocky young man posturing in front of him. "I see you're still humble as ever."

"Athletes don't get far being humble, Mr. Farley. A man should know his worth and never settle for less." Billy leaned forward. "All I'm asking for is one lousy tryout. I don't cut it, you never hear from me again. What do you say?"

Farley pulled on his eyebrow, pondering Billy's offer. "Let me be upfront with you. I got a slew of outfielders I'm paying a shit load of money to who are riding the pine because I don't have a place for them. I don't need another right fielder. What I need is a pitcher, a solid fifth starter. Look, I'm sorry, Billy. I'm afraid it's just not in the cards. Maybe next season."

Farley's secretary buzzed in, letting him know there was an important call on hold.

"I have to take this. Good luck, Billy."

"Wait. What if I told you I had an inside track to the greatest knuckleball pitcher since Hoyt Wilhelm? A pitcher who's managed to remain under the radar, with six no-hitters. His name is B.J. Popwell."

Farley paused before taking his call. "Never heard of him. Who does he play for?"

Billy hesitated. "A semi-pro team called... Highwater."

Billy could sense Farley might be leaning towards taking the bait, so he decided to put it all out there and reel him in - offering two for the price of one, assuming both he and Popwell blew him away in the tryouts.

There was something about Billy's crazy pitch and boyish naiveté that was both ridiculous, and yet intriguing. Farley scratched his head. "Let me give it some thought," as three more lights lit up on his phone demanding to be answered.

"What's there to think about? It's just a tryout," Billy urged.

"You still with Erikson?"

Billy swallowed hard. He couldn't blow it now. Not after he'd gotten this far. He had to come up with a name. "I'm... I'm... presently represented by... Frank... Frank Tortiricci."

"Tortiricci!" Farley echoed, and not in a good way. "That ball-busting, pain in the ass?"

Billy shrugged. "He may be a pain in the ass, but he knows talent when he sees it."

Farley nodded, begrudgingly. "Yeah. Yeah. Unfortunately, I know all about Tortiricci. He represents Kip Chapman, a bright young kid in our farm system. Tell you what, Billy, I'll give the little prick a call and set something up."

44

Highwater's field was deserted. To Billy's surprise, as he headed past the bleachers, the grass beneath his feet felt coarse and scraggly, most definitely in need of a thorough soaking. He also found it odd he never noticed the growing number of worn patches that could do with some re-seeding as well. He made a mental note to mention it to Miss Duncan. To be sure, if he and Popwell were going to get in some serious practice sessions before the tryout, he needed to insure the field was in tip-top shape. No sense risking a sprain or other stupid injury right now.

He sprinted to the back entrance, anxious to break the news to Popwell as soon as possible. He wondered if Popwell would be grateful. Billy figured he should be, seeing no one else at Highwater would've given a nut case with multiple personalities this kind of opportunity.

It didn't bother him one bit that without the pitcher's astounding skills he wouldn't have had a prayer persuading Farley to give him a look right now. So what if he was using Popwell. Didn't Popwell owe Billy for the all the times he used him? Didn't Popwell do his damndest to humiliate him when he first arrived at Highwater? Didn't Billy bust his hump learning how to catch his knuckleball? Darn right he did. Billy decided if this worked out, they'd be even.

He tugged on the door handle, but it was locked. So he decided to see if there was anyone hanging out in the Day Room that could let him in without having to walk all the way around to the front entrance.

It was hard to see in through the windows, with the dust and grime caked to the panes by the afternoon sun. He used a patch on the back of his sleeve to clear a small circle in the glass and peer inside, but spotted no one, not even the ever-present Rochester.

Undeterred, he scurried past the overgrown brush and bramble that grew along the side path and up the trellises like frightened children clinging to the safety of their parent's arms. He continued on toward the front gate with a joyous bounce to his step.

To his surprise, the entrance was locked as well, and a sign had been posted.

CLOSED FOR RECONSTRUCTION

He knocked on the solid oak doors towering above like sentries of old. Was it possible, he wondered, as he waited, that they had somehow grown larger, more formidable in his brief absence? When no one came to the door, he banged harder and yelled as loud as he could. Finally, he could hear footsteps growing closer across the tiled foyer.

"We're closed." Watermain shouted from within.

"It's me. Billy."

"Who?" The guard responded, in a voice suggesting Billy had rudely roused him from a mid-day nap.

"Billy Rubin. C'mon, Watermain, open up," he insisted, pounding once more until he heard the deadbolt unlock. The guard, looking weary and bedraggled slid one of the oaken doors just wide enough to poke half a shoe out into the courtyard.

"What the fuck's going on?" Billy demanded

"We're shut down," the guard admitted simply.

"Why? When?"

"Remodeling. After Sven went up to the roof, we discovered the whole foundation was shaky. The walls were beginning to crumble. You can't come in with all the construction going on."

"This is crazy!" Billy said. "Where's Popwell?"

"Gone."

"What do you mean, gone? Gone where?"

Watermain scratched his head thoughtfully. "Beats me."

"What about Henry or Huff? Maybe they know where I can find him."

Watermain soon grew weary of Billy's incessant stream of questions. "There's nobody here anymore. I was getting ready to leave myself."

Billy had to see for himself what remained of Highwater. More importantly, he had to find Popwell. There was no tryout without him. "Out of my way, Watermain." He shoved forcefully against the guard's strong shoulders, and pushed past. He raced up the stairs two at a time, then wandered down hallway after hallway, dotted with faceless work crews busily assembling scaffolds and equipment. He flung open doors that led into nothing but empty rooms.

Billy's eyes darted back and forth as he entered Popwell's room, searching, scanning, pulling open drawers and closet doors, upturning waste paper baskets, trying to find something that might indicate where Popwell could have gone. But there was nothing.

Billy's old room was shuttered and dark. He reached for the light switch on the wall, manically flicking it back and forth without success. Then gazed up at the ceiling. Even the light bulbs had been removed. His bed was stripped of linens. He dropped to his knees and swept his hand back and forth beneath the bed frame, feeling for his suitcase, for his photos and clippings... but they too were gone.

As he tore down the stairwell amid the incessant banging and clanging, he thought he heard a voice off somewhere, singing. He bolted from the stairwell, past carpenters ripping down walls, their sledgehammers smashing against the beams. The voice grew louder. It was coming from the Day Room. As Billy crashed the door open, the tables and chairs had been moved to the side. On the floor in the center of the room was a small turntable. An old Elvis 45 spun round and round in the dark. He felt as if he were about to take a header off a cliff again. His head throbbed beyond all reason.

From somewhere out in the hall, came a sudden, resounding crash. Thick chunks of plaster crumbled into mounds of dust in an instant. The sound of demolition increased. The constant din of the jackhammers pounded in his brain, growing louder and louder.

Then, for just a moment, he thought he heard Diablo's grotesque laughter rise above the clatter. His head was exploding. He couldn't think amid the swirling chaos. The only thing that remained clear was Popwell had to be out there somewhere – and Billy had to find him.

PART THREE

45

The sun surrendered and rose again across the river flowing between the steel and concrete skyscrapers of downtown Chicago. For the past thirty-six hours, Billy hadn't slept or eaten, showered or shaved. He roamed the city's parks, train stations, and shelters, peering through windows, searching in the shadows for any trace of Popwell. In truth, he knew so little about the pitcher's story that he could be anywhere – or nowhere.

Nearing exhaustion, he stumbled toward a hole-in-the-wall pub located in a tree-lined, residential neighborhood, wedged amid tattoo parlors, a bike shop, and a series of blue-collar clapboard row houses from the fifties.

As he descended the cigarette butt-littered steps, day became night within the establishment's dimly lit interior. The backroom pool tables stood idle, waiting for neighborhood hustlers to drift in as the day wore on. At this hour, there weren't more than three or four regulars hunched over the red lacquer bar. At the far end sat a patron hiding behind a pair of dark glasses, nursing a beer, a ratty-looking dog perched contentedly napping on his lap. The dog had a beer of its own up on the bar, and from time to time, the mangy mongrel would sit up, slurp a little beer, then curl back down into its owner's lap.

"Hey, pal, how's it going today," nodded the scraggly bearded man behind the bar, wiping his hands on his apron, as Billy edged his aching body onto a stool. "Afraid all I got is room temperature beer and warm soda. Damn power went out again," he complained, snapping a bar rag in the air, targeting one of the largest flies Billy had ever seen -- an insect with the skill of a dive-bomber, capable of evading a string of the bartender's frenzied attacks.

"That's okay," Billy replied. "I didn't come in for a drink. I'm looking for someone."

In temporary détente between man and bug, the barkeep nudged a bowl of roasted peanuts in Billy's direction. "Who isn't?"

Grateful for something to put into his empty stomach, Billy popped a few into his mouth. They tasted dry and sour. He started to gag.

"Hey, easy pal. Here... on the house," as he poured a shot of vodka. "Stoli, right?"

Billy nodded, and took a hard swallow. The peanuts and booze crash landed, creating a raw and churning inferno.

"Like I told you last night, my friend, it's a cold, cruel world out there."

Billy looked up surprised, fighting the urge to hurl. "Last night," he began, wondering if he had actually started doubling back on places he'd already checked.

The bartender grinned knowingly. "I'm not surprised you don't remember, pal. How's the head this morning? I'm guessing you didn't get much sleep last night."

"Why would you say that?"

The bartender reached inside the drawer beneath the cash register and took out a hotel key card. "Because... when you stumbled out of here, you left this behind," he said, slapping the card on the bar in front of Billy. "Joey hung around for a while thinking you'd be back, but I told him you were way too wasted."

Billy scrutinized the unfamiliar piece of plastic, then met the bartender's gaze. "This isn't mine. I've never heard of the New Leon Hotel."

"Look, chief... all I could tell you is Joey said you left it in the corner booth."

Billy's head swiveled in the direction the bartender was pointing with no memory of ever having been there before. A frightening reality took hold as he realized the possibility that he might have blacked out again. Unless of course, the bartender had merely confused Billy with someone else, some poor jerk who couldn't hold his liquor, or for that matter, hold onto his hotel key.

As he re-emerged back out into the sunlight, to his amazement, literally within spitting distance down the narrow street was the modest, three-story, New Leon Hotel. Since he was heading in that direction anyway, he thought he might as well drop off the key in the lobby.

The *New* Leon Hotel, Billy questioned, as he entered, eyeballing the bleak, birch wood paneled lobby and faded pink and yellow plastic flower filled vases. If this was *'new and improved,'* he could only imagine the dump it was before.

A middle-aged woman dressed in crisp white linen, with blue-black hair tightly coiled in a serpentine bun, stood poised behind the front desk nibbling a blueberry muffin. As Billy approached she stiffened, hastily shoved the muffin beneath the counter and made a grab for the phone.

"If you come any closer..." she said, brandishing the receiver like a can of mace, "I swear I'll call the police." Billy could tell from her tone she meant business. "We don't want no trouble," she added, tremulously excavating a muffin crumb embedded in the corner of her thick, deep crimson lipstick-painted mouth with a shaky, two-inch, dagger-like nail.

Billy didn't move a muscle. He had absolutely no idea what she was talking about, but it was clear the woman was frightened by his presence. The last thing he wanted was to cause a scene or have the police brought in.

A sudden breeze blew through the lobby, billowing the pale blue curtains keeping out the afternoon sun. A metal wind chime rustled somewhere from a nearby room. Billy could hear it tinkling in the background. It reminded him of Gunther's key ring. And, for an instant, as the lobby curtains swayed, he thought he might have spotted Armand stroll past the open window.

He turned back to the desk clerk, "Look, Miss... Miss Loretta..." he said, quickly noting the name plate pinned atop her left breast pocket, trying his best to appear nonthreatening. "I'm not here to cause trouble. I just wanted... to... return this key. Someone named Joey found it at the pool hall down the block." Billy placed it on the counter. Loretta's stiletto-shaped fingers gingerly inched it across the counter, while her eyes remained fixed on Billy.

"If you've come for the suitcase," she said, as firmly as possible through a quivering lower lip, "the manager left strict orders. I can't release it until the hotel bill is paid in full."

"The suitcase?"

"The brown suitcase with the photos and clippings. Do you want it or not?"

When Loretta produced the suitcase, there was no doubt as to whom it belonged. At this point it didn't matter how it got there. He wasn't leaving without it. He reached into his pocket for his Visa card. Loretta jumped back. Billy swiftly brought his empty hands up and out to the side. "Just looking for my credit card, that's all. Okay?" Loretta nodded warily. "How much is the bill?"

The desk clerk turned to her computer and hit a few keys. "Sixteen hundred and fifty dollars."

"WHAT!" Billy stated in shock. "For a room in this dump?"

"The room's paid for, but there's an outstanding balance for damages, including the bellboy's trip to the E.R."

Billy felt he had no choice. If he wanted to retrieve his belongings he had to pay the tab. So he offered up his card without questioning Loretta's wild assertions, grabbed his suitcase and left the hotel trying to reconstruct how his belongings ended up at the New Leon.

As he cut through the back alley, he was certain someone was trying to set him up. An elaborate, carefully constructed scheme involving not only the bartender at the pub, and the shady looking guy with the drunken dog, but Loretta as well. Or it could be Armand, or even Dr. Rasher, desperate to derail him and send him begging on his knees back into therapy.

He stared at his suitcase. There was of course one other possibility that frightened him even more – the chance he was still nutty as a fruitcake. Crippled by the fear of losing control, a wave of depression washed over him. He propped the suitcase against the back of the building and sat down on top on it. His lethargy quickly gave way to intense anger. He picked up a moldy apple lying in a discarded heap of trash by his foot and flung it against one of the dumpsters. The rotting core made a hollow clang as it crashed into the metal, followed by what he thought was the sound of something rustling inside the dumpster. A stray cat perhaps, or possibly a rat.

Billy decided it was time to move on. He picked up his suitcase, then stopped, as the rustling was replaced by a mournful whimper. He inched closer and peered inside the dumpster. To his shock, in amongst the filth, and mounds of garbage was the knuckleball pitcher. "What the… are you okay Popwell?" Billy asked.

"Popwell is gone," said a frightened little voice. "He left me here after Charley got into a really bad fight. Don't hurt me," he sniffled. "Please don't hurt me again."

"Nobody's going to hurt you. I promise." Billy struggled to make sense of what he was hearing. "But if you're not Popwell, and you're not Charley... then who are you?"

"I'm Timmy," he said, dabbing at his tear-streaked cheeks with the cuff of his sleeve. "If I promise to be good, can I go home with you?" he asked, gazing at Billy with wide, pleading eyes.

46

Julie's worst fears began when Billy left a somewhat cryptic message on her voicemail while she was locked in a closed-door meeting with the marketing team. He asked her to meet him at the apartment as soon as possible. He sounded weird, his voice hushed as if not wanting to be overheard, but he didn't mention by whom. He didn't say who he was with, or where he had been for the past two days. There was no way she could concentrate on work until she knew he was not in some kind of trouble.

She raced back to the apartment and waited. Forty-five minutes later she was still waiting. She feared something terrible must have happened.

When her efforts to reach him on his cell proved futile, she decided to try Dr. Rasher. When she hung up, she was more frightened than before. Rasher's cautionary explanation of Billy's abrupt decision to terminate therapy was disturbing. Julie shared his fears, as they were both deeply concerned by Billy's dogged denial; his resistance to accept his situation might worsen without on-going professional counseling.

She couldn't bear the thought of Billy out there alone, struggling to keep it together. No wonder he sounded so strange on the phone. He must be feeling adrift, more disconnected than ever. Without Rasher's help, Julie knew she was all Billy had. It was daunting, but she convinced herself she could somehow make it work, at least until she could get him to go back into therapy.

Her resolve was tested anew when Billy finally showed up, suitcase in hand. And he wasn't alone.

Before she could ask where he'd been, and what was going on, Billy leaned closer and whispered in her ear so Popwell wouldn't overhear. "I know this is awkward for you, but I can explain everything. I swear. I... I just need a few minutes. Is that okay?"

Her eyes filled with compassion, as she watched him walk into the den and close the door. She could hear muffled voices coming from inside as she waited in the kitchen.

When Billy came back out, he looked haggard and disheveled, twisting in his seat, trying to explain in guarded and hurried tones, not only to her, but to himself as well, the improbable series of events and circumstances as they unfolded.

He glossed over the recent blow up with Rasher, and she tried to keep an open mind while at the same time insisting they needed to find another therapist as soon as possible.

"I don't need therapy," Billy maintained, running his fingers absently through his mangled hair. "All I need is you and Popwell." When he told her about meeting with the general manager of the Cubs and the tryout, she wasn't absolutely sure if it was fact or fantasy, but she held her tongue. Then he told her what happened when he tried to get back inside Highwater to find Popwell, only to come up empty.

"Popwell is my entrée back into pro ball. Even Frankie can't fast-talk his way around a tryout for me without Popwell's arm. Don't you see? He's part of the package. I never meant to drag you into this – but I didn't know where else to go."

"It's okay, Billy. You can stay here as long as you need to." When he told her how he found Popwell and Timmy in a dumpster in an alley, she was horrified.

She tried not to over-react, but she needed time to think things through. "You look exhausted, Billy. Why don't you go take a shower, change into some clean clothes and let me fix you something to eat?"

"What about Popwell and Timmy?" he asked.

"Don't worry. I'll... I'll make enough for everyone."

When she heard him step into the shower, tears splattered down her cheeks. What in God's name was she trying to do? She wasn't a shrink; she was just a young, pregnant woman, hopelessly in love with someone who obviously needed more help than she alone could offer.

When Billy returned a short time later, he found her crying by the window as if her heart was breaking. "It's nothing. Really," she offered unconvincingly. "It's just... I wanted to make you omelets and... there aren't any eggs."

Billy folded her into his arms and dried her tears. "Forget about omelets. I'm not really hungry," he stated. "Besides, I think it's time you met them."

Julie stared straight ahead. Every part of her felt numb. Her heart was racing. "Maybe we shouldn't try to handle this on our own. Maybe you should go back and talk with Dr. Rasher. Maybe he can tell us what to do about Popwell and Timmy."

Billy sighed. "That's not an option. It would only complicate things more than they already are. Rasher would just use Timmy's emergence to reinforce his opinion the tryout is a big mistake."

"Have you even told Popwell about the tryout yet?'

Billy shook his head. "I haven't had the chance." He put his hands on Julie's shoulders. "But, here's the thing – I need Popwell to be Popwell; not Timmy, or Charley or God knows who else if I'm gonna pull this off. I can't risk losing him again. But, I'll understand if the whole thing is freaking you out. Maybe my bringing him here is asking too much."

He seemed so hopeful. She couldn't let him see how scared she was.

Billy squared his shoulders. "Now, to make this work... to get him to help me, I have to find a way to help him first."

Julie nodded with silent acceptance. "What if I say the wrong thing?"

"You won't," Billy smiled reassuringly. "Are you ready to meet him now?"

Julie paused, "Popwell or Timmy?"

Billy shrugged as he led her into the den. "I don't know. Whoever feels most like talking, I guess."

"Popwell doesn't want to meet you," said a small, shaky voice. "He told me he's too embarrassed under the circumstances, whatever that means."

Julie was nervous as she forced a smile. "So then, you must be Timmy. Right?" her voice wavered slightly, venturing into unknown territory.

"Uh huh." Timmy answered, hiding his face behind a pillow.

She stared at the shy, childlike man before her. He seemed so innocent. So vulnerable. "Are you thirsty, Timmy? Can I get you something to drink?" The pillow swayed back and forth as Timmy shook his head. Julie pressed on gently. "Was that a yes or a no? It's hard to tell with your handsome face hidden behind that big old pillow."

Ever so slowly, Timmy inched the pillow down until his wary eyes peeked out over the top. "Ahh. That's much better. Are you hungry? I think there might be some left-over spaghetti in the fridge I could heat up, or maybe you'd like some ice cream?"

Timmy was sorely tempted to let down his guard a bit as he dropped the cushion to his lap. Tempted, but cautious as he looked around the room. "What is this place?" he asked quietly.

"This is my apartment."

"Can… can Billy and me live here too? I promise to be good. I don't crayon on walls or anything like that," his young voice filled with pain cracked slightly as he spoke.

Julie sat beside him and gently nestled him against her shoulder. "That would be fine, Timmy," she whispered, soothingly stroking his hair.

Billy was moved by how Julie seemed to know exactly how to comfort Timmy. Moved and surprised to find his own eyes moist with tears.

For the rest of the weekend, Timmy was content he had found a safe place to stay and didn't feel the need to reappear. Popwell, as usual, kept to himself, avoiding direct interaction with Julie as much as possible. To Julie's credit, she told Billy none of them needed to hide from her, but Billy explained, Popwell wasn't hiding. He was pretty much a loner who preferred not to engage in conversation with anyone unless absolutely necessary.

The next morning, Billy was seated at the kitchen table helping himself to some coffee, when Popwell appeared. "Julie's not here," Billy said. "She left for work. Won't be home for hours."

Popwell looked out of place in a pair of borrowed slacks and one of Billy's old college sweatshirts. Billy's clothes didn't suit him, the fabric felt foreign and coarse against his skin. He reached up and tugged at the collar, chafing against his neck. But he had no choice since Julie insisted the filth from the dumpster had soiled his own beyond redemption, and threw them away.

Billy would have loved to know what the knuckleball pitcher was thinking, or how best he could engage, or befriend him long enough to accomplish his immediate goal. If he could just somehow keep him together long enough for him to strut his stuff for the Cubs so Billy could slide into the pros alongside him, it would be enough. Whatever happened after that didn't much matter.

But, as Billy stole a furtive glance, his apprehension grew. He had been around Popwell long enough to know the difference between his impassive indifference and complete and utter withdrawal. He had to do something and soon or Popwell might slip into the shadows and disappear altogether.

Billy decided it might brighten the pitcher's mood if he told him about the prospect of the tryout with the Cubs. He described his meeting with Farley, all the while carefully finessing his words in such a way as to make it appear as if what he did was completely altruistic, designed solely to help Popwell gain success, and nothing more.

"No!"

"No?" Billy stammered. "What do you mean, no?"

"I don't want Popwell to tryout for the Cubs. I don't like the Cubs. I don't even like baseball anymore," he remarked, hopping up from his chair. "And I really don't like these stupid clothes," he said, tugging at the sleeves of Billy's sweatshirt until they stretched down past his wrists. "They're way too big. I hate this icky color. It makes me look like a stupid girl!"

Billy quickly realized he was no longer speaking with Popwell. "Can we talk about the clothes a little later, Timmy? If you don't mind, I was talking to Popwell."

"I do mind. And besides… you can't talk to Popwell."

"Why not?"

"Because he's not here. Because I made him go away."

"Why?" Billy asked, puzzled and frustrated.

"Because… all you two ever want to do is talk about baseball. I'm bored. I want to go somewhere – or play something. How about hide and seek? Or we could play pirates."

Later that afternoon, Timmy grew weary as Billy ushered him through the long, never-ending aisles of Macy's, trying on a host of age appropriate clothing, some of which looked down right ridiculous on a grown man. Timmy complained his feet hurt, and he was still bored.

After half-heartedly agreeing on two new polo shirts, Timmy stubbornly flopped down into a chair and let his eyelids slowly droop shut. A short time later, he awoke with a start. He jumped up, his eyes searching for Billy, but Billy was nowhere to be seen. Timmy took off, running down the up escalators, and up the down, all the while oblivious to the annoyance he created, jostling past the mid-day shoppers.

As he headed up to the fifth floor, his face lit up like Christmas when he spied a young man with bright red painted circles on his cheeks, decked out as a life-sized toy soldier heralding the entrance to Macy's FAO Schwarz toy department.

Timmy leapt from the slow moving escalator, forgetting all about Billy, and took off down the aisles overflowing with most every kind of toy imaginable. He breezed past the frilly dolls and the shelves filled with puzzles and board games --

And then he saw it... the Air Hogs RoboCopter Recon Spin Master remote control robot plane. It was truly a thing of beauty. He reached for the only open model on display, but unfortunately, a pair of little hands got there first, snatching it from his grasp.

"Hey! Gimme that!" Timmy protested, "I saw it first."

"Did not!" wailed the bratty, combative youngster laying claim to the toy by shoving it behind his back.

In the heat of the moment, Timmy didn't know if he was going to burst into tears or bop this kid over the head. It didn't take long to decide. Within seconds, angry words became pushes, and pushes became shoves. The boy started screaming as Timmy pinned him to the floor.

The youngster's apoplectic mother stormed over, wielding her satchel-sized handbag above her head, threatening to call the cops if Timmy didn't get away from her son immediately. "A grown man fighting with a little kid over a toy? You should be ashamed of yourself. You're lucky my husband's not here, he'd beat the crap outta you!"

Timmy looked up, frightened beyond reason. "Please... please don't hurt me. I'm... I'm sorry. I just want to go back to Julie's." He dropped the coveted model plane and took off running as fast as his legs could carry him. He burst through the exit doors and out onto State Street, smack into the middle of traffic. Startled motorists screeched to a stop, as Timmy covered his ears. "I don't like it here," he screamed.

All at once, Billy came to his aid and guided him safely back onto the sidewalk. "It's okay, Timmy. Nobody's gonna hurt you. We can go home now."

As they headed back to the apartment, Billy's concern grew. If

Popwell couldn't keep Timmy under control during a simple trip to the store, what hope did he have of keeping it together during the pressure of a major league tryout?

47

If it's true that some people have 'all the luck,' it might explain why Marvin Rasher had none at all of late. Initially, his success betting on Wagner's Iowa Cubs lifted his spirits, his bank account, and his manhood once he optimistically informed Connie he might have the funds for her cosmetic overhaul sooner than anticipated. That was until the Iowa Cubs inexplicably went into a colossal slump. He even tried betting against the I-Cubs, and on those occasions, to his utter consternation, they would somehow manage to pull out a victory. He decided the minors were too unpredictable, so he placed a sizable wager on the Dodgers, who were overwhelming favorites against his hometown heroes, The Chicago Cubs.

As he hotfooted the eight blocks from Gaylord's Lube 'N Tune back to his office after dropping off Connie's BMW for an oil change, he figured the game was probably somewhere in the seventh inning by now.

Too fired up to wait for the elevator, he pounded up the stairwell. His heart thumped heavily against his ribs as he waited for his office TV screen to explode from black to picture.

Rasher was right. The game was in the bottom of the seventh, only to his utter disbelief, the Cubs were ahead, breezing along, 9-3. He slumped into his leather armchair, his head dumped into his hands; a portrait of human suffering plucked straight from the pages of a medieval morality play. "SHIT!" he moaned, convinced the only explanation for the highly favored Dodgers to be in the toilet right now was that he had money down on them to win.

He took out his cell, and clenched his jaw. Informing Connie she had to put her body sculpting on hold again was not going to be easy. First she sobbed, then she screamed a series of unveiled threats punishable by jail time in at least a dozen states.

That evening, Rasher eased Connie's freshly lubed BMW up the driveway with mounting trepidation. He turned off the engine and sat behind the steering wheel staring blankly at the vast collection of boxes stacked high in every corner of their four-car garage – testaments to his past extravagant indulgence of Connie's Home Shopping Network purchases. Sadly, he recognized her endless sense of entitlement wasn't entirely her fault. He had to admit he shared some blame. Throughout their years together, he had become her willing enabler, perhaps, in part to ease his guilt at having cheated on, and deserted the first Mrs. Rasher.

It was almost eight years to the day, when Marvin and his first wife were in San Francisco to celebrate their twelfth wedding anniversary. He had wandered into one of the high-end hotel shops hoping to find a simple token to commemorate the occasion but found Connie Hunter instead.

She was young and incredibly sensuous, with honey-blonde hair that cascaded down her back, barely covering a tiny scar on her left shoulder blade. She was dressed most inappropriately, in the briefest of halter-tops that showed off her nubile breasts, and skintight slacks that clung to the well-rounded outlines of her lower extremities. When she sashayed across the shop, the sharp V-shaped fabric crease that formed between her legs left little to Marvin's panting imagination. The ensemble may not have been haute couture, but togged out like that, the saucy, young salesgirl had no trouble selling the happily, yet complacent, married man anything she wanted that day.

From the second he laid eyes on her, he was hooked, powerless to walk away. To cloak his intense attraction, he proceeded to purchase over seventeen hundred dollars worth of merchandise he didn't need – or even want. All he wanted by then was Connie.

When the first Mrs. Rasher headed off to the hotel salon to have her hair and nails done to look her best for their anniversary celebration, Connie showed up at Marvin's room to personally deliver the items he had purchased earlier. Each one now attractively gift wrapped and tied with bright pearl colored anniversary ribbons. She placed them on the ottoman at the foot of the bed, then hopped up onto on the edge of the canopied, four-poster, suggestively straddling one of the thick, cherry wood posts between her thighs and coyly inquired if there was anything else she could do for him.

Haplessly succumbing to the siren's call, nothing else mattered from the moment she shed her clothes and exposed him to the dizzying world of clandestine, uninhibited, raw, wanton sexual pleasures.

Marvin had never experienced anyone like Connie before. The more he had her, the more of her he wanted. They managed to covertly continue their dangerous liaison undetected for the remainder of his stay.

On one of their final trysts, as Marvin, under the careful tutelage of his insatiable young instructor sensuously ran his tongue up and down her bare back, he noticed the small scar on her shoulder blade.

As they lay back against the pillows, spent and sweaty, Marvin happened to mention she could easily have the scar removed by a skillful plastic surgeon he knew of back in Chicago. At first Connie didn't appear interested. "It's just a teeny-weenie little scar – what's the big deal?"

"True," Marvin agreed. "But you are so close to absolute perfection... why not go for it all?" In an attempt to lure Connie to Chicago, Marvin offered to fly her out and pay for the surgery. The rest, as they say, is history.

Marvin continued to sit in silent contemplation in his garage. He sighed deeply, then picked up his briefcase and headed inside. He decided to forestall a face-to-face confrontation and made his way silently into the dining room without announcing his arrival.

On the elegant, Koa wood dining room table, was a cold, partially eaten Domino's pizza, unceremoniously sitting in an oil stained, cardboard box, and an uncapped, half-empty bottle of warm Diet Pepsi. Obviously, Mrs. Rasher had no interest in waiting to join her husband for dinner. Since their earlier acrimonious phone call, Connie had little interest in doing anything with her husband tonight. The longer he made her wait to go under the skillful scalpel of Chicago's finest plastic surgeon, the more miserable she decided Marvin's life would become.

Rasher glanced at the once flavorful pepperoni pie, now resembling a fourth grade science project gone bad. The succulent circles of pepperoni drizzled with fragrant oils had long since hardened into tiny, shriveled slabs, solid as Lake Michigan in winter. Having pretty much lost whatever appetite he may have once had, he reached over and closed the lid.

He headed into the den and poured himself a glass of Glenlivet and settled in on the couch. A short time later, Connie decided to make her presence known. Cold pizza and flat soda were to be the least of

Marvin's punishments tonight. She slithered into the den in a slinky satin robe that clung to her flesh, her blonde curls swept atop her head, tied with a black velvet ribbon, and sat down on the settee directly across from the couch without the slightest acknowledgement of Marvin's presence. She reached up and slowly undid the hair ribbon, releasing the soft, blonde tresses Marvin prized so dearly, and ran her freshly polished fingernails through her hair, then stretched all the way back, purring like a cat in heat. Marvin couldn't turn away as she teased back the hem of her robe, exposing just a hint of her naked flesh.

He sat up straight; his heart and groin began to pound as Connie continued her calculatingly cruel performance. Her sinewy fingers toyed with the front of her robe until it fully exposed her ample left breast, Marvin's favorite. She closed her eyes and began to moan as she played with her nipple until it stood hard and erect. Then seductively peeled back her robe, leaving absolutely nothing to her husband's tortured imagination. Her defiant, smoldering hazel eyes met his, confident she had made her point. There lay Connie, Marvin's bride of seven plus years, in all her bare-assed, lusty splendor – and there was nothing he could do. He couldn't have her.

It was too much for Marvin to take. He rose from the couch clutching his briefcase in front of him, hoping to conceal both his throbbing erection and his wounded pride.

Connie could hear his car tear out of the driveway and race down the street as she stood and wrapped her robe around her. She turned out the living room lights and made her way up to the master bedroom.

On her dresser was a framed photo taken perhaps a year or two earlier. She looked happy, and beautiful and perfect. She glanced at herself in the mirror above the dresser. She didn't like the image looking back at her. She ran a critical finger across her forehead and down her cheek, then climbed into bed and cried herself to sleep.

48

There was a message waiting on her voicemail when Julie got home from work. It was from her mother, Doris, announcing she was on her way to Chicago for a surprise visit. Well, more than a visit. Doris preferred to call it, a pre-emptive rescue mission. It seems Mother Hatcher had recently been booted off the Agoura Hills Country Club Steering committee by a secret, unanimous vote of her long-suffering, fellow board members, who had grown tired of her endless controlling demands and lofty expectations. Now freed from her duties as the self-proclaimed arbiter of pretty much everything, and despite the fact Julie was a grown woman expecting a child of her own, Doris decided it was time to refocus her attention on her daughter's appalling, ill-thought-out life choices.

Julie knew it was pointless to try and stop her. Any objections she might have raised would have fallen on deaf ears anyway. As long as she could remember, nothing and no one was ever good enough to earn Doris Hatcher's benign approbation. Not the friends Julie chose growing up or the way she wore her hair or even the grades she worked so feverishly hard to achieve. Or for that matter, her soft-spoken father, who had suffered in silence under his wife's intractable reign for eleven miserable years, until the day he left for work and simply never came home. Even at the tender age of nine, Julie understood why he left. She swore when she grew up, she would never be anything like her mother.

She couldn't very well ask Billy to leave, especially with the tryout coming up. But she couldn't risk having Doris stay in the apartment without the likelihood of running into Popwell and Timmy. Julie knew she'd get some flak from her mother, but the only way to get through the next few days would be to put Doris up at the hotel. She hated the thought of subjecting her co-workers to her mother, but at the moment, there was no other option.

As soon as Doris stepped foot into the apartment, she started in on

Julie. She felt it her motherly duty to point out how bedraggled and pale she looked. How terribly disappointed she was with Julie's choice of furnishings, and, as she ran her finger across the stove top, that it was painfully clear, the first thing Julie needed to do was hire a better cleaning service, or, as Doris archly pointed out, "Why not have Billy do it? Since he obviously hasn't anything better to do."

"Oh, but I do, Doris," Billy said, as he grabbed her suitcase in one hand and his car keys in the other. "I've got to get your bags over to the hotel and check you in." Before Doris could protest, Billy was half-way out the door. "You ladies have fun now. I'll catch up with you later at the park."

Julie's plan was to keep her mother occupied by showing her around the city. But Doris had little desire to sightsee or enjoy 'The Windy.' She managed to put a negative spin on just about everything. Chicago has too much crime. It's too cold in the winter, too humid in the summer, and definitely not a suitable environment to raise a child in. She didn't even like the deep dish pizza! She urged Julie to think about returning to Southern California, preferably to the lovely bedroom community of Agoura Hills.

"When and if we decide to move back to California, Mother, it wouldn't be to Agoura Hills," Julie finally stated in frustration. "Have you forgotten? Billy still has a lease on a wonderful beach house in Malibu."

"You can't be serious?" Doris gasped. "That bachelor pad has nothing to offer a child but sand. My granddaughter needs a proper backyard, with trees and a swing set, not ten-foot waves that could drag her out to sea! I can't believe what people are willing to pay for houses in that zip code. For what you pay in Malibu, you could lease a virtual palace in Agoura Hills." And then, revealing her true agenda, "In fact, there happens to be a wonderful three-bedroom condo right in my complex that's about to come on the market."

Julie shuddered at the thought, and prayed for the strength to get through the rest of her mother's stay. As they headed through the park, Julie caught sight of a bustling farmer's market up ahead. Bushels of fresh fruit and vegetable stands, and row after row of colorful booths displaying paintings and crafts by local artisans. If nothing else, it held the promise of a brief respite from her mother's endless diatribe.

Amazingly, Doris did manage to cease complaining long enough to inspect a peach. She held it up to the light, then to her nose, sniffing like a police dog rooting out cocaine. Following which, she proceeded to grill the poor vendor about pesticides and the like before determining if his wares were somehow worthy of the Doris Hatcher seal of approval. They weren't. So Doris moved on to the tables filled with object d'arte and oil paintings.

Billy entered the park and walked along the lake looking for Julie and her mother. The sparkling, clear blue water was quiet and serene. A parade of pint-sized ducklings trailed obediently behind their proud mama in one straight line, making tiny ripples in the water as they paddled by. Then suddenly, not three feet in front of him, suspended inches above the lake, swooping and splaying its magnificent plumage, was a majestic Peregrine Falcon. He could almost swear it was the exact bird he watched soar into the sky from Julie's terrace. It seemed to be staring at him, causing him to wonder if it might have actually followed him here.

Billy spun around, expecting to find everyone equally enraptured by the vision of the spectacular creature. But, to his surprise, no one else seemed to notice this wondrous occurrence. When he turned back around, the bird was gone. He gazed out over the lake, an empty sadness washing over him.

Julie ran her finger across the rim of a wine-colored, hand thrown, earthen bowl, admiring its aesthetic ornamental design and flow. Doris thought it was hideous and amateur. Mother Hatcher continued marching down her personal path of destruction inspecting each handicraft and canvas with a jaundiced eye. "Oh. Good Lord," Doris uttered full voice, indifferent to the poor artist perched on a nearby stool. "This has to be the ugliest painting here! I mean, this is not art. This is utter garbage. You have to see this, Julie. You have to take a look at what passes for art in this city."

Julie's cheeks flushed with embarrassment as she stood beside her mother. Her heart went out to the humiliated young painter pretending not to have overheard Doris trashing his work. She could hardly wait to get away when a sudden dull pain gripped her lower back, followed by a strong, tight tension in her abdomen.

"Be honest, Julie. A chimp with a turkey baster could've done better," Doris continued, positively giddy at the cleverness of her witty remark.

"Mom, I'm really not feeling too good right now. I need to call Billy."

Doris was just starting to enjoy herself for the first time since her arrival and had no desire to leave. "For crying out loud, Julie, you're five months pregnant. How do you expect to feel? When I was pregnant with you, I was either exhausted or in agony for nine whole months – but did I complain? No, I did not. Hatcher women grin and bear it. So suck it up and let's go see what other horrible things are on display."

Then, it was as if someone reached up and turned off the lights. The paintings and pottery swirled to a blur, the park grew silent, the sky and the faces around her disappeared as Julie swooned onto a ceramic-laden table and promptly passed out.

"The baby is fine," Sarah Constantine reassured them. "What Julie experienced was a simple panic attack." In Billy's mind there was nothing simple about it. Damn Doris and her unwelcome intrusion. "What I strongly recommend is a few days off from work and if possible, some quiet bed rest."

While Julie started getting dressed, she asked Billy if he'd please go find her mother and let her know what the doctor had said. She figured Doris was likely climbing the walls by now.

Julie was right. Doris was near hysterics, livid at having been made to remain in the waiting room like a nobody. Though Billy did his best to address Doris' concerns and bring her up to speed, Julie's mom was far from satisfied with Dr. Sarah's oversimplified explanation. She was not about to trust her daughter's health to anyone but the chief of staff at Cedars, or at the least, someone high up on the obstetrics pecking order at UCLA Medical Center. Most certainly not to some young, inexperienced woman barely out of med school at a second rate medical facility who refers to herself as Doctor Sarah! What kind of confidence does that inspire? None, according to Doris. What Julie needed was to return to California with her as soon as possible.

Billy was in no mood to deal with Doris' blistering tirade, but the thought of her threatening to take Julie back to California was unbearable. As was Charley's sudden unexpected appearance, despite Popwell's promise to keep him out of sight until Julie's mom left town.

"Hey asshole," Charley shouted. "I tailed you from the park 'cause I got a bone to pick with you. For your information, no one tells me what I can and cannot do. Got it?! I go where I please, whenever I please. I don't take orders from you."

"This is not a good time, Charley," Billy whispered, behind Doris' back.

"Why... because Julie's ball-breaking mother might overhear us? Jeeze what a wimp you turned out to be." Charley shook his head in disgust, and to Billy's horror marched directly up to Doris. "Hey loudmouth," Charley blasted, jabbing Doris on the shoulder. "Why don't you stop trying to run everybody's life and go home."

But it would take more than a poke to intimidate Mother Hatcher. "Excuse me? Just who do you think you are?"

"Now that's kind of a trick question," Charley responded. "Depends on who decided to come out. But I'll give you a hint – since you're new to the game. You see me pull out something sharp, get ready to run."

Doris spun on her heels with righteous indignation, coiled to strike. "How dare you speak to me like that?"

"Like what? Like you're a lousy excuse for a mother and Julie deserves better."

"You listen to me, you lunatic --"

"Lunatic is not a phrase we're especially fond of, Doris. The correct term is Dissociate Identity Disorder."

"You belong in a mental institution," she screamed, nostrils flaring.

"Been there. Tried it. Didn't really work for us."

Doris had enough. She strode past the receptionist with a 'don't even try to stop me' glare, and bolted into the exam room. Julie was buttoning her blouse when Doris marched in. "As soon as you're dressed," Doris announced, without fear of contradiction, "we're getting on a plane to California."

"What? Mom, what are you talking about? What's going on? I could hear you shouting all the way back here."

"We're going to see Dr. Tisherman at Cedars tomorrow straight from the airport. He delivered you and he's the only one I trust to deliver my granddaughter."

"But, Mom," Julie protested. "Doctor Sarah said all I needed was a little bed rest, and a little less stress."

Doris was way past caring about anything some wet-behind-the-ears physician had to say. "I'm your mother. I know what's best for you. Don't even think of arguing with me about it, little girl."

Julie reached for her mother's arm, hoping to get through to her. "That's just it, Mom, I'm not a little girl anymore. You have to stop."

"Stop what?" Doris shot back, pulling her arm away. "Stop being your mother? Is that what this city, with its rude, crazy people has done? Turned you against me?"

As her mother's agitation grew, Julie tried to remain calm for the baby's sake if not for her own. "Mom, please, for once -- just listen. Try to understand, I can't go back to California with you. My place is here with Billy." Doris' face contorted with disgust, her lips puckered as if sucking on lemons at the sound of his name. "He's the father of my child. He loves me and I love him. I think we can make it work – but not with you hovering and trying to run my life."

Doris was crushed. But her hurt feelings quickly twisted into anger. "So, everything is my fault?"

"I didn't say that. But, I think it might be best for all of us if you went back home."

Julie knew her words stung deep, but she refused to take them back. There was too much at stake. "This isn't about you, Mom. For once it's about me. What I want. What I need. You're my mother and I love you. I'll always need you, but right now..." Julie said, in a calm but firm manner while reaching for her mother's hand again. "You need to let me grow up and lead my own life. You need to go home."

49

"I don't see any Wonder Bread," Timmy stated, popping in unannounced as Julie fussed around the kitchen, dredging a dozen raw chicken fillets through seasoned flour.

"No Wonder Bread tonight, Timmy. I'm making Billy's favorite. Chicken Marsala."

Mealtimes had indeed become an interesting challenge. Popwell, when he'd admit to being hungry, took most if not all of his meals alone in the den. As for Timmy, his preferences were quite specific. Smooth Skippy peanut butter on Wonder Bread with raspberry jelly.

But tonight, Julie was craving something a little more grownup, a little more gourmet, something that might go nicely with candlelight and soft music. With Popwell and Timmy constantly lurking somewhere in the background, finding alone time with Billy had become a bit tricky. It required planning, resolve and cunning.

Julie had taken out books from the local library on multiples, and had done her homework well over the past few days. She believed, the more she knew about Dissociative Identity Disorder, the more help she could be to Billy, and the less unnerving sharing an apartment with Popwell and Timmy would prove to be.

Timmy hopped up onto a stool and wrinkled his nose. "Looks yucky," he offered, as he poked his fingers into the bowl then stuck them into his mouth.

"Don't do that!" Julie chided, latching onto his hand before he had a chance to try it again. "That's disgusting!"

Timmy dropped his chin to his chest, and flapped his flour-coated hand back and forth across his shirt. "Sorry. I -- I promise not to do it again."

Instantly regretting having scolded him, Julie tucked her hand beneath his chin and gently lifted his face. "It's okay, Timmy. Really. I'm sorry I raised my voice."

Timmy's eyes glistened with tears. "I didn't mean to do something bad," he sniffled.

"You didn't," Julie reassured him. "In fact," she said, sticking her own finger into the bowl. "I think it might be kind of fun." Then to Timmy's surprise, she dabbed her flour-coated finger to the tip of his nose. "Go ahead," she suggested. "Your turn."

Timmy wiped the tears from his face, and dipped a tentative finger back into the bowl. Then, with a little further coaxing from Julie, deposited a generous splotch of white flour on the tip of *her* nose. He started to giggle and so did she.

"C'mon. Why don't we go wash our hands and you can watch the Disney movie I brought home for you in the living room while I finish making dinner." Timmy excitedly jumped off the stool and happily followed her out. When she returned to the kitchen, she was feeling a little uncertain about how she handled Timmy. After all, it wasn't exactly easy having a conversation with an eight-year-old boy living inside a grown man's body.

"That was nice... what you did for Timmy."

Julie spun around surprised to find Popwell standing there. "Thank you, Popwell."

Popwell nodded, then headed back into the living room.

At a critical juncture in the cooking process, the phone rang. Julie called out, "Billy, can you get that?" No reply. The ringing continued. "Billy? Popwell? Timmy? Can somebody please get that? My hands are full."

Reluctantly, Popwell picked up the phone and held it to his ear.

"Hey, hey, buddy," said the voice on the other end.

"Who's calling?" Popwell asked, curtly.

"Very fucking funny, Billy boy. It's Frankie, as if you didn't know. And what's with the voice? Fuck, you better not be coming down with something. Look. I just got off the phone with that douche bag, Farley. I got you and your boy Popwell a tryout with the Cubs a week from Thursday."

Without a word, Popwell hung up and walked off into the den.

A moment later the phone rang again. This time it was Billy who picked it up, just as the TV screen was merrily scrolling off the final Disney end credits. Before he could so much as say, 'hello,' Frankie started in.

"What the fuck was that about?"

"Frankie?" Billy said with much relief. "I was hoping you'd call."

"Oh yeah? Well you got a funny way of showing it. Hanging up on me like that."

"What do you mean, hanging up? What are you talking about?"

"You just slammed the fucking phone down in my ear."

"What are you crazy? When?"

"Two fucking minutes ago. Hey, look, we must'a had a disconnect or something. Anyway, like I was saying, I called to tell you, I got you and that pitcher of yours a tryout. A week from Thursday."

Before Billy could respond, it suddenly hit him. It must've been Popwell or Timmy who picked up the phone the first time Frankie called. Billy looked around, but Popwell was gone.

"Hey, Billy," Frankie shouted. "You still there?"

"Yeah. Sorry Frankie."

"I gotta say, your enthusiasm is underwhelming! You sound like I just told you your fucking parakeet drowned in the toilet. This is the Chicago Cubs we're talking about. Let's hear a little excitement."

No... I'm... I'm excited, honest," he answered, half-listening, his thoughts focused on Popwell's abrupt disappearance.

"Good. But I'm telling you, this Popwell better be aces. If he blows, youz goes – straight out the fucking door. Got it?"

Billy let the phone fall from his hand as Julie came in from the kitchen balancing a savory platter of Chicken Marsala. "Who's hungry?" she asked, lyrically, as Billy bolted out the front door without a word. "Billy?" she called after him. "What's going on?" Then she spotted the phone dangling from its tangled cord near the floor. Frankie's distant voice still floating in the air. She set the platter on the coffee table and picked it up.

"Hello? Frankie?"

"What the fuck is going on, Julie?" he demanded.

Julie plopped herself onto the couch, sinking deep within the cushions. She took a long breath. "Have you got a few minutes? We need to talk."

50

He was sitting by the window at Iggy's, a friendly little diner known for its Chicago dogs and fries. It was packed with a hungry cadre of customers who had come to worship at its greasy altar while listening to the strains of a juke box that had been there since it opened in the fifties.

"What the hell's going on?" Billy asked. "Julie went to a lot of trouble to make us Chicken Marsala."

"Chicken Marsala is your favorite, not mine."

"Just the same, you could've stuck around."

"In case you forgot, I'm not Timmy. I can come and go as I please." Popwell unfolded his napkin and placed it on his lap.

"Of course you can," Billy said, backing down. "But, if this is about Frankie's phone call, you shouldn't have picked it up."

Popwell lifted his head, "She asked me to."

"She?"

"Julie."

"Okay, forget about who told who to do what. I still don't see how anything Frankie said could've made you bolt like that."

Popwell arched an eyebrow. "So then this… Frankie is it?

"Yeah. Frank Tortiricci.

"Did you go behind my back and have him set up a tryout for me with the Cubs?"

"No." Billy offered, a little too quickly. "Well, not exactly. I told you about it, or at least I thought I did. Unless… I was talking to Timmy."

Popwell leaned back against the faded, red leatherette, narrowing his eyes with a probing glare.

"Look, Frankie's my agent, but I got you the tryout. I thought you'd be on top of the world," Billy stated hopefully, as he leaned in closer. "Jim Farley, the Cubs GM had his eye on me since college. No shit. He's been trading calls with Tortiricci for weeks. I just didn't feel I was ready.

Not while I was still sorting things out at Highwater. But now I am. And so are you. So, I pulled a few strings, called in a favor and got Farley to check you out too. What do you say?"

"Not interested."

Billy was rattled. "What do you mean you're not interested?"

Popwell clammed up as the waitress arrived, her serving tray piled sky high. "Three monster dawgs with everything," she proclaimed loudly through iridescent, orange painted lips. "And a frosty pitcher of suds." She deftly placed the platter on the table. "Anything else?" Neither Popwell nor Billy spoke a word. "It's not that hard a question," she responded, shrugging her hefty shoulders. "Okay then. Enjoy!"

When the waitress sauntered off, Popwell picked up the first juicy offering as if Billy wasn't even there.

Billy refused to be ignored. "I know you're pissed. I should've made sure you knew what was going on before you heard it from Frankie. But what's done is done. You're too good not to play in the majors!"

Popwell speared a greasy fry, popped it in his mouth and remained mum.

Billy refused to give up. "There has to be something I can do to change your mind."

Popwell continued to ignore him, shifting his gaze to a heavy-set woman at a nearby table burying her face in a burger slopped with caramelized onions and relish. Frustrated, Billy threw up his hands. "Look, if I stepped over the line, I'm sorry. I hope at least we're still friends."

At first, Popwell said nothing. Then, after a moment, he gently nudged the sizzling sausage platter towards Billy as a gesture of reconciliation. Billy stared at the plump pink pile bursting with perfection, the tantalizing fries tempting him beyond his ability to resist.

"You know," Billy said, between guilty bites. "Julie busted her butt making dinner. She's gonna kill us both." Popwell nodded knowingly.

They ate in silence. Somewhere around the last of the fries, Billy tried testing the waters again. "I just don't get it. How could anyone turn down a tryout for a major league team? I'd really like to know?"

Popwell grinned mischievously, his eyes big and bright as motorcycle headlamps. "You know what I'd really like? A double hot fudge sundae with big red cherries on top."

"Popwell?"

"Popwell's done eating. It's my turn now. Besides, you wanted to know why he doesn't want to try out for the Cubs. He doesn't know why, but I do."

"Timmy?" Billy asked, pretty certain that's who had once again taken center stage.

"Uh huh." Timmy answered, taking a mighty gulp from the frosty mug in front of him. "Yuck," he winced. His face wrinkling in disgust and disappointment. That's not Pepsi! It tastes like puke."

Billy picked up the mug and placed it beyond Timmy's reach. "That's because it's beer and you are way too young to drink beer."

"Then are you gonna get me a sundae? Please, Billy. Please!"

"We'll see. But first you need to tell me what you meant when you said, you know why Popwell won't try out."

"I want my sundae first," the petulant youngster screamed. A handful of nearby customers turned, focusing curious stares at the sudden outburst. The woman with the sloppy burger rolled her eyes with distain, as pickle juice ran off her chin.

"Forget the sundae, Timmy," Billy said, quietly, yet sternly. "This is important."

"Why are you being so mean to me, Billy? I don't think you like me anymore." Timmy began kicking hard at the table leg. "I bet you'd get Popwell a sundae if he wanted one!"

By now Timmy's tantrum was generating more than a little ire amongst quite a few of Iggy's patrons. The waitress made a beeline to their booth just as Timmy grabbed a spoon and fork and started banging loudly on the Formica tabletop.

"Everything all right over here?" The waitress asked, glaring oddly at Billy.

"I want a sundae!" Timmy demanded.

"Well you coulda waved me over, 'stead of banging on the table like a loony tune. You're bothering the other customers."

Billy looked up, painfully aware of the disturbance Timmy was creating. "Sorry. I'd like to order a double hot fudge sundae, please," he said, then paused, as Timmy whispered insistently.

"Don't forget cherries. And some nuts."

"I'd like cherries on top. And some nuts."

"Big cherries," Timmy begged.

"Big cherries," Billy echoed, giving up the fight.

"Sorry," the waitress announced. "All we got is maraschinos." She shook her head and headed off for the kitchen, obviously not in the mood to cater to the wishes of an unruly table.

"Are you mad at me, Billy?" Timmy asked quietly.

Billy sighed. "I'm not mad. I just really need to find out what you can tell me about Popwell."

Timmy played with the silverware as he spoke, lining up the spoons and forks in a circle. "Charley doesn't like me to talk about Popwell with anyone. And I'm a little afraid of Charley."

"Me too," Billy admitted. "But you don't have to worry about Charley. I think he wouldn't mind if we talked about it if it'll help Popwell."

Timmy nodded, then whispered, "Charley doesn't want me or Popwell or any of us to go to Wrigley Field ever again."

"Again? Why not?"

Timmy hesitated for a moment, looking around for the waitress. "Do you think she'll put something icky in my sundae… because I was bad?"

"I promise. I won't let the waitress or anyone hurt you, Timmy. Now, go on."

Timmy seemed reassured. "Remember when I said I didn't like baseball? Well… it wasn't exactly a fib, but… I used to like baseball a lot, especially the Cubs. I'd watch them on TV all the time. I used to beg my daddy to take me to Wrigley so I could watch a real game, but he'd always tell me he was too busy, or too tired; or that he didn't have time for stuff like ballgames, and even if he did, he'd have to pay someone to stay home with my sister, and babysitters cost a whole lot of money. But I kept asking and asking anyway.

Then one day when I was getting ready for bed, he came into my room to say goodnight. He sat on the edge of my bed and told me he was gonna skip work tomorrow and take us to see the Cubs. I started jumping around the room. I didn't even care that we had to bring my stupid sister with us. I said he was the best dad ever! I got back into bed, but I was way too excited to close my eyes, so after he left, I got out my box of baseball cards and memorized every stat of every player.

We had really great seats… right by first base. As soon as I sat down, I shut my eyes real tight and pretended I was the pitcher and that everybody came just to see me. Then, Daddy got up to get us some Cracker Jack. He made me promise to keep an eye on my sister till he got back. Even though she wasn't a baby, she was a real pain. She kept pestering me the whole time.

After a while, I started looking around. Daddy had been gone a long, long time. My sister kept yelling she was hungry. I started getting kind of nervous; I couldn't even watch the game. Some more time went by and he still didn't come back. I guess I started to cry, and then my sister started to cry because I was crying. Then some lady called an usher, and he called the police. I still don't know what I did to make him go away. Why he left us there. But it made me feel real bad. Then they went and put me and my sister in a foster home."

"Why didn't you stay with your mother?" Billy asked.

"Because she was in heaven. She used to hear people talking in her head a lot. One day she said they were yelling real loud. Telling her to jump. The voices made her head hurt so much, she didn't even kiss me goodbye when I left for school.

Old Mrs. Catalfo found her stuck on a steel spike sticking out from the fence down below our apartment. Nobody at school wanted to play with me anymore. They called me lots of bad names. They said I was the freak whose crazy mother flew out the window. I felt so bad, I couldn't even look at anybody anymore."

Billy looked at Timmy's tears and felt like crying. All he could utter was, "Sweet Jesus. No little kid should ever have to go through all that." Billy felt a sudden need to try and comfort him. "But, Timmy, that was a long, long time ago. What happened with your mother, and what happened at the ball park wasn't your fault."

"But it was. Don't you see? I must've been really, really bad. That's why they all went away and left us."

"Sometimes grown-ups do stupid things for no good reasons. Do you understand what I'm saying, Timmy? It wasn't your fault. Popwell needs to know that too. I need to talk to Popwell again. Is that okay?"

"What about my sundae?" Timmy asked, hopeful.

"I'll have the waitress pack it up and you can eat it at home."

Timmy nodded reluctantly, then let Popwell return. When Popwell looked for his beer, he was surprised not to find it where he left it.

"Do you know what happened to Timmy at Wrigley?" Billy asked. Popwell stared straight ahead, his eyes blank and far away. "Could you hear him when he told me about it?" Billy paused. "Is that why you won't go back to Wrigley? Is that how this works?" Popwell weighed Billy's observation thoughtfully, as Billy continued to probe. "Did Dr. Rasher know what happened?"

"Timmy never met Rasher. Charley wouldn't let him."

51

When he got home, Billy placed Timmy's partially melted sundae alongside the foil-wrapped package of untouched Chicken Marsala. He scribbled a big T on the outside of the foil in black marker to ensure no one would mistakenly help themselves and risk disappointing Timmy when next he appeared, then sat at the kitchen table and buried his face in his hands. Without Popwell, Billy knew he could kiss his chance at a baseball career and all his grandiose plans for the future goodbye.

He lifted his head and stared out the window, wondering how nice it might be if the falcon from the lake would come back and carry him off. He closed his eyes, imagining how it would feel to fly free as a bird -- the breeze dancing across his body – the moonlit clouds rippling through his fingers. Until he thought about Julie and the baby, and knew he could never leave them behind again.

It was late when he finally tip-toed into the bedroom. He peeled off his matted clothes and stretched out against the cool, cotton sheets, listening to the drumming of the air conditioner as it shifted gears straining to stay in sync with the changing temperature. He turned silently onto his side and stared at the gentle curve of Julie's back, aching to touch her. She felt the weight of his body and turned towards him, rubbing the sleep from her eyes. "Are you okay? Where did you go? I was so worried."

"I'm sorry. There was something I needed to do. I'm sorry about dinner. I know you went to a lot of trouble --"

"Shh," she whispered. "It's fine. It's in the freezer. We can have it tomorrow or the next day. Do you want to tell me where you went?"

Billy proceeded to recount the night as it unfolded, careful not to mention succumbing to the heaping plate of Iggy dogs and fries.

"I need to help Timmy and Popwell come to terms with what might have happened to them."

Julie sat up and arched her back. "Might have? You don't think what Timmy told you is true? That it happened the way he said it did?"

Billy sighed, "I don't know anymore. You gotta admit. This whole multiple thing is pretty bizarre. I mean, how do we really know any of these things actually happened? Maybe they're just fabrications. It's all pretty crazy."

"I believe it. And so does Dr. Rasher. I really wish you'd reconsider calling him, Billy. Did you know he did a paper on D.I.D. for the American Psychological Association?" She flipped on the lamp, opened the nightstand drawer and retrieved a stack of pages she had printed off the internet. "Look. It's all right here. Dr. Rasher is convinced," she said, reading from one of the pages, "Validating traumatic childhood experiences provides opportunity for both alter and dominant to heal and move forward. See for yourself," she said, offering up the pages, which Billy promptly dismissed, placing them face down on the bed.

"I told you, I'm not interested in anything Rasher has to say. But I do have to do something, and I have to do it fast. I can't let the Charley alter win. I can't let him keep Popwell from going to Wrigley if I'm gonna have a shot, which means I have to make it right for Timmy first."

Julie turned to Billy, "Maybe we could take Timmy on a little adventure tomorrow. He's been begging to go for a ride on the L. We can make it a fun afternoon. We can get off at the ballpark stop and see how he reacts. If it doesn't freak him out, we could pick up some tickets and go see the game."

"But there's no game tomorrow. The Cubs are on the road."

"Even better. Wrigley should be fairly quiet and low-key. If we can find a way into the park, we can show him there's nothing to be afraid of anymore. If we can make him feel safe there, if we can convince him we understand the pain he felt was genuine, and that we know he did nothing wrong, it might give him the reassurance he needs to move on. Then maybe this Charley won't have to keep Popwell, or any of the alters out of the ballpark anymore."

The next day, Timmy was over the moon. He loved the whole idea of going for a train ride. He counted every step in a booming voice as they descended the wooden staircase. He skipped and jumped across the platform with bursts of childlike energy to the curious stares of everyone he passed along the way.

Billy, on the other hand, cautiously studied the faces of every person boarding and departing the train each time it stopped. Improbable though it was, he braced for the possibility he might once again encounter the loathsome visage of Diablo.

His heart began to race as a mountain of a man entered, his face buried inside a newspaper. He held his breath as the man took a seat and lowered the paper to his lap. To his relief, it wasn't Diablo. Not this time.

When the train pulled up and out of the tunnel into the sunshine, Timmy inched closer to the window for a better view. He pressed his nose against the glass as the buildings blurred past. Julie kept a close eye on him as the train lumbered into the Addison Street station, hoping he wasn't yet aware of their final destination. He seemed calm and content as they got off the train and headed for the exit, looking forward to a promised hot dog and strawberry ice cream cone. As they started down the long flight of stairs, Timmy's gait slowed to a crawl and then to a stop, gripping the handrail so firmly his knuckles turned white. "I… think I want to go home now," he said, sitting down on the steps, tightly squeezing his eyes shut. "Charley says we have to turn around. I have to do what Charley says or he might cut me, or maybe even try to cut Billy again."

Julie sat beside him and put her hand across his shoulders. "I swear Timmy, Charley will not cut you or anyone else." Timmy opened his eyes and looked at her. "Do you trust me, Timmy?" she asked. "I promise nothing bad is going to happen to you today. Billy and I will protect you. Do you believe us?" Timmy wiped away a tear and nodded bravely. "Now, we're going to show you just how good and brave we think you are. I'm sure Charley is only trying to do what he thinks is best for you. For all of you. But this time he's wrong, so you don't have to mind him." Julie took him firmly by the hand and led him slowly down the remaining steps.

They headed away from the El and onto the streets of Wrigleyville leading to the stadium. The neighborhood had an odd, vacant feel. No fathers and sons, no businessmen playing hooky from work on a weekday. No program vendors, or stealthy ticket scalpers lurking about. There was no smell of peanuts, hotdogs or energy. Just a few souvenir shops hoping to make a buck on an off day.

"Do you remember how much you liked watching the Cubs on television, Timmy?" Julie asked casually, as they paused in front of a pet shop window to watch a trio of Dalmatian puppies mischievously tearing up newspapers.

Timmy nodded, adding, "Yes. But that was before... you know."

"Well," Julie said. "Billy and Popwell and all their friends really like the Cubs too. And we thought it might be fun to walk around Wrigley and see the statues, and maybe even sneak into the bleachers and pretend there's a game going on."

He stopped and tugged at her arm. "But there isn't. Right?" he asked, cautiously. "The... the ushers and policemen and the noisy people won't be there today, will they?"

"Nope." She reassured him. "Just us."

And then, as they turned the corner, there it was. Wrigley Field. Timmy's chest tightened. Julie looked into his frightened eyes and drew him close.

They found their way into the ballpark through an open gate but were quickly intercepted by a security guard. "Can I help you?" the guard asked, polite but firm. Timmy did his best to fade into the background to ensure the guard wouldn't take him away.

"I'm from the Trib," Billy offered, in a moment of inspiration, flashing Middleman's I.D. as quickly as possible. And this is my associate, Miss Hatcher. "We're working on a special series of articles on Wrigley for the Sunday Magazine section. We want to feature the people who keep the ballpark going behind the scenes."

"Behind the scenes?"

"Yeah. You know. Vendors, ticket takers, maintenance, and of course... the ballpark's hard working security force. You guys are the backbone, the veritable gatekeepers of this hallowed shrine."

"Nobody said nothing to me about any magazine reporters coming by today."

"I know. I know. Look," Billy said, pulling the guard aside. "We weren't scheduled to be here until a couple months from now. But my associate here went and got herself knocked up and, well... the big brass thought we better move the project up while she could still squeeze through the turnstiles... if y'know what I mean," he winked.

The guard turned to Julie, who smiled meekly. "I suppose it's okay."

"Thanks," Billy said, as the guard walked off.

They headed from the concourse and out into the open air, greeted by a dazzling field of green. For most young boys, the excitement of entering any ball park would create a joyous moment that would last forever. But when Timmy caught sight of a particular row of seats along the first base line, he turned and bolted back up the steps, quickly disappearing inside the dark and sheltered concourse. Julie raced after him. As her eyes adjusted to the light, she found him cowering beside a shuttered souvenir stand. She approached with caution, softly calling his name. Timmy stood up and ran into her arms. She wiped his tears, and held him close, then brushed back his hair with her fingers and straightened the mottled, sweat-stained collar of his shirt.

"I'm sorry, Julie," he sniffled. "I'm ruining everything. I didn't mean to be bad. Did I ruin the new shirt Billy bought me? I... I couldn't help it."

"It's fine. You're fine. See," she reassured him, pointing to his reflection in the side of a nearby shiny metal girder.

Timmy stared at the image mirroring his own. "That can't be me," he stated with surprise. "I look too big to be me. I look as big as Popwell and Billy."

"That's just it, Timmy. You are big now. What happened here, the bad memory, happened a long, long time ago. It doesn't have to hurt you anymore. C'mon. Let me show you. Okay?"

Timmy took her hand as she led him back out toward the stands. The closer they got, the more hesitant his steps became.

"Is that where you sat with your dad and your sister?" Julie asked, pointing to the empty stream of seats, standing like silent sentries waiting for the next onslaught of frenzied fans. When Timmy didn't respond, she tried to gauge if he was still functioning in the present or had been pulled back into the horror of that long ago day. "They can't hurt you. I promise. They're just a couple of silly old chairs. That's all."

"Do... do I have to go over there?" Timmy asked, warily pointing to a row of seats nearby.

Julie nodded and smiled hopefully. "Billy and I think it might help make you better. You don't have to stay a frightened eight-year old forever. You can grow up and become the wonderful man you were meant to be instead of being haunted by a terrible nightmare."

With Julie by his side, Timmy cautiously lowered himself into the seat. "I didn't make it up. It wasn't a nightmare. It really happened."

"We know, and we're all real sorry it did. But that was many years ago. And you had nothing to do with why it happened."

Timmy looked around. "I don't think Billy or Popwell believe me," he whispered to Julie. "Popwell never let me come out and tell what happened to anyone; not Huff and Henry or Dr. Rasher, or even to that nice Miss Duncan. Popwell and Charley made me stay quiet and hide away from everybody for so long."

"That was a big mistake," she said, taking his hand. "And they're really, really sorry now. Can you look inside your head and see Popwell? I'm pretty sure Popwell is sorry he didn't let you come out before. I bet even Charley feels bad."

Julie watched, as Timmy's shoulders began to relax as if a terrible weight had been lifted.

"So, I don't have to be scared anymore?"

Julie nodded and smiled. "It's okay to let go of the pain."

"How?" Timmy asked.

"Well," Julie whispered softly in his ear. "Billy tells me, you grew up to have the best knuckleball he's ever seen? In fact, you might even find yourself playing for the Cubs one day. Would you like that?"

"You bet," Timmy beamed. "You really think I could do that, Julie?"

"I know you can."

A moment later, Timmy was gone and Popwell appeared in his place. He rose from his seat, walked onto the field and headed for the pitcher's mound. Not just any pitcher's mound, but the one smack dab in the middle of Wrigley Field. He picked up a baseball lying on the grass behind the mound, then toed the rubber. He focused on the square painted on the back of the batting cage, came set, reared back and threw. The ball arrived and kissed the strike zone right down the middle.

52

Frank Tortiricci stood by the dugout, resplendent in a cream colored blazer and beige Dockers with razor-like creases sharp enough to slice cheese. He had been at the stadium for hours, chatting up the scouts, and laying the groundwork for the tryout. He did his level best to appear confident, despite the unending cascade of sweat dripping from nearly every pore on his body. Of and by itself, this was nothing new to Frankie. For years he wrestled with perspiration under pressure. But tumultuous events leading to hyperhidrosic episodes in the past, paled in comparison to his present level of anxiety. There was a lot on the line today. On the one hand, should the day prove successful, it would undoubtedly increase his leverage with Cubs upper management. On the other hand, trotting out a 'nearly was' Billy Rubin and his crazy pal, B.J. Popwell, under the guise of a serious tryout, could land Frankie flat on his ass, a total laughing stock.

He bit off the tip of a finely wrapped seventy-five dollar Gray Cliff with the grace of a starving seagull, nearly choking on the tightly wrapped layer of tobacco hurtling from his gullet with an unrefined loogie. He checked his watch for the fourth time in the last three minutes wondering where the hell Billy was. His concerns were put to rest when he caught sight of him pushing open the gate and strutting towards him.

Despite Julie's words of caution, he had to admit, Billy looked great, more than great. He looked like an All-Star, poised to step back into the spotlight. His dazzling smile, well-defined physique, and confident swagger screamed major endorsements down the road. And, as any sports agent worth his diamond-studded tie clip knew, that was where the real money was. Untold millions waiting to be plunked down by fans eager to grab a small piece of someone else's hard-earned accomplishments. 'God bless America,' he thought to himself.

So what if an athlete has a few loose screws? Got a little depressed now and then – or had an occasional violent outburst or two? A player with anger management issues was certainly nothing new in the sports world. In fact it might actually add to his mystique if it surfaced Billy once tried to check out inside a Ziploc. Of course, it wasn't likely they'd be offered plastic bag endorsements anytime soon… but, hey, there were plenty other Fortune 500's up for grabs. And what did Julie call this Popwell guy again -- Dissociative? Okay. Different -- but definitely do-able.

The agent clamped the unlit stogie between his teeth and waved Billy over. "Looking fucking good, man," Frank said, sticking out his hand.

"Feeling good, Frankie," Billy said, slapping five against Frank's slippery palm. "Whoa." Billy chuckled, drying his fingers along the side of his 501's. "You trying to get me nailed for having a foreign substance on my bat?"

"Nothing foreign 'bout good honest sweat," Frankie cackled. "C'mon. Let's take a little walk and go over a few things before the scouts come back down."

Frank tucked the cigar back inside the breast pocket of his blazer. "Think I'll save this little beauty to celebrate after the tryout. Besides, we wouldn't want anyone accusing me of 'blowing smoke' up their ass today, now would we?" he chortled, a bit more tensely than he intended it to come across.

"Relax, Frankie. It's a lock. We're gonna impress the hell out of these guys. You already know how good I am," he said, punctuating the remark with his trademark wink, "and there's no way Popwell's gonna disappoint."

Frank stopped walking and looked Billy squarely in the eye. "About this Popwell. I spoke with Julie, and – just how is this supposed to work – between you, me and him? I got papers that need signatures."

Billy grinned. "Look Frankie, if you're worried about someone trying to screw you out of your commission, you can stop worrying. I've got it covered. You and me, we've got a history. Right?"

"Right," Frank answered, dabbing at the fresh layer of moisture beading across his brow. "But, I gotta tell you, I'd be feeling a whole lot better if I could hear that from this Popwell as well."

Billy took a moment, lowered his head, reached up and rubbed the muscles in the back of his neck. "Listen. Popwell's got a gift, an extraordinary arm. But we wouldn't want to risk doing anything that could throw him off his game before the tryout. Know what I mean?"

Frank nodded, though not entirely on board. "Yeah. Sure. What the hell, we'll worry about the details when the verdict is in."

Billy ducked into the locker room to change into his gear. He ached to be back in the game. He dropped his duffle to the floor, took a seat on one of the benches and glanced around the room. Caps and cleats were neatly displayed on the top shelves. Spotless uniforms with player names emblazoned on the back hung in the lockers. The fresh scent of linen lingered in the air. More so, the scent of 'major league' was everywhere.

Billy could feel the presence of the legendary Cub players wherever he looked. How many, he wondered, once sat on this very bench, lacing up their cleats? He was definitely pumped as he stood to square the peak of his cap in a nearby mirror, before striding confidently out onto the field.

He was greeted by Larry Watson, the assistant scouting director who introduced him to the two scouts who held his future in their hands. One was Russell Cambridge, who started in the Cubs organization back in the sixties. His weatherworn face was deeply wrinkled, topped by a thick mane of gray hair slicked back with Pomade. A stopwatch swung from his neck.

The second scout, Pete Brooks, was lithe and considerably younger, most likely a player at some point. Billy could tell by the way Brooks looked at him when he spoke, he remembered Billy from his days at USC. Unfortunately, Billy couldn't tell if that would prove to be a help or a hindrance.

They gave him a little time to loosen up, then pointed him to the outfield to run wind sprints, clocked by Russell's trusty stopwatch.

"How's your trigger finger this morning?" Billy shouted with a grin, as Russell paced off sixty yards of turf. "How 'bout a two second head start?"

The crusty scout was not amused. "Let's hope you don't need one, son."

Billy knew most scouts set a target time of under seven seconds. He wasn't worried. In the old days he could do that in his sleep. Besides, he'd put in enough pre-dawn practice runs, dragging a junkyard tire roped to his belt to ensure he could pass Russell's muster. He reached down to touch his toes and get in one final stretch right before Brooks yelled, 'Go,' and he was gone, full throttle motoring across the grass.

From the minute he pushed off, until he sped past Russell at the finish line, it felt good. With a quick sideways glance, he could see Brooks making notes on his clipboard. When the scout motioned for Billy to 'set up' again, Billy nodded; fairly certain Brooks was paying particular attention to see how well his knee would hold up during repetitive speed drills. The second and third sprint seemed a touch off his first, but not enough to dampen his spirits.

Without comment, Brooks told him to grab his glove and trot out to right field. The scout picked up a fungo bat and made Billy scamper, intentionally sending some flies into the gap in deep right center, way out of Billy or anyone else's reach, which ticked him off royally. But, despite the difficulty of the task, if Billy managed to get a glove on the ball, he'd catch it. "Eat that, scumbags!" he muttered beneath his breath. "It's gonna take more than a couple of tight-assed scouts to make Billy Rubin look bad."

Billy raced in after a short pop fly, dove, and made an incredible shoestring catch. In the process, he could feel the muscle behind his left knee tighten but refused to let it show. It was bad enough submitting to the indignity of their scrutiny like a never played, wannabe, but there was no way he was going to allow these scouts to sniff any trace of weakness.

"Let's see what kinda arm you got?" Brooks yelled, as he threw the ball high, blasting a shot out to deep right. Fortunately, this was where Billy had always excelled. He had a cannon for an arm since high school. Rarely, if ever, was he challenged by a runner trying to take an extra base, or tag up from second to third. And if they did, most often, they paid the price.

Billy snagged the long fly, then rifled the ball home. Unfortunately, the ball bounced between home and third and landed in the dugout. His accuracy was off. The next few pegs were no better. Then, Brooks hit a lazy looper to short right. Billy raced in, caught the ball on a fly, and in one fluid motion, fired it so far over the catcher's head, it caromed off the screen behind home plate and landed on the pitcher's mound.

Fuckingshit! Billy mouthed beneath his breath. Luckily, this part of the tryout wasn't a total disaster as Billy earned an 'A' for consistently hitting the cutoff man.

All things considered, Billy waxed philosophical; given a little time, he was certain his dead-on, split-second precision would find its way back to him. Surely, a sharp guy like Brooks would see that.

Billy sprinted back to the dugout, and grabbed his bat. He stepped into the on-deck circle, popped on a donut and took a few practice cuts.

The scouts had brought in a pitcher from one of their farm teams. Billy eyeballed the young buck waiting on the mound. An insidious hint of doubt began to gnaw at him, until, out of nowhere, he could swear he heard Henry and Huff shouting words of encouragement. Telling him he still had the chops to get it done! He headed to the plate with the old, shit-kickin' Billy Rubin grin plastered across his face.

But when Billy lifted the stick off his shoulder, he discovered his bat speed wasn't quite as fast as it used to be. The young southpaw had a good array of pitches, his fastball firing somewhere in the low nineties. And testing his mettle against a good curve or a tricky slider was something the steel arm of the batting cage couldn't provide.

Billy fouled a few off, then made good contact on the next two pitches, hitting two streaming liners that got lost in the ivy in deep left center. He was psyched. A couple more wicked shots to right and a blast that went foul in the upper deck in left. He was just finding his groove when Russell suddenly waved the pitcher off the mound. Billy was puzzled, as Russell approached. "Thanks, Billy. Nice job. We'll be in touch," he uttered in monotone, extending his hand.

At first Billy was too dazed to respond. Nice job? That's it, he thought. "I got a lot more to show you, Russell."

"No need, son. We saw what we needed to see."

"But, I was just starting to hit my stride."

"Like I said… we'll let you know."

By sheer social reflex, Billy shook the scout's extended hand. It felt weightless in his grip. The entire experience seemed surreal. It had all gone by in an instant. He stared down at his hand as if searching for an explanation.

He didn't see the expression on Frankie's face as the agent watched him disappear within the darkness of the locker room tunnel.

Frankie had personally assessed Billy's performance as, 'not half bad.' But, the wily agent had been in the game long enough to know it might not have been stellar enough to force Farley's intractable signing hand. He was nervous, realizing at this point his last hope of really impressing the scouts lay with a guy with multiple personalities and a pitching arm he had yet to see for himself. Aw, fuck it, he thought. I oughta go find Billy and talk to him. As Frank started for the aisle, he spotted the General Manager heading in his direction. Too late. No time to hold Billy's hand right now. Just enough time for some major grinning and spinning.

As Billy approached the locker room, the pain behind his knee intensified. He ripped off his jersey and flung it against the far wall. Blinding regrets clawed at his brain like howling furies. Hot, salty tears blurred his vision. The dream was over. He felt naked, exposed, imploding with self-loathing. His fingers grasped at his neck in desperation as his throat muscles choked closed with the venomous bile spurting up from his gut. He raced to the bed of sinks on the far bathroom wall. He tore at the faucets, cupping and thrusting overflowing handfuls of water against his skin. And then in an instant, everything stopped; the clatter in his brain, the fever beneath his skin.

"Guess I should be going out there," Popwell broke in, as if little of Billy's ranting had had the slightest effect on him.

Billy stared into the mirror dumbfounded. In his torment he had completely forgotten about Popwell.

The old scout stepped off the field for a minute to give his grandson, Chip, the Cub's newest batboy, a little encouragement and a few inside pointers before working his first game tomorrow. Chip was the only one of his grandkids who seemed to share Russell's devotion to baseball. Yes sir, Russell thought, swelling with pride. Working at Wrigley, even as a batboy was an honor.

"What did you think, Grandpa?" Chip asked, leaning against the rail. "This guy good enough to make the cut?"

"We'll see," Russell said.

"Holy crap," Chip whispered, pointing toward the field. "What the heck is that about?"

Russell spun around in time to catch Popwell emerging from the dugout dressed in his vintage Highwater uniform, looking like he stepped out of a time machine. Russell scratched his head in wonder.

Chip whipped out his cell phone in an attempt to capture a video of

Popwell striding toward the mound.

"What do you think you're doing?" Russell demanded.

"You kidding, Grandpa? This has got to go on YouTube. Like, right now."

The old scout quickly wrested the young man's phone from his eager fingers, and clamped his wizened hand sternly around his startled grandson's wrist. "You get this back, Chipper, only if and when I'm sure you understand the way things work around here. Nothing that happens during any of my tryouts goes anywhere. You got me, son?"

Up in the stands, Frank Tortiricci stood alongside Farley watching Popwell as he rubbed up the ball. "This some kind of joke, Tortiricci?" Farley spit out. "'Cause, I'm not laughing."

For once, Frank had nothing to say.

53

It felt like popcorn popping inside her. A surprising, wonderful sensation that took her breath away. It was weird knowing no one could feel or hear it but her. At this very moment there was a tiny, perfect person living within a person, poking at her ribs. She wondered if being pregnant felt anything like being a multiple. Having someone with separate thoughts and independent actions inside her, waiting to get out and find their place in the world. "Know what your daddy's doing right now?" she asked, leaning back in her desk chair. "He's at Wrigley Field showing off."

Her cell was within arm's reach on her desk, confident Billy or Frankie would be calling any second with good news. She desperately wanted to believe in the healing power of baseball as Billy did. That getting back his dream of playing in the majors would help him move beyond the emotional struggles that plagued him. She had to believe today's tryout would be the beginning of wonderful things to come. That soon the real Billy would be back, front and center stage. Cocky and self-assured, playing ball, signing autographs, and preening for his adoring fans.

Helping to sustain her positive posture was a bit of office gossip Howard let slip when she ran into him in the parking lot this morning. It seems, Michael Whitethorn, the second V.P. of Marketing would be exiting the Chicago branch sometime in the next few weeks and word had it they were particularly interested in filling the position with a woman this time to satisfy their diversity quota.

Julie wanted that position. The work would be far more challenging, and far more creative. Not to mention a healthy salary bump, which combined with Billy's anticipated salary from the Cubs, would easily allow them to hire a top-notch nanny. It might take a little finessing, what with planning to take a few weeks off when the baby arrives, but one thing was definite, she had no desire to be a stay-at-home mother.

She was about to order lunch when she looked up to find Billy standing in the doorway. She could read it all in his face.

"I never had a chance," his jaw tightening as he spoke. "I was just getting started when they cut me off. I never got to show them what I could do. This old scout, Russell... it was like he didn't even want to see the real me out there. He looked right through me, like he was doing me one big, fat favor just by showing up."

"What did he say?"

"That they'd seen enough."

"Well," Julie offered hopefully. "Maybe they did. Maybe it went better than you think."

Billy dropped the duffle to the floor with a noisy thud.

"What about Popwell?" she asked.

Billy shrugged, lost in his own anger and disappointment. "Don't know. Don't care."

"Then... then how do you know if... if maybe..."

"What the hell difference does it make!" he shouted, pounding her desk so forcefully the fringe on the lampshade rocked back and forth.

Julie tensed. "Stop it, Billy. Please don't do this here."

But Billy wasn't listening. "Don't you see," he spouted. "When the tryout was over they were supposed to want me – Billy Joseph Rubin, not Popwell. Me! I don't give a flying fuck how Popwell did."

Julie grabbed his hand. "C'mon. Let's get out of here for a while. We could go get something to eat, or just take a drive somewhere."

Despite her better judgment, she decided not to protest when Billy insisted on driving her car. They wouldn't go far – just far enough to put some distance from the tryout, and to hopefully gain some perspective.

As they pulled onto Lake Shore Drive, Julie broke the agonizing silence, hoping to lift his spirits. "I felt the baby kick this morning."

Billy took his eyes off the road for a second to glance at her stomach. "Oh yeah? What'd it feel like?"

"Like butterfly wings. I can't wait for her to do it again, so you can feel her too."

Billy returned his eyes to the traffic up ahead. "That's great," he nodded, with a deeply contemplative expression. She waited quietly, wishing she knew what he was thinking.

"I think it's time we got out of Chicago," he announced. Not exactly what she was hoping to hear. "Start fresh. Maybe your mother was right. Maybe we should go back to California. There's nothing here for me anymore."

Julie could have dealt with maudlin hyperbole, self-absorbed tears, or even a volatile outburst, but this... this was unacceptable. "First off, my mother is *never* right, and second, we can't just pick up and leave. I don't want to leave Dr. Sarah... and what about my career? I'm just starting to make contacts here, to network. I can't just pack up and go, not with a possible promotion coming up. If I move again there's no guarantee I can find this kind of opportunity anywhere else."

Billy's eyes clouded with intensity. He knew on some level he was being selfish but, how could she compare her stupid job to what he was going through? If it were up to him, they would keep driving and never look back. But he did look back. There, in the rear view mirror was a late model green sedan maneuvering dangerously close to his rear bumper. Billy sped up, but so did the sedan. He pressed down harder on the accelerator. Julie's head snapped back against the headrest. "Billy, please slow down."

"I can't. Some asshole's trying to run us off the road."

"What! Why would someone want to run us off the road?" Julie craned her head around to see what Billy was talking about. Incredibly, the driver behind them was in fact on their tail, smacking his horn, wildly waving with his free hand.

It was impossible to tell what he was gesturing about, but he obviously had no intention of slowing down. "Pull over," she urged. "Maybe he just wants to pass."

But Billy was in no mood to be bullied. Not today. Rather than pull over, he eased his foot onto the brake pedal and slowed, forcing the sedan to cut its speed as well. The driver tried to maneuver into the left lane, but the flow of traffic prevented it. So he sat on his horn instead. The grin on Billy's face spread as he began to enjoy this little contest of wills.

A half-mile down the road the green sedan found an opening, and slid into the right lane. Too soon to let the game end, Billy floored the accelerator, and zipped out in front of him again.

"Billy!" Julie screamed, as she gripped the armrest, closed her eyes and prayed, suddenly finding themselves inches from the back of a flatbed truck directly up ahead.

Billy slammed on the brakes, miraculously avoiding a collision with the flatbed. The sedan however, unable to stop in time, barreled into the rear of Julie's car. Julie shrieked as the airbags deployed.

There wasn't much of a shoulder on this part of the Drive, just a narrow stretch of grass. Billy pulled the car as far out of the lane as possible, as did the front-crumpled green sedan. "Are you alright?" he asked. Julie nodded, brushing the airbag residue from her blouse.

The surrounding cars slowed to a crawl, pausing to gape while attempting to circumnavigate the unfortunate fender-bender. Before Julie could stop him, Billy kicked open his door and leapt out with blood and vengeance on his mind. The driver's door on the green sedan kicked open as well.

"What the fuck were you trying to do back there," both men screamed in unison.

Billy blinked his eyes; his jaw flopped open, dumbfounded upon discovering the other driver was Frankie.

"What the..." was all Billy managed to utter.

"I'll tell you what the, you lunatic. I've been trying to flag you down for fucking miles, then you go and make me wreck my fucking rental. I'm telling you this much," Frankie blustered, surveying the damage to his car, "this is definitely coming out of your first week's pay. And another thing, why the hell wasn't your cell phone on? Huh? Huh? Answer me that!"

Billy remained mute, hearing perhaps only every other word beyond 'your first week's pay,' as Frankie scurried around to the passenger side of Julie's car. "Jeeze. You okay in there, Julie?" he asked, with concern.

"What are you saying, Frankie?" Billy called after him.

"The scouts liked what they saw," Frankie shouted, above the swirling din of cars blurring past. Julie was too excited to stay inside the car a moment longer. Despite angst driven reservations about standing inches from the mid-day crush, she stepped out and excitedly threw her arms around Frankie's neck.

It took Billy a full ten seconds to compute, but when it did, "You better not be shitting me," Billy warned.

"Hey! Who's shitting who here?" Frankie grinned. "You think for one fucking minute I believed that cocky-assed ego of yours thought you wouldn't make the team? I'll tell you this much, the pitching fucking blew them away! They never saw nothing like it, I swear on my mother."

"Sure. Fine," Billy piped in. "But, what about my fielding? The shoestring catch? I could tell Brooks was eating it up. Man, I wish I could've been a fly on the wall when he reported back to Farley. C'mon, Frankie. Do I have to beg? What else did the scouts say about me?"

"They said you were --" Frank hesitated for a moment, "-- you did good. Very good," he offered, whipping out a large white hanky to wave off the on-coming traffic.

"And?"

"And what? They wouldn't be signing you if they didn't want you."

Though not quite enough to satisfy Billy's appetite for praise, he let it pass. "Okay. So what happens next?"

Julie hugged the side of the car as she inched closer. "Hey guys, could we maybe talk about this somewhere else? Somewhere a little safer, like not out in the middle of Lake Shore Drive?"

"What happens next is..." Frankie repeated, turning to Julie with a smile. "We can start forwarding Billy's fan mail care of the Iowa Cubs."

"The I-Cubs?" Billy said, his face suddenly dropping. "The minors?"

"Hey," Frank jumped in, "You're back in the game. Even A-Rod did a month in the minors before re-joining the Big Club. And that was after eighteen years playing in the majors. You were in the majors for what? Eighteen fucking minutes!"

Frank made his point. The important thing was Billy would be back playing ball again. "Okay," the young athlete admitted begrudgingly. "You're right... but, Iowa?"

"What's wrong with Iowa? The corn is fresh, the natives are friendly, and the sky is a hell of a lot bluer than Chicago. You and Julie are gonna love it there."

Billy shot a quick glance in Julie's direction. Right now, he could tell she was as caught up in the excitement as he was and he loved her for it, but was it fair to ask her to follow him to Iowa, to give up everything she had going for her in Chicago to go watch him play ball? Besides, once they got there, they wouldn't have much time to be together anyway. He'd be spending every day with the team. And what about when the I-Cubs went on the road? She'd be stuck in a strange new town without any friends or even a career to occupy her time. That kind of sacrifice can grow old pretty quick. She might even come to resent him before long. And that was a chance he didn't want to take, especially with the baby on the way.

"Wait a minute, Frankie. Let's not get ahead of ourselves. I don't see why Julie has to pick up and move to Iowa with me?"

Julie looked startled by Billy's remarks.

"Well, I just thought," Frankie continued, stumbling over his words. "I figured you'd wanna... you know... especially under the circumstances... "

"I know the circumstances," Billy quickly countered, "and just so you know, as long as I'm playing baseball, I can keep it together. I don't need a babysitter. I don't want Julie shortchanging her own career to follow me out there."

"I appreciate that Billy, really I do," Julie offered sincerely, "but I think it's important that I go to Iowa with you."

"What about the possible promotion coming up? And, didn't you just tell me you didn't want to leave Dr. Sarah right now?"

"I know, but... Dr. Rasher is concerned that..."

"I don't answer to Rasher anymore," he said, carefully keeping his anger in check. "Look, it's not like I'll be away all that long. The regular season will be over in a month or two. I'll be back way before the baby's born, and in between, you can take the train down for some of the home games. We can make this work for both of us. Besides, I know how these things go. Once I get down there and show them what I can do, it won't be long before I'm called up to the majors. I'll be back in Chicago before the ink dries on the contract. So there's nothing to worry about. Isn't that right, Frankie? Go on, tell Julie there's nothing to worry about."

Frank nodded slightly and bit his lower lip. "Yeah. Sure. Hey, what the fuck? I'm not worried about a thing," he lied. "But all the same," after clearing his throat and taking in Julie's anxious expression before proceeding. "Maybe we'd all feel a lot better if you gave us your word you'll find a good shrink as soon as you got settled in out there. We know you can handle yourself on the field. It's off the field we're talking about. We could keep it on the down low. No one else has to know a thing about it. If you'd like, I could ask around. Please, let me do this for you."

Billy rocked back on his heels and stood his ground. "All you have to do for me," he bristled, "is tell me when we leave."

54

Billy handed his credit card to Ceasare Balaban, owner of Balaban's Auto Body for banging out the dents on Julie's car. As he stood at the counter, he noticed a team photo of fifteen cherubic little boys in baseball uniforms hanging above the cash register. "One of those Little Leaguers yours?" Billy inquired, making small talk as Balaban ran his card.

"All are mine," Balaban boasted. "I am part time, after-school Pee Wee league coach. Six years I coach. Sometimes..." he grinned, displaying a mouthful of teeth yellowed by decades inhaling Karelia cigarettes, "...sometimes I think I like spending time with the little boys more better than working on broken cars."

Popwell, decidedly uncomfortable, mumbled something incoherent, and took off.

"Receipt?"

"Huh?" Billy said, distracted by Popwell's abrupt departure.

"Receipt," Balaban repeated, sliding Billy's paperwork across the counter.

"Yeah. Thanks," Billy replied, as he took off for the parking lot. "What gives?" Billy asked, as he slid into the driver's seat and started the engine.

"He made me wanna hurl."

"Who? Balaban?"

Popwell grimaced. "I couldn't take the stink of grease on his filthy hands."

"Well," Billy suggested, "roll up the window 'til we get on the road and maybe it'll pass. We'll be back at Julie's in no time."

"Julie's?" he said with vacant eyes. "Who's Julie?"

"Who's Julie? My Julie. Julie Hatcher." Billy paused, quickly realizing Popwell was no longer there.

The newly emerged alter said his name was Cal. Barely more than a boy. A boy with a secret. His manner bespoke a loss of innocence. His lack of candor made communication all the more difficult.

He seemed however to know all about Billy and Popwell's tryout, admitting he had watched from the shadows on numerous occasions as Popwell threw his mystifying pitch; a pitch Billy was about to discover began with young Cal, and not as he had believed with B.J. Popwell. Billy was intrigued to discover Popwell wasn't the only alter who possessed the ability to throw the extraordinary knuckleball.

As long as Popwell remained sequestered at Highwater, Cal was content to leave things as they were. But now that Billy was about to bring Popwell's knuckleball out into the world, Cal could no longer remain silent.

"Popwell needs to know the truth about Jeremiah, before it's too late."

"Who's Jeremiah?"

"The one who taught us..." Cal started to reply, then quickly covered his face with his hands, trying to hide the fact the corners of his lips were twitching, his cheeks puffing and pulsing beyond his control. He hated the bizarre, facial tics that made people stare and pity him. He didn't want Billy's pity. He wanted his help. "I have to make things right. I've got to find Jeremiah. I need you to take me back to Belleville."

"Belleville?" Billy leaned forward, resting his hands on the steering wheel. He felt a familiar tightness in the back of his neck he hadn't felt since Highwater. Not ten feet away, he could see Balaban and a few of the mechanics standing around wondering why Billy hadn't left the lot yet.

"Look, Cal... I'd like to help you out, really. But, Belleville is like... a good two hours from here. And, Popwell and I, we've got a lot to do before we leave for Iowa, so if you don't mind..."

Despite his youth, Cal was determined not to cave. "Popwell's not going anywhere with you. Not until I can make things right. You have to help us. There's nobody else."

Billy didn't even pretend to understand Cal's plight. It was all pretty confusing, not to mention exhausting, and he was fast running out of time and patience. He certainly didn't need some new crisis on the eve of his return to pro ball. But one thing was clear, either he was going to end up dragging this new alter down to Iowa and hope he could persuade him to let Popwell re-emerge in time to suit up and play, or he was going to drive to Belleville.

Since he couldn't will Cal away, he threw the car into gear and squealed out into traffic heading north on Jefferson toward the Dan Ryan Expressway. Though not exactly familiar with the route to Belleville, he figured he needed to get onto the I-55 south, trusting somewhere along the way Cal would guide them to their final destination.

He knew he should let Julie know where he was going, particularly since he was taking her car without running it by her. But for now, he figured she was better off not knowing any of the particulars. Hell, *he* didn't know the particulars yet. Nonetheless, he had to admit there was a part of him that was curious to meet the mentor behind that astounding pitch.

No further disclosure or even simple conversation passed between them as they traveled down the highway. Though Billy tried, it was obvious Cal had no intention of divulging anything more than he had unfinished business with this Jeremiah person.

Billy fiddled with the radio, hunting for a familiar station, only to have it sputter and fade each time they drove out of range. As the first Belleville exit sign came into view, Billy went to switch to another station. When he reached for the buttons, he felt a strong hand encircle his wrist.

"Pull onto the shoulder, jerk wad," Charley growled, refusing to relinquish his grip.

"What are you doing, Charley!" Billy shouted, trying to maintain control of the wheel. "You trying to get us all killed?"

But Charley wouldn't let go. "You'd like that, Billy Boy, wouldn't you? You can't stand that the Cubs are more interested in Popwell than you. That's why you're going to Belleville. To get back at Popwell. Turn the car around! Nobody needs to go to Belleville and dig up the past." Billy struggled to maintain the upper hand, but Charley grabbed the wheel, forcing the Honda up onto the shoulder. Billy hit the brakes hard, turned off the engine, and bolted from the car.

"Damn it, Charley!" he said, slamming his fist on the roof of the car.

"Ow! Please don't do that," Timmy suddenly pleaded, covering his ears with his hands. "Big, banging, noises make me nervous."

Billy didn't know why Timmy chose this moment to return, but there he was behind the wheel. The angrier Billy became, the more frightened Timmy became, quickly locking the car doors. Billy's frustration grew beyond words at his inability to exercise control over the rapid infusion of alters. They seemed to be popping out and switching so rapidly of late, it was becoming a challenge just to keep up with the growing cast of characters.

"Timmy!" Billy demanded, "You have to let me talk to Cal again, or even Charley."

The last thing Timmy wanted was to witness another scary fight between Billy and Charley. Panicking, his fingers found the ignition key and the Honda purred to life, bucking its way back onto the road. Timmy managed to maneuver but a few hundred yards of highway, traveling at speeds no greater than ten to fifteen miles per hour, while traffic swerved and screeched around him, blasting their horns.

A panel of red and blue lights flashed in the Honda's rear view mirror. The voice of authority barked from a loudspeaker ordering him to pull over. Timmy had no choice. When he yanked the key from the ignition, the car slowly drifted to the side of the road and stopped. He pushed open the door and jumped out.

Two Highway Patrol officers pulled up and exited their vehicle, their hands suspended gingerly above their gun holsters. One officer had a round, rosy red pudgy face, flush from a surge of adrenalin. His partner was tall as a lemon tree, with a bushy yellow mustard colored mustache that made Timmy giggle as it wriggled back and forth each time he spoke. "I need you to get back inside the vehicle, sir," ordered the mustard mustache.

"I'm not a sir. I'm Timmy," he responded, smiling with unabashed innocence.

"Back inside the vehicle, sir. I don't want to have to tell you again."

The sternness of his voice made Timmy exceedingly anxious as he crawled back into the front seat and gripped the wheel with ten trembling fingers, hoping Billy would come find him. The officer motioned for him to roll down his window.

"License and registration," he demanded.

"I don't have a license," Timmy whimpered. "I'm… I'm only eight." Timmy looked up into the hard-jawed officer's face and burst into tears, but the officer wasn't buying it. "Please don't take me away, Mr. Policeman. I like where I live now. I'll be good. I promise."

"Have you been drinking, sir?"

Timmy sopped up the tears that trickled down his face with the cuff of his sleeve. "I had a root beer," he thought to confess. "A&W. It was good. But, it was really, really cold. Billy told me if I drank any more it would make my brain freeze. So I didn't."

The officer peered inside the vehicle. "Is that yours?" he said, pointing to the soft brown wallet wedged between the two front seats.

"Uh-uh. It's Billy's," he replied, handing it over through the open window. The officer removed the license, passed it to his partner, and handed the wallet back to Timmy.

"Step out of the vehicle please, sir." When he asked him to walk a straight line, Timmy thought they were playing a game. So at first, he kept his gait nice and steady, putting one foot in front of the other, but then he figured he might earn extra points by hopping backwards. He didn't.

The yellow mustache crinkled in the fading sunlight like a dried up Kleenex as he stepped forward and told him to blow into the Breathalyzer tube. Timmy was confused. He thought the officer wanted to take his temperature.

"I'm not sick," Timmy told him. "Honest. Cal just wants Billy to drive us to Belleville."

"He's clean," the officer said, as his partner returned from the patrol car and handed the license back to Timmy.

"The vehicle is registered to a Julie Hatcher," said the round pink face, squinting down at Timmy, "You know this Julie Hatcher?"

"Uh huh. She's the nice lady who lets me stay at her house. She makes me peanut butter sandwiches."

"You wouldn't happen to know her phone number, would you?"

Timmy brightened, then proudly reeled off the numbers just the way Julie had taught him.

Though Julie had no idea why Billy, and apparently Timmy and God knows who else were on their way to Belleville in her Honda or why Billy had seen fit to let Timmy drive, she thought it best not to try to explain the complex bizarre behavior occasionally exhibited by someone with Dissociative Identity Disorder to a patrolman standing by the side of a busy highway.

Thinking quickly, she decided her best shot at defusing the situation was to appeal to what she hoped would be the officer's sense of patriotism. She proceeded to tell him the man behind the wheel was a returning vet, a decorated war hero, who had recently returned from proudly serving his country in Afghanistan and suffered from occasional spurts of inappropriate behavior. She assured him he was currently in the care of a well-regarded therapist who was certain he was not a risk to himself or anyone else. She also insisted the Honda was not taken without her permission, so there was no need to press charges.

The officer cast a compassionate eye in Timmy's direction as he sat quietly a safe distance from the traffic, contentedly drawing stick figures in the dirt with his finger.

"I sympathize, Miss Hatcher. I got a brother who served in Afghanistan. I hate what this damn war did to him, but I can't just let him back on the road. Maybe," the officer considered, "if you're willing to come out to Belleville and pick him up... "

With a huge sigh of relief, Julie promised to leave immediately, but first asked if she might be able to talk with him and tell him she was on her way.

The officer handed Timmy the phone and watched as his face lit up at the sound of her voice. After he told her what happened, she made him promise to listen to the officers and not go off anywhere on his own ever again. That he needs to tell Billy everything as soon as he shows up, and that he should let Billy handle things until she gets there and takes them home.

It wasn't long before Timmy found himself looking up into Billy's worried face.

"It's okay, Billy. The policemen aren't mad anymore. The man with the funny mustache spoke to Julie and she explained everything. Only, she doesn't want any of us to drive her car right now. She's coming to pick us up. She told me not to say another word... to anyone," he said, locking his lips with an imaginary key. "Just to wait here quietly 'till you showed up again."

The pink-cheeked officer drove Julie's car into the historic little town of Belleville, and as arranged, pulled into the parking lot of an all-night diner.

"I just wanted you to know, we understand what you've been through, soldier," the officer remarked. "My own brother served two tours over there. When he came home the first time, he screamed in his sleep like a banshee. My cold-hearted sister-in-law took the kids and left him. You're lucky you got a good woman who understands."

Billy nodded silently, trying to make sense of what the officer was saying and all that must have transpired in his absence. The little he'd been able to piece together from Timmy led him to believe Julie had come up with some kind of fabrication that seemed to satisfy the officers. He considered it wise not to contradict anything she might have told them if he intended to do what he could for Cal, then get the hell out of Belleville as quickly as possible.

"Now what?" Billy asked, to no one in particular, as the officers drove off. "This has to stop," he said, slapping his palm on the dashboard in frustration. "I can put up with Popwell, but everybody else has got to leave me alone." As he raised his hands to massage his throbbing temples, Timmy spoke up hopefully. "Could we get some ice cream at the diner?"

Billy sighed again. "No. No ice cream. No nothing. Not now. I think we can both agree you've caused enough trouble for one day."

This time it was Timmy who sighed, then promised he'd do anything if Billy would stop being mad at him.

"You can let me speak with Cal."

Timmy nodded, then closed his eyes allowing Cal to re-emerge. Cal looked around, oblivious to the earlier events, as if no time had passed since he and Billy first set off for Belleville. "Take a left at the next light."

Billy wasn't too keen on doing anything that might invite further run-ins with the law. But, he also knew at best, it would take Julie some time to get there. So after checking to make sure the highway patrol had left, they headed off down the road.

Cal's directions led them to a quiet tree-lined street, dotted with modest two-story houses with shingle roofs and white vinyl siding. Though Cal attempted to remain calm, the facial tics returned. Billy couldn't help but notice how tightly his hand gripped the door handle when they pulled up in front of the third house on the right.

Without a word, Cal got out, and slowly made his way up the flagstone path leading to the front porch. The young alter hesitated briefly, then rang the bell. He flinched as the yellow porch light went on, painting him with its eerie amber glow. An elderly woman with hair the color of fresh fallen snow cracked open the door. It seemed to Billy, no more than a brief exchange followed before the woman went back inside and turned off the light, leaving Cal alone, silhouetted in the deepening umbers of waning daylight.

Cal bolted from the porch, and raced down the block. He ran with the speed of a tireless teenager, up one street, down the next, crisscrossing backyards and alleyways until he scaled the chain link fence behind Signal Hill Elementary School.

Billy called out after him. He had to get back to the diner before Julie learned he was out chasing after another of Popwell's maddening delusions. He searched behind bushes and out buildings until he found him cowering behind a row of bleachers in the back of the schoolyard.

"Cal, we've got to get back to the diner." But Cal wasn't going anywhere. "Whatever it is," Billy offered, "it's gonna be okay. I mean it. C'mon. Tell me what we're doing here. Maybe I can help."

"You can't help. No one can anymore."

"Why'd you take off like that? Was that where you used to live?"

After a moment, Cal choked back his anger. "No. It was his house. But not anymore. The old woman said Jeremiah's dead."

"I don't know what to say... I guess... I'm sorry," Billy offered in sympathy.

"Don't be. I'm only sorry I didn't get to tell him how much I hated him before the bastard died."

Billy failed to understand Cal's anger toward the person who taught him and Popwell the art of perfecting a perfect knuckleball.

"Popwell didn't know Jeremiah like I did. He wasn't there when it happened."

"I don't understand."

"Popwell couldn't know what happened in order to survive. But, I knew what Jeremiah did. I couldn't take anymore. That's why I had to disappear and let Popwell take over."

"What happened here, Cal?" Billy whispered, almost afraid to ask.

Cal stood up and walked over by the schoolyard fence. He curled his index fingers through the chain links, reconnecting with the dark, twisted images of his past. Reliving the pain only he could remember. The young boy began to tremble.

Billy was overwhelmed. He wished he had waited for Julie. He wished he hadn't followed Cal. He wished he'd never come to Belleville.

A cool night breeze whistled through the schoolyard, lifting and swaying the creaking tree branches in a dance above their heads.

"He used to hang around the schoolyard," Cal began in a haunting monotone, "and watch us play ball when he wasn't down at the garage fixing cars. His hands smelled like grease, but we didn't care. Everybody liked Jeremiah. He wasn't like other grownups. He didn't treat us like a bunch of stupid kids. We called ourselves the Belleville Bellevederes. Sometimes, after a game, especially if we lost, we'd pile into the back of his pickup and he'd take us all out for pizza and soda. Sometimes, if we won, he'd even sneak us a sip or two from his beer mug if no one was looking.

He was always telling me how special I was. Why he chose me instead of the other kids to learn his knuckleball. At first I didn't get it. But Jeremiah wouldn't let me give up. We'd practice four, five times a week until it got too dark to see the ball. Sometimes, if we didn't feel much like practicing, we'd go back to his house. He had this really neat model train set he put together. He told me he bought it for his kids, but something happened and they didn't live there anymore. I felt kind of bad for him when he told me, but I was secretly happy I didn't have to share the trains with any other kids.

Whenever things were bad at home, I wished I could stay at Jeremiah's forever. He didn't care how much TV I watched, especially if the Cubs were on. He never yelled at me for messing up, or pushed me to do homework. He didn't even care if sometimes I had to bring my sister with me. He'd just sit and talk with her while I played with the trains or went out back to practice my pitching.

One day I came home from school and found my sister crying on our back steps." Cal paused as the words became more difficult. "I asked her why she was crying, but she wouldn't tell me. I wanted to make her stop, so I took her hand and told her we could go over to Jeremiah's and I'd let her play with the trains. She started kicking and screaming, saying she didn't want to go. But, I made her go anyway. The whole time we were there, she didn't say nothing – not even a word.

Later, when we were walking home, she told me she never wanted to go back there ever again. She ran into the house, right up to her room and slammed the door. She wouldn't talk to me, or anyone. I figured she was just being a brat like she always was.

That night when I was trying to finish my math homework, she came into my room. Her eyes were all red and puffy looking. When I asked her what was wrong, she told me, Jeremiah was a bad man. I got angry. I told her to shut up, that she was just jealous because he was my friend and I didn't care what she thought.

She started to cry again and told me he made her touch him in bad places, and that he touched her in bad places too, and that it hurt. Then he told her not to tell anyone or she'd be in a lot of trouble. He said child services would take her away. Maybe take me away too and they'd make us live somewhere else.

I didn't believe her. I told her to take it back, but she wouldn't. I said she better stop making up stories or else, then I yelled at her and told her I wished she wasn't my sister and to get out of my room. In the morning, my foster mom said she ran away. Everybody was going crazy looking for her. It made me feel like for once, I was the 'good' kid, the one that wasn't causing any trouble. I was still pretty mad at her for fibbing, so at first I didn't care where she went.

Two days later they found her… at the bottom of the lake. She was all blue and still. Everybody said it was an accident, but I knew it wasn't. 'Cause I knew how good she could swim. I should've believed her, y'know, what she said about Jeremiah. But I didn't. I didn't do nothing to help her, nothing to stop him," Cal added, overcome by guilt and shame.

"You can't blame yourself for what happened," Billy offered, hoping Popwell might have heard Cal's tragic tale as well. He needed to know, to heal and move past it. "There are a lot of bad people out there. I think you were very brave to come back to confront Jeremiah."

"It's too late to make him pay for what he did. I hate that he's dead," Cal admitted, solemnly.

"It isn't right," Popwell intoned without emotion, re-emerging with young Cal's tears still fresh upon his cheeks. "I was given the gift and all Cal was left with was the pain."

Billy couldn't help but be moved by Popwell's words. "We need to help Cal make things right."

The moon was out in full when they tiptoed through the unlocked gates of the local cemetery and wound their way in the darkness, past neat rows of headstones searching for Jeremiah's gravesite.

When they found it, they quietly emerged from the shadows. Billy, Popwell and Cal, seeking revenge for the theft of a child's innocence. Cal turned away, unable to face the patch of overgrown weeds that covered Jeremiah's remains. Popwell stared at the simple burial plaque which revealed for all eternity little of Jeremiah's ugly past. Billy knelt down and traced the raised lettering with his fingertips;

BELOVED HUSBAND, SON, AND FATHER
MAY HE REST IN PEACE

Nowhere was it written how he preyed on helpless children. How he tricked them. How he hurt them. Cal stepped forward; a pocketknife clutched in his trembling outstretched hand. He offered it to Billy who offered it to Popwell.

There, on a starless summer night, the past and present collided. Each took their turn, hacking, scratching and slashing repeatedly against the headstone until Cal was satisfied the world now knew who truly lay beneath the dirt. He stepped back to admire their handiwork --

CHILD MOLESTER -- MAY HE ROT IN HELL

PART FOUR

55

The left field gate burst open and Arabella, a 250-pound show pig wriggled and squealed her way out onto the field to the crowd's delight. It was Honey Baked Ham night at Principal Park, and the company was sponsoring a raffle with the promise of a year's supply of sausage links to the lucky winner. Arabella was none too pleased with the grand prize and chose to exhibit her displeasure by wresting free of her restraints and running amok. A handful of wranglers gave chase, ultimately hog-tying the little porker, but not before she managed to dump a sizable load on the beautifully manicured infield.

Kip Chapman thought it was a hoot-and-a-half and let out a raucous belly laugh as he emerged from the dugout. Sunshine played off his toothy smile and backlit his golden hair like Apollo ascending the heavens. He loped gracefully toward the crush of fans squashed along the rail like anchovies wedged inside a can. Scraps of paper clutched in their eager hands, hoping for his autograph.

The charismatic Chapman, barely out of his teens, was a church going, fun-loving good ole boy from Tupelo, Mississippi, bound for greatness. At least that's what the big-city sports agent told him the day he convinced him to scrawl his signature along the bottom of the contract spread across the mud-crusted hood of his daddy's John Deere tractor. From the morning Kip left the farm, he put his unwavering faith in God, family – and Frank Tortiricci.

Up in the stands, Billy felt a pang of envy as he watched Chapman sign autographs and pose for pictures with his fervent fans who continued to rush the rail and scream his name. It didn't help that Frankie was convinced Kip was nothing short of the second coming of Mickey Mantle. A boast that was starting to get under Billy's skin.

Moments later, a group of local cub scouts, whose proud parents paid twenty-five dollars a head for their progeny to have the privilege of singing the National Anthem, made their way onto the field. Cameras flashed non-stop as family and friends recorded the moment for posterity. When the small-town fanfare subsided, the Triple A, Iowa Cubs took the field amid boisterous cheers.

The visiting Oklahoma Red Hawks hadn't won a game in weeks. So the I-Cub fans had every expectation of an easy rout as they stuffed their faces with Casey's pizza, Stew's BBQ and Principal Park's infamous Hot Meat Sundaes.

But, when the visiting Red Hawks posted a surprising five, coupled with the I-Cubs anemic bats that found it impossible to get off the schnide through six, Principle Park became as quiet as a dropped call. Even the weather took a sudden turn, as the sun fell behind a procession of dark, ugly clouds slowly drifting across the Capitol building beyond the right field stands.

Through it all, Popwell maintained a position of silent observation, watching the game unfold through Billy's eyes, sensing his Highwater teammate's restlessness growing.

For Billy, the spectacle on the field showed little to support Frankie's overblown estimation of Chapman's abilities. Thus far, the fabulous farm boy had produced little more than two groundouts to short. But it wasn't just Chapman's lack-luster performance that occupied Billy's thoughts at present. His focus kept drifting back to their meeting with David Wagner earlier that day.

From the moment Billy entered Wagner's office, the manager seemed to eye him like a slab of moldy cheese, well past its prime.

"I pride myself on instilling a solid work ethic in my team. As long as you work hard, keep your nose clean, and dedicate yourself to what we're trying to do around here, who knows. As time goes on, you may be in line for a spot in the starting lineup."

Billy was rattled by the notion he might for one second be relegated to being a sub. Billy Rubin doesn't ride the pine anywhere, let alone in the minors. Though Popwell appeared unfazed, Billy was starting to believe Rasher might have something to do with Wagner's lackluster welcome. Who else could have poisoned the well? Who else had an axe to grind and an inside track to Wagner's ear? It certainly wasn't Frankie. There wasn't any profit in it. It had to be Rasher, licking his professional wounds after being abruptly dismissed. He had to fight the urge to storm from Wagner's office, take the next flight back to Chicago and wring the doctor's miserable neck.

Billy's head began to pound. He couldn't wait for Wagner to shut up so they could leave. When he couldn't take it any longer, he offered a half-hearted, 'yeah, thanks, it's great to be here,' and bolted from the room. He took a few shaky steps down the hall, then leaned back against the wall to steady himself.

"Hey! What's with the lousy 'tude?" Frankie barked, barreling down the hall after him. "That didn't go so bad in there, did it?" The agent paused, assessing the situation. "Hey. Level with me. You okay? 'Cause you're sweating like a choir boy caught whipping on his dummy by a nun."

"Yeah. Sure. I'm fine. It's just…Wagner could've been a little more receptive. But hey, that's cool. I'll live. Right?"

"Fucking right, you'll live," Frankie offered. Then taking a step closer and lowering his voice by half. "But… look… if it'll help, I got a couple Valium in the trunk of the rental car and…"

"No." Billy fired back. "I don't need pills."

"Okay. Okay. I get it," Frankie responded, raising his palms, backing off. "The happy pills weren't my idea anyway. Julie just thought, y'know… in case you might need something to take the edge off from time to time. That's all."

"I told you, I'm good," Billy insisted.

A thunderous wallop rang out in the seventh as the ball exploded off the bat, returning Billy's focus back to the game in progress. Chapman had just lined a three run homer pulling the team within two. And in the ninth, he sent the crowd home happy with a monstrous grand salami, and an Iowa Cubs come from behind win.

"Did I tell you Chapman was the fucking man," Frankie exclaimed, leaping to his feet. "C'mon," he motioned with a, 'follow me' wave. "Let's get down to the locker room. I wanna introduce you guys."

The clubhouse reeked of aftershave, talc and up-beat conversation. Several players had already changed into street clothes, and were ready to head out. Wagner was all smiles as he wended his way among the team, slapping backs, and shaking hands. As of today, the I-Cubs were firmly ensconced in second place; just three behind Nashville, and a weekend sweep against Omaha could really keep the pressure on.

Chapman stood by his locker, a thick white towel slung around his slender hips, responding politely to an endless list of questions posed by a local reporter. When asked if the hero of tonight's game expected to get called up to the majors to help with the playoff run, Chapman grinned sheepishly. All Kip expected right now, he insisted, was to put some juicy beef ribs in his belly and continue to give his all to the Iowa Cubs and their wonderful fans.

"Besides," Kip opined, "getting called up ain't up to me anyhow. That decision is up to God in Heaven, Mr. Farley in Chicago and," he added, spying Frankie entering, "my agent, Mr. Frank Tortiricci. Now, Mr. Tortiricci is who you ought to be talking to. Not me. I'm just a simple farm boy living his dream because of that man right over there."

Billy found Chapman's self-deprecating modesty as nauseating as he did watching Frankie sashay up to the reporter like a proud papa. Billy felt like an outsider, with Chapman fast becoming the poster boy of his resentment. The broader Chapman smiled, the more Billy disliked the self-proclaimed, 'simple farm boy,' and his oh-so-humble routine. It didn't help that Kip played the same position as Billy. His obvious talent wouldn't be so hard to swallow if he were, say, a third baseman. But, he wasn't. Billy took a deep breath and tried to channel his thoughts elsewhere. But every sappy homily and quip that dropped from Chapman's lips, made Billy feel like gagging.

When Frankie beckoned him over, Billy stood his ground. There was no way he was going to bow and scrape to Chapman, especially in front of a reporter. If Frankie's flavor of the month so much as tried to smart mouth him, he'd deck him flat, Press or no Press.

As soon as the interview was over, Kip headed directly up to Billy and extended his hand. "I can't believe I'm actually shaking hands with the great Billy Rubin from U.S.C. and The Kansas City Royals!" he gushed. And then, careful not to leave anyone out, "And of course, Mr. Popwell, with the golden arm. Welcome. I am honored to be playing on the same team with y'all. Oh. And by the way, Billy," Kip added, taking him into his confidence, lowering his voice to a whisper only a long-eared bat could hear. "Just so you know… you don't have to worry about me. I'm cool with it."

Billy squared his shoulders and took a quick step back, eyeing his chatty, new teammate guardedly. "What I mean is," Kip continued, "about Mr. Popwell. I've got an uncle back in Pelahatchie… Uncle

Findley, by name. Findley Kip Chapman. Fact is I was named after him. Well, anyway, people thought Uncle Findley was a little… y'know… different too. But me, I just thought of him as special."

Decidedly cynical, Billy couldn't help but wonder just how much information Frankie had already shared with Chapman. Regardless, Kip's enthusiasm and boyish naiveté were fast becoming difficult to ignore.

Chapman tightened the towel around his waist. "Hey, I don't know about you all," he said, poking at his washboard abdomen, "but my belly is a growling something fierce. I was fixing on heading over to the Raccoon for some down-home eats. How 'bout you all joining me? I got a whole mess of things I'm just dying to ask you about. I mean… for example, you and me, Billy. We got us a lot in common. You know, 'specially with us both being right fielders and all. What do you say? You like ribs?"

Kip's charm was totally lost on Popwell, who had no interest in making a new friend. It was obvious Popwell had depleted his tolerance for socializing with strangers by now as he opted to retreat quietly from the scene. Frankie had several crucial business calls to make, and so declined as well. But Billy found it increasingly hard to say no to Kip.

When they got to the restaurant, Kip requested a quiet booth in the back, but it hardly mattered, for wherever Kip Chapman sat within a hundred miles of Principal Park, he rarely could partake of an uninterrupted meal. All eyes were riveted on him as he ripped into his third slab of barbequed beef. "Best dang ribs this side of Tupelo!" Billy couldn't agree more as he leaned back with a gentle groan, loosening his belt a notch or two.

A youngster, a few years north of potty training, sporting an I-Cubs baseball cap, half covering his tiny, apple-cheeked face, shyly walked up to ask for Kip's autograph. Kip searched the tabletop for an unsoiled paper napkin to write on. He joked about how many autographs he'd signed accompanied by a dab of hot 'n spicy barbecue sauce, then took the time to carefully straighten the little guy's cap before sending him on his way with a freshly signed napkin and a big smile.

Despite his earlier resentment, Billy was starting to get a kick out of Kip's folksy, down-home demeanor. After all, it had been awhile since he had the chance to kick back and talk baseball with someone who wasn't crazy or on meds. It even fleetingly crossed his mind that

Chapman might be the real deal, a genuine, guileless young ballplayer who shared Billy's total absorption with the game.

Conversation and pitchers of Raccoon River Lager flowed freely as the hours drifted by. To help maintain his buzz, Billy graduated to Boilermakers. He lowered his eyelids to a squint, and stared at the row of shot glasses brimming with Tequila on the table before him, shimmying like a pack of impatient puppies pleading for his attention.

"Ever had one of these back in Tupelo?" Billy asked, reaching for a glass.

Kip shook his head, "Nope. Beer's pretty much been it for me."

"Well, I guess to each his own," Billy said, as he jerked back his head, and tossed the golden contents down his waiting throat, quickly followed by a long pull on his beer stein. "Here's to the hero of today's game," he offered, hoisting another shot.

Kip picked up his beer, then placed it back down, opting for one of the remaining Tequila shots instead. "Hey, what the heck. Here's to the up-coming Omaha series. Let's sweep those pea-pickin' mothers!"

Mimicking Billy, he threw back his head and swallowed. The alcohol rocketed through Kip's untempered gullet like battery acid sucked from a tractor. His eye sockets burst with tears, as the Devil's flames licked at the inner lining of his chest.

Billy started to laugh as he picked up the pitcher, topped off Chapman's glass and nudged it across the table. "Here. You gotta follow it up right away or it just might kill you."

Kip grabbed the glass with both hands, and drank until the burn subsided. Billy shook his head sagely. "I guess Boilermakers are an acquired taste."

As the evening wore on, Kip set about acquiring the taste. Conversation became less lucid, but remained honest and sincere, none-the-less.

"Sometimes," Kip slurred in confidence, "I swear I love baseball even more than gettin' laid. I bet you think I'm crazy as a June bug?" Before Billy could respond, Kip leaned across the table, and pressed a lazy finger to his lips. "Never mind. You don't really have to answer that." Kip was feeling no pain as he slid Billy's drink back across the table and grinned. "C'mon. Drink up and let's go shoot us some pool."

Kip's legs buckled as he rose from the table cradling the frosty pitcher in the crook of his arm. "Follow me," he babbled, as he wobbled off.

Billy fired off a sloppy salute and attempted to stand up a touch too quickly. He steadied himself by grabbing onto the edge of the table, then barely managed to drop a fistful of dollars to cover the bill before venturing off to find Chapman.

Meanwhile, Kip was attempting to make his way through the crowded restaurant. Unfortunately, he was far too wasted to realize just how wasted he was. Too drunk to notice the burly Red Hawk fan who had driven in from Oklahoma to attend today's game and had chosen this very moment to get down on one knee and propose marriage to the girl he had loved since high school.

With a thunderous crash, Kip toppled over him, showering the contents of the pitcher, and ending up face down in the lap of the young man's intended. The startled young lady began screeching like a hoot owl. In an instant, six of the man's closest, and largest friends, dressed in matching Red Hawk t-shirts, jumped up en masse like a crimson-colored mountain rising from the sea. Kip barely managed to lift his head in time to see the first of many fists slam into his face.

The diners seated nearby couldn't believe they were witnessing their beloved Kip Chapman being pummeled at the bottom of a pile of human flesh. An English teacher from the local elementary school scrambled from his chair yelling for them to leave Chapman alone or he'd call the police. His skittish wife, fearing her husband was no match for a bunch of out of town, drunken hooligans, grabbed his arm and pulled him back inside their booth.

Billy stumbled to Kip's aid, along with half a dozen local I-Cub fans. Chapman fought back valiantly, but his alcohol-soaked brain was having difficulty distinguishing friend from foe and the last thing he wanted to do was bloody the nose of one of the faithful.

Chairs flung, punches flew, as the Red Hawk contingent realized not only were they engaged in defending a lady's honor, but that the man who so rudely crashed their party was none other than the I-Cub right fielder responsible for the heartbreaking Red Hawk loss.

While the free-for-all continued, Billy somehow managed to pull Kip out from under the pile of testosterone driven brawlers and slip him out the back as police sirens wailed off in the distance.

56

Four hundred miles away, the stench of rotting flesh roused her from sleep. Julie threw back the bed sheets and sat bolt upright. It was two a.m. The room was black as a witch's cauldron and twice as hot. Noticeably silent was the usual hum of the air-conditioner. She covered her mouth and staggered into the living room, but found it no better out there. She pulled open the terrace door, grabbed onto the railing and nearly heaved the spicy enchiladas she consumed earlier over the side to the street below. This was definitely not morning sickness.

She chalked it up to fatigue and having eaten dinner much later than usual, due to the fact some co-workers decided to throw an impromptu bachelorette party for one of the hotel clerks at a nearby Mexican restaurant. At first, Julie planned to decline the invitation since she barely knew the bride-to-be and wasn't particularly close to any of the other women who would be there. But, by the end of the day, the thought of returning to an empty apartment with nothing more enticing than peanut butter and jelly, provided all the excuse she needed to change her mind.

The evening proved more fun than she thought it would. Mariachi music blared; conversation was lively, the restaurant festive and the food fantastic. But being pregnant took its toll.

So here she was on her terrace staring at the city lights below, knowing the first glint of sunrise was a mere few hours away. She desperately wanted to crawl back into bed, but the noxious bedroom odors would make her puke for sure. She considered curling up on the terrace, but an unexpected flock of noisy birds, swooping perilously close to the railing made her dart back inside to the safety of her living room. How odd, she thought. Even the birds can't sleep tonight. As much as she hated to wake Mr. Theophilous, the building super, she really had no choice.

Gregor Theophilous, arrived at her door a short time later dressed in rumpled, blue striped pajamas beneath a thin cotton robe that did little to hide his formidable middle-aged pouch. Had it been anyone other than Julie, his favorite, sweet little pregnant tenant, he never would have picked up the phone at this ungodly hour.

As soon as he walked through the door, there was no denying something was very wrong. Mr. Theophilous insisted she wait in the hall while he checked things out. About fifteen minutes later, he came back out holding a wadded hand towel up against his mouth and nose and announced in muffled, broken English, "Eatz boidz, Mizz Joolie. Boidz in your valls."

Julie stared back blankly. "It's what?" she asked.

"Boidz," he said, dropping the towel to felicitate communication. "Boidz," he repeated, flapping his beefy arms up and down.

Mr. Theophilous concluded, several wayward birds had managed to fly in through an air duct that connects to the roof, and set up nests. They must have gotten trapped in the electrical wires and died somewhere inside her walls.

It may have been the heat, or lack of sleep, or the thought of frantic mother birds and their precious little babies perishing that gave rise to the trail of tears that rippled down her cheeks like summer rain.

The creases in Mr. Theophilous forehead burrowed into a frown. "Oh, Mizz Joolie, pleeze, no cry. Gregor will fix. Apartment be fine as new."

After a scant two hours of sleep, Julie eventually dragged herself into work an hour later than usual. She was armed with little more than fresh clothes, a few layers of concealer to mask the dark, puffy circles beneath her eyes, and a decaf Caramel Macchiato she picked up along the way to wash down her baby vitamins. She closed the door to her office, flopped into her chair, turned on her computer, peeled back the lid of her coffee and took a sip, determined to get through the day as best she could.

She swiveled in her chair eyeballing her email, hoping Billy might have written. But he hadn't. Though he'd only been gone less than twenty-four hours, she already missed him like crazy.

She was lost in thought when Howard poked his cheerful face in through the doorway.

"Hey, Jules, got a minute? I need the Pharma convention dates. I don't want to overbook. Those 'pill-pushers' get kinda testy if they can't drop their suitcases and head for the open bar the minute they arrive." He took a step inside, then stopped, folding his arms across his chest. "By the way, you look like total crap this morning."

"Thanks for pointing that out, Howard," she murmured, stifling a yawn as he dragged a chair up to her desk and sat down. "You always know just how to cheer me up."

"Must've been quite a fiesta last night. I thought it was frowned upon for pregnant women to tie one on nowadays."

"Virgin margaritas only," Julie corrected him, reaching for the Starbucks on her desk. "And this," she smirked, "just in case you're keeping track of all my bad habits, is baby-friendly decaf, thank you very much. And -- if I look like *crap*, as you so delicately put it, it's because I've got birds. Dead birds! At least a dozen of 'em."

Howard rocked forward in his chair, resting his elbows on her desk. "Birds? Where?"

"In my walls. In my bedroom. In my living room. Everywhere," she said, throwing her arms about. "I had to sleep on my super's couch last night."

Howard listened with sympathy as Julie somberly explained it could be weeks before she could stay in her apartment again... due to the fact they have to rip out some walls, replace the air ducts and the mangled wires, then seal it back up and re-paint.

"So whatcha gonna do? Where you gonna stay in the meantime?"

"Haven't got a clue. My super's been great, but I don't think I could wake up to the smell of souvlaki every morning without up-chucking."

Howard eased back against the chair giving her dilemma thoughtful consideration. "The way I see it, Jules, you basically have two choices; you could bunk here, or you could sleep on the pullout bed in my spare room."

Julie groaned, resting her chin in her hands. "Now why would anyone want to take in a fat, old, sloppy pregnant woman, Howard?"

"Hey. You're not... old," he offered, hoping to put a smile on her face. Julie started to laugh, causing a mist of Macchiato to spray from her lips in a most unladylike fashion. She reached for a napkin. "Thanks for the offer, but a pregnant woman needs her personal space. And, as for staying here, I'd have to be pretty desperate to sleep in my office."

"Who said anything about sleeping in your office? With one click of a mouse, I could set you up with a junior suite."

Julie took another sip. "Says who? The hotel's booked solid."

"Says me. There's always a vacancy if you know where to look. And since I don't believe the Queen of England is planning a visit anytime soon…"

"Like she'd really stay in a junior suite."

"Hey, everyone's looking for a deal. C'mon, Jules. It'd be fun. You could be like Eloise. Terrorize the night staff. Keep them on their toes. Order up room service at four in the morning. What do you say?"

57

Billy awoke surprisingly clearheaded following his night of merrymaking at the Raccoon. On his way to the ballpark he decided to make peace with his present circumstances. It isn't all that bad, he rationalized, being a big fish in a small pond for a little while anyway. And, having learned a thing or two from his Highwater days, he decided to make an effort to try and be 'just one of the guys' this time, instead of trading on his past accomplishments.

He was pumped as he sauntered into the clubhouse with a cheerful smile, looking forward to playing in his first game. Only, once his new teammates caught sight of him, his friendly, open smile was either ignored or met with glacier-like stares. Not quite what Billy expected. He decided not to dwell on it and go about his business.

As Billy looked around for a locker with his name on it, he literally backed into Marty Granville, the equipment manager, carrying an armload of dirty uniforms.

"Hey, sorry. I'm Billy Rubin. I'm looking for my locker."

"Yeah. I know," he shot back, ignoring Billy's outstretched hand. "Follow me."

Marty led him to the far corner of the clubhouse and pointed to a locker. "The name plate's on order. I'll tape something up in the meantime, when I get around to it," he muttered, before heading out, leaving Billy with the impression Marty couldn't get away from him fast enough.

He looked around for Chapman, hoping his Boilermaker baptism the night before hadn't left him with one hell of a hangover. He grinned, remembering how totally innocent yet smashed Kip looked right before that Oklahoma Red Hawk fan sucker punched him.

As he slid the top button of his crisp, new uniform smoothly through the hole, the third base coach walked up and told him Wagner wanted to see him in his office, a.s.a.p.

Billy nodded and grinned, pleased that Frankie must have interceded on his behalf, letting the manager know he wasn't quite 'feeling the love' upon his arrival. He was relieved to think Wagner was man enough to want to correct any poor first impressions. Billy decided for the good of the team to react with class, more than willing to forget the slight ever happened.

He knocked politely before entering. "You wanted to see me, Mr. Wagner?"

The manager sat back in his chair and fixed Billy with an unforgiving stare. "Do you know the legal drinking age in this state, Mr. Rubin?"

"Um. Twenty-one? Nineteen?" he answered, unprepared, crinkling his eyes against the harsh streaks of late afternoon sun splintering in through the window slats. Obviously someone informed Wagner that Billy had seen fit to explore the local brewery on his first night in town. "But, I can assure you," he added, flashing his most charming smile, "no matter what you might have heard, it was just a few beers," he lied," and I am well over the legal age."

"It's twenty-one," Wagner scowled. "Which means Kip Chapman is ten months and seventeen days shy of legal age. Which means," he repeated for emphasis, "if I didn't know the right people in the sheriff's department, my best player would be sitting in some sorry-assed jail cell right now thanks to you."

Billy's jaw dropped. He honestly had no idea the Mississippi hayseed was underage. It was becoming abundantly clear Wagner hadn't summoned him here to make nice and discuss the starting lineup. Clearly uncomfortable, Billy muttered a hasty apology then did his best to try and back-step from the room.

"Sit down," Wagner barked. Billy froze, respectfully removed his cap and obediently slumped into an armchair across from Wagner's desk. "As a result of your stupidity last night, Kip got busted up pretty good, injured his back. No telling how long he'll be out of the lineup." Billy could hardly believe the little scuffle at the Raccoon would sideline the young athlete. "Which leaves me without my star player going into the most crucial series of the year. And that, fucking pisses me off."

Wagner stood up behind his desk and jabbed a menacing finger in Billy's direction. "You wanna fuck with your own career, that's on you.

But you don't get to fuck with my ball club. You get it!"

Billy pushed against the arms of his chair, and rose to his feet. "I can fix this. Let me make it up to you. I'm as good as Kip, probably better. Give me his spot in the lineup and I guarantee we can still beat Omaha."

Wagner's fiery eyes locked with Billy's. "You got a lot of balls suggesting that, Rubin," he spit back. "Too bad your balls are bigger than your brain. Let me tell you something. Farley can send down anyone he damn likes, but that don't mean I have to play 'em. So you can just cool your heels. You'll get yourself up for every game, put on your nice, clean uniform and then, you'll get to play when and if I say so. You got me?"

Billy drifted from Wagner's office in a daze, nearly colliding with a few members of the team heading out to the field. As he fell into step behind them, not a one looked his way. The frosty behavior of his teammates back in the locker room made sense to him now. They all blamed him for Kip being scratched from the lineup.

It wasn't long before the sold-out crowd at Principal Park learned Chapman wasn't in today's lineup. Rumors and wild speculation surrounding last night's incident and the young ballplayer's condition rapidly spread like a child's game of telephone. Despite Frank Tortiricci's valiant efforts to downplay his clients' involvement in the circumstances leading to the fisticuffs, few in the local Press were buying it. The unabashedly shameless agent went so far as to suggest the possibility that young Kip wasn't even inebriated at the time. That he had in fact, displayed heroic valor under fire, with little regard for his own personal safety when he threw himself into the fray to break it up, hoping to prevent injury to others.

What Frankie and the Press failed to get was the simple fact, the fans couldn't care less if Chapman was underage when he downed a few at the Raccoon. The only thing on their minds was just how bad off was he?

There were those who believed he'd merely miss a game or two, while others predicted it might be weeks, maybe months before his return. One gentleman, clad in a postal uniform, swore on his honor as a United States civil servant, that Kip was in intensive care on life support. That he had nearly been stomped to death by an angry mob of Arab terrorists.

David Wagner had little time to concern himself with addressing public misconceptions. He had a game to manage. An important game he desperately wanted to win, with or without Kip Chapman.

Nick Thompson, the I-Cubs ace was able to hold Omaha to one run through six, but it was the only run of the game thus far. Each time the I-Cubs put men on base, the rally fizzled as fast as it began. Through it all, Billy sat quietly hoping Wagner might change his mind and put him in. But he didn't. In the ninth, the I-Cubs managed to load the bases with one out, hoping to pull out a victory, but their scrappy shortstop, Dustin McAllister grounded into a game ending double play. Omaha prevailed, 1-0.

As the players hung their heads making their way back to the clubhouse, Billy spotted Kip through the steamy glass doors of the training room, submerged in a whirlpool from the neck down. A purple welt, the size of a golf ball hung above Kip's half-closed left eye. A fresh stitch or two adorned his swollen lower lip. Apparently, Wagner hadn't over-stated the extent of Kip's injuries. Billy tried to piece together what happened last night, and just how much they had to drink. But, all that came to mind were some hazy images of ribs dripping with hot sauce, Kip mentioning something about wanting to shoot some pool, or get laid or something, and a bunch of jerks in red jerseys piling on top of them. He was hoping Kip didn't blame him for what happened the way Wagner did. At this point, he could use all the allies he could get. Then again, why should Chapman blame him, Billy reasoned, with his baser instincts. If Kip chose to drink, was it Billy's responsibility to stop him? And yet, watching Chapman boil in a vat of bubbling water like a Friday night chicken didn't make him feel any less culpable. So, Billy surmised, there was no time like the present to find out where they stood.

"Yo, Billy!" Chapman hollered, with a lop-sided grin, hampered by his ballooning lower lip. "Were we as snookered as two pigs staring at a wristwatch, or what?"

Billy couldn't help but grin. Chapman was definitely one for the books. No doubt, one day when they both took their place in the annals of baseball history, the incident at the Raccoon Brewery would find its way into baseball folklore.

As badly as Kip felt about missing the next few games, he confided in his new best friend, he wouldn't have traded last night for anything.

His first boilermaker, his first man-sized black eye and fat lip, not to mention the very special attention and phone number he got off this real pretty red-headed nurse at the E.R. At least he thinks she was a looker. It's hard to know for sure, since he was drunk as a skunk and could only see out of one eye. And then, with a concerted amount of effort on Kip's part, he leaned in closer, out of earshot of the trainer, and whispered in Billy's ear. "You gotta help me. I was so shit-faced I'm afraid I might have asked that purdy little nurse to marry me."

Billy stared back blankly, thinking, what the hell did Kip get himself into, until the young ball player roared his head back with laughter. "Gotcha!" Chapman howled, slapping at the water until it spilled up and over the edge onto the floor.

Billy shook his head. Damn, if hanging out with Chapman didn't make him forget his own problems – at least for the moment.

The following afternoon, the two teams met again with pretty much the same result. Wagner could barely look in Billy's direction without spitting. Billy thought back to the first time he met the surly manager in Dr. Rasher's office. How flattered he felt when Wagner recognized him. How he tried in vain to push Rasher into putting in a word to jump-start his return to baseball. Never in his wildest dreams did he think it would come to this, benched without a single turn at bat, watching Wagner watch Omaha beat the hell out the I-Cubs.

The next day, Wagner held a pre-game, closed-door meeting with the hope of salvaging the series by taking both ends of today's twin bill. The meeting wasn't meant to chastise. It was intended to boost morale and energize the troops by telling them this is not and never will be a one-man team.

"We need to put the last two games behind us," he said, as he paced the floor and emphasized the positive in a commanding voice. "Each and every one of you is capable of stepping up and getting this team back on track. So let's get out there and square this thing."

The motivational pep talk that spurred the team in the clubhouse quickly evaporated when Omaha easily rolled over the I-Cubs in Game One. The onslaught continued in Game Two as Omaha racked up a commanding seven run lead by the end of the fourth inning.

To Wagner's way of thinking, this game was over and done. He knew it. The crowd in the stands knew it. Hell, he was pretty sure by now his team knew it too. It ate at him that he still had to burn another pitcher after using six in the first game. He conferred with his pitching coach, who suggested he bring in his middle reliever, who had only pitched to two batters in the previous game.

Wagner paused in reflection, considering his options. He shut his eyes and massaged his temples, then reached for the dugout phone to inform the bullpen coach of his decision.

The coach set the receiver back on its cradle, cleared his throat, pointed to Popwell and yelled, "You're up." All eyes followed, as Popwell without expression, grabbed his glove, and started warming up.

As Omaha loaded the bases, hoping to add to their seemingly insurmountable lead, Popwell trotted in from the bullpen and took the mound as the public address speakers announced the change of pitchers. Murmurs buzzed through the stadium as fans scoured the pages of their programs looking for his name. But the programs had been printed days in advance, so no mention could be found.

Popwell got down to business, quickly striking out the next two batters on six straight pitches.

For the rest of the game, the fans sat in awe as his knuckleball continued to frustrate the opposing team. He struck out ten in the remaining five innings without giving up a hit. Although the I-Cubs wound up losing, 7-3, and the long, disastrous, winless weekend was finally over, everyone, including Wagner realized they had just witnessed something very special.

58

The I-Cubs had lost five in a row when Kip Chapman trotted out onto the field to take his place back among his teammates, smiling, waving, and acknowledging the huge outpouring of emotion accompanying his return. The hometown crowd was starved for the sight of their beloved Kip back in uniform again and doubly starved for a win. It didn't take Kip long to justify their loyalty, blasting not one, but two homers against the Memphis Redbirds in his first two at bats.

In a move to confirm B.J. Popwell's dazzling performance against Omaha wasn't a fluke, Wagner brought him in to relieve in the eighth. And he didn't disappoint, saving the game with two scoreless innings. Sugar plum dreams of vying for the division lead seemed possible again, though the I-Cubs were still seven games behind first place Nashville.

For Billy, the moment was bittersweet. Popwell's success should have been a testament to Billy's belief in his extraordinary gift. But it wasn't enough. It wasn't Billy driving the team to victory. It wasn't Billy the crowd was screaming for. It was Chapman and Popwell. Though Wagner's mood and spirit improved exponentially, Billy remained in the doghouse, yet to play a single inning.

By weeks end, the Cubs trailed Nashville by only five games, with Chapman racking up an additional six home runs while knocking in fifteen RBI's, and Popwell saving another three games before being moved into the starting rotation.

Billy trudged down the hall at a funeral pace to his tiny furnished apartment. He wasn't in the mood to talk baseball, pander to Timmy's childish whining, deal with Cal's constant need for reassurance, and certainly not for any of Charley's loud-mouthed opinions. Co-habiting with Popwell was like living in an army barrack. If he didn't feel responsible for dragging Popwell to Iowa in the first place, he'd be long gone by now. Why hang around if Wagner won't play him?

As his key turned in the lock, he could hear the house phone ringing. He knew who it was. Julie had already called several times today. As much as he missed her, he wasn't in the mood for another of her thinly veiled attempts to prod him back into therapy. All he wanted was to play baseball and be left alone.

He chortled, as it suddenly hit him how much like Popwell that sounded. The further irony being, the more like Popwell he became, the more Popwell got to live the life Billy wanted. Screw going back to some analyst's couch. All he needed right now was a little liquid therapy.

The phone finally fell silent. Billy grabbed a nearly-full bottle of vodka from the back of the kitchen cupboard and drifted into the living room. The Iowa Register was spread across the couch, rife with stories by local scribes touting Chapman's triumphant return and the team's intriguing new knuckleball pitcher. Billy shoved it onto the floor with the heel of his shoe, flipped on the TV and proceeded to drink himself into a numbing stupor.

A short time later, the strident rings from the phone positioned inches from his head, startled him awake. In his semi-functional state, his arms flailed outward, accidentally knocking the receiver from its cradle. It dangled, bobbing up and back like a flaccid bungee cord. He rolled off the couch onto his knees, and managed to crawl over and hold the receiver to his ear.

"Is that you, Billy?" Julie asked. "Please, tell me you're alright?"

He wanted to tell her he was, but he couldn't quite bring himself to, because he wasn't. "Yeah, it's me. I... I just got home. Sorry. Guess I knocked the phone over rushing to pick it up." He found himself instantly wishing he had never left Chicago and the sweet comfort of her arms.

The strain in her voice began to ease. "Well, I'm glad I finally got ahold of you." He closed his eyes, remembering how soft and full her lips looked when she spoke. "Mr. Theophilous called," she continued. "It looks like it's going to be at least a month or more before I can move back into the apartment."

Billy's bloodshot eyes darted to the bottle of vodka now tipped onto its side, slowly trickling its prized contents onto the carpet, drop by precious drop. "Christ!" he yelled, as he let the phone fall, scrambling to retrieve what he could salvage.

"It's really not so bad staying at the hotel. I don't want you to be concerned, Billy. Billy? Are you still there?" her voice called from across the room.

"Damn it, Julie. This is not a good time," he mumbled. Then, aware she most likely didn't hear him, scrambled back over to the phone and picked it up. "I can't talk right now."

"Okay. I just wanted to update you on the apartment, and..." she continued, but Billy wasn't listening.

"Fine. Stay wherever you want. What the hell's the difference?"

"What's going on, Billy?" When he failed to respond, she asked the obvious, "You're not drinking again, are you?"

"What's that supposed to mean?"

"Nothing," she murmured. "How's Popwell?" she asked, changing the subject.

"Haven't you heard?" he sneered. "B.J. is making quite a splash down here. He's starting his first game Friday night."

Julie paused briefly, then pushed on. "That's great. Isn't it? Maybe I could come out and see the game. I can talk to Frankie and..."

Billy felt sick. His head was throbbing. His stomach was churning. I gotta go, was how he left it, as he hung up the phone and tore off into the bathroom.

59

Popwell sat calmly in the dugout, oblivious to the mounting excitement of the sold-out crowd anxiously awaiting his first start. Suddenly, a captivating sound began to weave its way into Popwell's soul. The sweet, intoxicating voice made him rise from the bench and turn towards home plate.

There in the sunlight stood a vision with delicate, tapering fingers softly caressing a microphone. He watched entranced, as she sang the National Anthem to the unworthy crowd who failed to hear her hypnotic notes the way Popwell did. It was almost as if she was singing to no one but him.

A gentle breeze blew through the infield. Her simple dress of peach petal gossamer floated and fluttered around her goddess-like frame. Though he tried, he couldn't look away. She was beautiful and perfect. No doubt a person of enormous refinement.

"Ain't she the purdiest thing you ever seen?" Kip intoned wistfully, pointing to the object of their shared desire. "Miss Felicity Flattery. Her daddy owns the biggest horse ranch in Tennessee. In fact, I think he owns half of Tennessee. He's also a close personal friend of Mr. Jim Farley, which is why she's out there warbling. I'm afraid it would take more than playing in the minors to get into those silk panties my friend. Take my word for it, that little lady is way out of both our leagues."

Until Chapman brought it up, the thought of actually meeting her hadn't even occurred to Popwell. The mere suggestion made him weak in the knees. He sat back down on the bench and fiddled with the laces on his cleats. He had a game to play and he didn't like being distracted.

As Felicity was escorted from the field to a smattering of polite applause, Popwell thought she may have glanced in his direction and smiled for a second or two. A moment later, when Kip grabbed his glove and led the team onto the field to the roar of the crowd, the besotted pitcher rose from the bench and headed toward the mound.

Popwell had yet to give up a run in his first three relief appearances and Wagner was hoping the streak would continue as a starter. Popwell worked fast, pausing just long enough to get a sign from his catcher.

For the first three innings, he retired all nine batters, but when he returned to the mound in the top of the fourth, by sheer misfortune, there, on the fuzzy edge of his peripheral vision was an unexpected glimpse of the winsome Miss Flattery, seated in the third row behind home plate. With every warm-up he threw, Felicity's enchanting face, crowned by lustrous auburn hair, appeared in his sight line. He tried to zero in on the pocket of the catcher's mitt and block out everything else, but found he couldn't.

He was uncharacteristically wild with the first batter, walking him on four pitches. The image of Felicity's smile was branded in his brain. It unnerved him. He didn't come anywhere near the strike zone with the second batter and ended up walking him as well.

Wagner studied his pitcher long and hard, hoping his control hadn't abandoned him. Popwell stepped off the mound and turned from his catcher, staring off into the outfield, wishing he could erase her from his mind.

The minutes ticked by until the umpire peeled off his mask and headed toward the mound, demanding Popwell get on with the game. Wagner raced over. "Is everything okay?"

Popwell didn't respond, his eyes straying to where he last spotted Felicity. But she was gone. Maybe, he convinced himself, she was never there at all. He re-took the mound, and proceeded to set down the side.

By the end of the sixth, murmurs began to buzz through the stands as the fans realized Popwell had yet to give up a hit. He cruised through the seventh, retiring Nashville in order. When he returned to the dugout, his teammates immediately moved as far from him as possible, as is customary when a pitcher has his sights on a no-hitter.

When Popwell came out for the eighth, no one left their seats. The concessionaires sat on their hands, beer taps and soda fountains stood idle. The stands exploded each time Popwell sent another frustrated Nashville player back to the dugout. In the bottom of the eighth, Popwell sat alone, eyes straight ahead, concentrating on nothing. His teammates couldn't help but sneak a peek every now and then, but their stolen glances quickly darted to the ground, for fear of jinxing him.

The decibels rose as Popwell set the first two batters down on strikes in the top of the ninth. The next batter swung at the very first pitch and connected – a long blast to deep right. Kip Chapman raced back as far as the outfield would allow. He squinted up to the clear blue sky and...

An explosion of fiery flashes lit up the stadium, crackling and popping as thousands of cameras and cell phones raced to capture the moment.

To avoid being trampled by his teammates and the fans pushing onto the field, Popwell made a dash for the dugout. In addition to escaping the swarm, he hoped with a little luck he might be in and out of the clubhouse before the local reporters had a chance to corral him. He had no appetite for the Press, or for their stupid hyperbole and idiotic, questions.

He dipped the brim of his cap, lowered his head and made it as far as a few steps into the dugout, when a woman's voice shot over the railing and stopped him in his tracks.

"You were amazing! I'm so glad I was here to see it," Julie shouted with excitement.

Popwell muttered thanks, and continued moving swiftly past.

"Wait. Please. I need your help. I didn't exactly tell Billy I was going to be here today," she admitted. "Could you let him know I'm here and that I'm hoping he can meet me at the Bluebird restaurant for dinner tonight?"

60

Billy brushed past the crowd milling about the entrance to the Bluebird, one of the town's trendier establishments. The restaurant's dimly lit lounge was filled with stylish women sipping champagne from fluted glasses, tittering inappropriately across intimate, burnished rosewood tables with silver haired gentlemen old enough to be their fathers. Dotted among their ranks was a smattering of lonely Iowa singles hoping to discover soul mates before the night was over.

Billy couldn't help wonder why Julie chose to meet here. Any one of a dozen local greasy diners seemed far more appropriate given his current situation. But then again, before she took it upon herself to show up in Iowa uninvited, she may have mistakenly thought they had something to celebrate. After all, before today, she had no way of knowing his baseball career had fallen so far off track. Damn, how he wanted to stop by the bar and throw back a stiff one before having to face her with the ugly truth. He really didn't want to see the look of disappointment on her face fully sober.

As Billy wrestled with his resolve, a man in a cashmere sport coat stood up and blocked his way. "Excuse me," he asked, politely explaining it was his wife's birthday, while reaching for his cell phone. "Would you mind?"

Billy stared back blankly. "What? Why?" he asked in earnest.

"We're both big I-Cub fans," he said, pointing to himself and then to his nodding spouse. "Season ticket holders in fact," he added, proudly. Before Billy could react, the wife sidled up alongside him, and CLICK... FLASH, it was over and done with. Billy blinked, trying to wipe the blinding flash from his field of vision. When his eyes re-focused, he caught sight of Julie seated by the glistening Baby Grand piano. The pianist's agile fingers danced across the ivories with passion and skill. It might have been something by Mozart or Beethoven. Billy didn't know which, nor did he much care.

His heart quickened as she turned around, her face brightened at the sight of him. She stood up and leaned forward to greet him. Her lips tasted of fresh strawberries. Sweet and moist from the virgin daiquiri in front of her.

The moment's pleasure quickly faded when Billy discovered Frankie and Kip seated alongside her. He hadn't planned on having to share Julie with anyone tonight.

"Well, look who fucking decided to show up," Frankie groused. "C'mon. I'm f-ing starving," he added, signaling the hostess.

Billy managed to remain remarkably quiet through the rubbery shrimp cocktail, choosing to let Frankie hold court instead. He sat in stony silence as the agent prattled on about his latest self-aggrandizing accomplishments. Billy dredged his spoon through the lobster bisque, praying somehow the evening would end before anyone could get around to mentioning he had yet to add a single grass stain to his clean, crisp uniform. From time to time, he could tell Julie was hoping he would open up and contribute to the conversation. But he didn't, and thankfully, she didn't press. While waiting for their main course to arrive, Billy was grateful that Kip started asking Julie all kinds of questions about her job and the baby on the way. Billy had to admit, it wasn't hard to see why women found Kip so attractive. And that was sort of okay at first.

But when the Iowa Cubs superstar began regaling Julie with storied tales of his bucolic boyhood days on the farm, Billy watched her face. He couldn't believe she actually seemed to enjoy hearing every idiotic tractor pull and corn festival story Kip cared to tell. Laughing at all his jokes, regardless of their merit. As the evening wore on, he began to feel she might be enjoying Kip a little too much. Billy eyed Frankie's scotch and soda longingly.

When the waiter returned to refresh Frankie's drink, and inquire if he could get anything for anyone else, Billy twisted the linen napkin in his lap until it looked as if it had been pulled through a wringer. *Yeah,* a voice inside him screamed, *let's have a little something to get through this miserable night without losing it.* But Billy merely looked up at the waiter and shook his head.

Then, without warning, the conversation turned to the I-Cubs, and Billy became increasingly uncomfortable.

"You're right, Mr. Tortiricci," Kip said. "I have to admit, tonight was something special. A no-hitter sure doesn't come around all that often."

"Didn't I tell you he was something else? One of a kind," Frankie said, bending Kip's ear, then adding, "I'm telling you, true talent doesn't go unnoticed. We'll all be up in the fucking majors before you know it."

Julie smiled, then reached for Billy's hand beneath the table and held on tight. Billy wrested his clammy palm from her grip and used it to summon back the waiter. "Let's hear it for all the talented young players going to the majors. I think that calls for a celebration. Don't you, Julie?" he asked, rhetorically.

She held her tongue as Billy ordered the first of several vodka and cranberry juice cocktails. Instead, she looked to Frankie with pleading eyes. But Frankie, not wanting to create a scene in a place like the Bluebird, merely shrugged, implying they should let it go for now.

By the time dessert arrived, Billy was feeling no pain. The alcohol coursing through his system loosened his previously silent tongue. "Go on, Kip. Why don't you tell Julie about the time you smacked three homers in a row against Fresno? That ought to impress the hell out of her. Or... or... tell her about the night you were so wasted you proposed to the ugliest nurse in the E.R."

Billy slapped the table and laughed himself silly. Now it was Kip's turn to feel uncomfortable. He shifted in his seat, embarrassed both for Julie and Billy as well. No one spoke as Billy peered into his empty glass, then waved it high above his head.

"Hey!" he bellowed, above the muted mix of Mozart and dinner conversations filtering through the room. "What's an I-Cub got to do to get another fucking drink around here?"

Heads spun in their direction. Julie couldn't take much more. If Frankie or Kip wasn't going to do something, she would. She clamped onto Billy's wrist and lowered his glass to the table. "Billy, please. People are staring. You don't need another drink."

Billy shoved her hand away. "Sure I do. It's a party! What I don't need is you treating me like a dumb kid. I'm not freakin' little Timmy."

"Whoa. Let's just hold on there," Kip offered. "We don't need a repeat of what happened at the Raccoon."

Julie's questioning eyes darted back and forth between the two men. Billy grabbed onto the arms of his chair and tried to raise himself to a standing position. By now, his words were slurring together. "Thass-juss-great, Kip. Tell Julie all about the night at the brewery. Tell her how Billy Rubin got the great, under-aged hero so plastered he had the cow manure kicked outta him while good ole Billy wound up benched for eternity. Tell her how Wagner's turned me into a fucking joke. Go on. Run your mouth, farm boy."

Julie's eyes widened. "What are you saying, Billy?"

"It's nothing, Julie," Kip offered, his voice low, attempting to cool things down.

"Yeah," Frankie added. "He's drunk. He's not making any sense." Frankie swiveled in his chair to quell the unwanted attention they were garnering from the other diners. "Show's over, folks. Just a little joke among friends. That's all. Enjoy your dinner."

"Shut up, Little Frankie," Billy yelled, as he leaned in against the table, then turned to face Kip. He tried to focus as the blurry image of the young ball player seemed to double, then triple before his bleary eyes.

"Hey, Julie. Look!" he said, pointing a bobbing finger towards Chapman. "Three different Kips. Guess Popwell's not the only multiple on the team."

"Sit down, Billy. Please."

Billy grabbed onto the back of her chair. "Get your purse. We're outta here," Billy proclaimed, pulling his car keys from his pocket, only to have them slip from his fingers to the floor.

"I'm not going anywhere. And neither are you," Julie said, as she bent over and picked up his keys.

Billy rocked unsteadily on his feet and held out his hand, but Julie wouldn't hand them over. "Fine. Then fuck you, Julie," he spit back, and then, with a sweeping gesture of his arm to include the entire restaurant, yelled, "fuck all of you!" He staggered from the table, pushing wait staff and patrons out of his way. Julie felt a hard knot in her stomach like a tiny fist, as she felt their baby stir inside her. She couldn't let Billy leave like this. She had to fix things. She had to go after him.

"Let him go, Julie," Frankie urged, placing a firm hand on her wrist. "Don't get me wrong, I love the guy too -- but sometimes I swear I don't know why we put up with all his crazy-ass crap." Billy's outburst had put Frank in a lousy position and an even lousier mood. "It's hard enough signing and keeping talent on the right road without having to worry about putting out fires every other day."

"Stop it," Julie demanded, yanking her hand away. "You know that wasn't Billy talking."

"Yeah. Yeah." Frankie muttered. "I know."

"And, don't tell me not to put up with his crap. Can't you see it's killing him? You of all people know what baseball means to Billy. You can't turn your back on him. He deserves your respect. Seems you've forgotten, without Billy you never would have had the chance to represent Popwell." Not knowing who she was most angry at right now, she grabbed her purse and started to get up from the table.

Kip thought it best not to get in between his agent and Billy's girl, but felt the need to say something. "I don't think Mr. Tortiricci is saying you should walk away, Julie. Just, maybe you shouldn't go running off after him just yet. Maybe give him a little time to cool his heels and sober up first."

Julie looked into Kip's kind and thoughtful eyes, realizing what he said made sense.

A short time later, Kip drove Julie over to Billy's apartment and offered to go inside and check on him with her. God knows it would be nice to have some support if Billy was still raging out of control. But she also knew the last thing Billy needed right now was an audience.

Kip smiled weakly, and gave her a lame, 'thumbs up.' "It's gonna be alright. You'll see. Billy's a great guy and a hell of a ballplayer. He's gonna get it together and turn this thing around, you just watch."

Julie waited for Kip to leave before knocking. As her knuckles rapped against the wood, the door swung open, singing like an un-oiled gate.

She took a tentative step into the darkened foyer. It was quiet as a tomb. "Billy? It's Julie." Her voice echoing off the empty entry walls, as she closed the door and felt around for the light switch in the dark. A small table lamp went on in the living room. Its 40 watts splaying an eerie shadow over someone sprawled face down across the couch. "Billy? Popwell?" Julie asked, with no response. As she drew closer, it became painfully obvious who lay before her reeking of alcohol. "C'mon, Billy. Wake up and talk to me," she said, speaking firmly, as she prodded him on the shoulder. He grunted incoherently, briefly arched his back, then collapsed with the full weight of his body, his right arm dangling off the couch like a lazy metronome abruptly brushed against her leg. Julie jumped back. "Jesus, Billy," she fumed. "I didn't come all the way from Chicago for you to shut me out like this."

"I didn't tell you to come," he mumbled. "Go home, Julie. We don't need you here," he said, turning his face away, burying it deep into the upholstery.

"I'm not going to leave you alone like this."

"Alone!" Billy chortled. "I'm never alone thanks to Popwell and his band of merry mad men."

Julie grew angrier by the second. She felt like shaking him, but the baby began pressing against her bladder. Frustrated, she left him there snoring while she went off to find the bathroom. When she returned, Billy had turned off the lamp. The only light spilling into the room was a soft glow coming from the refrigerator that had been left opened. It was all too apparent there would be no chance for any kind of meaningful communication between them tonight.

She made her way into the kitchen, turned on the overhead light and slammed the refrigerator door, not caring if it woke him or not. A calendar held in place with a magnet, fell to the floor. Her eyes began to moisten as she read Billy's handwritten entries. He had written down every one of her scheduled baby check-ups, some of which she could barely recall, and had set up a countdown to the baby's due date. How could she feel all this anger and resentment at his totally outrageous behavior, yet continue to love and need him as much as she did? It was nearly impossible. He was impossible. How many times had she tried to convince herself it could work? She curled up on the loveseat opposite the couch and watched her hopes drift away once again.

It was a mistake to come to Iowa. She could see that now. Somehow she had lulled herself into a false sense of believing Billy was making real progress. The months of therapy and the promise of resurrecting his baseball career let her believe the demons that plagued him had been overcome. Tonight was a hard reminder of how far Billy still had to go.

Tears from a shattered heart streamed from her eyes. And in the morning, when Billy awoke – she was gone.

61

It was getting harder to drag himself down to the ball park each day, let alone summon the desire to suit up. What for, he lamented, staring at the uniform hanging in his locker. No one really cared if he showed up or not. It was like he didn't even exist – at least not the Billy Rubin he once was.

Adding to his misery was Julie, the one person he thought he could always count on. She made him look like a fool in front of everyone last night. Right or wrong, she should have backed him up. She should have been in his bed, lying next to him in the morning when he awoke. But she wasn't. He didn't even know where she slept last night. Or even where she was right now.

Billy looked up as Kip Chapman entered the locker room. Ugly images began to form in Billy's head. Ones he couldn't shake. Of Kip, putting the moves on Julie at the restaurant. Of Julie flirting like a school girl, hanging on his every word.

If Chapman felt Billy's suspicious eyes upon him it wasn't apparent, as he stripped down to his briefs and changed into his uniform. Suddenly it was clear to Billy why Julie didn't leave the Bluebird with him. Why she never showed up at his apartment last night. There was no other explanation. She went home with Chapman.

His mind tormented by the thought of Kip pawing her. Julie's breath quickening as he explored her body until she moaned with pleasure. Kip's filthy hands sliding between her legs. Julie inviting him deeper inside her with every thrust. The two of them sweating like rutting farm animals.

And now, here stood Chapman in the middle of the clubhouse unrepentant, his mere presence humiliating Billy beyond human endurance.

As Chapman ran a quick comb through his hair, he caught a glimpse of Billy standing behind him. "Hey. How's it going, Billy?" he said, spinning around with a sunny smile.

Chapman never saw it coming, as Billy pounced, knocking Kip into his locker, screaming, "Son of a bitch," his fist, poised to deliver a punishing blow to Kip's jaw.

But this time, there were no boilermakers to mire Kip's defenses. Chapman's arm flew up to block the punch. He grabbed Billy's arm, twisting it hard behind his back. "Shit, man," Kip yelled. "What'cha gone and done that for?"

"Don't play innocent with me, fuck face! You think I'm stupid? I know what's going on. Keep your goddamn hands off Julie!"

A couple of teammates raced over, attempting to separate the two, as the rest of the I-Cubs crowded around. Billy stood his ground, flailing his free arm and kicking at anyone in his way.

David Wagner stormed into the clubhouse. "Break it up!" he shouted, brushing players aside like leaves before a storm. "What the hell is going on here?"

Kip released his grip and took a step back. "It's nothing, Mr. Wagner. Just a little misunderstanding."

Wagner glared at Billy, not buying it. "What the hell's going on here, Rubin?"

"Hey, Kip," Billy hissed, between clenched teeth, while his teammates continued to restrain him. "You go tell Julie something. Tell her not to bother to come looking for me when she decides to crawl out from between your filthy sheets."

Wagner shifted his glare to Kip, who stared back flustered.

"I don't know what he's talking about, Mr. Wagner. I swear," then turning back to Billy. "Nothing happened last night. I don't even know where Julie is. I haven't seen her since I dropped her off at your place."

"Fucking liar!" Billy screamed, bursting free, trying to go after Kip again.

Wagner stepped between them. "You're out of control, Rubin. Go home and cool off."

Billy kicked open the door to his apartment. It crashed against the wall, swung back on its hinges and crashed into the wall again. The fury of the impact loosened plaster chips that fell from the ceiling like snowflakes. A few pieces of the cheesy knick-knack collection Timmy had talked Billy into buying him, bobbled their way off the edge of a nearby shelf like toy soldiers dropping off a cliff. With one angry sweep of his hand, Billy quickly finished off the rest. It felt good. It was the first thing today that did. Wagner was wrong. He wasn't out of control. He was finally taking control.

"Bring it on," he grumbled. He couldn't wait for Wagner and the rest of the team to learn the truth about Kip and Julie, and how they set out to deceive him. Even Wagner would have to admit what Billy did was justified. Unless – if Kip somehow managed to snow Wagner; to convince him Billy was a total piece of shit – someone to be barred from the clubhouse forever. He couldn't let that happen. Frankie! He had to find Frankie. Frankie could make it right with Wagner again. And maybe… just maybe, he'd finally have a shot of getting into the starting lineup.

He paced impatiently, waiting for the agent to answer his phone. When he did, Billy launched into a rambling, manic tirade. Frankie tried to get a word in, but Billy barely paused to breathe.

"You gotta stop this Billy," the weary agent finally offered. "I can't do nothing. My hands are tied. Wagner can run his ball club any way he wants to. You just got to stop giving him ammunition to use against you. And, for what it's worth, I don't believe for a fucking second Julie spent the night with Kip."

Billy lowered the phone from his ear and held it out in front of him. He stared at the slim, shiny piece of metal with disgust. "Are you my agent, or not?"

"Of course I'm your agent."

"Then start acting like it. Do something! Fix this thing with Wagner," Billy demanded.

Frankie paused, choosing his words carefully so not to upset Billy more than he already was. "I can't help you unless you help yourself first. And the booze isn't helping anyone. You gotta get back in therapy. Or at least get your ass to a couple of AA meetings."

Billy didn't want to hear any of it. "I don't have a drinking problem. I have an agent problem. So just fix this for me or you're fired."

62

A driving rainstorm had been falling for hours, saturating most of downtown Chicago. The streets, washed clean of their late summer soot and grime, replaced with a steamy-gray haze that rose eerily from the pavement like wandering soulless spirits in search of unsuspecting victims. Right now, Julie felt very much a victim. Worn and threadbare like a pair of old jeans.

Upon her return from Iowa, she was greeted by the hotel doorman with a friendly, 'Welcome home.' But her impersonal suite of rooms didn't feel much like home. She wasn't expected until tomorrow, but she thought as long as she was back, work might help keep her mind off her problems. It didn't. She felt miserably alone as she thought of her friends and family back in California, most of which had warned her not to follow her heart. Not a one could she call without being judged at this point given the mess her life had become. Certainly not her mother.

When the doorman told Howard that Julie came back early, he decided to check in on her during his lunch break. Howard was just what she needed -- a nonjudgmental friend and a good listener. She needed to open up to someone. She hadn't planned on telling him everything, but somehow, once she started talking, it all came tumbling out. She told him about Popwell, and Highwater, and Billy's drinking, and his on again off again horrible temper. And of the calendar taped to the fridge, and how she sat and watched Billy sleep for hours before she got up and walked out on him. Possibly for good.

Howard sat quietly as she vented and cried. If he was shocked or disturbed by what she revealed, he didn't let it show.

"Maybe I've been fooling myself. Maybe Billy and I just don't work anymore," she stated, half hoping Howard would tell her she was wrong. But he didn't.

"I can't answer that for you, Julie. But, one thing is obvious, you definitely could use a break from all the drama."

"Easier said than done. I still love him. I still can't shake the feeling we could have a great life together if he can just get healthy. I honestly thought I could make it happen if I did all the right things, said all the right things. It's just… every time I try it blows up in my face. I wind up hating him and hating myself even more. I can't keep doing this, Howard. Please. Tell me what to do."

"Look, maybe there's nothing more you can do at this point… except try to get him back into therapy."

Julie sighed, and leaned forward, her elbows propped upon her knees, her chin resting on her palms. "He'll never go for it. After his experience with Dr. Rasher, he doesn't want to start over with somebody new." Julie leaned back against the seat cushion, drawn and exhausted.

"Just think about it, okay?" he said. "In the meantime, how about we order up something for you from room service? Then you can turn off your phone and try to get some rest."

As if on cue, Julie's cell phone rang. She checked the caller I.D. It was Billy. She looked to Howard, who seemed to say with a shrug, it's up to you. She looked back at the phone, and waited for it to go to voicemail.

Howard offered to stay and keep her company if she didn't want to be alone. But Julie shook her head. "No. Thanks. I'll be okay." She jumped when her phone started to ring again. Howard could tell from her expression it was Billy again. He reached for her phone and turned it off.

As she walked him to the door, the hotel room phone began to ring. They both knew it was Billy, and let it go to message. When the little orange light began to blink, Julie pressed the button, and played it back. Billy's drunken, angry words slopped together. Over and over, he screamed for her to pick up, insisting until she did, he would continue to call and call and call. She replayed it for Howard. As soon as he placed the receiver back on its cradle, it started to ring again. Julie looked to Howard. Tears filled her eyes. Without a word, he went over and picked it up, curtly explaining Julie couldn't come to the phone right now.

Billy didn't take it well. "Who is this?" he demanded. "Who the hell are you?"

"Howard Caldwell. I work with Julie at the hotel."

"What the fuck are you doing in her room?" Billy demanded. Without waiting for a response, he ordered Howard to put Julie on immediately. When Howard refused, Billy lost it; making threats, accusing Howard of taking advantage of a stupid argument he had with Julie. Billy's fury escalated, demanding to know if Howard was fucking her.

Through it all, Howard maintained his composure, refusing to sink to Billy's level. He simply informed Billy his calls were upsetting Julie. She didn't want to speak with him and that if he cared anything about her, he would stop calling. With that, Howard hung up.

With that, Billy fired his phone across the room. A wrenching pain tore through his gut. Terrible thoughts of Julie screwing some hotel flunky, of her rolling in the sheets with Chapman, of Rasher's smirking face, of Wagner's bullying stance, of Frankie's betrayal. He wasn't making it up. These things actually happened. They were still happening. He needed to put an end to it all. Not by suicide. Not by death. Not this time. This time, they would pay. All of them. Each in their own time.

He looked to see where his cell had landed, ultimately finding it wedged beneath a bookcase. First things first, he thought. Wagner can't continue to torment him if he's not there to let him. He punched in the manager's private line and bereft of amenities, left a single terse message. "Listen, you miserable bastard! It's Billy Rubin. I quit!"

Now… it was Julie's turn to pay.

63

The only thing on his mind was vengeance. Sweet, satisfying, vengeance, as he gunned the engine on his rental car. Two can play Julie's game.

In his college days, it wouldn't have taken more than a short stroll across campus to charm some young co-ed into bed. They were everywhere back then. Girls with tight little butts in painted-on jeans. Juicy-ripe breasts in skimpy halter-tops jiggling across the Quad, all begging for a taste of the campus all-star's ready cock. He went to great lengths back then to ensure Julie wouldn't find out when he cheated. But tonight was different. Tonight he would make sure she learned of each and every delectably deceitful detail. He wanted her to suffer. He needed her to feel the same pain he felt by her betrayal. Even more, if possible.

Billy clutched the steering wheel tightly as he trolled through the desolate downtown streets. He fantasized Julie watching him screw another woman. He could hear her voice begging him to stop. Begging him to forgive her. To take her back. But he wouldn't stop. The thought excited him as he angled the car over to the curb near the front of a string of deserted buildings. A sinewy, bottle-blonde with gigantic breasts, dressed in bright yellow hot pants and six-inch, clear plastic heels, sidled up and stuck her head inside the open passenger window.

"How 'bout a ride to McDonald's, honey?"

Billy chuckled. In L.A. or Chicago a clever hooker might've come up with Starbucks, or at least a Jamba Juice to cover her thinly veiled proposition. But hey, here in the dregs of Des Moines, he's probably lucky she has teeth.

"So?" she queried, arms akimbo, "You lookin' for a date or what?"

Billy tipped his head toward the window and grinned. Not his carefully practiced grin reserved for adoring ballpark fans, but an expression of anticipated pleasure, both physical and mental, as he reached across the passenger seat and pushed open the door. The woman hopped in, popping the snaps on her blouse, proudly displaying her wares.

"Nice tits," Billy murmured appreciatively.

"Thanks. I'm Charity. What's your name, sweetie? You look familiar?"

"You follow sports?"

"Not really," she admitted.

"The name's Kip Chapman," Billy said, with a sadistic grin.

A patrol car cruised slowly down the street. Charity covered her naked breasts, lit up a cigarette, and suggested Billy drive around the corner and head toward the Levee. She took a deep draw on her extra-long filter tip, then absently flicked the ashes through the open window. A glowing, red-orange spark flew back into the car and landed on her thigh. She slapped at it with her palm.

"You know," Billy offered, "cigarettes are dangerous."

Charity leaned back in her seat, satisfied her fishnet stockings weren't about to go up in flames, then turned to Billy and smiled. "Oh. I don't usually inhale... but," she added proudly, "I am the only girl on the street who can blow smoke rings with my cunt!"

Billy pulled the car behind a boarded-up building and turned off the engine.

"It's twenty for a blow job, thirty-five to watch me get off and sixty to fuck me doggie style. But if you go for the whole package, I could throw in the smoke rings for free."

Billy laughed. There was something about Charity, or whatever her real name was, that was endearing. In this light, she could have been seventeen or forty-seven, it was hard to tell. But she seemed simple and sweet and eager to please.

She led him down a darkened hallway amid piles of rotting lumber and months, perhaps years of discarded trash left behind by faceless Johns, trespassers and transients. She unlatched a door and stepped inside. A bare, well-traveled mattress lay in the center of the room.

"So, what'cha looking for, Kip? A fuck or a suck?"

"Revenge," Billy admitted, reaching into his pocket for his wallet.

"A cheating wife, huh?" she asked, as she slithered out of her shorts.

"Something like that," Billy responded, as he watched her squat, spread eagle on the filthy mattress.

"Let's see the money, honey. And come give mommy's juicy pussy a little taste."

Then, a cold chill shivered through his body when he thought he heard her say, 'I'll even let you call me Julie while you fuck me.' Only, she didn't say that. She couldn't have. He was certain he never mentioned Julie's name.

A wave of fear and shame engulfed him. The room reeked of beer and urine. Charity reeked of cigarettes and the streets. In this light, there was nothing sweet or simple about her. She was a twenty-dollar whore. He pulled his empty hand from his pocket and stumbled backward towards the door.

"Hey! Where the fuck you think you're going?"

He reached for the door, his heart thumping wildly, threatening to burst through his ribcage. "Look. I'm... I'm sorry. You... this place... it's all a really bad mistake.

"You're the mistake, asshole," boomed a voice that rattled the boarded-up windows. The darkness obscured everything but the shadowy outline of a massive form in the doorway. Billy watched, as a man barreled past, yanking Charity off the mattress by her hair like a rag doll.

Charity whimpered as she struggled beneath his vice-like grip. She called him by name, begging for mercy. Whatever streetwise moxie she exhibited moments earlier vanished, replaced by a frightened, submissive shadow of her former self. He called her a worthless piece of filth, and brutally kicked her with the tip of his heavy black boot.

Billy wanted to run, but something wouldn't let him. He reached out and caught the man by the sleeve of his jacket. "Leave her alone!"

The man spun wildly, flinging Billy halfway across the room, then charged after him, encircling his neck with his massive hands. Billy was on the verge of losing consciousness, when the pimp's gnarled fingers began to spasm, releasing their hold on Billy's throat. The salty taste of blood was upon Billy's lips. But the blood was not his own.

Charity held the rusted, crumpled end of a steel pipe in her trembling hands. Then let it drop to the floor with a hollow clang. The pimp's body lay lifeless before her.

Billy was scared sober as he sped past the Levee. His throat still bore the imprint of the pimp's crushing hands. The night air was uncomfortably hot and muggy, but Billy's blood ran cold.

64

Forty-eight hours later, after throwing another one-hit shutout against the Nashville Sounds in Tennessee, Popwell sat alone in his hotel room unable to sleep. His somber visage reflected in the flat-screen mounted on the wall. He thought about Billy's abrupt departure from the team. No point even trying to find him. If and when Billy chose to return, he would. The boy had a talent for baseball, of that Popwell had no doubt, but his hair-trigger temper and obsessive need for recognition and adoration was something Popwell would never understand, even if he wanted to.

He lay back on the bed, and closed his eyes, but sleep continued to elude him. As the restless hours crept by, he hoped perhaps a glass of warm milk might help him drift off. But when he called room service and was told they wouldn't be able to send anyone up for at least an hour or two, he decided to sneak downstairs and try the little coffee shop off the lobby. At this late hour he was fairly sure he wouldn't have to worry about running into members of the Press or having to duck any crazed autograph seekers.

He kept his head down as he slid onto a stool at the far end of the empty counter and waited for the waitress to finish restocking the dessert case. As the parade of freshly baked pies revolved atop their doily-covered plates, he decided to have a slice of blueberry pie with his milk. After placing his order, he got up to wash his hands. As he made his way past a booth tucked away in the back, his heart began to race. There, engaged in quiet conversation, seated across from a distinguished, silver-haired man in his fifties, sat Felicity Flattery. Her sweet voice as lyrical as the first time he heard it at the ballpark in Des Moines. She looked up briefly as he passed. He averted his eyes, stepped into the men's room and locked the door.

He waited an interminable period of time before cracking open the door and peering back out into the restaurant. The booth once filled with her angelic presence was now empty. Once again, it gave him pause to wonder if she had ever been there at all. Or had it simply been another tired trick his restless mind created to confuse and torment him?

Popwell returned to the counter and halfheartedly picked at the outer edge of the once hot wedge of pie with the tip of his fork. The waitress offered to reheat both the milk and pie. But Popwell silently shook his head, effectively ending any attempt on the server's part to engage him in discourse on pie or anything else. It was obvious he wanted nothing more than to be left alone. Not wishing to offend him, the waitress started off down the counter, then stopped, suddenly remembering something. She reached inside her apron pocket, pulled out a carefully folded slip of paper, and scurried back over.

"The lady in the corner booth asked me to give you this before she left," she said, placing the handwritten note on the counter.

Popwell didn't budge. He stared at the slip of paper, but couldn't bring himself to pick it up. For if he did, it would mean his fingers would touch the same piece of paper Felicity's delicate hands held moments earlier.

The waitress pretended not to notice his odd behavior. She waited for him to finish eating before walking back over. "It's got to be hard," she said, inching closer while pretending to scour a nearby section of spotless counter top with a fresh damp cloth. "I can only imagine what it's like being famous," she continued, "being pestered all the time. Everybody always trying to get close to you. Take a picture with you. I mean, I recognized you the minute you walked in. Just didn't want to... you know... bother you for an autograph or nothing. Unless, of course... you wouldn't mind?" she asked, hopefully. "Ever since your no-hitter, my nephew can't stop talking about you. He thinks you're the greatest pitcher to come along in forever. Forever! That's his word, not mine. He's gonna be pretty excited when I tell him I got to serve you a wedge of blueberry pie."

Growing increasingly uncomfortable, he stood up and fished around his pockets for his wallet. Seeing her chances of getting his autograph diminishing, the waitress picked the note up off the counter and offered it to him. "You forgot something."

Popwell's hands began to tremble as he continued searching for his wallet. He wanted to run as fast and far as humanly possible.

"This can't be your first mash note from a fan, now could it? Not a big handsome ballplayer like you. I'll bet you get hundreds of 'em."

Popwell turned away, awkwardly shifting on his feet. The muscles in his back began to spasm beneath his shirt. He took a deep breath, exhaled, and then turned back with a devilish wink and reached out his hand. "More like thousands," he said, grinning like the baseball hero she knew he truly was, as he slipped Felicity's note into his pocket.

"Look, sweetheart," he murmured, oozing charm. "I seem to have left my wallet somewhere. Why don't we just charge the pie to room 746. If that's okay with you?"

"Of course," she said, giggling like a schoolgirl, as he headed for the exit. "Wait," she called, rushing from behind the counter, quickly producing a pen and fresh paper napkin from her apron. "Would you mind?"

"Anything for a fan, sugar," he grinned, as he scrawled his signature across the napkin. Then blew her a kiss and headed out.

She stayed in the doorway blushing, watching until he disappeared down the corridor. She sighed, then cast her eyes on the napkin clutched in her hand. She tilted her head to the side, her excitement turned to confusion. On the napkin, clearly written – 'For my favorite waitress. Love ya, Charley.'

Back up in the hotel room, Charley popped open a beer from the hospitality fridge, and took a long, hard swallow. Things were definitely looking up as he slid Felicity's note from his pocket. Not only were Popwell's athletic abilities beginning to garner some well-deserved praise, but his newly acquired fan base was getting more interesting by the minute. This Felicity Flattery was a definite ten in Charley's estimation. While she was kind of young and innocent looking, he certainly hadn't failed to notice the superb pair of lungs she had on her the day she sang at the ballpark. He was thinking, easily a 34C – no -- maybe even a D.

Not wishing to get ahead of himself, he decided to see what the charming Miss Flattery had written in her note.

"I truly hope you won't find this too bold of me, but I've had the immense pleasure of seeing you play on three separate occasions now and simply had to tell you how very exciting it is to watch you on the mound -- even when you're decimating our very own beloved Nashville

Sounds! Just so you know, I had considered asking our mutual acquaintance, Mr. Jim Farley, if he might one day oblige me by arranging a more formal introduction, but when I saw you in the coffee shop, I now truly believe we are most certainly fated to meet. If you think so too, please call me."

There, right below her phone number, she closed the note with, *Sincerely yours, Miss Felicity Flattery,* and where the dots should be, above the i's in Felicity, she had drawn two tiny hearts.

Charley swirled the beer around his tongue. Jesus, he thought. Now, how sweet would that be? He reached for the phone on the nightstand, but Popwell blocked his way.

"Don't," Popwell stated, with more emotion than Charley had ever heard him use before.

"Why not?"

"Because I don't want to see her again. It's too risky."

"For you maybe, but not for me. Trust me, Ole Charley can handle this."

"I don't want you to handle this. It's my note."

"Hey. If you want to call her yourself, fine. Say the word and I'll back off. But, how rude would it be if no one responds to the lovely lady's invitation?"

"You know I can't do that," Popwell simply stated.

"And that's why you have me. To jump in when anything threatens you. Look in the mirror, B.J. You. Me. She'll never know the difference. They never do."

65

A hard-driving Country Western tune thundered from the radio, as Charley made his way down the narrow Tennessee back roads. Following the I-Cubs sweep over Nashville, the team had a much needed two-day break. Charley could think of no better way to pass the time than to accept the charming Miss Flattery's invitation to join her for a taste of southern hospitality at the family horse ranch, before having to head back to Iowa, and watch Popwell toss a little white ball around a field.

Charley didn't really *get* baseball, not the way Popwell did, but he was more than ready to enjoy the perks it brought, like a day in the country with a beautiful woman.

His fingers drummed the steering wheel as he motored through the gated entrance down the winding road that led to the baronial, English country estate.

The Flattery Ranch was festooned with elegant landscaping, nestled in a manicured forest of imported trees. He drove slowly past the rolling, fenced-in blue-green pastures, and the massive, European style barn, until finally cruising to a stop at the main house.

He was greeted by the same distinguished gentleman who was seated across from Felicity at the coffee shop. Charley fervently hoped the geezer was her old man, and not some sugar daddy who might possibly put a crimp in his plans for a little afternoon delight. Not that Charley minded a little healthy competition. He knew the ladies found him attractive in the past, and now with Popwell's increased celebrity, he figured he was a shoo-in to score.

His host, who indeed turned out to be Felicity's father, Franklin Stonewall Flattery, proved most hospitable, and almost as eager to meet the young ball player as was his daughter. He escorted Charley up the hundred-year-old barn-wood steps to the sweeping stone veranda where the lovely Miss Felicity stood waiting. The sight of her took his breath away. Her fiery-red hair tamed by white satin ribbons that trailed down the side of her elegant, patrician neck, their tapered edges resting lightly upon her bare, sun-kissed shoulders. She wore a pale green sundress that perfectly set off her luminous emerald flecked eyes. She extended her delicate hand. The immediate sensation of her skin inside his palm sent shock waves shuttlecocking down his spine, causing him to wish he had thought to bring her flowers, or at least a box of candy.

Within seconds, a host of uniformed servants appeared, wheeling serving carts laden with a tantalizing array of southern dishes, the likes of which Charley had never seen before. He dug in with gusto, savoring each tasty morsel.

Throughout the meal, Charley managed to deftly deflect as many inquiries as possible about Popwell's famous knuckleball, choosing instead to profess great interest in every aspect of training and breeding champion stallions. For the most part, Miss Felicity rarely spoke up, allowing her father and their guest to dominate the conversation.

The sweet scent of late-summer honeysuckle drifted across the veranda as the servants went about clearing the table. That was when Felicity chose to politely remind her father, if he still wished to attend the horse auction in Kentucky and dallied any longer, he'd most certainly miss his plane.

For a moment, Charley was actually disappointed when the engaging Mr. Flattery stood up to leave. Until now, he was having such a good time he almost forgot the primal urge that prompted him to accept Felicity's invitation in the first place – the chance to discover if her panties were in fact made of silk, as Kip Chapman had implied. Until now, they hardly had a moment in private since he arrived, let alone an opportunity to make a move. Despite his usual pattern, Charley decided to take things slow.

Once Mr. Flattery took his departure and the servants discreetly vanished, Felicity inquired if he might be interested in seeing the new foal that arrived that morning. They barely made it inside the stable before she tore open his shirt and thrust her full, insistent lips hard against his mouth. Charley had success with women in the past but never had it been this easy. More often, the women he seduced took a touch more finessing.

Felicity swiftly unhooked his belt buckle and slowly slid down the zipper on his jeans. Her fingertips lingered, skillfully stroking his responsive organ which by now was firmly committed, and bursting for relief. As they tumbled into an empty stall smelling of fresh laid straw, Charley thanked his lucky stars that good ol' screwed-up Popwell was indeed an up-and-coming, genuine triple 'A' team celebrity. With any luck, Popwell would make it to the majors, and subsequently, if today was any indication, so would Charley's sex life.

Minutes turned to hours. Hours to days. Two days to be exact. Felicity's appetite for sexual fantasy and pleasure seemed boundless, as they lustfully explored one another in every building, room and closet of the enormous estate. Had the ranch been any larger, their impressive exploits might have killed Charley altogether.

When evening fell, they watched the sun dip below the hills beyond the soaring windows that opened out onto the lilac-clustered meadows. There were tender, delicious lingerings entwined in each other's arms, sipping vintage wines before a blazing, stone fireplace in the great room. But for Charley, nothing was more beautiful than the sight of Felicity's breasts bouncing provocatively amid the frothy foam swirling in the marble whirlpool tub in Franklin Stonewall Flattery's private master bathroom. Charley almost felt guilty being this happy.

Early into their third morning together, a nagging voice crept into Charley's consciousness. His temples started pounding. Something was telling him to jump into his rental car and head back to Des Moines. Even Charley knew that ball-buster Wagner didn't take kindly to players showing up late on game day. So, despite his baser instincts, he reluctantly urged his body from Felicity's warm satin sheets and slid into his boxers, carelessly slung over the back of a priceless Charles Eames divan.

Felicity stirred, with heavy-lidded, bedroom eyes. "Where you going, honey? It's sooo early. Come back to bed and keep me warm," she purred.

Charley smiled, as he stuffed his button-less shirt inside his pants. "Wish I could, baby doll. But, I gotta get back to work."

Felicity pushed back the covers exposing her luscious, naked body and suggestively spread her long legs wide in invitation. "I'll put you back to work, honey."

Charley heaved a sigh, then slipped into his shoes. With Popwell's neurotic voice ringing in his ears, he leaned over, and gave her a quick, no-nonsense kiss goodbye.

The final erotic image of Felicity stayed with Charley for the first two-hundred and seventeen miles of highway until replaced by the recognition there might be hell to pay if Popwell missed tonight's game. Then again, he reasoned, wasn't he entitled to a life of his own? After all, Popwell had a promising career in baseball ahead of him, why shouldn't Charley have Felicity and a horse ranch?

He was glad that self-centered, pain-in-the-ass Billy Rubin had disappeared. Had he still been sniffing around, bending Popwell's ear, he'd undoubtedly try to pull some crap to get in Charley's way. Let him try, Charley thought, with a smirk. If he stepped out of line, he might just have to show him the tip of his blade again. Remind him who's really running the show around here.

The cell phone resting atop the dashboard hopped up and down as it rang. A quick glance confirmed it wasn't Charley's long-limbed, horse ranch heiress, but that irritating, little prick agent, Frank Tortiricci. He promptly ignored the call as he had all the other calls while at the ranch.

As the Iowa City limits came into view, Charley was feeling rather smug, until he gazed into the rear view mirror and found Popwell's irksome image staring back. Something in Popwell's expression led him to conclude Popwell was not about to sit back and enjoy the ride, especially not since he was already some three hours late checking in.

Charley wasn't in the mood to be taken to task for spending a little time getting his rocks off. So, before Popwell could speak his mind, Charley handed him the phone. "By the way, I think your agent called."

Popwell checked the long list of missed calls, two from David Wagner, and forty-three from Frankie. But whatever Frankie had to say would have to wait. A string of repressed emotions swirled into Popwell's consciousness. This time, unlike in the past, he knew he couldn't push them away. If he did, Charley might try something like this again. No matter what the consequences, the time had finally come for Popwell to stand up to him. He knew he couldn't banish Charley, but perhaps something Dr. Rasher told him weeks earlier was true. He needed to find a compromise that would work for both of them. Popwell decided to offer Charley a deal. A dénouement, if you will, between two symbiotic yet conflicting personalities. What he wanted was for Charley to stop seeing Felicity. But, as Charley archly pointed out as they headed off the ballpark exit ramp, "giving up Felicity was not about to happen."

So, Popwell suggested, if Charley promised not to allow his time with Felicity to interfere with baseball, Popwell would continue to disappear when Felicity was around. It wasn't perfect, but it could be a positive first step towards a more workable co-existence.

The team was already on the field as the start of today's game was less than thirty minutes away. Popwell raced into the empty clubhouse and grabbed the uniform from his locker. As he shoved his arm through the sleeve, the pitching coach came into the locker room and told him Wagner wanted to see him, a.s.a.p.

Wagner looked up from his paperwork as Popwell stepped into his office. The manager glanced up at his starting pitcher, still sporting Charley's scraggly two-day beard. "You're scratched from the line-up." Popwell nodded penitently, not entirely surprised by Wagner's decision. "Pack your bags," the manager continued. "You're out of here." Popwell just stood there, shifting his weight from one foot to the other, his lips clamped tightly together. "So, that's it?" Wagner baited, expecting more of a response from the superb athlete whose incredible arm he'd come to rely on. "Don't you have anything to say?"

Popwell raised his head slowly, "It's your call, Mr. Wagner."

Wagner shook his head and grinned. "You never cease to amaze me. I'm not tossing you out. You've been called up. You and Kip both. Kip left yesterday. If I could've found you, I would've told you sooner." A simple nod was Popwell's only response. Wagner wondered what could possibly be going through this odd, young man's head right now. "And, there's no need to thank me," Wagner added. "Cause it wasn't my decision. When the Cubs' General Manager calls, I got no say in the matter. I'll be honest," Wagner continued, as he came around to the front of his desk. "I never wanted you or Rubin on my team in the first place. Billy was nothing but trouble from day one. But at least he said what was on his mind. While you," he said, shaking his head thoughtfully, "I never had a clue." Popwell looked him directly in the eye without changing expression, as Wagner extended his hand. "Anyway... good luck in Chicago, kid."

66

It was late. Very late, as Langston Hargrove, manager of the Chicago Cubs pored over a stat sheet illuminated by a splash of light from a green-shaded banker's lamp. Despite the fact his team was currently in first place in the Central Division, he couldn't shake the feeling the dreaded 'Billy Goat Curse' might yet rear its ugly head.

He was confident he had a solid team. But with twenty-seven games left in the regular season, what he needed was a little something to tip the scales in their favor.

The following day, on advice from his eccentric Aunt Tootsie, Hargrove drove out to the Chicago suburb of Oak Park. A woman named Chandari greeted him in the doorway of an old two-story wood frame house, dressed in a flowing, magenta sari that failed to fully disguise the, 'It's better in the Bahamas' T-shirt she had on underneath.

Langston followed her into the dining room, which apparently doubled as her parlor of psychic predictions. Up atop a chipped Formica table, amidst the ubiquitous crystals, was a longhaired, mangy-looking terrier earnestly gnawing on some crusted leftovers stuck to the morning's breakfast plates. After pausing to tie the wild little mutt to the porch out back, Chandari returned and ran down a list of available fees and services. Hargrove was unsure, never having visited a psychic before. Eventually he opted for the basic twenty-five dollar tarot card reading.

The psychic gazed at the colorful cards spread before her and announced they told of a young man with a rich twang to his tongue, toiling in a field, surrounded by cows and sheep and goats. "If you use this young man wisely, he will be of great help to you."

Then, to Langston's surprise, Chandari threw back her head and emitted a spine-tingling wail. She claimed to have had a powerful vision of the future. Of Langston, holding a large, silver trophy with thirty gold plated, hand-furled flags above his head. Langston's throat went dry. He couldn't resist temptation. He dug deep into his pocket and quickly forked over an additional fifty bucks.

Chandari leaned forward, narrowing the distance between them. Her voice, a raspy whisper. Her vision included another man, a strange, quiet man, atop a mountain. One possessing the power to slow the movement of time with his bare hands.

The psychic warned without both these men, Langston's future appeared less rosy, cautioning there could be dark days ahead if he didn't heed her words. Langston sat spellbound, his head spinning. Then, a sudden torrent of water lashed against the windows like a Greek chorus, echoing the psychic's prophecy. Chandari's mutt yelped, scratching wildly at the porch door, begging to be let back in.

Langston rose from the table, and covered his head with his jacket, anticipating a soaking from the unexpected downpour as he ducked through the front door and headed out. To his surprise, the skies above were clear. The sudden downpour was nothing more than Chandari's rusty, garden sprinklers, spurting out of control against the windows.

He rushed back to his office. He knew what had to be done. He penciled in Chapman to replace Bennett in right, and tossed the ball to Popwell to make his first start this weekend against Houston.

67

"How's work?" Dr. Sarah Constantine inquired, as Julie slipped her slender arm through the sleeve of her blouse.

"Fine. Busy. We've got a slew of trade shows coming up. Why? Need a hotel room?"

"No. But it might be a good idea to start cutting back a bit. Have you put in for maternity leave yet?

"No. Not yet. I was kind of hoping to work right up to delivery... unless..." Julie searched Sarah's face for answers.

"Relax," Dr. Sarah said, calmly. "There's no cause for alarm. But, your thyroid level is a little low and your blood pressure is somewhat elevated. I'd like to see you eating a little better and getting more rest. Maybe let the baby's handsome daddy spoil you a bit."

Letting Billy spoil her right now seemed a complete pipe dream, so Julie nodded meekly, and let it go at that. She had no desire to open a discussion of her screwed up relationship. Or reveal the fact that it had been almost two weeks since she had any meaningful contact with Billy at all. Fortunately, she didn't have to get into any of it, as an office assistant popped her head in to announce a Mrs. Cooper was in advanced labor at the hospital, screaming bloody murder.

"Triplets," the doctor sighed, gathering up her things. "I want you to promise you'll try to cut down your workload and find ways to have a little more fun. Okay?"

When she got back to the hotel, she ran into Howard in the Break Room helping himself to a donut. Her face fell. "Howard, please tell me that wasn't the last one."

"You know the rules, Jules. After eleven, it's every man for himself. Hey, I came by your office earlier with those convention numbers you wanted. But you weren't there."

"I had a doctor's appointment. Baby checkup."

"Oh. If I'd known I would've saved you a donut. Here," he said, gallantly offering her a piece of his. "How'd it go?"

"Great," she answered after swallowing it whole. "Only my doctor wants me to eat better, work less, and totally chill."

"Sounds like good advice. You're off to a great start with that donut," he laughed.

"I was wondering," she asked, poking at the leftover crumbs in the donut box. "If you're not doing anything special tomorrow, would you wanna go to a museum or see a movie or something?"

Howard could barely respond. For all the time he spent trying to come up with legitimate-sounding excuses to spend time together away from the office, it was beyond his wildest dreams that she might actually suggest it on her own.

He savored the moment before responding, then heard himself ramble without thinking. "I'd love to, but I have to go up... I have this cabin out on the lake... near Saugatuck. I really need to deal with some leaky windows before the next big rain. And... this guy, Jerry... who's got a cabin down the road, offered to come by and talk me through it... and..." No sooner had the words tumbled from his lips than he regretted having said them. What was he thinking? Julie Hatcher was offering to spend an entire day with him. So what if the whole cabin floated down the street next time it rained.

"I didn't know you had a cabin," she said, with interest.

"Yup. Bought it about a year and a half ago. It's beautiful up there. Sugar fine beaches, lots of trees. Real peaceful."

"Sounds wonderful."

"You're welcome to come with," he offered tentatively, convinced she never would.

"I'd love to," she responded, catching him off guard. "But I have to warn you, I'm not much good with a caulking gun."

Howard's cabin was like something out of a storybook. From the moment Julie arrived, she felt transported to an enchanted fairyland, complete with brilliant cerulean skies, dazzling sunshine, and unsurpassed beauty as far as the eye could see.

A host of colorful, sweet smelling wildflowers lined the flagstone path that led to the cabin's front door. As she made her way from the car, she half expected a bluebird to land on her shoulder and start chirping a happy little Disney tune.

Howard's neighbor, Jerry arrived not long after in paint stained, worn-out overalls and a sea-blue beret, fixed at a rakish angle. He peddled his way up the driveway perched atop a rusty, fire engine red Schwinn, circa the '60's. Julie liked him right from the start. He was open, and friendly and funny. She instantly pegged him for one of those deeply creative artist types that subsist on wild berries and pine nuts. The kind that wakes at noon, drinks gallons of strong, black coffee, and sets up their canvas by the lake's edge waiting for the sunset to awaken their muse.

She was surprised to discover Jerry couldn't paint a sunset if his life depended on it, and was actually a licensed psychotherapist with an advanced degree from Yale, and a bustling practice in Ann Arbor.

When she offered to help with the windows, Howard insisted she was here to do nothing but follow doctor's orders and relax.

"Besides," Jerry grunted, pounding his chest, delivering his best caveman imitation, "fixing windows is man's work."

Outnumbered two-to-one, Julie agreed to make herself scarce and let them play handyman without her getting in the way. While they tackled the windows, Howard kept a watchful eye on Julie as she sat by the lake, happily dipping her toes beneath the cool, sparkling water. A blush of color returning to her cheeks. He was filled with conflicting emotions. He felt guilty wanting her. She belonged to someone else, carrying someone else's child. But he couldn't help himself, as he watched her lean back on the sand, her perfect face capturing the shimmering rays of sunshine.

When the chores were done and Jerry had gone home, Howard threw together a platter of rustic breads and cheeses from the local market and headed out to join her.

"I think," she said, tearing off a hearty chunk of the Rosemary Olive bread, "I could stay here forever."

Howard agreed, as he stretched out on the warm sand, shielding his eyes from the sun with his forearm. "Oh, by the way... try not to fill up on the bread. If it's okay with you, Jerry invited us over for dinner. He's hoping to dazzle you with his culinary skills."

"Fixing your windows and cooking dinner – what more could you ask for?"

There was a lot more Howard could ask for as he lay by Julie's side.

He longed to tell her how he felt, but was afraid it might ruin everything.

"C'mon," he offered, as he rolled onto his stomach and sat up. "I've got a couple of poles in the garage. Let's walk down by the pier and see if the fish are biting."

Julie laughed, free and easy. "You've got to be kidding! Do I look like Huckleberry Finn? The closest I've ever come to fishing was picking a lobster from a tank at a seafood restaurant."

With a little prodding, Howard got her to agree to at least go see how the neighboring fishermen were doing. As they walked along the lake, conversation flowed like the gentle water lapping up onto the banks, slapping against their bare feet. Julie had almost forgotten how good it felt to spend the day with someone as uncomplicated as Howard. She was just about to thank him again for bringing her up here, when she clumsily lost her footing on a slippery patch of wet grass and stumbled backwards. Fortunately, Howard managed to grab her before she could tumble and fall.

"Whoops," she giggled. "I'm such a total spazz, and big as a whale to boot."

"No. You're not," he whispered softly, steadying her in his arms. "You're incredibly beautiful."

She held his gaze for a moment, then didn't protest as he slowly drew her closer. His kiss was tender and warm. Despite the fact it wasn't Billy, she felt herself responding. That it didn't feel wrong was more confusing than anything else that was happening.

As their lips parted, Howard's heart was racing. He couldn't speak – and even if he could, he had no idea what to say next. He searched her eyes for the slightest hint the kiss meant as much to her as it did to him. But the only thing he saw was surprise, which wasn't a bad thing, since at this point he was almost as surprised by the kiss as she was.

Several endless moments passed before Howard spoke up. "I don't want this to be awkward. That didn't have to mean anything... unless you want it to," he said hopefully.

"To be honest, I don't know how to answer that right now."

"Then don't. Look. I'm not naive. I know no matter what you say, you still have feelings for Billy. It's complicated. I get that. But I swear I will respect your decision. Whatever it is. I just wanted you to know how I feel. And that I'll be there if things don't work out between the two of you. But I'd never want to be the reason they don't."

"Thank you, Howard. And thank you for bringing me here. The cabin... the lake... it's a very special place."

"Then here," he said, taking a key from his pocket and pressing it into her hand. "I want you to have this... so any time you feel the need to get away... to relax... to sort things out... with or without me... I want you to feel free to use it."

Over the next few days, despite how often he found himself thinking about the sensation of her lips on his, he never pressed her for anything more. He tried to convince himself that Julie's friendship was enough. But he knew it was a lie.

Then, despite his resolve, he couldn't resist asking her out to dinner to celebrate her new promotion. She looked so radiant he was sure he was the envy of every man who watched them enter the restaurant together. When the waiter asked Howard what his wife might like for dessert, Howard didn't bother to correct his misimpression. And neither did Julie.

68

Sarah Constantine's words continued to echo as Julie stared at the mountain of paperwork threatening to slide off her desk. How foolish to think an assistant might come with her new promotion. She glanced at her watch. It was almost noon. She pushed back from her desk, knowing full well the files would still be there when she returned.

A gentle breeze came in off Lake Michigan as Julie strolled through the north entrance to the Lincoln Park Zoo. She was instantly drawn to the children's carousel. A whimsical fantasy ride where little ones rode atop smiling painted pandas, shimmering zebras and elegant giraffes. Each tiny rider waved excitedly to doting parents watching a few feet away. Julie imagined how sweet it will be to watch her own child glide past on an elephant one day, her eyes alive with wonder, her precious, little girl giggle blending with the magical music of the calliope.

The ride slowly wound down. Moms and Dads hopped aboard the platform to un-strap their youngsters from their galloping mounts, as a bright yellow bicycle slowly pedaled past the far side of the carousel. Something about the rider caught Julie's eye. She couldn't be sure, so she called out after him. When he didn't stop, she decided to follow. She saw him turn down the path toward the pond, then lost him in the crowd. Although not totally convinced it was who she thought it was, she quickened her pace.

By time she arrived at the pond, neither rider nor bicycle was anywhere in sight. She checked her watch, no point wasting what remained of her lunch hour chasing a false alarm. After all, she only saw him for a second. She thought about heading back to the carousel, then decided to stroll on with no particular destination, meandering down the circuitous paths that lace together the zoo's exhibits.

As she came upon the primate house, she spotted the yellow bicycle chained to a tree by the entrance, and decided to go inside and have a look around.

The interior was dark and shadowy, crowded and clammy. A group of rambunctious kindergarteners on a field trip were pressed up against the glass enclosed gibbon habitat, vying for the animals' attention. A rather large, male gibbon peered back with contemptuous snorts, then latched onto a vine and launched himself at the gathering of little people, causing all but the bravest to scurry behind their teacher's skirt.

Julie stepped back as well, bumping up against someone standing in the crowd behind her. "I'm so sorry," she offered. Then, as her eyes adjusted to the light, she gasped, startled to actually see him standing directly behind her. "What are you doing here?"

"Hello," he mumbled, awkwardly, lowering his eyes. "Timmy wanted to see the zoo."

"No. I mean, what are you doing in Chicago? I thought you were still in Iowa?"

"We got called up by the Cubs."

"Oh my God! That's fantastic."

"Billy wasn't called up. Just me and Chapman."

An awful feeling shivered through her body. She didn't know how to react at first, then found the courage to ask. "How did Billy take it?"

Popwell shrugged his shoulders. "Like Billy."

There were so many questions she wanted to ask, but feared it might run him off. Popwell shifted his gaze to a pair of young, white-cheeked monkeys sitting on a tree branch. "What about you? Are you okay?" She waited for Popwell to respond. Instead he continued watching the monkeys lovingly grooming one another, until a larger monkey started screeching up above them.

"Why does he do that?" Popwell said aloud.

"The monkey? I don't know. Because he's a monkey, I guess."

Popwell continued to stare straight ahead. "I asked him to stop seeing her. It's going to turn out bad for all of us."

"What will turn out bad? Who are you talking about?"

"Charley and Felicity. The woman who sang at the ballpark. Charley's having sex with her. He might even be in love with her."

Julie gagged, as the smells of the monkey habitat entered her throat. A wave of nausea swept through her. She covered her mouth with her hand, frantically searching through her purse for a tissue.

Popwell turned toward her. It was awkward. She looked so pale. He hadn't had much experience with pregnant women about to vomit.

"I'm fine," she offered, reassuringly, forcing air in through her nostrils, willing the nausea to subside. "It's just... I honestly never thought, Charley... or... for that matter any of you... I mean, any of them could even have a separate... relationship."

Popwell's eyes darted toward the exit. "I need to go."

Julie grabbed his arm. "Wait... I can see it's upsetting you. But maybe Charley doesn't have any real feelings for this woman... this Felicity. Maybe she means nothing to him. What does Billy think?"

Popwell shrugged and told her they never talked about Felicity. Billy may not even know she exists.

69

Connie insisted they take her BMW and not Marvin's crappy little hybrid if he expected her to accompany him to the Cub game today to watch one of his stupid, former patients play ball. She wouldn't have agreed to go anywhere with Marvin had it not been at David Wagner's personal invitation. She couldn't care less about The Cubs, or baseball for that matter. But the chance to be photographed seated next to someone as rich and famous as the charming rapscallion, David Wagner, was something she couldn't resist.

She tried not to frown as she scrutinized her reflection in the drop down visor mirror. At the rate it was taking Marvin to scrape together the money for her procedure, she couldn't afford to add any new creases to her forehead.

Connie hadn't uttered a word since she and Marvin left the house. Marvin had grown used to his wife's punishing silence. And today, it seemed a blessing, for he had other things on his mind. His reaction was mixed when Wagner first invited them to Wrigley to watch Popwell's first major league start. Rasher hadn't seen Popwell, or Billy, for that matter, in quite some time. Upon learning only Popwell was called up to the majors, he couldn't help wonder what happened to Billy. To say the psychiatrist felt a keen sense of personal failure regarding Billy's mental health told only half the story. In truth, he still bristled at Billy's abrupt dismissal. He was thoroughly convinced neither Billy nor Popwell were capable of succeeding without his professional guidance. Then a horrible thought occurred. Could he possibly have been wrong? Would watching his former patient flourish on the field today be proof Rasher wasn't quite the brilliant therapist he believed himself to be?

He shook his head to jettison the preposterous assertion from his brain. No more mental masturbation, he thought, deciding instead to focus on the miserable cross-town traffic.

Connie hid behind a pair of over-sized sunglasses that managed to stylishly conceal half her face when Wagner greeted them at the VIP entrance. She smiled seductively as he kissed her cheek. Then, as they made their way through the Players entrance, she proceeded to walk three steps ahead, to insure Wagner couldn't miss the one part of her anatomy she still felt supremely confident about.

Despite the considerable vacuum created by losing his two best players to the majors, Wagner's Iowa Cubs still managed to finish out their minor league season in second place – an achievement that hadn't gone unnoticed by the Cub organization. So David Wagner was feeling pretty good about attending today's game. And, having the pleasure of Rasher's bimbo wife seated up against his restless thigh for a few hours would be a delightful perk. He wasn't blind. He knew Connie had the hots for him since the day they met, and given the right opportunity, might easily be persuaded to offer up a bounteous grope or two when Marvin wasn't looking. Even more -- if he so desired. He wondered if the good doctor knew, or even cared.

Connie waited for Wagner and her husband to catch up as she stood in the clubhouse corridor feasting on the athletic, rippled bodies lining the locker room. The aphrodisiac of power, money and half-naked men made her shiver. Even the baby-faced ball boys looked delicious. When Rasher and Wagner showed up, Connie slipped her arm through Wagner's hoping to create an illusion of greater importance for her grand entrance.

Marvin stood patiently by as introductions were made. Connie immediately whipped out a camera, giggling and batting her eyes at each player she met. Rasher grew increasingly uncomfortable with every idiotic photo-op. When he could tolerate his wife's embarrassing behavior no longer, he wandered over to the soft drink cooler, feigning interest in the rows of chilled bottled water and Gatorade. Reflected in the cooler's glass door was Popwell, seated across the room lacing up his cleats.

"I just wanted to wish you well out there today," Marvin offered, as he walked up, and extended his hand with a disingenuous smile. Popwell nodded in recognition and politely shook his hand. Any further conversation was abruptly interrupted when Connie flounced over. "Ooo, I know who this handsome hunk is," she chirped. "My dear, dear friend David Wagner told me all about you."

Popwell shifted his weight awkwardly, then looked from Connie to Marvin.

Rasher began hesitantly, "... this is my wife, Connie."

"Oh my gosh," Connie gushed. "I can't believe I'm standing this close to greatness. Look at me, I've got goose bumps all over. But, I bet you have that effect on all the girls," she said, nuzzling in beside him, thrusting her camera into Marvin's hand. "Here. Take two, just in case you mess it up."

Kip crunched a mouthful of sunflower seeds like a nervous squirrel as he peered out at the crowd from the dugout. He missed the instant recognition he'd grown accustomed to back in Iowa; the rabid autograph hounds, the adoring fans, and the pre-game confidence it inspired. Today the only familiar face he could spot was Wagner's, sitting next to that hot little blonde from the clubhouse. Frankie was around somewhere, he just didn't know where. This was definitely a whole new ballgame for Kip in more ways than one. He knew he'd have to prove himself all over again. He toed the top step of the dugout, closed his eyes and prayed, crossed himself twice to make sure it took, then raced out onto the field.

When Popwell took the mound to warm up, many in the crowd, especially the lunatic bleacher bums in right and left, who never seem to agree on anything, found themselves on the same page questioning Hargrove's decision of letting a rookie start.

As Popwell focused in on his catcher, Timmy suddenly began struggling to re-emerge. Popwell tried to suppress the feeling, but Timmy couldn't be stopped. The frightened young alter didn't want them to be there. Despite past efforts to take Timmy beyond his childhood trauma, the sight and smell of the crowded ballpark was too much for the little boy left behind to handle. Dissociative Identity Disorder was not quite so easily conquered. It was an on-going process requiring patience and time.

Popwell needed to settle Timmy down, to get him to leave quietly and soon, as the ballgame was about to begin. He assured Timmy he was safe here, promising to look out for him and protect him from harm.

Timmy seemed comforted by Popwell's words, grateful to feel understood, and protected by someone other than Charley. Almost immediately, he could sense Timmy's presence leaving his body.

Popwell kicked a few particles of dirt off the rubber, and then, to the delight of the crowd, delivered three straight knuckleballs, badly fooling the hitter, and recording his first ever major league strikeout.

To Marvin's annoyance, Connie stood and cheered, blowing kisses to every single Cub who came up to bat. The more attractive and sweaty the player, the louder she cheered. But, by the bottom of the third, having lost all interest in the slow moving game, Connie decided to amuse herself by marking her souvenir program with little stars and hearts beside each athlete's name. Jimmy Wilder, the young, strapping shortstop garnered three stars. Apparently, the fact that he flubbed his last two routine grounders had little impact on Connie's rating system.

When Popwell struck out his sixth batter to end the fourth, Connie started pumping Wagner with an endless string of stupid questions about him -- none of which had anything to do with baseball. Marvin couldn't take it anymore. He had to shut her up.

"The man is a psycho. Okay!" he blurted, in utter exasperation. "That's all you need to know, for Christ's sake!"

Connie became indignant over her husband's ludicrous claim and looked to Wagner to back her up.

Wagner merely shrugged. "Who gives a shit? If his knuckleball can get the Cubs into the World Series, nobody cares if the guy thinks he's Mickey Mantle or Mickey Mouse."

Popwell scattered six hits in seven innings of work without allowing a run. But when the Houston catcher doubled with two outs in the top of the eighth, Langston Hargrove felt his rookie had done yeoman's work in his first outing, and pulled him to a standing ovation.

Far less inspired, was Chapman's major league debut, as Kip never quite managed to shake his big league jitters, going hitless at the plate, striking out three times. Then, to make matters worse, in the top of the ninth, with a runner on first, the Houston shortstop lined a single to right. As the base runner raced around second heading for third, Kip took off after the ball with a frenzied attack. In his overzealousness, he came up firing. The ball sailed over the third baseman's head into the stands, where a startled, yet excited fan leapt from his seat and snagged it in his beer cup.

Kip kicked up a clump of sod, cursing his performance, knowing, had it not been for his miserable throwing error allowing Houston to score, the game could have ended with a shutout.

As he headed for the locker room, despite knowing his error proved inconsequential to the final outcome of the game, Kip changed into street clothes, and left without speaking to anyone. Had he stuck around, he might have realized aside from himself, not a person in the clubhouse gave a moment's thought to his overly anxious, rookie misstep. The Cubs remained in first place, and that was all that really mattered to anyone.

70

The cracks in Highwater's walls had been plastered over and repainted a pleasing shade of robin's egg blue. Huge dormer windows had been added, splashing the once darkened corridors with newly found clarity. Miss Duncan's ginger-colored hair floated freely around the edges of her collar, no longer tightly twisted in a knot at the nape of her neck, as she walked alongside Billy past the Music Room on their way to Group.

With Armand's departure and the dissolution of the Titans, the Music Room was no longer used to foment schemes designed to divide and conquer. Melodic strains of Prokofiev sang from its open doors, greeting Billy's ears and hastening his footsteps.

Billy wondered how different the sessions would feel without Popwell holding sway over the group's every thought and action.

Henry, Huff, Benish and Scooter were seated inside, as usual, buried chin-deep in the sport sections of the morning's paper. As Miss Duncan entered, the men snapped their papers shut, placed them beneath their chairs, and looked up, catching sight of Billy's return.

"Wow." Scooter said, all smiles and excited, "Billy's back."

"Well, look who's here," Benish chortled, as Billy took a seat. "I thought for sure you'd been captured by aliens and was playing ball on Mars."

"Shut up, clown," Henry warned.

"Why else would he disappear on us like that?"

"Billy don't need to hear your stupid shit the minute he comes back," Henry bristled, plowing a fierce elbow into Benish's ribs.

Huff and Henry nodded in agreement, while Benish tried to straighten up, rubbing his ribcage. "What's so stupid about wanting to know where he's been hiding out? After all, he didn't just bail on the Bellevederes and hot-foot outta Highwater, he bailed on Popwell. He let us down. He knew we was all counting on him and Popwell to help get the Cubs into the World Series this year. Then again, I guess the way the Cubs been playing, they don't really need Billy." Though merely stating the obvious, Benish's words hit a nerve.

"Don't pay Benish any mind. We know you tried your best," Huff interjected. "After all, not all of us are cut out to play in the majors."

"What's that supposed to mean?" Billy shot back. "Let me tell you something. I would've been the one making headlines if I hadn't been benched because of a two-bit, yokel who couldn't hold his liquor."

"Who we talking about?" Henry questioned.

Billy didn't respond. All he could think of was Chapman's miserable, toothy grin. The concept of holding the rookie accountable for Billy's misfortunes began to grow. Every miserable thing that happened could be explained by Chapman's plot to push Billy off the team. How else could an unseasoned kid from nowhere hope to succeed?

"Is this something you'd like to explore further in Group today, Billy?" Duncan inquired.

Billy remained silent. His eyes darted from Henry to Huff to Benish to Scooter, then back to Henry again. Could he possibly make them understand what he went through, what he was still going through?

"I'm talking about Kip Chapman. He's the one who set me up. Turned everyone against me. He wasn't satisfied manipulating the truth and ruining my career. No. That wasn't enough. He went after Julie next, working her with his dumb-ass, country-boy shit. He didn't stop 'til he got her into his fucking bed."

Henry leapt from his seat. "We should kill the miserable son of a bitch," he shouted, swinging his fist like a wrecking ball. Benish joined in, threatening to set Chapman's testicles on fire. Billy felt vindicated.

"Now wait a minute," Huff spoke up calmly, reaching out to lower Henry's angry fist. "Just stop and consider," Huff continued, addressing everyone but Billy. "All we've heard so far is Billy's side of the story."

"You calling me a liar, Huff?"

"I didn't say that…"

"Because you weren't there." Billy spun on his heels, jabbing an accusing finger toward the group. "None of you were."

"Do you have any proof Chapman slept with your girl? Did you catch them doing it?"

"I didn't need to. I know what I know."

Huff lowered his eyes and shook his head slowly. "You know, old friend, you and Barney are a bit more alike than you'd care to admit."

"Barney," Billy snorted. "Fuck you. I'm nothing like that paranoid lunatic. Tell him, Henry. Tell him he's talking crazy. Tell him I'm nothing like Barney." Henry searched Billy's eyes for the truth, then sucked in his lower lip and sat back down. "That's just great! What about you, Scooter?"

"I… I'm sorry, Billy. I'm not sure what to think."

"What about you, Benish?" But Benish simply looked away. "Nothing?" Billy spit out. "Not even a lame-assed pun?" Billy didn't like what was happening, not one bit. He felt like an outsider. "Don't you find it funny, Benish… I come back to Highwater looking for a little support, and get stabbed in the back by a bunch of losers who couldn't last a day on their own in the outside world? Guess the joke's on me. You're all just out for yourselves. You don't give a damn about the shit I'm going through. I'm outta here."

The late summer sky, teetering on the brink of autumn, held the threat of certain showers, as Billy burst through the Day Room doors and barreled out onto Highwater's field. A cool, moist wind whipped against his pant legs, swirling the sea of unruly, yellowing blades that now covered the outfield beneath his feet. He squinted, searching for the familiar chalk lines, but they had all but faded away as did the camaraderie once felt from the members of his team. Right then and there, Billy resolved he was through with group therapy. In fact, he was through with the whole lot of them.

Over the next few days, Billy's only ally was the affable guard, Watermain, who would stop by after rounds each day to shoot the breeze, and share a laugh or two. Billy liked the fact Watermain had no therapeutic insights and best of all, made absolutely no judgments on Billy's behavior whatsoever.

When Watermain failed to show one afternoon, Billy went looking for him, only to find him sprawled across a couch in the guards locker room, his feet propped atop a coffee table reading the sports section of the morning paper.

"Can you believe it!" Watermain sputtered. "Jesus! Bases loaded, bottom of the ninth, and this new kid Chapman couldn't even buy a lousy single. Now the Cubs are in a dead heat with St. Louis with ten games to go." Watermain tossed the paper aside, then dug into the salty remains of the crumpled pretzel bag on the table. "Hargrove oughta get his head outta his ass and sit Chapman down if we want a decent shot at winning this thing. This rube hasn't got the skills or the sense God gave an aardvark."

Something in the guard's callous, offhand remark irritated Billy. He picked up the paper and zoned in on a photo of reporters gathered in the Cub locker room for post-game interviews. Off to the side behind a disappointed yet still hopeful, Langston Hargrove, sat Chapman, eyes sad and vacant, looking to all the world like a whelped puppy caught in a clothes dryer. He was batting a paltry one-ninety, with no home runs and just six RBI's in seventeen games.

He stared long and hard at Chapman's image; gone was his boyish grin, and the uncomplicated, pure love for a game that once brought him so much joy. Billy knew the feeling well. Watermain was right. This was the Bigs; you either cut it or you're out.

When he returned to his room, Billy tried to wash away all thoughts of Kip. He peeled off his clothes and ran the water in the tub. Though he tried to concentrate on other things, memories of his erstwhile teammate continued to play out. The brawl at the Raccoon; Kip's battered body submerged in the whirlpool; the way Wagner and the rest of the team reacted when he went after Chapman like a maniac in the locker room, and how Kip never even once tried to fight back.

Billy sunk into the tub, letting the water rush up and over his ears. But it didn't help. He could still hear Kip's voice, open and honest, without the slightest, telltale hint of guile, nor trace of bitterness. Nothing but that stupid Southern drawl telling him how he wouldn't trade their night at the Raccoon for anything. And then later, when Billy accused him of seducing Julie, how Kip swore he got it wrong. That he was only trying to help patch things up between them.

Billy had to own up. He pegged Kip Chapman as the competition from day one. Maybe even before that. Maybe from the moment Frankie began throwing it in his face that Kip was on the fast track for major league greatness. The very thought of having to share the spotlight with the small town hero infuriated him. And when Kip's injuries caused him to sit out the next six games, it was Billy who went to Wagner coldheartedly suggesting he take Kip's place in the line-up, thoroughly convinced, once the fans got a chance to see him strut his stuff, Chapman would be all but forgotten.

Had he possibly misjudged Kip? He really had no proof beyond his wild imaginings that the kid from Tupelo had betrayed him.

Billy stepped out of the tub and stood naked and dripping before the mirror, finally accepting the fact that he held on to his mistrust and anger because it gave him someone to blame. Now the question became, could he let it go? Was he ready to move on?

71

The wide-body jet fell a few hundred feet in a matter of seconds, tumbling through a dense cloudbank somewhere high above the Rockies.

"What the fuck?" Frankie yelled, clutching the top of his head to ensure his pricey hairpiece wouldn't slide from his scalp amid the turbulence.

He hated flying. He much preferred driving or taking a train if necessary, but when Kip called and told him he was thinking about packing it in and going home to the farm, Frankie knew he had to get back to Chicago, and fast.

The seatbelt sign was flashing. The miniature Kettle One bottle and complimentary peanuts rolled back and forth across his plastic tray table like dice in a craps game. Sweat pooled from Frankie's neck and forehead as he dug his nails into both armrests. His very first thought was, Shit! We're going down. His second, was of Air Paraguay Flight 22 that ditched into the sea last month, killing all on board because some birds had gotten sucked into the engines. Stupid, useless, miserable birds that had no business being up that high in the first place!

The possibility of dying could not have come at a worse time. There were still too many things left for him to do. Too much to prove; to himself, to his smarmy detractors, and to his basement-dwelling father, who never believed Frankie would amount to much of anything.

Most of all, he had to prove he wasn't wrong about Chapman; that he hadn't put in all that time and energy for nothing. He was firmly convinced Chapman just needed a little handholding. And if that didn't work, he'd just drop-kick some sense into him. That is of course, if the Lord hadn't already decided Frankie wasn't going to make it back to Chicago.

If only he hadn't tried to light up that fucking Camel filter tip in the back of the rectory when he was ten, accidentally setting Sister Catherine's Easter pageant costumes ablaze, which led to his immediate expulsion from Catholic school, Frankie might've had a prayer or two to call on at a time like this, but nothing sprang to mind.

He peered through the porthole at the mountaintops below and shrugged, realizing it probably wouldn't do much good promising to repent for his mortal sins at this point. Chances were pretty damn good God would know he was lying in a desperate attempt to save his fucking hide.

Passengers shrieked as once again, the plane violently lurched downward. Then, moments later, to Frankie's immense relief, the Captain's voice came over the intercom, calmly apologizing for any discomfort during the brief roller coaster ride, and to assure Frankie and the rest of the passengers it looked like clear skies ahead for the duration of the flight.

As soon as they touched down at O'Hare, Frankie grabbed his cell, called Kip and told him to unpack his bags, heat up some grits and wait for him to get there.

They stayed up half the night talking. Frankie did his best to convince Kip the farm would always be there, but quitting now would prove to be the biggest mistake of his life. "You don't throw it all away just 'cause you're stuck in a little slump. It happens to everyone. All you need to do to get unstuck is to fucking relax." Kip looked at Frankie with trusting eyes, wanting to believe him. "Look, kid, I don't want you cooped up here brooding on your day off." The wily agent sprinted from the couch, and yanked up the window blinds. "C'mere. I want to show you something. This is fucking Chicago, man. You need to get out there and have some fun." Despite his encouragement, Frankie could tell his client was obviously still feeling out of place in the big city. "Look, Kip, Chicago's no different from Iowa or even Tupelo — it's just got more people and less cows. But that don't mean you can't go do the same fucking things you used to do between games. Go bowling, pick up a bimbo, see a stupid movie, or ride the fucking El all day if that'll make you happy."

"I dunno, Mr. Tortiricci. I just don't think I got it anymore."

"Lemme ask you something, Kip. Have I ever fucking lied to you?"

Kip lowered his head and looked out the window. "No sir."

"Then trust me on this. Talent like yours doesn't just up and disappear. It's right there," he said, poking him lightly in the chest.

"You've still got it."

Thirty-seven hours later, the Cubs were back at Wrigley to face the Brewers. Despite a strong suggestion from batting coach, Don Delephant, that they give Chapman a rest, Hargrove wasn't quite ready to tempt fate just yet. Even though it made perfect sense to sit Chapman down at this point, Hargrove was still pulling for the cut-rate fortuneteller to have the inside track. So he decided not to bench Chapman, but to move him down to the eighth spot in the lineup instead.

In the meantime, Kip had taken his agent's advice to heart and showed up for today's game far more relaxed, and ready to play.

The Brewers started early with a quick two in the first, but in the bottom of the fourth, the Cubs loaded the bases with two men out. The fans were ecstatic until they realized the next batter up was Chapman.

Hargrove began having second thoughts. Maybe Delephant was right. He tugged nervously at the collar of his shirt, pulled a shiny St. Jude medallion from his pocket, and lifted it to his lips, praying he wasn't making a huge mistake. He still could put up a pinch hitter, but he had to go with his gut, which, despite the relentless flow of churning acid, was telling him to keep Chapman in. He lifted his cap to swipe his brow as Kip stepped into the batter's box.

The first two pitches were high and outside. The next, a nasty cutter, right around the strike zone. Kip met the ball with a vicious swing and launched it over the left field bleachers out onto the street. The crowd went crazy as he trotted around the bases, head down, humbled by their exuberant cheers.

Kip continued to crush the ball the rest of the game, going three-for-four, with two homers and a long double. The slump was definitely over. The Cubs went on to rout the Brewers. Hargrove felt vindicated as he glanced at Delephant, who could only shrug, happy to be proven wrong.

With nine games remaining in the regular season, the team hit the road for the next six, hoping to gain some ground on second place St Louis.

They swept three in Cincinnati, with Kip garnering six hits and Popwell pitching another gem. Then marched into Pittsburgh, taking two of three from the lowly Pirates. With the Cardinals dropping a day-night doubleheader to Milwaukee, the Cubs were now within a game of clinching the Central Division title as they boarded their charter flight back home to O'Hare.

Frankie found a new way to keep pace with his clients on the road. Following his terrifying near death experience at the hands of the 'not so friendly' skies, Frankie decided to keep his feet planted closer to the ground, and travel by rail.

The Capitol Limited idled in the station as Frankie sat by a window in the dining car scowling at a parade of filthy pigeons strutting across the tracks pecking at garbage. "Fuck you, pea brains," he muttered smugly, as he launched into his turkey on whole wheat. "You're on my turf now my fine, feathered friends. Things are a little different on good ol' terra firma. I'd like to see you try and fuck with the engine on this hunk of steel... see how far that gets you!"

The birds began to scatter as the Limited chugged from the station. Frankie lowered the window shade, leaned back in his seat, and closed his eyes. He was feeling pretty good -- actually, more than pretty good. The sky's the limit, he thought, wishing he could meet with Cub management and renegotiate both players' contacts right now, but he knew that wasn't possible. For the next six years, his two star clients were locked into their present contracts at league minimum, with scheduled bumps per year over the next three years. After that, if they continued putting up great numbers, Frankie knew he could request salary arbitration and likely bump them up a few million each. But, even that was small potatoes compared to what sweet year seven could bring.

Frankie opened his eyes and slid the shade back up. As the scenery rumbled past, he pulled a pen from his briefcase and scribbled some numbers on a napkin. In his estimation, there were approximately two thousand days to go before he'd be able to get a clean shot at Farley's checkbook again. All he needed to do until then to put the Tortiricci Sports Agency firmly on the map was exercise a little patience. Unfortunately, patience was not one of Frankie's greatest attributes.

72

Marvin Rasher's financial woes were expanding exponentially. It was no longer just Connie's obsessive desire to remain anatomically perfect straining his finances; it was everything. More than a few of his cash clients began to cut back on the amount of sessions they could afford to pay for out of pocket. To make matters worse, the damn insurance companies were squeezing him so tight on the ones that had coverage, he barely had room to breathe. He was also falling behind on his ex-wife's alimony checks; was currently two months late on the payments for Connie's BMW, and of course, there was his mounting gambling debt.

Hard choices had to be made. He never thought that once again, he'd be forced to borrow against the equity in his home, as he did several years back when Connie convinced him to buy her a chocolate shop that quickly went belly up. Unfortunately, what he wasn't aware of, upon checking with his banker, there was barely enough equity left on the house to finance a chocolate bar.

What he was aware of, was the subtle change in his wife's behavior as of late. She tended to smile more, bitch less, and actually seemed to take an interest in Marvin's work. On more than one occasion, she even made a point of asking when he'd be home and what he'd like for dinner. All this should have made him happy. But it didn't. It made him suspicious.

"Hi Honey," Connie sang out from the kitchen, as Marvin walked through the door a little earlier than usual, pausing briefly to sift through the fresh stack of bills waiting for him atop the antique lacquer table in the foyer.

He sighed in resignation, stuffed the mail into his briefcase and followed the scent of something delicious coming from the kitchen.

Connie stood by the stove diligently preparing his favorite dish; pork loin with French plum sauce and double stuffed potatoes. Marvin was ecstatic. She hadn't put that much effort into cooking since the last time they had hot, passionate sex, over three months ago. Connie's impressive multiple orgasms in the past were often followed by an insatiable desire to express her ardor in the kitchen as well, apparently sexual gratification made her hungry. One of Marvin's fondest culinary sexual memories occurred a few weeks into their marriage. The newlyweds had spent the entire morning sweating up the sheets before the new groom managed to pull himself away and pop into the office for an hour or two. Upon his return, he found his young bride clad in nothing but a 'Kiss the Cook' apron and spiky high heels, up to her elbows in cream, trying to whip up a chocolate mousse from scratch.

When the electric mixer accidentally zipped into high gear, waves of cream dotted with chocolate bits flew in every direction, leaving Connie spackled with the sweet, sticky concoction, head to toe.

Marvin burst out laughing. Connie reached into the mixing bowl, scooped up a handful of the messy glop, and promptly shoved it down Marvin's pants. Rasher took her right there on the kitchen floor. Shamelessly tasting one another like starving, shipwrecked survivors discovering coconuts for the first time. Oh, if only there was a way to recapture the passion they once had, Marvin wondered wistfully, as he took in the heady aroma. "What's the occasion?" he asked

"No occasion," she replied, stirring the plum sauce with a large silver spoon. "Just thought you might enjoy a nice home-cooked meal after a long day at the office, that's all." Then, as she lifted the spoon to Marvin's lips for a taste, "Oh, guess what?" she mentioned. "I heard on the radio your former patient... you know, the one who plays for the Cubs, is having a *no runner*."

"A what?" Marvin asked, licking his lips, as the savory sauce graced his palate. "You mean he's pitching a shutout?"

"No," she answered, pressing her index finger to her forehead, trying to remember. "That wasn't what they said. I'm sure it was a 'no' something."

"A no-hitter?" Marvin asked, the long-suffering Cub fan in him suddenly stirring in his chest.

"Yes. That's it. A no-hitter."

Despite the fact he was convinced someone wrestling with Dissociative Identity Disorder wasn't stable enough to play pro ball, there was no way he was going to miss the thrill of witnessing a no-hitter, no matter who was pitching. He couldn't believe with all his problems, he had completely forgotten the Cubs were playing the Cardinals today and could possibly clinch the division. Hoping the no-hitter was still alive, he turned to Connie. "Would you mind?" he asked, excitedly.

"Go ahead, Marvin. If it's that important. I guess dinner can wait a little."

Marvin sped into the den and turned on the TV. He could hear the Cub commentator's raspy voice yelling, 'Strike two!' Rasher swallowed hard, too excited to sit. He dared not blink for fear he might miss something.

A deafening roar rose from the stands. But, on the mound, Popwell heard nothing but the sound of his heart beating with a solitary, intense desire. He stepped off the mound, fiddled with the rosin bag, then scuffed up the ball. In the Rasher den, Marvin could hear his own heart thumping, waiting on the next pitch.

The second stringers, along with a handful of coaches were leaning halfway over the dugout rail, pulling for him. Popwell stepped back onto the hill and toed the rubber, his steely gaze focused on his catcher. Not that he was waiting on any particular sign. He knew exactly what he was going to throw.

The batter tightened his grip, his stance opened slightly, desperate to put some wood on the ball and break up the no-hitter. Popwell wound up and threw – the pitch sailed as it left his grasp, chin level, maybe higher, at least two feet above the strike zone. Then suddenly, with a will of its own, the slow, wobbly pitch dropped at the last second. The hitter never got to lift the bat from his shoulder as the umpire rang him up with a bellowing, strike three!

The dugout and bullpen emptied as the entire team rushed the mound. For the first time all day, Popwell looked truly terrified.

Marvin fell back into his armchair, dying to talk about the game with someone... anyone. Too bad Connie didn't share his passion for the sport. Trying to have a meaningful conversation about baseball with his wife was as pointless as discussing God's miracles with an atheist. She just didn't get it and never would. "Is it over yet?" Connie called from the kitchen. "Dinner's on the table."

Marvin didn't want to tick off Connie by having her fancy pork roast get cold, so he pulled up a chair as Connie brought out the potatoes. Just as Marvin was about to place his napkin on his lap, Connie's cell began to ring. She glanced at the caller ID, then darted back into the kitchen, claiming she left the gravy ladle on the counter.

He could hear her speaking in muffled whispers, her hand cupping the mouthpiece. When she returned, she looked flush and flustered informing Marvin the call was from a friend of hers, a woman named Dimita, who apparently was very, very ill. So ill, she was afraid to be home alone. Connie felt compelled to bring her friend dinner and sit by her bedside until her relatives could get there, quickly adding, Dimita's family lived out-of-state and might not arrive until sometime tomorrow.

She picked up the carving knife and began lopping off two hearty portions of pork, siphoning a hefty amount of the plum sauce, packing up the potatoes and sealing them in a plastic container.

Marvin surmised Connie wasn't thinking clearly when she chose to pack up both mouth-watering crusty ends of the loin, knowing full well they were Marvin's favorite part of the roast. Then, he started to wonder about the peculiar nature of her friend's dire illness, and why anyone would bring pork roast to a seriously ill person?

"Shouldn't you be bringing chicken soup instead?"

"There really isn't time, Marvin, and you certainly don't expect me to show up empty handed, do you?"

Marvin began to suspect the authenticity of his wife's sudden mission of mercy. To the best of his knowledge, Connie didn't have many friends, certainly not any she'd run out the door at the drop of a hat to care for.

Upon further grilling, Connie was forced to own up. Dimita wasn't really a friend. She was Dr. Kingston's receptionist. Connie was only trying to make the best of the situation Marvin put her in. She'd been forced to keep in close touch with the woman, hoping if they forged some kind of friendship, Dimita might prove helpful, if and when Marvin was able to scrape together the money for her procedure. Unfortunately, due to his endless foot-dragging, she may have lost any chance of getting put back onto the surgeon's schedule for years. And that's where her friendship with Dimita would hopefully come in handy.

For the first time in a long time, Marvin felt guilty. After all, it was his fault Connie had to cancel the procedure twice before.

"Of course," Connie continued, her voice cracking with emotion, "if what I want isn't important to you. If you think I'm not doing the right thing, offering to help Dimita. If you prefer I stay home to serve your dinner, I'll just call back and say I can't make it."

An ache crept into Marvin's previously hardened heart. Maybe Connie was actually trying to be helpful in her own screwed up way. After all, he had to admit he had intentionally kept her in the dark about the true state of their shrinking finances, fearing she would leave him if she knew.

"No. Y'know what, Connie," he said, helping her pack the food into a Bloomingdale's shopping bag. "This Dimita obviously needs you more than I do right now. You go ahead. You're doing the right thing. Don't worry about me."

As Connie's car roared from the garage, Marvin sadly surveyed what remained of his special dinner. He pushed his plate away and went into the kitchen for a beer. There, on the counter, partly hidden beneath a dishtowel was Connie's cell phone. He raced out the front door and looked down the street. But the BMW was gone. He knew eventually she'd discover it missing, and didn't want her worrying needlessly. The problem was Marvin had absolutely no idea how to get hold of her. Then it occurred to him, since Dimita called on Connie's cell, all he had to do was check the number of the last incoming call.

To his surprise, the call wasn't answered by an ailing woman named Dimita, but by a towel boy in the Cub's locker room.

Marvin dropped the phone to the counter like a lump of burning coal. He took a moment to let it sink in, then calmly walked into the den, turned on his computer and ran a search for the name of a good private investigator.

73

The Wrigley crowd emptied onto the sidewalk en masse. T-shirts and caps boasting 'Central Division Champs' flew out the door at Sports World as fast as salesclerks could tag 'em, and bag 'em. Though, even the most naïve Cub fan knew the Central Division title was only the beginning of a long road ahead in the quest to make it to the World Series, but for now, nothing could shake their dogged optimism.

Champagne corks were popping, spurting sticky-sweet geysers in every direction as Langston Hargrove ducked 'n weaved past flapping sheets of plastic draped across the clubhouse lockers like flea market shower curtains.

'A proud and satisfying moment,' was what he told the assembled members of the Press in his postgame interview, the Korbel sluicing off the brim of his cap. 'Proud and satisfying -- the culmination of a season's worth of hard work by an outstanding group of young men.' Not a mention was made of the role Chandari's psychic vision may have played in the outcome.

Popwell was halfway out the door before Hargrove managed to block his path. "What d'ya mean you're outta here? You just pitched a no-hitter. You gotta talk to the Press."

"I don't talk to reporters."

Hargrove was torn. He had managed his fair share of screwed-up athletes over the years; everything from narcissistic, ego-maniacs who'd gladly run down their own mothers for a little extra ink, to pill heads, wife beaters, boozers, and even a certain unnamed power hitter with a predilection for wearing lacey, women's undergarments beneath his uniform. Shielding a player's unsavory peccadilloes from the Press was part of a manager's job. Sometimes it worked. Sometimes it didn't. While Popwell's bizarre trainload of emotional baggage could pose a serious distraction for a team hoping to keep its winning ways alive, he had no choice. It was a risk he'd have to take.

"Look… I know you prefer to keep a low profile, and I respect that, but I'm afraid you can't *not* talk to the Press today. I know most of these guys. Just take a few quick questions, keep it simple, stick to the game and I promise, it'll be over in no time."

With Hargrove blocking Popwell's only means of escape, it didn't take long for the TV cameras and the pack of reporters to sniff him out.

"When did it start to sink in you were throwing a no-hitter?"

"It didn't."

"C'mon. There had to be a moment somewhere in the game."

Popwell felt trapped. He didn't say anything. He merely shook his head.

"What's it like being the number one starter after only a month in the majors?"

When Popwell didn't respond, an attractive young reporter, fresh out of journalism school elbowed her way up front. "Annie Fuller, Chicago Herald. What about the curse? Think you're the man to break it and finally get the Cubs back into a World Series?"

Popwell stared at the floor. He closed his eyes. His shoulders started to twitch as Charley began to stir inside him. "You're killing me in here," Charley whispered. "Say something clever. Turn on the charm. It's not that hard. See if we can get her number."

"No! That's not gonna happen."

"Did you just say the Cubs *won't* get into the World Series?" The red-headed newbie shoved a microphone into Popwell's face.

"C'mon, B. J.," Charley pleaded inside Popwell's head. "Open your eyes. She's practically begging for it. Look how she comes dressed to a Press conference, you can see her pointy pink nipples right through her shirt."

"Shut up!" Popwell spit back.

"Hey! I didn't just slam the Cubs," remarked the bemused reporter. "You did."

Popwell clamped his jaw, attempting to choke Charley back, but instead found himself slipping further away from the advancing army of reporters.

As Popwell withdrew deeper into the shadows, Charley emerged displaying a devilishly charismatic smile. "Sorry, Popwell," Charley whispered inside his head, "but someone's got to save our ass before you say something that gets you slammed by every sports writer in the country."

Charley laughed easily. "I really had you going for a minute there, didn't I gorgeous," he said, with a wink and a playful nod to the Herald reporter.

The redhead stared back, unsure where this was going. "Was your statement meant as a joke?" she remarked, furrowing her brow.

"C'mon now, sweetheart. What else could it be? Seriously, we both know with the great team Langston Hargrove put together and with me on the mound – it's gonna happen. It's our year. I know it. You know it. And the fans know it. Didn't you hear them screaming out there? They love me," he grinned with bragadocious immodesty. "Nobody can beat us."

Hargrove was beaming. He couldn't have asked for a better sound bite if he had scripted it himself. Then a voice rang out from the middle of the pack. "What about the Mets?" sniped Jim Marsden, from USA Today.

Charley's eyes narrowed, as he went on the offensive. "What are you deaf, or something? I said *nobody*, especially the Mets. The Mets suck!" Charley shouted back.

"That's a pretty bold statement seeing they beat you guys eleven out of twelve in the regular season. It was like batting practice for Woznewsky every time he came up. The homers just kept coming."

"Screw the regular season. Most of that was before I got here. Things are a lot different now. And screw Woznewsky while you're at it. The Woz is a wuss! In fact, lemme tell you somethin' else, the Mets are ready to choke. Yeah, that's it. The whole team is a bunch of limp-wristed, over-paid chokers. I can't wait to get to New York and beat the crap outta those girls." Charley was loving every moment of his bad boy posturing.

While the media devoured each and every stupid slam sprouting from his lips, Hargrove had an uneasy feeling the interview might be heading down an ugly path. Unable to gauge what his wacko pitcher might say next, he thought it best to put an end to the press conference. After all, this wasn't a prizefight, it was baseball, and baseball by centuries old tradition is far more civilized.

74

Frankie leaned back against the coarse, green fabric that covered the five-cushion couch doubling as his father's daybed. The fringed pillow backs reeked of stale cigars and vapor rub. He cast his eyes up to the basement ceiling. He could hear his mother's ancient Electrolux sputter and grumble, making intentional, angry, zigzag patterns across the threadbare carpets on the floor above their heads.

"Shut that goddamned vacuum, you miserable witch. We can't hear the fucking TV down here," his father bellowed, ratcheting up the volume on the 60" flat screen, a recent gift from Frankie, purchased with part of his commission money. Frank Sr. had the volume hiked so loud, Frankie thought his ears would split. But despite the familiar pattern of his parent's mutually abusive relationship, little could shake the high he was on right now.

"Hey, Pop. Turn it the fuck down, will ya? I wanna ask you something."

Frank Sr., far more intent on listening to the end of the post-game interviews, dismissed his son with a *shush,* and an indifferent wave of his hand. When an irritating ad for a constipation aid came on, the old man hit the mute button. "Eat a prune, you moron," he barked at the screen, curling his thumb and forefinger around the barrel of the acrid, half-smoked stogie wedged into the recesses of a large ceramic bowl.

Frankie saw the opening he waited twenty-eight years for. "So, Pop... what'cha think of your Cubs now?"

Frank Sr. shrugged, reflecting philosophically. "Eh. The Cubs are still the Cubs."

Frankie couldn't believe his ears. "The Cubs are still the Cubs? What the fuck you talking about?" The veins in his neck began to throb. "That's fuckin' crazy, Pop. Thanks to me, your Cubs could win the whole fucking thing this year!"

"Thanks to you," his father grunted, rummaging through his pockets till he found a crumpled book of matches.

"Yeah! Thanks to me. And if it wasn't for me, you and the rest of the long-suffering Cub fans would be crying in their beer again, moaning, 'wait until next year.' Do you think for once you could fucking tell me I did good?"

Frank Sr. drew in the harsh, peppery smoke, then belched out three short, gray puffs that hung suspended in air punctuating his next remark. "Proud of you? For what? What the fuck did you do beside skim some money off the top of someone else's talent?" he sputtered.

Despite years of being trivialized by his father, Frankie stood his ground. "I found them, Pop. I dragged Chapman's ass off a fucking plow, and I handed Farley a crazy knuckleball pitcher the likes of which nobody's seen since Phil Niekro. Without my clients, your lovable losers would be just that."

Frank Sr. took another pull on his spit-soaked stogie, then exhaled a cloud of brown, noxious smoke that saturated the room. "Son, you coulda dug up the Mick and Cy Young to play for the Cubs and it ain't gonna make no difference. If anything, you went and made things worse."

Frankie sucked in his lower lip and swiped at the sweat puddling in his shirt collar. "What the fuck you talking about, Pop?"

"All you did was go and get everyone's hopes up. It's pretty stupid if you ask me, seeing you already know they're just gonna come apart when it counts most. Wise up junior, the Cubs ain't getting into no World Series, this or any other year. That's just how it is." Frank Sr. let out a wicked laugh. "You think the Cubs sat on their asses for a hundred years waiting for Little Frankie to come along and save them? But hey... don't take it too hard. It ain't entirely your fault. It's the fucking curse."

Frankie lowered his head and choked back tears. Why did he think anything he ever accomplished would elicit an ounce of praise from his father's lips? In this moment, deep in the bowels of his childhood home, he was the one who felt cursed.

"Now, go do something useful for a change. Go tell your fat slob of a mother to fix us something to eat while I see what else is on the tube."

As Frankie trudged up the basement steps, his cell began to ring. It was Billy. The two hadn't spoken since Billy disappeared from sight.

A fine mist spattered against Frankie's face as the center jet of the massive, pink marble fountain soared a hundred fifty feet above his head. His eyes shot back and forth searching the darkened, nearly deserted section of the park until he spotted Billy hunched forward, alone on a bench, the brim of his USC Trojan cap pulled halfway down his familiar face.

"I messed up, Frankie. I need your help."

It seemed like forever since he and Billy stood in the shadows of Buckingham Fountain, a couple of innocent kids stretching their chubby little arms and sticky, candy-coated fingers in the water, vying to see which of them could touch one of the four spouting sea horses flanking the fountain's basin. Everything was so less complicated back then. Needs could be met with a quarter, battles could be fought and won in the back of the schoolyard, and friendships were meant to last forever.

Frankie took a seat on the bench beside him.

"You're probably mad as hell," Billy began, "and you have every right to be, the way I screwed things up, walking off the team and all. I was confused. I blamed Kip for everything. I know now I was wrong."

Frankie leaned forward and sighed. "Look, Billy… things happen. Sometimes it's for the best. Maybe I was pissed at first, but I ain't anymore, so let's just leave it in the past. Okay? Me and you – we're cool, alright?"

Billy searched his face for signs Frankie was on the level. The intensity of Billy's gaze made the agent increasingly uncomfortable. It wasn't that he didn't want to help, he just no longer knew how. "Look, it's getting' kind of late," he muttered, as he rose from the bench.

Billy reached for his arm. "Don't walk away, Frankie. Please. I've given it a lot of thought. I know Chapman didn't cause any of this. He's a good guy, and a hell of a ball player. He deserves to be where he is. But so do I. You know it's the fucking truth. I should be there too. It should be me the fans come out to see. I deserve it. I earned it. You know I've still got the goods. You're the only one who can get me back into the game. Everybody else deserted me. Even Julie."

"Is this about Julie?" Frankie asked, sitting back down. "'Cause there's no fucking way I'd ever believe she'd give up on you. She said you two were just taking a break 'cause no matter what the fuck she did, she couldn't get through to you." Billy turned away but Frankie grabbed him by the shoulders, forcing him to hear what he had to say. "You fucking want my help, Billy? Then lemme tell you something. I'd give my left nut to have someone like Julie in my corner, someone who'd love me the way she does you, no matter how fucked up I got."

"This isn't about Julie," Billy spit back. "It's about figuring out the rest of my life."

Frankie was fast losing patience. He wanted to smack Billy up both sides of his head, right here, right now in the middle of a public park. "What the fuck is your problem? Can't you see how that girl's turned herself inside out for you, while you're here whining that Billy Rubin's pretty face isn't plastered on tee-shirts and bubble gum cards? Well, fuck you Billy! You're as messed up as I've ever seen you. And let me tell you something else while I'm at it. If you think I miss representing Billy Rubin for one fucking second – I don't. I'd rather represent Popwell any fucking day of the week. You better get yourself back into therapy, get your act together, and beg Julie to forgive you before you lose a lot more than you think you already have. And if you think I'm not your friend," Frankie hammered, jabbing his index finger at Billy, "think again, 'cause this is the best advice any friend could ever give you."

A short time later, Billy found himself standing alone in the alley across from Julie's hotel, watching as hotel guests bustled up and down the steps of the main entrance. He thought about going inside to look for her, but didn't have to, for a moment later he saw her walk out through the front doors. She paused at the top of the steps and motioned to the beefy doorman stationed down at the curb, looking quite heraldic in his shiny red uniform trimmed with braided golden epaulets. With three short blasts of his silver whistle, he summoned the attention of a cab heading in the opposite direction. As the taxi swirled past executing a perfect U-turn, Billy closed his eyes remembering the first time he and Julie shared a cab in Chicago. It was the amazing day he learned he was going to be a father. It made him smile, but the smile faded as soon as he opened his eyes. Walking toward Julie was a man Billy had never seen before. A man with a big wide grin and an even bigger stuffed white Panda hidden behind his back. She looked so excited and happy when he surprised her with it. Was this guy just a friend, or co-worker? When Julie reached up to brush a wisp of hair that had tumbled across the man's eyes, a wave of anxiety washed over Billy. There was something painfully intimate about the way they interacted. The way he touched her shoulder, the way she smiled back up at him. Frankie was wrong. Julie had moved on.

Billy lowered his eyes and drew further back into the alley. He couldn't bring himself to witness anything more.

75

Two days later, die-hard Met fans, emboldened by a flurry of scurrilous blogs and provocative tabloid headlines, all but calling for the head of the loose-lipped Cub pitcher, began arriving early at Citi Field for the start of the National League Division Series.

A rabid, attention-seeking contingent sporting papier-mâché goat heads, toting scurrilous, homemade placards, screaming, 'Choke on this Knucklehead,' and 'Nobody beats the Woz,' rushed the turnstiles. When the Cubs came out for batting practice, nothing was off limits – catcalls, death threats; whatever pumped-up Met fans deemed appropriate to ensure the Cubs felt more than unwelcome.

But the real ruckus began when Popwell entered the bullpen. Even the most civilized New Yorkers couldn't resist the urge to boo and jeer, hoping to unnerve the phenomenal young pitcher and get inside his head. But Popwell's pre-game concentration never wavered. Not even when a raucous few sent half-filled plastic beer cups hurtling down from the upper deck.

When the game finally got under way, the Cubs exploded with four in the first, as Chapman homered with a man aboard and Cubs catcher, Dan Dobbs doubled in two.

In the Mets half of the first, Popwell struck out the first two batters he faced, then fleet-footed right fielder, Dusty Castillo legged out a slow roller for an infield hit. The hometown crowd went wild as Vince Woznewski made his way to the plate.

'WOZ! WOZ!' they screamed, from every corner of the stadium as the Mets' home run blaster planted his feet firmly in the batter's box, then leveled his bat directly at Popwell's head. "Let's see who the wuss is now," he challenged.

Popwell came set, checked Castillo at first, then threw. Woz choked his stick with his massive hands, waiting patiently for the slow knuckleball to arrive, then pounced and connected. The ball took off, outstripping the wind, soaring high and far, way over the right field stands, smashing into the bottom of the eye-popping, neon Pepsi sign. The Met fans went berserk as Woznewsky cut the score in half, 4-2.

For the next two innings, neither team managed to produce a run. The scoreboard stood unchanged until the Cubs sent the Mets' starting pitcher packing, tattooing him for four more runs while Met fans sat quietly on their hands.

In the bottom of the fourth, with two men out and nobody on, Woznewski came up again, and promptly cranked a triple off the center field wall. Popwell remained composed, quickly striking out the next batter on three pitches to end the inning.

The Woz definitely had Popwell's number, as he doubled to left center in the seventh for his third consecutive hit. But the rest of the team had very little success against the crafty knuckleballer.

When Popwell retired the side in order in the eighth with the Cubs still ahead by a comfortable eight-two margin, waves of disgusted Met fans began streaming through the exits in droves. They trudged up the long flight of stairs leading to the elevated Willets Point train station, insisting they'd rather poke out their eyes, than sit through the bottom of the ninth and watch their beloved team succumb to the inevitable.

When Popwell toed the rubber for the Mets last chance, only the most loyal New York fans remained. It was eerily quiet when the leadoff batter popped out to short, but there was a growing noise inside Popwell's head.

"Psst! Hey, B.J.," Charley began, in an urgent whisper as the next Met batter stepped into the box. "We need to talk."

Popwell lowered his head and covered his lips with his mitt. "We had a deal," he whispered. "You don't come out during a game."

"Yeah, I know, but... this couldn't wait. I wanna pitch. Let me finish off this last inning." Popwell turned his back to the batter and stepped off the mound. "Look. I wouldn't ask, 'cept, Felicity's in the stands, and..." As Popwell paled, Charley continued. "I thought just once I could be the one she saw out on the mound. C'mon, what d'ya say? You got a six run lead. This game's history anyway."

Popwell scuffed up the ball as both his catcher and the umpire wondered what the holdup was. Despite Popwell's protests, Charley was relentless. Little by little, he managed to wear Popwell down. By time the umpire headed for the mound to motion Popwell to get on with the game, it was Charley who stood ready to pitch.

Inside a hot, crowded subway car, disheartened fans continued their lament while a scrawny young man in a tattered Mets cap slumped against an exit door, a radio glued to his ear. "The Mets have first and second," he shouted, unable to contain his excitement.

"Big deal," someone groused. "They still need six just to get even."

"Holy shit!" the young man screamed, "Bobby La Cava blasted a three run homer." The entire train erupted.

"C'mon. Shuddup!" ordered a sweaty barrel-chested fan. "Let the kid listen."

As the crowd grew silent, the young man shouted, "Wilson lined a double."

"How many outs?" screamed a woman, half a car length away.

"One. The Cubs' manager is coming out to the mound."

On the field, Hargrove signaled the bullpen to bring in the right-hander, then held out his hand, motioning for Popwell to give him the ball. But, Charley would have none of it, tucking the ball tightly in his mitt, then holding it behind his back. "Nobody tells Charley what to do. So I suggest you get the fuck back in the dugout if you know what's good for you!"

For the first time in his career, Hargrove was truly at a loss. He knew he could have him removed by security, but that was exactly the kind of spectacle he'd been trying to avoid from the moment he realized as off-balanced as his pitcher may be, he was key to their hopes for a championship. Having him carted off kicking and screaming in the bottom of the ninth would most likely land him in a nut house and the Cubs back 'waiting 'til next year,' once again.

Up in the broadcast booth, Met commentators were having a field day. No one had ever seen a pitcher refuse to relinquish the ball. Sure, over the years a few disgruntled pitchers may have balked a bit, but no one ever stood his ground and refused to be taken out of the game.

The hell with it, Hargrove reasoned, telling the confused relief pitcher standing on the mound to follow him back to the dugout. After all, the odds were still favorable the Cubs could finish the inning and come away with a victory with no one being the wiser.

On the subway, as the train motored out of the station, the young man pressed the radio as tight to his ear as he could without drawing blood.

"Mullen's up." The packed commuters waited in silence. "Ball four! First and second. Still one out. Tying run at the plate." When the train doors whooshed open at the next station, not a person left the car. The tension mounted. "He walked Peterson! Bases loaded," the young man screamed.

On the mound, Charley swallowed hard. The Cubs were on the brink of blowing a six run lead and Charley definitely didn't want Felicity to see him looking like a bum.

"Okay, B.J.," Charley reluctantly owned up. "You can take over now. This isn't as much fun as I thought."

But Popwell stood his ground. Despite the fact Charley had served him well over the years, he had to make sure he wouldn't try to challenge his dominance on the baseball field ever again.

Charley squinted up into the stands, catching a painful glimpse of Felicity's disappointed face as she followed his pathetic pitching attempts. He had to do something. "C'mon, Popwell, name it. What'll it take for you to come back and save this shitty game?"

"The ballpark is off limits," Popwell demanded. "Especially for Felicity. I mean it, Charley. It can never happen again."

"You got it," Charley whistled, breathing a bit easier. The base of Charley's spine began to tingle as he felt Popwell slowly returning. "Now, make us look good," he whispered, as Popwell's fingers closed around the ball in Charley's outstretched palm.

The riders crushed closer, surrounding the scrawny young man like disciples waiting to hear the word of God, as the train plunged into darkness, making its underground descent.

"Who's up next?" someone yelled from the far end of the car. But the radio was losing reception.

"I dunno. I can't hear. I think the announcer said Castillo, but I can't be sure." A hush fell over the subway car as it pulled into Roosevelt Avenue Station. Again, no one got off. The cramped commuters waited breathlessly for the play-by-play. A single thought on everyone's mind – why the hell did they ever leave the ballpark?

"Ground ball to third," the young man yelled. "Play at the plate! And... he's... he's..." as his voice dropped lower, "out." A collective groan trailed through the train.

"Two outs, bases still loaded. Here comes Woznewski."

The stage was set. Vince Woznewski, lumber in hand, was heading for the plate.

The anticipation was unbearable as the train squealed into Queens Plaza. This time no one even moved. "Ball one," the young man announced. "C'mon," he pleaded, "a walk is as good as a hit."

On the field, Popwell looked in for a sign, came set and threw. High and outside. Two balls, no strikes. Woznewski fouled off the next two pitches. Soon the count was full. Three balls, two strikes, two outs, bases loaded, eight-seven in favor of the Cubs. Popwell peered in for a sign, then came set. The muscles in Woznewski's arms rippled as he swung at the slow moving knuckleball and connected. The few thousand people who remained roared, as the ball rocketed from sight. But the euphoria quickly vanished, when the ball landed just to the left of the fair pole in deep left field.

"Foul ball," yelled the umpire, wildly waving his arms toward the stands.

Dobbs removed his catcher's mask and ran out to talk to Popwell. It was brief. Just a few words from Dobbs, and a return gesture from Popwell. A moment later, Dobbs was back, squatting behind the plate.

Woznewski stepped back into the box. Again, he pointed his bat at Popwell, shooting a nasty, unspoken spear toward the mound. Dobbs gave Popwell a sign, pounded his mitt, then set up his target on the outside part of the plate. Popwell came set -- but this time the ball zoomed from his grip, jet propelled. A hundred-and-five mile-an-hour fastball. A pitch no one had ever seen him throw before.

As the subway car rattled to a stop, many of the embittered riders threw up their hands as they stepped off the train. "We'll get 'em tomorrow. You just watch," they grumbled.

"Glad I didn't hang around for the ninth. Got an early day tomorrow," lamented a downcast fan as he elbowed his way off the train.

"Yeah," agreed another, prying the sticky collar of his shirt from his neck. "But this was one hell of a subway ride."

The following day, the Mets were more determined than ever to even the series at one game apiece. After all, this was their park, their city. Even the Mayor came out to cheer them on. They scored often and early and by the third inning the Cubs trailed the Mets, six-one. But Chicago's lovable losers still riding a high after yesterday's win, managed to claw their way back, tying it up in the eighth, then pulled ahead in the ninth for good, on a bases loaded double by Chapman, taking a solid two game lead back to Chicago, hoping to wrap it up in front of the hometown fans.

76

The contents of the laundry hamper lay scattered on the floor as Marvin Rasher inspected each and every discarded garment his wife had worn in the past few days with forensic dedication. He was looking for something, anything that might point to an act of indiscretion. To date, his pricey private investigator hadn't turned up a thing, so Marvin decided to take matters into his own hands. Connie wasn't stupid, just arrogant enough to pay little mind to covering her tracks.

Sitting cross-legged on the floor, sifting and sniffing wasn't the way Marvin planned to spend his afternoon when he left for work this morning. But, after three of his four scheduled clients cancelled, it became apparent no one wanted to delve into their emotional issues when they could be elsewhere, watching the all-important Game Three between the Cubs and the Mets. So he packed it in early and headed home.

He glanced at his watch, wondering where the hell Connie was. Lately, he didn't have a clue what she did with her days or who she did it with. But, little red flags began popping up on a daily basis, telltale signs too on the money to ignore. Like her newly acquired fascination with the daily sports section. Less than a month ago, Connie couldn't tell the difference between an RBI and the NFL. Nor did she care. Yet now, beneath the bouncy blonde curls lay a mind eager to absorb everything and anything related to baseball.

The other morning at breakfast, as she poured over Jay Mariotti's column, she riddled Marvin with questions concerning each issue Mariotti raised. 'Did Marvin agree the Cubs could actually make it into the World Series this year? If they did, how many games would be in Chicago? Is it true some players are superstitious about having sex before a game?' That last one nearly caused Marvin to choke on his cornflakes.

Initially, he considered the possibility that his illustrious patient, David Wagner, might have opted to graduate from spending time on

Marvin's couch to crawling into bed with Marvin's wife. If it was true, Wagner was beyond contempt. It made his stomach lurch to think how he might've wasted his expert counseling on a miserable S.O.B. the rest of the civilized world had rightfully vilified for being the lying, cheating bastard that he was. Marvin wasn't blind. He had occasionally noted the flirtatious looks and secret smiles that passed between Connie and the philandering former ballplayer, and knowing Wagner's character flaws as well as he did, an illicit affair would not have been out of the question. The mere thought of Wagner or any of his patients getting a taste, not only of his wife, but of his favorite part of his roast, ate at him.

However, as far as he knew, Connie hadn't set foot out of Chicago in years. And Wagner's infrequent appearances in town simply didn't match up with the times Connie slipped out, only to return home with a smug, lusty smile plastered across her cheating face as she raced up the stairs to shower away her lover's fingerprints. No, he wagered, Wagner was probably not the likely rival for Connie's affection. It had to be someone on the current Cubs roster.

When he heard her car pull into the garage, he scooped up the delicate unmentionables and shoved them back inside the hamper, then raced out to surprise her.

"What are you doing home?" she asked, a bit rattled, hastily wrapping her light, summer raincoat tighter around her body.

"I had a few cancellations," Marvin admitted, "and thought it might be nice to spend some quality time at home together." He studied her face as she made a move for the staircase without even pausing to take off her coat.

"That's a lovely idea, Marvin, but... unfortunately I've got a really bad headache. I think I'm going to go take a shower and lie down for a while."

"Can I get you an aspirin, dear?"

"No thanks," she answered, brushing past him up the stairs.

Marvin leapt up behind her. "At least let me hang that up for you, Connie," his hands slipping the raincoat from her shoulders, leaving Connie in nothing but a satin bustier and panties.

Marvin stood dumbstruck until he found his voice. "Who is he!" he demanded, looking as if he might actually haul off and strike her.

"It's not what you think," she cowered, momentarily frightened. "So calm down and let me explain."

Marvin flung her coat over the banister in a rage. "Don't lie to me, Connie! I demand to know where the hell you went dressed like that!"

"I went... to... the dry cleaners," she blabbered off the top of her lying head. "If you had picked up my clothes last week like I asked, I might have had something decent to wear."

Marvin fixed his wife with an icy stare. "So where is it, Connie?"

"Where is what?"

"The dry cleaning. Where are the clothes neatly wrapped in plastic? Huh, Connie? Huh?"

Connie leaned back provocatively against the stair rail and smiled down at him. Her chin nearly resting atop her propped up, heaving breasts, threatening to burst out of the lacey trim top of her bustier. "Unfortunately, I didn't have enough cash on me, sweetheart. If you'd like, as soon as I get out of the shower, I can run right back over and pick them up. Unless of course," she added, swaying her hips like a ten dollar pole dancer, "you'd prefer watching me run around the house half-naked for a while."

Despite her ridiculous attempt to throw Marvin off the scent, she failed to distract him from his enraged state. "I'm not an idiot, Connie! I know you're seeing someone," he screamed. "I don't know who it is yet. But when I do, I swear I'll kill him."

"That's sick, Marvin. And stop screaming at me," she screamed back. "You sound like one of your crazy patients."

"Is that who you're sleeping with, one of my crazy patients? You should be ashamed. Deeply ashamed."

"I've done nothing to be ashamed of. You're the one who should be ashamed. You swore you'd get the money for my procedure weeks ago. You're pathetic, Marvin," she howled, as she turned and stomped up the stairs.

"Get back down here, Connie. This is not over. We're not finished yet."

"Keep it up, Marvin, and we just might be," she threatened without looking back.

Fifteen minutes later, Connie reappeared at the bottom of the stairs, suitcase in hand.

"Where do you think you're going?" he sputtered.

"My sister's. And I'm not coming back until you apologize and put together every last cent you promised me."

The front door slammed behind her with a thunderous shudder. Marvin didn't know who he despised more right now -- his unfaithful wife or those despicable Cubs. He kicked her coat up off the floor, marched into the den, slumped down onto the couch and flipped on the TV. As a catchy soft drink jingle faded and the network returned to the game in progress, he turned from the screen and buried his tortured face in the sleeve of her raincoat, breathing in the remnants of her perfume, cradling her coat tightly against his chest.

After a moment, he found the strength to lift his head. Who knows, maybe the Mets were killing the Cubs by now. He could sure use something to buoy his spirits. Until he knew for sure which one of them was screwing his wife, he prayed the Mets would win the next three games and crush the Cubs into oblivion. But Marvin couldn't concentrate. He was far too frustrated, far too filled with rage. Damn, Connie! It was bad enough she was sneaking around behind his back. Did she have to go and ruin the playoffs for him too?

His heart sunk to the depths of his mortal soul as fireworks lit up the ballpark and Cub fans were dancing in the aisles. Wrigleyville was one mass party. Thousands filled the streets in celebration.

Connie's raincoat dropped to the floor as Marvin rose to his feet. He could barely believe what he was seeing. The Cubs just swept the Mets in three to win the National League Division Series.

After decades of Cub loyalty, he found he couldn't quell the rush of emotions stirring inside him. For one brief second, Marvin almost forgot how much he hated the Cubs.

77

Rasher grew more desperate by the hour. His beautiful young wife didn't want him; income from his practice was dwindling, and his ill-placed wagers had pretty much depleted most his savings. He had nightmares of ending up lonely and alone. A penniless, old man, cast off by a trophy wife, left to spend his declining years getting sponge baths from foreign tongued women in a state run assisted living facility.

"No," he sighed. There had to be some way to turn his fate around. With nothing much to lose, he decided to risk the penalties, withdraw the money from his I.R.A. and make a hefty wager on the first two games of the upcoming National Championship Series between the Cubs and the Dodgers. Even though the Dodgers had let him down against the Cubs in the past, the Cubs well-established history of choking in the playoffs led him to conclude the Dodgers were still the way to go to recoup his losses.

Though publicly, Langston Hargrove projected a cautious degree of optimism about his team's chances against the Dodgers, privately he was more than a little concerned about Popwell's erratic behavior in the final inning against the Mets in Game One. And he certainly didn't want to risk another confrontation on the mound should one of the troubled pitcher's less agreeable alters decide to emerge and challenge his authority again. So, Hargrove decided the safest way to go was to shake up the pitching rotation and hopefully give Popwell a little more time to re-group before sending him back to the mound. He figured he'd have Dunaway start Game One and perhaps use Scottie Wolter, in Game Two, saving Popwell to open up in Los Angeles.

The next day, when Hargrove entered the clubhouse to go over his line-up card, he was feeling pretty confident about his game plan. Unfortunately, the Dodgers blew into the Windy City with a solid game plan of their own. The Cubs fell behind early, and didn't produce a single run other than Chapman's homer in the seventh, as the Blue Crew went on to take the opener, five-one.

In Game Two, thanks in large part to the pathetic play of the bumbling Cubs infield, the Dodgers ran all over them. The Cubs were simply outplayed at every turn, committing error after error and doing a sorrowful job of hitting with runners in scoring position. The fans were suicidal as the Cubs went down to defeat once again. There was only one logical explanation. The curse! The dreaded curse!

Marvin Rasher sat behind the wheel in the parking lot alongside a Starbucks with the radio playing and the engine running. He was giddy as a schoolboy as his bookie counted out Marvin's ill-gotten gains from Games One and Two, and placed them into his eager hands. The good doctor shoved the wad of crisp, new hundred-dollar bills into his pocket. He was feeling particularly lucky, so without hesitation, decided to bet his winnings, and then some on the Dodgers to take Game Three in Los Angeles. Who knows, if his luck continued, he might even be able to make enough to resculpt every blessed inch of Connie's body and win her back. Maybe even take her on a cruise when her scars faded, or replace her year-old Beemer with a shiny new Bentley.

The oft quoted adage, 'managers are hired to be fired,' played over and again in Hargrove's head like a jammed CD. As he locked the door to his office and sat at his desk, he realized keeping Popwell on the bench until Game Three could very well cost him his job if the Cubs fail to come back and take the series. And with the way the Cubs played against the Dodgers in the regular season, and given the fact the next three games were in Los Angeles, winning two out of three seemed like a tall order.

Hargrove unlocked the bottom drawer of a steel file cabinet and removed a faded manila envelope sealed with strapping tape. Inside the envelope was an old unopened pack of Marlboro Reds. He toyed with the cellophane, then knelt down by the air-conditioning vent. Inhaling slowly, he took it deep inside his lungs, then blew a thin ribbon of smoke out into the open vent.

The tobacco felt harsh and bitter at first, then comforting, like a long forgotten friend. Who could blame him for slipping? He resolved to quit again tomorrow as soon as they got into L.A. But tonight, he justified his actions, believing it was the only way to calm his jangled nerves.

78

Dr. Sharon Edwards' voice had a calming effect, despite the interfering crackle on the line. Billy was convinced she was the only one who could help him now. He was even willing to fly back to California immediately, and swore he'd do anything she asked, short of going back to Dr. Rasher, if she would find the time to meet with him. She was his last hope.

The moment their jet touched down at LAX, Langston Hargrove, haunted by the team's abysmal performance in the first two games of the series, whisked them directly from the airport to the stadium to work on fielding fundamentals.

The stink of burnt sagebrush was everywhere. Kip Chapman's red-rimmed eyes stung like the devil from the recent California wildfires. The thick, suffocating smoke and ash seemed to cling to his skin no matter how many times he tried to wash it off. What kind of place was Los Angeles anyway, he wondered, and why would anyone in their right mind want to live here?

Yearlong sunshine, gorgeous women, glamorous movie stars, white sandy beaches and fancy cars. That's the exciting L.A. portrait Billy painted when they were both playing for the I-Cubs. But back then, Kip had to admit, everything seemed more exciting, and a whole lot more fun when Billy was still around.

He rubbed his eyes with the back of his sleeve, coughing up black, slimy globs of spit, trying to make out what he could of the ash shrouded, San Gabriel Mountains off in the distance. How he wished he could be whitewater paddling back in Bear Creek, Mississippi right now, instead of shagging flies in Chavez Ravine on what was supposed to be a travel day.

About an hour into the drill, Hargrove began to second-guess his decision as he watched the team struggling to rise above the heat and acrid Santa Ana debris-filled winds. Fearing it might do more harm than good, he called them off the field and sent them to the hotel, then proceeded to phone the office of the Baseball Commissioner, suggesting he consider postponing tomorrow's game.

A short time later, the Commissioner's office phoned and said they'd take Hargrove's concerns under advisement and maintain a wait-and-see policy based on tomorrow's weather and air quality report.

That night, the top story, practically the only story on the local eleven o'clock news was rain, or at least the suggested possibility of rain in the immediate forecast. The Channel Seven News staff fell all over themselves, wagging effusively as if reporting the discovery of human life on a distant planet. Results of today's highly contentious, International Summit Talks were relegated to a later time in the broadcast, sandwiched between a report on designer doggie rain boots, and a few 'man-on-the-street' interviews with Angelinos rushing about, loading up on sandbags so not to risk life and limb navigating the wet, oil-slicked highways once the rains began.

As the gorgeous, model-thin, anchor woman with ridiculously stiff, flaxen hair that wouldn't move if she was struck by a tornado, offered an impassioned plea for calm and caution during the anticipated treacherous morning commute, Popwell turned off the T.V. and got into bed.

He slept like a dead man, as the much heralded storm blew into town between the hours of two and five a.m., leaving a trail of downed trees and muddied hillsides in its wake. Yet, its promised sheets of cleansing rain managed to push much of the abusive ash and smog out over the ocean, making it a perfect day for a ball game.

Popwell rolled onto his back. A sweet scent of jasmine teased the tip of his nose, gently nudging him awake. He turned his head to the right, then blinked and tried to catch his breath. There atop the sheets lay Felicity, in nothing but a string of expensive pearls. She stirred and stretched in her sleep, absently displaying the heart-shaped tuft of soft, curly hairs nested between her open thighs. Popwell shielded his eyes, but it was too late as he felt his body responding. He ducked his head beneath the sheets, and was shocked to discover he was as naked as she, minus the pearls of course.

He silently crept from the bed and tiptoed to the bathroom seeking sanctuary. What was she doing in his bed and where the heck was

Charley?

Felicity called from the bedroom as Popwell fled into the shower and turned the water full blast to block the sound of her voice. He was determined to stay there until Charley reemerged. How could Charley do this, he questioned, struggling with his emotions. The least he could have done was warn him Felicity might be spending the night!

The shower curtain billowed as Felicity opened the bathroom door. A cool breeze swooshed into the room as she entered. Gooseflesh sprouted across Popwell's wet, naked skin. Then, to his horror, she promptly slid into the shower beside him. He hastened to cover his privates and without a word, turned his back to her.

She was almost purring as she reached for the bath gel and began to slather his back with long, lathered fingers. She lingered playfully, swirling her fingertips around and beneath his buttocks. When her hands ventured between his thighs, making a beeline for his guys, Popwell panicked. He swiveled from her grasp and spun around, only to find himself inches from her breasts, the shower bouncing off her nipples like windshield wipers. His eyelids fluttered, his body shuddered, as Charley rushed to the rescue.

"I'll take it from here," Charley whispered urgently inside Popwell's head. Then noting the pitcher's engorged member raised in full salute, added, "And don't worry, I promise to put that to good use."

Charley knew eventually he had some explaining to do, but for the moment, he was grateful Popwell obligingly stepped aside and disappeared.

79

In the warmth of the midday sun, Billy sat at a table at the Kings Road Café in West Hollywood. He was nursing his second cup of coffee, as he thought about the session he had with Dr. Edwards earlier. He stared out onto Beverly Boulevard, as a procession of exotic, late model cars filed into the car wash down the block to be detailed following last night's downpour. He couldn't believe there was actually a time when owning a fancy car mattered to him. Now all that mattered was getting back with Julie before it was too late -- before Howard had the chance to steal her away for good.

He hoped Dr. Edwards understood how important that was, but he wasn't sure she did. For no matter what he said, she kept going off topic, making him talk about Highwater, and all the crap that happened in Iowa with Kip and the I-Cubs.

Talking about Highwater and his stint with the I-Cubs made Billy think about Popwell, and how he probably should've stuck around long enough to offer his congratulations when Popwell got called up to the majors. Billy figured he owed Popwell at least that much.

He knew the Cubs were in town for the playoffs. The L.A. Times mentioned the team was staying at the Hilton, so Billy figured, what the heck, maybe he should see if he could connect with him before the start of tonight's game.

"Here's the thing," Charley said, as he looked in the mirror to straighten the collar of his shirt. "I didn't plan on you coming out to play so early this morning. When I'm with Felicity, I have a habit of losing track of time. But don't worry, I know we have a deal and I plan on stickin' to it. So, sorry for the slip up." He tried to read Popwell's expressionless face staring back from the mirror. "Oh, and a little heads up. You might find a few new items in your closet after today. Felicity headed for Rodeo Drive after our morning shower." With a sheepish smile, he reluctantly admitted, "She thought you could use some new duds to spruce up your wardrobe. The ones you got don't quite cut it with the horsey set. She should be back any minute. If you'd like, I'll head her off in the lobby."

"You have to end it, Charley. It's not going to turn out good."

"You're wrong," Charley insisted. "It's all good. And not just for me. I'm looking out for you... for all of us. Just like I've always done." Charley ran some gel through his hair. "Baseball careers don't last forever. We need to consider our options. We could all do a lot worse than hooking up with a gal who's gonna inherit a big fat horse ranch."

"I don't want a horse ranch, Charley."

"That's because you've never been to one. I'm telling you, you'll love it. And so will Timmy and Cal and the others. Felicity and her old man can be damn hospitable once you get to know them. I've been giving it some thought and... I'm thinking about asking her to move in with us for a while. Like a trial run. See how it goes?"

Popwell turned pale. "She knows about me and the others?"

Charley shook his head. "I didn't want to spring it on her too soon. But I know she'll be cool with it. Women have a way of dealing with that kind of stuff. Look how well Julie Hatcher took to Timmy. She's okay, that Julie. Maybe we should introduce her to Felicity. They might like each other."

"I don't think Billy would like that," Popwell said.

Charley sneered, "I don't give a damn what Billy likes. And neither should you. It's none of his damn business what we do anymore. He's out of our lives. Gone for good. He may have helped get you the initial tryout, but beyond that you owe him nothing. You don't need him. You got me to watch your back. We were all doing fine before he showed up at Highwater and since he decided to abandon you, I say, the hell with him."

A short time later, just as Billy appeared at the hotel, Charley swaggered through the lobby, then grabbed Felicity from behind, struggling under the weight of armloads of shopping bags. He smacked her on the butt, and began nuzzling her neck, moaning and groaning like a love-sick gorilla, right in front of everyone. Billy couldn't believe his eyes as Felicity giggled with pleasure, squeezed his buttocks, and stuck her tongue down his throat.

The flagrant display of crude public behavior angered Billy. It was bad enough the Hilton staff and few hotel guests took notice. What if there had been reporters around? It certainly wouldn't be good for Popwell's image, or for his fledgling career in the majors. Despite Charley's lustful efforts, he couldn't keep Felicity from heading off to try on a twelve-hundred dollar pair of Louis Vuitton sunglasses she spotted in a boutique window off the lobby.

Billy saw an opportunity and took it. "You're a real pig, Charley. Y'know that?"

"Whoa. Look who's got the nerve to show his ugly face again. What's a matter Billy-Boy?" Charley smirked. "Can't stand to see somebody getting some when you're not? I heard Julie dumped your ass."

Billy's hand tightened into a fist. He wanted to deck Charley right there and then, but fought the impulse. He shoved his fist inside the pocket of his jeans and willed his fingers to uncurl. He kept his voice slightly above a whisper. "I don't want to fight, Charley. I'm simply trying to point out groping some strange young girl in a hotel lobby is bad for Popwell's career."

"Popwell's career is doing just fine. I see to it he eats right, gets his rest and steers clear of nosy reporters." Billy did his best to control his temper and quietly asked if he could please speak with Popwell now. "Afraid not," Charley gloated. "Me and Popwell made a deal. I don't show up at the ballparks, and he disappears when I'm out with Felicity."

"Felicity?" Billy asked, uncertain if he had heard the name before.

"Yeah. That's right, Felicity Flattery, the cream of southern society. So, eat your heart out, Rubin, 'cause that's one righteous piece of ass you'll never touch. Matter of fact, you just missed meeting my 'sweet future' in the flesh.

"Your future?"

"Yeah. Screw playing baseball. Me and Felicity are gonna bring Popwell and the others to live on the biggest fucking horse ranch there ever was. And our plans don't include unwelcome guests. So if you're thinking about trying to piggyback off Popwell's good fortune again, you can forget about it."

"This Felicity… she knows about the alters? About the D.I.D.?"

"Take off, Rubin. You got no business with any of us anymore,"

Charley hissed.

"You can't make Popwell live on a dude ranch, Charley. He's got to play baseball or he'll shrivel up and die!"

"Excuse me?" Felicity asked, as she approached. "Whose gonna die, honey?"

"It's nothing, sugar. Don't listen to him. He's an asshole."

"Huh?" Felicity uttered, looking confused.

Billy grabbed her arm. "I don't care what you think of me, but you can't let him do this to Popwell. Charley's selfish and... violent. He could decide to cut you one day, and you'll never see it coming."

"This is crazy talk," Felicity said, with a nervous laugh. "C'mon, sugar. Let me in on the joke."

"You wanna know crazy?" Billy continued. "I'll bet you don't even know who you're sleeping with. He ever ask you to make him peanut butter and jelly on Wonder Bread? Sometimes he's an eight-year-old. You've been fucking an eight-year-old. I bet you didn't know that! Or you could be waking up in the morning with a teenager suffering from nightmares 'cause some pervert raped his sister and she ended up at the bottom of a river."

"Shut the fuck up, Billy!" Charley screamed.

People were beginning to stare. Felicity scrunched her face, and placed an irritated hand on her hip. "I don't know what's going on, but keep your voice down honey."

"Don't tell me what to do. Nobody tells me what to do!"

"I'm just saying, sweetie..."

"This is what I'm talking about," Billy spat out. "You better run while you can or he just might kill you in your sleep."

"This is starting to scare me," she whined, reaching for his arm.

Charley brusquely shook her off. "Stay out of this. This is between me and him."

"Are you going to tell me who *he* is?"

"Go on, Charley. Tell her," Billy demanded, no longer caring who overheard him. "I dare you."

Charley's hand reached for Billy's throat and as he dug his fingernails deep into the skin, Felicity was horrified.

"Stop it!" she pleaded, grabbing at his hand. Charley peeled her fingers from his own and shoved her hard. She stumbled backwards, nearly falling to the ground. When he took a step toward her, she grew more frightened. "Stay away from me!" she screamed, hysterically. The hotel manager rushed from behind the counter, coming to her aid. "You're an animal!" Felicity yelled.

"And you're a rich, spoiled cunt!" he railed back.

Under the manager's watchful eye, Felicity was safely escorted through the front doors of the hotel. As Charley watched her flee, his dreams, and future plans began to fade with her. He forgot about Billy and raced after her. "Wait! Stop! Don't do this," he shouted, as the doorman hurried her into a waiting cab.

Felicity ducked inside. "We're done, you fucked-up crazy bastard! Stay away from me or I'll have you arrested."

Charley pounded on the trunk of the taxi as it screeched down the driveway, sped onto Santa Monica Boulevard and disappeared. Frustrated and helpless, oblivious to the curious stares, finger-pointing and animated whispers of those who had witnessed the scene, Charley stormed back toward the hotel entrance.

"I strongly suggest," the manager muttered uncomfortably, stepping in to block his way, "you look for accommodations elsewhere."

"Do you know who the hell you're talking to, moron?" Charley blasted. "Cause I don't think you do. You're asking the starting pitcher for the Chicago Cubs to vacate your rinky-dink hotel? That bitch was a hooker. You hear me? A low-life tramp. You should be thanking me for booting her skanky ass out of here."

With that, Charley brushed past him and strode back inside the lobby. He reached into his pocket and pulled out a knife. He looked around, but Billy was nowhere to be seen.

Later that evening, as Popwell warmed-up in the bullpen, he felt as if a heavy burden had been lifted. He hadn't as yet heard Charley confirm it, but he could almost sense that Felicity was gone from their lives. It was enough for his focus to return to the task at hand. Popwell pitched a masterful three-hitter, going all the way, shutting down the Dodgers, five -- nothing. His inspiring performance served to ignite his teammates as they swept the Dodgers in their own house in front of a somber, celebrity-laden home crowd, taking the next two in grand fashion – scoring sixteen runs in Game Four and another nine in Game Five to clobber the Blue Crew and take the series back to Chicago.

80

It was still some five hours before the start of Game Six, but the booze had been flowing steadily throughout Wrigleyville since early morning. Team spirit, exhibited as raw emotion, heightened by liquid libation, caught fire through the streets, culminating in one giant party.

Over by the Players entrance, a crowd of wildly enthusiastic devotees crushed against the fence shouting frantically to anyone even vaguely connected to the team. When Chapman arrived, a cluster of teenage girls screamed themselves hoarse.

Kip trotted over to the fence to press the flesh and sign a few autographs before heading into the stadium for some early batting practice.

"Hit one for me, Kip," pleaded a pretty brunette, verging on nervous hysteria, as she shoved a scrap of paper with her phone number written in bright orange lipstick through the chain links.

"We love you!" screamed another, elbowing her way closer, then yanking up her shirt, revealing a bright red, white and blue tattoo of Kip's name etched across her naked left breast. Kip couldn't keep from blushing, as the young woman pushed into the fence, the tip of her stiffened nipple poking through a tiny opening in the fence like a turkey timer in a ripe, juicy watermelon.

"Looka here. I love you too," he laughed, back-stepping his way to the Players entrance, waving his arm in a sweeping gesture.

As game time grew closer, scalpers appeared like sandpipers at low tide. Some positioned near Addison Street station, some more brazenly hawking their ducats within the shadows of the stadium entrance itself, all the while keeping a watchful eye out for any sign of Chicago's finest.

At 7:05, all eyes lifted skyward as four jets soared above the stadium nearly breaking the sound barrier, along with several sensitive eardrums in the upper deck. A stately American eagle swooped down from on high, then posed grandly on the index finger of its baldheaded trainer standing like a beacon in the night atop the pitcher's mound. The capacity crowd rose from their seats for the singing of the National Anthem, performed by the inspiring, Acme Baptist Church Gospel Choir. Heads were bowed, and hopes and prayers were sent up to the heavens.

Hargrove elected to start Dunaway, knowing if the Dodgers took tonight's game, he'd still have his ace knuckleball pitcher waiting in the wings for tomorrow's crucial Game Seven.

The game was rocky right from the start for the hometown boys. The Dodgers had at least two men on in each of the first six innings, and twice loaded the bases. But like a cat with nine lives, Dunaway managed to somehow wriggle out of a jam each time, keeping the ballgame scoreless. It was hard for the fans to watch as the Cubs managed only two paltry singles as the game headed into the seventh.

Hargrove stood in the far corner of the dugout. Half the time with hands tightly coiled inside his jacket pockets, the other half, nervously gnawing on what was left of his ravaged fingernails. It was just a matter of time, he thought, before the Dodgers finally get on the board. And, given the way the Cubs non-existent bats have been performing thus far, one Dodger run might be all they'd need.

The bullpen got busy when the first Dodger batter led off the seventh with a walk. One more base runner and Dunaway is history, Hargrove concluded. But as Dodger left-handed batter Andre Perkins stepped up to the plate, Hargrove liked Dunaway's chances, especially since Dunaway had already fanned him in his two previous at bats. But Dunaway began having trouble finding the plate, falling behind in the count, dangerously close to putting two men on with nobody out.

Hargrove's stomach churned. What absurd hubris had ever led him to believe that he, Langston Hargrove, from Wichita, Kansas, would be able to turn things around, when all those who had recently come before had failed? He wasn't young anymore. He knew the fate that awaited him if the team failed to win the pennant again this year, and how slim his prospects were of being hired to manage another major league team any time soon.

Caught in the dark drama of his personal nightmare, Langston couldn't help but wonder why he didn't choose to go into his father's hardware business instead of baseball when he had the chance. Nuts, bolts, screws – a weekly paycheck for an honest week's work. Life might have been boring, but it would've been better than the ulcer-producing stress he was going through now.

"BALL FOUR!" The ump yelled. With first and second and nobody out, Hargrove leapt from the dugout. He turned to his middle reliever, Roberto Escalante, who made short work of the next two Dodger batters.

The game dragged into extra innings with the score tied at zero. After the Dodgers went down in order in their half of the tenth, the Cubs, with two men out and very little to crow about, managed to load the bases on two singles and a walk. The stadium reverberated with a roar that could be heard clear across to the south side, as Kip Chapman headed for the plate.

The team locked arms in the dugout. Hargrove shut his eyes and prayed. Kip laid off the first two pitches; slow breaking curve balls that nicked the outside part of the plate for strikes. Kip dug in. The pitcher came set, checked the runners, then reared back and fired a hard, blazing fastball that tailed in on him. Kip arched his back. When the bat flew from his grip, Kip grabbed his hand and set to hollering like a freshly branded calf, insisting he'd been hit by the pitch. The umpire disagreed, claiming the ball hit the bat.

The reaction from the fans was swift and ugly. Kip's finger swelled to double its size, the nail was fast turning blue, as he shoved it into the umpire's face. The umpire inspected Kip's finger, then without hesitation, switched his call and signaled Kip to take first.

As Kip took off, and the runner from third advanced toward home, the entire park went berserk. The furious Dodger pitcher charged after the home plate umpire with fire in his eyes, and murder in his heart, insisting his original call should stand. But the umpire just turned his back and started off the field. The frustrated pitcher lost it. He leapt onto the unsuspecting umpire's back, knocking him to the ground. Both dugouts emptied and raced onto the field.

'What a way to clinch the Pennant!' – the headlines screamed – 'with bloody, battered bodies bouncing all over the infield.'

Throughout the state, and across the country, Cub fans everywhere rejoiced. A day that began like every other, ended like no other. For the true-believers, the earth stood still, the oceans parted --

The boys from Wrigley were going to the World Series.

PART FIVE

81

The small muslin sack felt nearly weightless as he sprinkled its powdery contents beneath the dugout bench, chanting, "Haedus Vomica Pepulli." He felt ridiculous, but he was determined to follow Chandari's instructions to the letter. The mystical mélange allegedly contained ground goat eyes, taro root extract, ginger, and a laundry list of impossible to pronounce, spooky-sounding ingredients.

He had to be as nutty as his pitcher, Langston thought, to buy into the psychic's curse-removing concoction, particularly at four hundred dollars an ounce. But, hey, what the hell... Chandari's psychic prowess had gotten them this far. He stuffed the empty sack inside his pocket and took a seat on the dugout bench.

Last night, Langston, the team, and about a dozen front office bigwigs dined together at a local steakhouse. The top brass toasted the players, wished them luck and expressed the enormous pride they felt having the Cubs in their first World Series since 1945. But, Langston wanted more than just being in the series. He wanted to be remembered as the manager who brought a World Championship back to Chicago after taking it on the chin for over a hundred plus years.

He lifted his head and watched as streaks of lavender crowned the still and silent stadium as the first hint of daylight emerged.

Frank Tortiricci was on top of the world. Not only was he about to watch his clients play in the opening game of the World Series, but he would be doing it from the owner's box by personal invitation from none other than Cub's General Manager, Jim Farley. This was his golden opportunity to schmooze with the Big Boys, and he didn't intend to blow it. He checked his watch. He was woefully early. He didn't want to appear over-eager by showing up before Farley, so he decided to head to the clubhouse and check in with his clients.

Frankie strode into the locker room with a confident air, and an unlit cigar clenched between his teeth. "How's it going guys? I just stopped by to wish you luck and to tell you to fucking kick some Boston butt out there tonight."

"Thanks, Mr. Tortiricci," Kip beamed, grabbing Frankie's hand. "And thanks again for seeing to all the arrangements so my family could be at the game today. Shoot, my kin are so excited. Mama hasn't eaten a lick in days."

"Happy to do it, Kip. Glad they all could make it."

"Oh wait, I almost forgot," Kip said, pulling a ticket from his pocket. "I've been meaning to get this one back to you. Cousin Vernon wasn't up to making the trip."

"Is he sick?"

"Nope. Just scared. He's like a long-tailed cat in a room full of rockin' chairs when it comes to flying. Imagine that, a grown man 'fraid to fly?"

"Yeah... imagine that," Frankie casually remarked, as Kip stepped away to check out a fresh shipment of bats that just arrived from Louisville.

Frankie looked around the clubhouse, taking in the impressive array of well-heeled athletes; some of which, he surmised, might well be bagging groceries had not fate and a great agent intervened. He was also acutely aware just how many of these undeserving, lucky bastards were sitting pretty with long-term, eight figure deals, while his guys were making little more than a newly licensed dentist in Peoria. It hardly seemed fair. It began to grate on Frankie, particularly in light of the undeniable truth that his two clients embodied the Cubs best hope for a World Series win.

Frankie had yet to approach Popwell. Mainly because he still felt a little uncomfortable around him. He worried even a heartfelt pat on the back before the game might set off one of the crazy alters. But he couldn't avoid him altogether. So a simple, 'have a great game' was what he settled on. And a simple 'nod of the head' from Popwell was what he got in return.

Langston was unable to get a decent signal on his cell inside the clubhouse, so he headed back out through the tunnel to try his ex-wife again. In the twelve years they were married, Victoria had never once been on time for anything. As he recalled, she was even late for their wedding. If it hadn't been the opening day of the World Series, he would've picked up the kids himself. It would be just like her to drop them off late, or not show up at all on one of the most important days of his career.

His irritation flared by the time he reached the dugout. He toggled down his speed dial to C, for cunt, then used his middle finger to dial his ex. "Vikki... is that you? Where the hell are you?"

At the other end of the dugout, a member of the grounds crew was quietly reeling up a long length of hose. Langston glanced at the fast drying puddles beneath his feet and paled. "Jesus! What happened here?" he shouted.

The groundskeeper looked up. "Something wrong, Mr. Hargrove?"

Langston waved him off. The deed was done. The dugout was sparkling clean. Not a trace of Chandari's curse-removing powder remained. Langston cut off his ex in mid-rant and immediately tried to phone Chandari. But the psychic failed to pick up. Langston and the Cubs were on their own.

When Frankie arrived at the owner's box, he was disappointed to discover Farley had invited six other guests. It hadn't occurred to the agent's overblown ego that he might not have Farley's ear all to himself. Aside from Frankie and the General Manager, there was Farley's wife, Margaret; the Mayor and two of his kids; one of which unfortunately was seated directly to Frankie's right, covered in sticky cotton candy. To his left was a somewhat pixilated councilman, and a fast fading, one-time movie star in her late eighties, with the intriguing name of Ramona Desdemona.

A small legion of brightly uniformed, military servicemen and women marched out onto the field to unfurl an enormous American flag. A whipping October wind blew in off the lake, setting the noble banner aflutter. The public address announcer's voice boomed through the speakers asking the crowd to please stand and join the members of both teams as they paid tribute to our great Nation.

Ramona Desdemona lurched forward and clutched onto Frankie's arm for support as she struggled to remain upright, teetering unsteadily in six-inch platform heels in the wind's blustery wake.

At home plate, performing the National Anthem, was Illinois-born, multiple Grammy winning, hip-hop solo artist, actor, and restaurateur, Georgie Z, splendidly decked out beneath the lights in shimmering sequined shades of red, white and blue.

Fans of baseball everywhere watched in patriotic silence through his final, stirring, emotional note, as the teams flanked the baselines facing the flag in center field. Frankie pried Ramona's claw-like fingers from his shirtsleeve and sat down. Bottle rockets and swirls of multi-colored floodlights lit up the stands illuminating the excited faces in the upper deck. 'Go-Cubs-Go,' flashed across the Jumbotron, and the Bleacher Bums went crazy, tossing bright blue beach balls and a rubber blow-up doll sporting a Red Sox uniform back and forth across the bleachers.

The crowd roared as the Governor jogged to the mound and threw out the ceremonial first pitch. To avoid any awkward embarrassment, the quick-thinking catcher lunged forward and grabbed the ball before it hit the ground. And Game One got underway.

The Cubs got on the board in the first, as Fitzpatrick walked and Chapman doubled him home to take a one-nothing lead. And in the fourth, Chapman tripled off the ivy in dead center, scoring two more. But the real story of the night was Popwell, who, as he strode off the mound to end the top half of the seventh, had retired all twenty-one batters he faced. The buzz of a 'Perfecto' soon wound its way through the crowd, the Press box, and out into the chilly night air of Waveland Avenue and beyond.

When Farley got up to use the restroom at the start of the seventh inning stretch, Frankie decided to tag along. He hadn't had much of a chance to say more than a word or two to the GM through most of the game thus far. He was hoping once they got inside Farley's office, he might be better able to discuss a little business.

To Frankie's surprise, Farley didn't head for the privacy of his office, but chose instead to join the masses queued up in front of the men's room on the concourse. Apparently, Farley had a fondness for being out among the fans, a genuine desire to mingle with the people who supported his team through good times and bad.

As the two men inched closer to the entrance, Farley turned back to Frankie and smiled broadly, patting the startled agent on the back in an unexpected gesture of camaraderie. "So what do you think of our team?"

"What do I think, Mr. Farley? I think you deserve a fucking medal. My hat's off to you. You've put together a helluva squad this year."

"Y'know, Tortiricci, I have to admit, you're really not the little prick I always thought you were."

"Thanks. I appreciate that, Mr. Farley."

"Why don't you call me Jim, Frankie?"

"I'd like that, Jim," Frankie grinned.

"Y'know, Frankie, I honestly believe we're gonna win this thing. You feel it too, pal, don't you?"

Farley was in such a good mood Frankie figured now would be as good a time as ever to go for it. "Absolutely, Jimbo. And, if you don't mind me saying so, I'm sure we also agree you wouldn't be making room on your mantle for a World Series trophy if it weren't for the extraordinary talents of my two clients."

"Absolutely," Farley responded, as he stepped up to the men's room trough. "Your boys were the missing pieces of the puzzle."

"Y'know, Jimbo," Frank began, as he stood shoulder-to-shoulder alongside Farley, peering straight ahead as men's room etiquette dictates, "some might say it's a tad premature, but I was thinking maybe we two pals should put our heads together and see if we couldn't come up with a way to do right by my guys. I mean, why not spread a little of that World Series cheer around. Keep everybody happy. Right? How about we try banging out a new deal for my clients?"

"Look, Frank, there'll be plenty of time to talk about that during the off-season."

"I'm only saying, my guy's out there about to pitch the first perfect game in the World Series since Don Larsen in 1956. That ought to be worth something."

"There's still two-and-a-half innings to go. Let's not jinx anything by putting it out there before it happens. How 'bout we just try to win this thing first and then we can see what's what."

"Yeah. Sure. I get that. But, look… I'm not trying to be unreasonable here, Jim. I just think what's fair is fair."

Farley realized Frankie wasn't about to back off. And he didn't like it one bit. "You actually expect me to renegotiate while I'm taking a piss? What the fuck is wrong with you?" Farley zipped up and headed for the sink.

Frankie quickly followed. "All I'm saying, Jim, is…"

Frankie could tell by the way Farley turned his head and glared, calling him 'Jim' had definitely been taken off the table. As the GM's mood darkened, Frankie tried to look contrite, even if he wasn't. "Okay. I get it, Mr. Farley. Maybe we should shelve it for another time. How 'bout after the game? We could go back to your office and talk some numbers. Preliminary, of course. Just to get the ball rolling…"

"How 'bout you shut up and I forget you're even here!"

Farley stormed from the men's room. Frankie followed him onto the concourse like a dog sniffing after a rib eye. "Wait a minute, Farley. This isn't right. What do you think the Cubs' chances would be like without my guys? Huh? Think about that for a minute."

"What's that supposed to mean?" Farley turned, getting in Frankie's face. "Are you threatening me, you little fuck?"

"Me? What? No. Okay. Look," Frank backpedaled. "Like you said, let's just go back and enjoy the rest of the game. Forget I even mentioned it. What do ya say, pal?"

Shortly thereafter, Frankie found himself exiled to the seat originally intended for Kip's cousin Vernon.

In the top of the eighth, the Boston third baseman ripped a double down the leftfield line, ending Popwell's bid for a perfect game. Frankie slammed his bag of peanuts to the ground. For the remainder of the game, the brooding agent sat uncomfortably among the simple band of Kip's jubilant, southern farm folk. There were tears in Kip's father's eyes as he watched his son with pride. There were also a few in Frankie's as he watched the Cubs take Game One, and wished he had waited until after the series to put the screws to Farley.

82

The gangly branches on the towering maple tree bowed and twisted in the blustery, early morning light. Its flame-red leaves scratched against the beveled panes of the stained glass window in Rasher's den like a harpy's fingernails. Perhaps if Marvin had been able to pay the gardener, the tree might have been properly pruned, instead of threatening to crash through the house with the next gust of wind.

Marvin sadly took in the unkind world beyond his windows, as he stood barefoot, unshaven, un-showered, and distraught, still lamenting the small fortune he blew betting against the Cubs in the Dodger series. He hadn't gone into the office for close to a week now or even bothered to answer his phone, fearing it might be a bill collector, or a friend or family member he had managed to hit up for a few bucks.

His groundswell of self-pity was interrupted by the front doorbell. It was the freckle-faced paperboy dropping off the morning edition of the Trib, hoping to finally collect the twelve dollars-and-fifty-cents the Rashers owed him. When Marvin made no effort to answer the door, the boy went around to the side of the house and peeked in through the window. Marvin quickly ducked behind the sofa.

It pained him to see the paperboy's face pressed against the window; his sad almond shaped eyes hoping to discover someone inside. But what was Marvin to do? He needed to hold onto his few remaining dollars to keep the private investigator on Connie's tail. At least the paperboy still had youth on his side, Rasher reasoned, and the chance to work hard and carve out a prosperous future for himself one day. Without Connie, what did Marvin have? Nothing.

Eventually, when the boy gave up and left, Marvin inched open the front door, snuck in the paper and ambled into the kitchen, where he scraped together the last of the gourmet coffee grounds and turned on the machine. The full-bodied scent of the rich Moroccan brew was a bittersweet reminder of the good life he enjoyed before everything came crashing down around him.

He took a sip, and leaned forward to peruse the Trib, zeroing in on a little article written by a nay-saying pundit named Morris Klumpsky. Klumpsky had the temerity to suggest that the unprecedented run of luck the Cubs enjoyed in front of their fanatical hometown fans in Game One and again in Game Two, as the Cubs went on to whip the Red Sox, 7-3, would likely disappear beneath Fenway's less-adoring lights when they faced off in Boston in Game Three tonight.

Marvin sat back in his chair and contemplated the likelihood that this obvious Cubs detractor made an excellent point. While everyone else in Chicago seemed to have completely lost their minds in the blind belief the Cubs were unstoppable, this wise and clever man, this Klumpsky, was definitely onto something.

In his opinion, wagering on Boston in Game Three was as close to a sure thing as Marvin was ever going to get. He re-read Klumpsky's article a second time, wrestled with his conscience for a good ten seconds, then called his bookie and laid down a sizable bet. It didn't matter to Marvin that he wouldn't be able to cover it if he lost. He was that certain of the outcome. So certain, he thought it might be nice to celebrate his anticipated good fortune with the one person who might actually still be happy to hear from him.

Later that evening, a jovial Marvin stood in the kitchen wriggling the cork from a bottle of vin ordinaire as the Red Sox came up to bat in the bottom of the third, already up three - nothing. He carefully poured the contents into two art deco goblets, tucked a chilled can of Reddi-wip under his arm, and sauntered into the living room, where his longtime 'friend-with-benefits,' Dixie Duquette had been waiting for his return.

But Dixie was no longer seated on the couch. All that remained was a tantalizing trail of her blouse, skirt, stockings, bra and panties that led invitingly up the stairs to the master bedroom.

Miss Duquette was delighted with the prospect of enjoying a naughty night playing house in between the doctor's satin sheets, rather than the usual quickie in a squeaky office chair, ending with a few hickeys and an aching back. Tonight marked the first occasion Marvin had ever invited Dixie into his home. She was flattered and intrigued, and though the shrink was merely hoping for an evening of meaningless sex, Dixie was intent on making the most of it.

Marvin cast a final glance at the TV on the living room wall to reassure himself the Red Sox were still in the lead, before stripping down to his watch and tennis socks and bounding up the stairs.

Once he set down the wine goblets and the whipped cream, he wasted little time with formalities. He literally dove on top of her, 'Little Marvin' already rock-hard, and began hurriedly slathering her Rubenesque body with his tongue, his eager hands grabbing and pawing at her most private places.

Dixie squirmed beneath him trying to catch her breath. "Ow! Slow down, Marvin, you've got my hairs caught in your watch."

It took a moment before Marvin sat up and disentangled a few of the twisted pubic strands caught in the links of his expandable, metal watchband. Dixie slid off the bed to inspect the irritated, mottled mound between her thighs to ensure Marvin's ardor hadn't caused any serious damage, then picked up her wine glass and headed for the bathroom.

In her absence, he decided to check in on the game. To his alarm, the Cubs had tied the score in the fourth, and were still batting with the bases loaded and two outs.

"Strike two," roared the ump, on a pitch Kip Chapman thought was high and outside.

"Strike him out!" Rasher screamed, jumping off the edge of the bed, his naked reflection a shadowy outline in the plasma screen.

Chapman's bat cracked into the next pitch like the blade of a tomahawk viciously slicing into a tree stump. The Red Sox leftfielder barely turned his head as the ball zoomed over the 'Green Monster' and out onto the street. The entire city of Boston was stunned as Kip crossed home plate, giving the Cubs a seven – three lead.

Stupefied, Marvin just stood there. Within seconds, Little Marvin began to cower and shrink. By the time Dixie returned, the fountain of Marvin's manhood was dead. He sunk back onto the bed. To her credit, Dixie was supportive in her own self-serving way. For the next half hour, she rubbed and licked and sucked like a stranded motorist trying to siphon gas through a straw from a stranger's car. But it was no use. Little Marvin simply refused to come out and play.

This never happened with Connie. Even when she denied him her guilty pleasures, all he needed was a glimpse of her in the shower or getting undressed for bed, and that was enough ammo to facilitate a stiffie, which he could at least enjoy alone in his den.

While Dixie redoubled her efforts, Rasher craned his neck above her naked shoulder to catch the final play of the game, as the Red Sox pinch hitter popped out to short.

Shortly thereafter, Dixie gave up. As she got back into her clothes, Marvin rolled onto his side and gazed upon his fallen soldier in disbelief. The devastating blow to his ego couldn't have come at a worse time. Not when he so badly needed to believe things would turn around.

He gave Dixie a peck on the cheek, packed her into a cab, then sat head-in-hands on the bottom of the staircase. When his cell rang, he could see it was his bookie, probably calling to make sure Marvin hadn't skipped town.

He panicked. How was he going to come up with the money? The only remaining object of value he still possessed was his late model, Toyota Camry. After checking the Blue Book value, he believed it just might be enough to show good faith and partially cover his losses. But time was of the essence. Placing an ad, even on the Internet, might not assure a quick enough sale to keep his bookie at bay.

And then it came to him. Why waste time and energy trying to sell it, or haggling over price with low-balling prospective buyers when he could simply have it stolen.

A short time later he entered his garage dressed in black from head-to-toe like something out of a bad ninja flick, then took off for the scariest, crime-ridden part of Chicago he could think of and still be able to catch a bus home without getting himself killed. He parked the Camry with the keys in the ignition in front of a liquor store, then casually sauntered into a 24-hour Laundromat directly across the street and waited.

As the hour grew late, Marvin became increasingly irritated that not one of the degenerate, criminal-types passing by seemed to notice his shiny little vehicle sitting there begging to be snatched. Desperate to move things along, Rasher darted back across the street, rolled down the windows, turned on the engine and left the motor running.

As it became more and more obvious Marvin wasn't hanging around to do laundry, the burly, heavily tattooed proprietor, began eyeballing him in a most unpleasant manner. Not wishing to be kicked out, Marvin swiftly removed his shirt and socks and dropped a few coins into one of the washers.

The clothes swirled in hypnotic, looping circles, dwarfed inside the double-load machine. Marvin's weary eyelids began to droop. Despite his best efforts to maintain a watchful vigil, his head bobbed down to his chest and he promptly nodded off.

When he awoke, the washer had stopped and the Camry was still out front. The car had run out of gas and all four tires had been stolen. There was nothing left to do but call the Auto Club and have it towed home.

Come morning, Marvin had another brilliant idea. He went down to the basement, spun the tumblers on the hidden floor safe, and removed an envelope containing the original copy of his life insurance policy naming Connie as beneficiary. He figured, at this point he owed more loyalty to his bookie, Arnold, than he did Connie. After all, his bookie had treated him far better than she had recently.

He researched it thoroughly and discovered it was perfectly legal to cash in his whole life policy if need be. He was delirious with joy when it hit him that the bottom line would be enough to not only cover his losses, but would leave him two-hundred-and-fifty grand to play with. There was no way the Cubs were going to sweep Boston in four. Even if the demoralized Red Sox showed up half-tanked and on crutches, they still had to win tonight's game. If for no other reason than the TV networks and the powers that be would lose way too much advertising revenue if the Series didn't continue. Now all he had to do was convince Arnold to take the bet on Game Four tonight.

The bookie was skeptical at first, until Marvin promised to draw up a notarized statement attesting to the terms of their arrangement. Arnold agreed, figuring he could always lay off a good portion of the bet on the street in case the Red Sox were to win.

Marvin's heart raced out of control. There was no way he wouldn't succumb to cardiac arrest if he tried to watch the game. He dare not even risk staying home, as having the remote an arm's length away would prove too strong a temptation to resist. So he hopped a bus downtown and walked around looking for a safe haven for the next few hours. But every place he passed, from coffee shops and taverns, to the local dry cleaners had a TV tuned to the game. The only sanctuary he could find was a pew in the back of Saint Matthews Church.

Marvin fell to his knees and prayed for a Red Sox win. He lit at least a dozen candles, then prayed some more. Badly in need of spiritual comfort, he spotted a young, novice priest in a nearby pew, engrossed in deep contemplation. A Bible resting atop his lap.

"Father," Marvin whispered, leaning forward. "I wonder if I could speak with you?" When the priest didn't turn around, Rasher got up and hastened closer down the aisle. "If I could have a few minutes of your time, Father..."

The startled young priest looked up. "Huh? I'm sorry," he responded, a bit embarrassed at having been caught watching the game on an iphone tucked between the pages of his Holy Bible. "What did you say, my son?"

Marvin blinked in disbelief and raced from the church.

As soon as Rasher got home, he fired up the computer to find out who had won. To forestall a possible shock to his system, he concealed the final score with a piece of cardboard, which trembled in his hands as he inched it down the screen little by little. The Red Sox only scored three. This worried him as he thought it was hardly enough the way the Cubs had been playing. He paused, hoping the number alongside the Cubs would be less. He slowly slid the cardboard across the screen, and there it was... Chicago Cubs - two.

Rasher leapt onto the couch and bounced up and down like a five-year-old overcome with joy. Flush with his new found winnings, he couldn't wait to call Connie at her sister's and tell her if she'll come back home, he's ready to spring for her surgery.

When his sister-in-law informed him Connie wasn't there, Marvin did his best to react with charm and candor. He asked if she'd be kind enough to have Connie call him when she got back. There was an awkward pause, followed by his sister-in-law's simple, but unexpected admission, "Connie's not here, Marvin. In fact, I haven't seen her in weeks. I'll tell her you called if I hear from her, but maybe you should try her cell?"

Marvin hung up. He was crushed. He knew Connie wouldn't pick up once she saw it was him. Just then, his cell began to ring. It was the private investigator informing him Connie left for Boston two days ago. She was registered at The Hyatt under her maiden name. While Rasher tried to absorb as much of the unfolding, damning drama as possible, the knot in his stomach grew tighter.

"My contact in Boston observed her chatting it up with a few of the Cub players who are also staying at the hotel."

Marvin hung up, poured himself a glass of Glenlivet, then went upstairs to pack a suitcase. In the back of the walk-in closet, behind Connie's faux leopard skin jumpsuit was another hidden safe. His eyes blazed with indignant rage as he spun the combination and removed a small handgun. He checked the safety, released the clip, then packed it in his suitcase, anchored between his socks and a new pair of lightweight Dockers. He wasn't worried about airport security. It was perfectly legal. He had a license to carry ever since a psychotic patient threatened his life seven years ago.

The only person with something to worry about was the man having sex with his wife.

83

A crowd eight deep, kept at bay by police barricades, jeered the Cubs as they pulled up to the Players entrance in an unmarked chartered bus. Despite the fact the Red Sox were playing in their own backyard, the odds-makers tabbed them decided underdogs for tonight's game, due to the fact Popwell was on the mound.

The moment Popwell stepped off the bus, Marvin Rasher sprang from the shadows, and blocked his way. How he got past security was anyone's guess.

"I need to talk to you."

"I've got a game."

"This can't wait. Listen," he forged on with desperation, his voice a notch above a conspirator's whisper. "Someone on your team is screwing my wife." Rasher leaned in closer, his fingers grabbing the pitcher by the front of his shirt. "I was your therapist, damn it! If it weren't for me you'd be dead by now. Help me out here."

Popwell barely reacted. Rasher released his grip. "Look. You know these guys. You see them all the time. You can't tell me you don't hear the trash talk in the locker room. Think. Did you ever hear Connie's name mentioned?"

Popwell just shrugged. Rasher pressed on, whispering through clenched teeth. "What about that oily Latin guy -- the one who wears all those gold chains? Or the third baseman with the dreadlocks? You ever see him and Connie together at the hotel?" Popwell fixed Rasher with an empty gaze. "For God's sake, let me talk to Charley then," Rasher demanded. "He knows everybody's business."

"Charley doesn't come to the games anymore. We made a deal."

"Make an exception," Rasher pleaded. Popwell shook his head and began backing away. "I know why you won't let me talk to Charley. It's because he's the son of a bitch who's fucking my wife," Rasher accused, the veins in his forehead popping to the surface, a rich, royal blue.

"That's it, isn't it? He's screwing Connie and you're covering for him!"

"Hey, what's going on? Everything okay?" Kip yelled, stepping off the bus.

Popwell waved him off. "I told you, Dr. Rasher, I've got a game."

Marvin was out of time as Popwell started for the Players entrance. He needed to force Charley's appearance one way or another. "Is Charley too chicken to face me?" he baited. When Popwell ignored him, Rasher spun him around, reared back and cold cocked him, splitting his lip and sending him crashing into the door.

The doctor got his wish, as Charley instantly emerged with fists flying. Marvin managed to duck, sending Charley reeling to his knees by the sheer force of his own flailing body. Security raced over.

"I'll kill you if you ever lay a hand on Popwell again!" Charley threatened, struggling to free himself from security's grip. "You're a fucking loser, Rasher."

Rasher's blood raced, as the strong arm of the law slapped the cuffs on him and hustled him into the back of a waiting police van.

Amid a swirl of unwanted attention, Popwell abruptly re-emerged to find himself seated on a bench in the locker room, an ice pack pressed to his lip, another harnessed to his shoulder. He winced as the team doctor attended to his scrapes and bruises.

Kip stood off to the side with the rest of the team, waiting anxiously. Hargrove dredged his fingers through his thinning hair as if digging for grub worms, agonizing over his decision. "Maybe we'll sit you out today," he reasoned, stooping down alongside him. "I need you at your best – a hundred percent."

Popwell stood up and dumped the ice pack into the trash, mildly irritated by Hargrove's foolish assessment and concerns. "I'm good."

All eyes followed as Popwell walked to his locker, pulled off the shoulder pack and began dressing for the game. You could feel the mood in the locker room shift. One by one his teammates eased into their pre-game rhythms, as their indomitable pitcher headed off into the tunnel.

It wasn't long before Popwell heard the sound of familiar footsteps in his head. He stopped mid-way through the tunnel, as the footsteps quickened. It was Charley.

"I asked you not to be here," Popwell chided.

"Yeah. Right." Charley balked, rubbing his sore chin with his hand.

You think I'd stand by and let that lunatic beat the crap outta you over nothing? Especially right before the biggest game of our life."

"It's not *our* game, Charley, it's my game."

"Fine," Charley acknowledged, fast losing patience. "Your game. I get it. So let's get out there and do your thing."

"You need to leave."

"I don't think so. What if another jerkwad decides he wants a piece of you? The stands are full of 'em. We're one game away from winning the World Series. These crazies might do just about anything to take you out of the game. You need my protection."

"Not anymore."

"C'mon. Give me a break. You owe me for getting Rasher off your ass. Not to mention, I cut Felicity loose for you, didn't I? I'm sure I don't have to remind you how fine she was. And you didn't even say thanks."

The fans began filing into the stadium. Both Popwell and Charley could hear them clomping and stomping to their seats. Popwell raised an eyebrow, "What about Rasher's wife? Are you sleeping with her now?"

Charley looked amused by the accusation. "Me?" he laughed, cocking his head. "And what if I was? It's not your concern. I look out for you. Remember? Not the other way around."

Charley's character, or lack thereof, was beginning to spill into Popwell's daily existence in an increasingly negative way. "This isn't working anymore, Charley."

"Sure it is. End of conversation. It's time to get out there and start warming up." Charley gave Popwell's shoulder a playful jostle, but Popwell didn't budge.

"Things have changed. I don't want you looking out for me anymore."

Charley stared in disbelief, never having had his position challenged by Popwell before. His lower lip drooped like a forgotten Christmas stocking, sagging off a mantle in late February. He turned his head as the rest of the team began filing down the tunnel. There wasn't time for a private, protracted disagreement. "You're making a huge mistake," Charley warned. "You're not prepared to go it without me. Who's gonna keep everyone safe? You?"

Popwell took a breath. "Maybe. But we won't know till I try."

On a night in which the Red Sox would either stay alive or pack it in for the winter, Boston's finest were not about to waste their time on an out-of-town psychiatrist who took a little poke at the starting pitcher for the Chicago Cubs. Hell, if it were up to the cops, they might have pinned a medal on him. Anything to ensure their beloved Sox would take game five. And since no one from the Cubs came forward to press charges, with a wink and a warning to keep away from the stadium and stay out of trouble, they promptly sent Marvin Rasher on his way.

After briefly stopping by his hotel room, Marvin decided to go out, have a drink and bide his time, as he sat alone in TC's Lounge, on Haviland.

As the Red Sox took the field on the big-screen above the bar, Marvin's fingers gingerly reached beneath his jacket, reassuring himself the gun was still tucked securely inside his waistband. Tonight he would reclaim his bride, one way or another.

84

He didn't regret banishing Charley. Yet, an eerie, sudden sense of foreboding gripped him, as if Charley was somehow being wrested from his body as he stood on the mound about to toss a few warm-up pitches. He didn't notice the river of red and white banners flowing through the stands, or the Red Sox revelers sporting grotesque Billy goat masks in the bleachers, booing and waving their arms. Nor did he hear their bleating, repeated taunt, 'Long Live the Curse!'

His fingers encircled the baseball. He could feel the stitching against his palm. It had a comforting effect. He adjusted his cap and turned toward Dobbs waiting at the plate to receive. The moment the ball left his hand he heard them. Two, three, maybe more, it was hard to decipher at first. Startled, he spun around expecting to see them standing behind him. But no one was there. He threw another warm-up pitch and the chaotic, frantic whispering began anew. A host of distinctly different voices, yet not a one addressing him directly. They were talking among themselves. He felt like an interloper within his own mind.

As his grip tightened around the ball, the voices became increasingly louder and more agitated. Someone was shouting. Someone was crying.

He refused to be distracted. He looked to his catcher, nodded and threw; the perfectly synchronized missile landing squarely in the center of Dobbs' mitt.

"You ruined everything for us!" a voice in his head yelled out.

"Take me home. I don't feel safe," whimpered another.

Popwell turned from his catcher, covered his mouth with his glove and muttered, "What do you want from me?" He waited, but no one answered. Then they all began speaking at once, interrupting one another, yelling and crying, creating a discordant jumble of words and wails impossible to ignore.

"Hush now, children," pleaded a mature, melodious, female voice among them. "Be good. Can't you see Popwell's trying to pitch?"

When the voices grew silent, Popwell turned back toward home, and threw his first official pitch of Game Five. The knuckler danced its way toward the overanxious, leadoff batter, who swung wildly and missed as the ball dropped like a stone to the dirt. Two pitches later, Popwell sent the batter back to the dugout.

"Who's gonna protect us if Charley's gone? What's going to become of us?" a tearful voice piped up, as the next hitter stepped into the batter's box.

"Shut up, Susie. No one wants to hear your stupid whining anymore," someone fired back. Susie began to cry. Her mournful sobs rippled through Popwell's chest causing him to step down off the mound.

"I'm scared," cried a shaky, male voice. "No one cares about us anymore."

"Helen still loves us, even if Popwell doesn't."

"It's not enough. She can't keep us safe," an angry voice insisted. "Why didn't he throw yet? What's happening? Get out of the way. I can't see."

Popwell lifted his cap and ripped his fingers through his hair. "Enough!" He yelled. "Stop it! Everyone stop talking!"

Hargrove watched with growing concern from the dugout steps. His eyes riveted to the Jumbotron displaying the unsettling sight of his starting pitcher losing control.

Popwell dropped to his knees pretending one of his laces had come undone. With his face turned from prying cameras, he quietly asked, "What will it take to make you go away?"

"They just want you to hear them. They need you to understand what happened to them," he heard Cal respond.

Popwell was actually relieved to recognize Cal's familiar voice amidst the surrounding chaos. "Okay. I'll listen. After the game, not now." There was a brief silence, followed by a flurry of heated, muffled discussions between Cal and several of the others, until Cal seemed to get them to agree. Popwell stood up and resumed play. Another six pitches and the inning was over.

Popwell headed for the far side of the dugout away from his teammates. Several of the voices sprang back to life, refusing to remain silent as Cal had asked. After all, Cal was not the boss. Without

Charley's presence, it was everyone for himself.

"Are you okay?" Hargrove asked, as he approached, peanut shells and spittle crunching beneath his feet.

Popwell nodded curtly. There wasn't time to explain what was happening. Besides, if he did, the voices might butt in and try to speak to Hargrove directly. And Popwell couldn't let that happen.

The venerable, 'Voice of the Red Sox,' Carl Beane, boomed through the speakers, "Your attention please. Now batting for the Cubs, left fielder, number thirty-seven, Mickey Fitzpatrick, number *thir-r-r-r-ty-seven*."

Fitzpatrick flexed his massive arms and promptly roped a double to left center. Hargrove's attention shifted back to the field. Whatever was screwing with his pitcher's head would have to wait.

But the Red Sox defense stiffened, and the Cubs came away empty to the delight of the revved-up Boston crowd.

Popwell headed back out to the mound in the second. The Boston fans hoping to get some runners on, thundered their encouragement by stomping on the ground. The vibration nearly shook awake the ghost of former Red Sox owner, Thomas Yawkey, who legend has it, returns to the ballpark in the guise of a pigeon in times of crisis and glory.

The first two batters lifted lazy fly balls to the outfield that were easily caught. Then, hard-hitting Red Sox catcher, Jose Montoya stepped in.

"I'm bored," intoned an irritated voice in Popwell's head. "If I have to stay here just to talk to him, I think he ought to let me pitch."

"Yeah. Why not," another joined in. He let Charley pitch once. Why not one of us?"

"We all should have a turn. It's only fair."

The voices started coming like fastballs spit from a ball machine. Popwell did his best to shake their plaintive requests, but they were starting to take a toll. Montoya laced a sharp single to left. The noise from the Red Sox faithful escalated. But it couldn't drown out the voices.

"I could throw better than that. C'mon. Let me pitch next."

Popwell walked behind the mound and pounded his glove. "No!" he screamed, "No one pitches but me."

"Now batting fourth for the Red Sox, number forty-one, *Tra-a-a-vis-s-s* Pendleton, number forty-one." Popwell felt the hairs behind his left ear bristle and flitter like ill-fated moths en route to a crispy death in the stadium floodlights. His hand reached up and swatted absently.

"Don't do that!" someone hissed in his ear. "You'll hurt Helen." Popwell spun around, creating a moment of confusion, as the infielders thought the runner might be breaking for second. But the runner hadn't moved a muscle.

"I think I see Felicity," Cal shouted.

Popwell clamped his eyelids shut, his face buried in the crook of his arm afraid he might find her in his field of vision if he looked up.

"Nah, that's not her. Billy Rubin made her go away," Timmy offered wistfully. "I liked looking at her big boobies. Didn't you?"

Popwell jammed his thumb inside his ear hoping to muffle the voices.

"Don't call them boobies, they're tits. That's what Charley called them," a gravelly baritone responded.

"Is Charley still doing her?" a throaty voice cut in. "Is that why Popwell sent him away?"

"Nah. Popwell thinks Charley's got a new girlfriend. The shrink's old lady."

"Ugh. I didn't like her. She's trouble."

"Shut up!" Popwell yelled, pounding his mitt, circling the mound. "Leave me alone." The fans started booing, taking the pitcher's antics as a ritual employed to psyche himself up. But the voices continued.

A snow-white pigeon nestled atop the rim of the Green Monster, ruffled its wings, and swooped down across the infield, circled back, then perched upon the top rung of the ladder above the scoreboard. The Red Sox fans took it as an omen Yawkey's spirit was watching over them.

Popwell looked in for a sign and threw. Pendleton swung mightily, barely making contact, tapping a slow roller right to Popwell. The perfect double play.

Timmy screamed, "Throw it to first."

Popwell picked up the ball and looked toward first. But in the corner of his eye, he saw the lead runner heading for second. Cameras flashed throughout the park obscuring his vision. He swiveled toward second, still time to make the throw and nail the runner. Then, another voice yelled, "No... third. Throw it to third." Popwell fired the ball to the third baseman. Both runners were safe. The Boston fans were stunned by

Popwell's confusion, but loved every bizarre minute of it.

As the next batter stepped in, Popwell's once impenetrable concentration was shot. He barely came set as he delivered the ball with nothing on it. No flutter, no dip, no nothing. The crowd rose from their seats in unison, as the batter connected and cracked one into the night. Kip Chapman galloped to the deepest part of the park, then with split second timing, scaled the wall, robbing the Red Sox batter with an unbelievable catch, ending the inning.

Popwell raced for the safe haven of the dugout. He dropped his head into his hands and pressed tightly against both ears. But the voices had become so terribly loud, he was certain everyone could hear them by now.

He rose from the bench and dashed into the tunnel. He couldn't help them, and they wouldn't leave. The tunnel stretched endlessly before him. Halfway through, he staggered back against the cool, gray walls, his arms outstretched like Christ upon the Cross. He couldn't take another step. The back of his knees buckled, succumbing to the pressure of the escalating battle raging inside him. His palms, damp with sweat, slid slowly down the wall as he crumbled to the ground. His brain fragmenting into a million, shattered pieces.

On the field, Dan Dobbs was about to strike out and end the inning. Some part of Popwell's conscious mind knew it was the fifth game of the World Series, but when he peered back through the tunnel, the pitcher's mound seemed miles away. The Fenway organist began to play. He struggled to pull himself back up, teetering on two unsteady legs, then heard an infant wailing with a pain far deeper than his own. Timmy began screaming for his father, begging him to come back, and Cal's panicky voice swearing his sister's molester was still out there.

Popwell mopped his brow with his sleeve. He had to escape. He had to find a way to make them feel safe again, or it would never end.

85

The pitching coach took off down the tunnel heading for the locker room. He kicked open bathroom stalls, and called out his name. But Popwell was nowhere to be found. He raced back out to Hargrove to deliver the news.

The home plate umpire removed his mask and headed for the Cub dugout. "What's the holdup?" he barked.

Hargrove stepped onto the field to meet him halfway. "There's a slight problem. I need to bring in a reliever."

"Well get somebody out here. We ain't got all night."

Reliever, Pete Nobles jumped to his feet, shoved a wad of gum into his mouth and trotted out from the bullpen.

"Hey, Petey No-Balls," mocked a cadre of Beantown fanatics, as his name was announced. "You suck!" The bleacher crazies proceeded to run through their repertoire of occasionally clever, yet absurdly juvenile remarks, as Nobles took his warm-ups. Others used the unscheduled intermission to replenish empty beer cups, relieve bursting bladders, or load up on over-priced Fenway franks and try to figure out why the Cub manager pulled his starting pitcher, although he had yet to give up a run.

In Chicago, Julie had barely settled back into the apartment before the parade of Doris Hatcher's baby gifts began arriving. It was still a few weeks before the baby was due, but Doris was not about to leave her granddaughter's needs to chance. Howard was watching the game in the den while busily adjusting the guardrail on the brand new changing table he just assembled. "That's strange," he said, as Julie came in with some sandwiches.

"What is?"

"That..." he said, pointing to the screen.

Julie turned up the volume and watched as one of the color commentators questioned the merits of Hargrove's surprising decision to pull his star pitcher so early.

"I wonder what happened," Howard mused. "He *was* acting kind of weird."

Julie stared at the screen, fearing the worst.

TC's Lounge exploded into ear-shattering decibels that could scramble eggs when the Red Sox squeaked out a 3 – 1 victory over the Cubs, insuring the Sox would live to play another day with both teams heading back to Chicago for a Game Six.

Marvin didn't give a rat's ass about the outcome of tonight's game. By now, he was on his third or fourth gin and tonic. To be honest, he'd lost count. Yet, somewhere within his alcoholically challenged state, he knew he had to keep it together if he was going to confront Connie and her lover face-to-face.

But, what the hell, he surmised, the game just ended. Plenty of time for one more drink to bolster his courage before heading back over to The Hyatt.

The plan was to scope out a covert location from which he could observe their arrival without tipping his hand. He thought about confronting them in the lobby. Then thought better of it, concluding it would be best to try and catch them in the act.

Connie would be exquisitely vulnerable, utterly defenseless. He would threaten to divorce her. He would threaten to keep the house, the cars, the bank accounts. Even the dog, if they had one. She would be left with nothing but the scarlet stigma of a wanton adulteress. And, as a delicious added bonus, if his suspicions were right, her psycho lover would soon face the scrutiny of a scandal hungry, eviscerating Press.

Hargrove adjusted the microphone, preparing to spin the truth, as he sat at a table in a packed room addressing the media. He cleared his throat and chose his words carefully. "I pulled him after the second inning because his shoulder tightened up. I know what you're thinking. This ain't sandlot ball. It's the fifth game of the World Series, and maybe I should've let him play through the pain. But…" as Hargrove crossed his fingers beneath the table, hoping the Man Above would forgive him for bearing false witness, "the God's honest truth is… I believe no game, not even a World Series game, is worth jeopardizing the health of one of my players."

A hand went up in the back of the room. "Steve Causey, New York Newsday. Is it possible he could pitch Game Seven if the shoulder responds, seeing that he only threw two tonight?" Hargrove covered his mouth with a coiled hand and choked back the phlegm lodged in his throat.

"Unless you know something I don't, Steve, there's still Game Six to play on Saturday. So, let's see what happens when we get back home to Chicago."

About an hour went by before Connie waltzed in through the revolving doors of the Hyatt in a rhinestone-studded tee shirt and jeans, looking more like a teenager than a suburban, Chicago housewife. Her eyes had a sparkle Marvin hadn't seen in a very long time.

He looked around for her lover, but so far, she appeared to be alone. Which of and by itself was conclusive of nothing. Given the nature of their clandestine coupling, it was not a reach to think the Cub's starting pitcher might have wished to put a discrete distance between their arrival times. It was also possible, given he was pulled after only two innings, that crazy psycho might not show at all. Perhaps by now the entire team had been whisked to Logan Airport and was already on their way to Chicago. But, if that were the case, why would Connie stay on in Boston alone?

At present, she was far too busy flirting with the front desk clerk to notice Marvin sitting in a remote corner of the lobby with a newspaper two-thirds up his face. When the clerk produced an armload of Bonwit Teller shopping bags he had been holding for her, a bellboy instantly appeared and insisted on taking them up to her room.

As Marvin watched them head for the elevator, a startling thought crossed his mind. Could he have possibly been mistaken about her trip to Boston? After all, the P.I. had yet to turn up anything damning or conclusive. Maybe there was no illicit affair. Maybe she flew to Boston just to piss him off... or to shop at Bonwit's? He had to know for sure.

As soon as the doors closed, Rasher sped over to see which floor their elevator landed on, then slipped into an adjoining one and headed up. When Rasher arrived on the fifteenth floor, the bellboy was making his way back from one of the three rooms at the far end of the hall.

Connie had to be in one of them.

Connie leaned back against the cool marble rim of the over-sized bathtub, and closed her eyes. Life was good. There was no need to rush into bed for a quick little slam-bam-thank-you-ma'am with her big, strong, major league beau. Tonight would be all about romance. Connie had orchestrated everything with great care. There would be perfectly chilled champagne, gourmet goodies from room service, and the outrageously naughty negligee she purchased at Bonwit's earlier. So what if his team didn't win tonight. When she was through making love to him, any earlier lingering disappointment would evaporate in the heat of their passion. She would certainly see to that.

The mere thought of his young, rock-hard, naked body pressed against her own made her long for him more. She arched her back and dipped a slender hand beneath the silky bath water, slipping her wet fingers in and out between her tingling thighs. Her heartbeat quickened, her muscles tightened, her nipples stiff as stones, anticipating the exquisite rush of warm pleasure that would soon shudder through her body. Then, on the brink of climax, she pulled her hand away, inhaled deeply, then grasped the side of the tub and sat up. Not yet. Not yet, she told herself. She wanted to wait for him to take her to the mind shattering, teeth chattering, quivering explosion only he could bring her to. So, she forced herself to exercise restraint, to wait for the taste and touch of her lover's lips. More importantly, she wanted to pleasure him beyond his wildest fantasies, to make him need her with the same intensity she felt for him.

The affair may have started as an easy way to punish her aging, unappreciative husband, but somehow, it had evolved, at least for Connie, into something deeper. Perhaps even, she thought, giggling to herself as she smoothed the rose scented bath oils across her breasts, perhaps, after all these years, she was actually, finally, truly in love.

Marvin pressed his ear against each of the three doors, but heard nothing from inside. He had hoped he might catch a break and come across a chambermaid willing to take a bribe in exchange for a little guest information, but unfortunately, none were around.

He couldn't wait any longer. He stiffened his resolve and knocked on the room in the middle. When the door opened, Marvin staggered backward, disappointed to discover it belonged to Kip Chapman.

"I'm... I'm sorry I disturbed you," Marvin stammered. "I... I was looking for someone else. I must've knocked on the wrong door."

The power hitter folded his arms across his bare chest and leaned against the doorframe, fixing Rasher with a defiant glare, recalling the scuffle with Popwell outside the Players entrance. "If you're looking to start something up again, fella, the guy you're looking for ain't here. So why don't you just mosey back where you came from? Unless, you wanna go a few rounds with me this time."

The last thing Marvin needed was to get into it with a young bruiser like Chapman. "My mistake. Sorry to bother you."

"What's taking so long, baby?" a breathy, female voice called out from inside the suite. "Just give the kid a tip and send him on his way."

Rage swelled inside Rasher's brain as he charged past Kip, and flung open the bathroom door.

"Get out, Marvin!" she screeched, sinking beneath the suds, with eyes wide as Dunkin' Donuts.

Marvin was speechless, his head darting back and forth between Connie and Kip, who burst in to her rescue.

"Hey, man. What the fuck you think you're doing?"

"I came for my wife," Rasher spit back. "Get outta that tub, Connie. We're going home."

Connie stood up, the water trickling down the sweeping curves of her body like an alabaster goddess in a Greek fountain. The sweet smelling bubbles clinging to her bare wet skin. She glared back indignant, her wrists propped against her hips. "I'm not going anywhere with you, Marvin!"

"You heard the lady," Kip said, stepping forward.

Rasher panicked. Despite his anger, despite the gin and tonics, he knew he was no match for young Chapman -- that is until he remembered the gun hidden in his waistband.

Rasher took fast aim at Kip's crotch. The ballplayer's hands flew to shield his privates, "Relax man. Y'all don't want to be doing anything stupid now."

Connie casually stepped from the tub. Neither man moved, as Connie, standing stark naked, positioned herself between her husband and Kip, who remained pressed flat against the tiled wall. "You might as well shoot me too, Marvin. Because I'm not going anywhere without Kip."

"Get out of the way, Connie," Marvin cautioned, motioning with a sideways jerk of his gun.

But Connie didn't flinch. She took a calculated step closer until she stood a mere inch from the muzzle of the gun. Marvin braced himself, clasping the pistol's grip unsteadily between two sweaty hands. He could feel her warm breath against his skin. In his irrational state, his desire to touch her was overwhelming. The scent of her hair fueled his sense of entitlement. He couldn't stop himself. His eyes drifted down her body. He wanted to suckle at her nipples, to cup each shapely cheek of her buttocks in his eager hands; to fall to his knees and taste what lay hidden just beyond his reach below the damp patch of light brown curls between her legs. He didn't even care that the very man she betrayed him with was still in the room. Nothing mattered except possessing her again. He would do anything, abandon his pride, sell his practice just to keep her. He would give her anything she wanted. But, unfortunately the only thing she wanted was Kip Chapman.

"Look at me, Marvin," she demanded. "All of me, not just my boobs. God I hate when you do that."

"I'm sorry," he whimpered. "I… I don't know how to make things right with us anymore."

"You can start by putting that stupid thing away before you wind up shooting yourself in the foot."

Marvin stared at the gun in his hand. "I can't do that, Connie. Not 'til you say you'll come back to me."

Connie sighed as she walked to the towel rack and wrapped herself in a royal blue bath wrap. "That's not gonna happen. For a man with a PhD, you're really pretty stupid. We are so over."

"That's not true," he said, turning toward her. "Damn it! You're still my wife."

"Not for long," she remarked. "Look, this doesn't have to get ugly. Just go home."

"But, I love you."

"But, I don't love you. Probably never did. We had an arrangement. You paid the bills and I pretended to like it when you fucked me."

Marvin's ego took the hit, and went on the attack. "Who's going to pay your bills now? Him?" he said, waving the gun at Chapman. "I read the papers. He doesn't make a tenth of what I make in a good year. The Cubs got him dirt cheap. Couple of seasons, he gets injured they'll cut him. Then what? You'll be old with no one to pay for your lifts and tummy tucks. Think about that, Connie." He waited for the truth to sink in.

"Fuck you, Marvin. Fuck you!" she screamed, "I'd rather be old, broke, or dead than spend one more day living with you."

Whatever hope he once had, Connie and that uneducated half-wit cowering in the corner destroyed. He felt like a beaten dog. The hand holding the gun dropped limply at his side.

"Connie, please. I'm begging you."

"Goodbye, Marvin," she said, coldly, without a shred of compassion.

The room service waiter hurried down the hallway, commandeering a cart brimming with everything Connie had ordered for her special evening. He was hoping the sexy, long-legged blonde who favored him with a wink and a sizable tip the last time he was summoned to her room would answer the door. Who knows? With a little luck, she might be alone and looking for some company. He paused briefly in front of her suite to brush a stubborn crumb clinging to the front of his otherwise, impeccably clean uniform.

As he raised his hand to knock...

Two gunshots rang out.

86

She thought she was dreaming. But seconds later she heard it again. It was four in the morning and someone was pounding on her door. In the darkness, she felt around for her robe, then shuffled across the living room, turned on the light and peered through the peephole.

There he stood, still in his uniform. Through the peephole his face appeared drawn and elongated, as if crafted by Modigliani. "What are you doing here?" she asked, as she slid back the chain lock and opened the door.

"I didn't know where else to bring them," Popwell responded.

"Didn't I tell you she was pretty?" Timmy warbled, as they stepped inside.

"She's not nearly the looker you said she was," grumbled a contrary voice. "She's soooo fat!"

"Hush now, boys," spoke a stern, motherly voice. "She's not fat. She's pregnant."

"Lemme see. Lemme see," shouted another, jockeying for position. "Oh gross. It looks like she swallowed a watermelon. She's not gonna eat us too, is she?"

Popwell covered his ears. "Shut up!"

"What's going on, Popwell?" Julie asked patiently. "Who else is here besides us?"

Popwell lowered his head and shuddered. "It's me, Timmy."

"Oh. Hi, Timmy," Julie responded warmly, taking his hand in hers. "I've missed you. Did you want to tell me something? Is that why you brought Popwell here?"

Before Timmy could respond, another alter rudely broke in. "Hey! Talk to me now. Timmy had his turn. It isn't fair. None of this is."

Julie pulled back her hand. "Okay. I understand. Can you tell me who's speaking now?"

"None of your damn business, that's who." Popwell's head swiveled sharply toward the door, as the alter continued, "Y'know what, I'm outta here. We all should go. We don't like being here."

"Why not?"

"Because Popwell tricked us. We thought he was taking us to Charley."

Julie placed a gentle hand on his arm. "It's late. Where will you go?"

"Screw you, fat lady. Stay outta our business!"

Popwell's breathing became labored as he struggled for control. "They're angry because I sent Charley away. Maybe they're right. Maybe I need to bring him back."

Julie searched his eyes. "I'm pretty sure that's not a good idea."

"Could you protect us?" A small voice queried.

"I'd like to," she whispered, "but I honestly don't know what more I could do. You need to speak with a therapist. Someone who knows how to help you."

"Noooo," someone wailed like a drowning man.

"Can we stay here, Julie? Please? Please?" Timmy asked. "Just for tonight? I'm really, really tired. It took so long to get here."

Before she could stop him, Timmy curled up on the couch and closed his eyes. He looked so peaceful she didn't have the heart to ask him to leave. She thought of calling Dr. Rasher, or Frankie, or even Howard, but it was barely sunrise, so she turned off the light, and drew the curtains so the rapidly approaching day wouldn't disturb him.

Come morning, Julie tiptoed into the kitchen, opened the blinds a crack and let the soft, early-morning sunlight spill across her face. Then, downed her usual handful of morning vitamins with the last of the orange juice straight from the carton, keenly aware little else was likely to be even close to usual today.

Giving in to near exhaustion, she sat at the table and rested her head in her arms. She had almost nodded off when she was startled by the phone. It was Frankie.

There was barely a chance to say hello, before the half-crazed agent began jabbering a mile a minute. "Slow down, Frankie," she pleaded. "I can't understand a word you're saying."

"I need to know if you heard from Popwell. Or even Billy. I'm desperate. I gotta find that fuckin' lunatic before I blow my fucking brains out... before I blow *his* fucking brains out!"

Julie looked up to find Popwell in the doorway. Or at least she was pretty sure that's who it was.

"What's going on, Frankie?" she asked, wondering if he had witnessed any of the alters frenzied performances firsthand.

"What's going on?" he yelled. "The shit's hit the fan. That's what's going on! Farley wants my head on a platter. Popwell went AWOL in the second inning. If I don't produce him, a.s.a.p., I'm finished! The GM thinks I've got him stashed somewhere so I could shakedown the Cubs for more money."

"Why would he think that?"

"How the fuck should I know!" Frankie exploded. "What the hell's the difference? Farley's a dick head! All I know is if I can't find him, I'm a dead man."

She could feel Popwell's eyes upon her. "I'm sure he'll show up. Maybe it's not as bad as you think. I mean, it was just one game."

"One game?" he said, incredulous. "What the hell are you talking about? It was Game Five of the fucking World Series! Can you believe it? He just walks out. Not a fuckin' word to nobody. I spent half the fucking night looking for him. He could be anywhere by now. Hargrove's doing what he can to keep it quiet. But, it's only a matter of time before the Press gets wind of it. They're already having a field day with Chapman, caught in the middle of that juicy murder/suicide."

Julie's jaw dropped. "Caught in what!?" she gasped.

"You haven't heard? It's all over the news."

Popwell picked up on Julie's flustered reaction. But there was no way she would dare say anything that might set off any of the alters again. Though her heart was pounding like a jack hammer, she waited for him to step back into the living room before she spoke again. "Is Kip okay?"

"Yeah. Yeah. Kip's fine. A little freaked-out though. I'm down at the precinct now, holding his hand. He's one lucky bastard, I'll tell you that much. Lucky that crazy, fucking shrink didn't shoot his pecker off when he caught him screwing his wife. Instead, this Rasher guy offs his wife then turns the gun on himself and... *splat*... leaves his brains all over the hotel bathroom." There was stunned silence on Julie's end, as she gripped the phone tightly. "Two bloody corpses and lover-boy Kip walks away without a scratch."

She pressed her fingertips to her temples and inhaled deeply. "Look, Frankie, I have to go. I haven't heard from anyone," she lied.

"But if you do…" he pleaded.

"I'll call, I promise." She hung up and went inside the living room. Popwell was by the front door. "We're leaving," he stated simply. "We can't stay here. Cal thinks the cabbie may have told someone where he dropped us off."

Despite trying to distance herself from anyone and everyone associated with Billy right now, she still felt somehow accountable. "Please… wait," her mind racing ahead of her words. "I know a place where you could stay for a little while. It's not that far. And no one would ever think to look for you there. We can leave as soon as it gets dark. I just need to pick up some supplies first."

Julie sat motionless, listening to the news on the car radio in the parking garage. Frankie hadn't exaggerated about the non-stop, lurid accounts of the Rasher murder/suicide. She couldn't understand how someone as brilliant and seemingly in control as Dr. Rasher could be driven to an act as irrational and insane as murder/suicide. Then she thought about Kip, and how terrifying it must have been for him. Kip had been so kind and helpful to her, she wished there was something she could do to help him. But right now she had problems of her own to deal with.

By two a.m., the streets on the Westside of Chicago were pretty much deserted; save for an occasional delivery truck rumbling by, or a late-night dog walker stumbling, half-asleep behind his pooch. Julie was thankful their escape went off without a hitch, and that at least for now, the expanding troupe of alters seemed content to return to whatever mysterious place they dwelt in.

The six-lane highway eventually gave way to long, narrow stretches of endless blacktop, illuminated only by the Honda's headlamps. Staring into the unfurling blackness that stretched before her, Julie hoped she was doing the right thing for everyone. She felt guilty lying to Frankie. But Frankie was still in Boston, and if she had let slip who was in her apartment, he would have found a way to make things worse.

When they pulled off the blacktop onto the curving, tree thick, dirt roads, a light rain began to fall. She parked as close to the cabin as possible and got out. She could smell the damp, sweet scented pine needles rustling, as the wind off the lake whipped against her body.

Inside, the cabin was warm and inviting. She was grateful Howard and Jerry had fixed the leaky windows before the rains came.

In the morning, Julie awoke later than usual. It may have been the deepening black clouds swirling above or simply, sheer exhaustion. She searched her purse for her pre-natal vitamins, then went into the kitchen to find something to wash them down with. To her surprise, a pot of freshly brewed coffee was waiting on the counter. She couldn't quite imagine Popwell fussing about in Howard's kitchen and wondered if perhaps one of the alters had taken the initiative. In any event, she didn't care. Real coffee was the one guilty pleasure she occasionally allowed herself during her pregnancy. Without thinking, she lifted the steaming mug to her lips and took a hard swallow. "Damn it, that's hot!" she cried, as it burned her tongue.

"Shame on you for swearing in front of the wee young ones, missy." Julie looked up, startled at the sight of Popwell standing by the fireplace. "The wee young ones can hear everything we say. They're very impressionable, don't you know."

Julie placed her cup on the counter. "Is that you, Popwell?"

His body began to sway, his arms shot forward, his fingers grasped the lip of the mantle for support. His eyelids blinking wildly. Julie trembled, as yet another new alter roared forth in a dark and menacing voice. "Popwell's gone. He got no patience for girlie small talk. But then, you already know that, don't you? That's why he disliked Miss Duncan so much. Talk, talk, yak-yak. That's all that woman ever did. That's why Charley had to jump in from time to time to show her who's boss. That shrew had no business meddling in our lives. And neither do you! Leave us alone," it shrieked. "Get out! You're a whoring witch who should be burned at the stake."

Julie stepped back. A shiver shot down her spine. "But, Popwell…" she cried, hoping he'd return. "It's me… Julie."

"I know who you are," the alter hissed. "You're the lying slut who tricked Billy Rubin. Everybody knows you got yourself knocked-up just to keep him under your spell. Well, you can't control me, or Charley or even Popwell. Not anymore," he bellowed, as he snatched a vase off the mantle, strangling its delicate blooms within his fist. "It would be so easy to choke you in your sleep, and dump your body in that big old lake back there… but, I'm thinking slicing you up would be a lot more fun." Julie jumped as he smashed the vase against the fireplace. Shards of glass flew everywhere. Blood spurted from his hand, as he made his way toward her.

She ran from the cabin and stumbled down the road. Thunder crackled from the sky as a driving rain began to fall. Tree branches tore at her arms. Jagged rocks along the path dug into her bare feet but she kept running until she finally reached the cabin she was looking for. Her heart was pounding. Her knuckles bleached white as she pounded her fists against the door, praying Jerry had come up this weekend.

87

"Hello, Popwell. My name is Jerry. I'm a friend of Julie's."

"I'm afraid Popwell can't speak to you right now, Jerry," said a soft-spoken female alter, blotting her hand with a paper towel. "It's important he rest now," she said, dropping the bloodied towel into the sink before drifting back into the living room. "And I'll thank you not to stand there dripping all over the nice clean floor."

Jerry obediently removed his jacket and muddy shoes, soaked from biking up to the cabin in the rain, then followed into the living room, and quietly lowered himself into a chair by the fireplace. The therapist thought he had detected a slight accent in the rhythm of her speech, Swedish or Dutch, perhaps. "Would it be okay to ask who you are?"

"Of course you can, dear. I am Helen. I care for the young ones."

"Are there many of them?"

Helen nodded gaily. "Oh yes. Indeed there are, lots and lots," then added wistfully, she used to watch over Timmy as well, but unfortunately, young Timmy no longer seems to want to hear her anymore. He just pulls away. She leaned back and sighed, admitting, it didn't keep her from worrying and fretting about him all the more.

"Do you think Popwell would mind if the two of us had a little chat?"

"Mind? I can't imagine why he would. I'm not even certain the poor dear knows I exist. Very few do. Charley and I thought it best to leave it that way. After all, Popwell never seemed to want to know anything about me or the babies. He sealed off that part of him a long, long time ago. But the wee ones can't look after themselves. They need me to tend to them; to see they are loved properly. And Charley, to make sure no one tries to hurt them ever again. Popwell may not want Charley to fight his battles for him anymore. But Popwell isn't up to taking care of and protecting the wee ones by himself. Popwell may have hurt Charley's feelings, but Charley will be back. If not for Popwell, then for the wee ones. Don't you see… Popwell can't replace Charley. That's not who he is."

"Could I meet the young ones? Would they speak to me?" Jerry asked politely.

Helen's face flushed with defiance. She wagged a crooked finger as if Jerry was one of her disobedient little charges. "No one speaks to the young ones except me, not even Charley. Besides, the littlest one is barely more than newborn, so I doubt you could understand what he says. He can only communicate through me."

"Perhaps," he said, calmly pressing, "I could speak to the Little One through you. Would that be alright?"

The alter sprang from the chair, viciously grabbed Jerry by the throat and threw him to the floor. "Get the hell away from her you goddamned, son of a bitch! You heard her. No one speaks to the Little One!"

Jerry struggled to catch his breath then cautiously rose to his feet. "You must be Charley, protective and strong." Julie had warned him of Charley's temper and violent nature, but Jerry was far too intrigued to walk away at this point, no matter what. "We need to find out what happened to the young ones, Charley. There's no other way." Charley glared back, fists clenched at the ready. "I'm not the enemy, Charley. I don't want to fight you. In fact, I admire the way you stand up and protect Popwell and the others. But they don't need protection from me. I'm here to help. To help all of you come together."

Jerry watched and waited as Charley's eyes opened wide in protest, then began to flutter as if struggling to maintain dominance. His menacing fists began to unclench. After a moment, he took a long, slow breath, his hands hanging loosely by his side, as the fight drained from his body.

"I'm very pleased you didn't try to take on Charley," Helen spoke up, as she returned. "It's so terribly upsetting to the Little One when grownups fight. The loud angry voices, the senseless thrashing about. He becomes quite agitated. It takes me so very long to calm him down afterwards."

"Can you tell me what happened to the Little One, Helen? You know, don't you?"

Helen turned and lifted her arms as if cradling an infant to her bosom. "We swore never to tell. I gave the Little One my word and I won't break my promise." Helen raised her arms close to her ear. "What's that, my sweet, precious one?" she asked. "No. I don't think that's wise. I'm not sure we can trust this stranger with your secret. How do we know he isn't trying to trick us? Grownups can't all be trusted. They pretend to love their children... but they don't. They are capable of bringing horrible, shameful pain on them. Besides, what took place is much too vile to speak of."

Helen walked to the window carrying the unseen infant in her empty arms. "Hush now, my darling, Helen will keep you safe," she whispered, as she reached up and closed the shutters, shielding the Little One from the lightning shattering across the sky. "There now, isn't that better my beautiful boy? Close your eyes and dream sweet dreams. You're such a good little boy. The monster lied. You're not bad. You are innocent, as are all little babies."

"Who was the monster, Helen?" Jerry asked.

Helen looked down at the floor, her heart quickening as she anxiously whispered, "What if *he* is not ready to hear it?"

Jerry gently touched her arm. "I believe he is. Do you think you can manage to keep Charley away for a little while?"

"I could try."

And with that, Helen sat down, closed her eyes and bowed her head. Her weary shoulders drooped forward, her limp body jerked back and forth by a series of involuntary spasms. After a moment, she lifted her head, and opened her eyes, as if waking from a deep sleep.

Jerry was fascinated to observe how the posture and facial expressions had changed, the lips, fixed and hard, the eyes blank and uninviting, yet the therapist couldn't be certain. "Helen? Are you still here?"

"Who?" he replied, eyeing Jerry with a blank and distant gaze. This alter seemed familiar with its surroundings, but not with the therapist staring back at him. The nurturing caregiver was gone, replaced with someone who showed little interest engaging in conversation. Instead, his eyes were focused on his hands; turning them over and back, staring with idle curiosity at the dried rivulets of blood crisscrossing the palm and back of his hand. He leaned forward in the chair as if to stand and leave.

"Wait. It's still pretty nasty out there. Can I get you some coffee before you go," Jerry offered, making his way into the kitchen. "It smells great. By the way, I'm Jerry, a friend of Julie's. I'm also a licensed therapist. And you are…?" There was a moment of awkward silence, as the alter stared at Jerry, sizing him up.

"B.J. Popwell."

"Ah. Popwell. Right. I was hoping to get the chance to meet you today. How do you take your coffee?" When no reply was forthcoming, "I don't see any milk around, so I hope black is okay."

Popwell said nothing as Jerry handed him a cup of the aromatic brew. "I just met Helen. She seems very concerned about you."

Popwell took the coffee and placed it on the floor, then stared back up at Jerry. "I don't know anyone named Helen."

"I believe she's one of the alters," Jerry said, matter-of-factly, taking a seat across from him. "I'll level with you, Popwell. I don't pretend to have all the answers, but I do know the right questions. I had a patient last year, a nurse, suffering from Dissociative Identity Disorder. Before I could help her, we had to unearth the original trauma. I think this Helen may hold the key to unlock the past."

Popwell brushed the doctor's words aside saying he already knew about his lousy childhood, thanks to his sessions with Rasher. He knew that his mother killed herself and his father deserted him.

"But, what if there's more?" Jerry cautioned. "What if Helen knows secrets even you can't recall. She's part of the mystery, as is I believe, someone she calls the Little One. I really think she wants to help you. All you have to do is be willing to hear her out."

Popwell looked up. His eyes fixed on a dimly outlined figure slowly forming in his mind.

"Are you ready to hear us?" Helen asked. Popwell remained motionless as she appeared beside him inside his head.

Popwell closed his eyes, allowing Helen to speak through him. Jerry quickly grabbed the mini recorder he brought with him and turned it on. He didn't want to miss a word of what might be revealed. A pronounced silence filled the room… then Helen began.

"I can tell you some of what you want to know and some of what you don't… but must. I came to care for the Little One because no one else could. He speaks only the truth because that is all the tiniest of little ones can do. He is very fragile and badly scarred, but not where most eyes can see. He's given me permission to tell you of his earliest memories. And I will do my best. But I will not let you judge him. Only God can judge him and I assure you God loves this little one very, very much."

Helen spoke softly of a newborn, lying alone in a hospital nursery for three full weeks after his difficult birth. He had been left behind because he had been so terribly pale and sickly when he came into this world. The infant wondered why there were no hands to hold him or faces to smile down on him as he lay in his hospital bassinette.

His mother had been sent home from the hospital weeks before, and had been forbidden to visit her infant son by her husband. He didn't want her to bond with her newborn, in case he died before they could take him home. And then, of course there was his twin sister, born strong, healthy and beautiful, who was whisked home from the hospital amid much joyous fanfare. The mother was needed at home to care for their good baby girl.

When the doctors felt the Little One was finally strong enough to leave the hospital, he wasn't released into a mother's loving arms. It was the father who came for him. The Little One was frightened. The familiar hushed tones of his lonely hospital quarters were soon replaced with unfamiliar sights and sounds, loud and disturbing.

His mother did her best to comfort him when he fussed. But, whenever she came to him, her hands would tremble as soon as the man who brought him home entered the room. Occasionally, the Little One thought he heard his sister call to him from a room down the hall she shared with their parents. For nine months they had shared their mother's womb – and now -- he was separated and alone. It seemed to the Little One that no one could love him and he wondered why.

One night, as he cried out for his mother in the darkness, anticipating her gentle arms, he was yanked from his crib by a strong pair of hands, lifted into the air, and shaken till he had no tears left to cry with. The monster with the deep, gruff voice shouted and told the Little One that he was a bad little boy. He warned him repeatedly not to cry. It was his father's harsh voice he heard. It was his father's calloused hands that landed hard and often against the tender skin of his sweet little bottom. Somehow, he managed to survive his cruel treatment and the months went by. But, the Little One grew older, cursed with the knowledge he was bad and unwanted. He could hear his father blaming his mother for the bad little boy she had brought into their lives. He would strike her repeatedly. With each blow the Little One would wince, feeling her pain as his own, aching to make it stop and powerless to defend her.

Then Helen stopped speaking. It was as if the memory of what came next was too horrible to speak out loud. She was shivering, trying to hold back the bitter tears pooling in her eyes.

"Can you continue, Helen?" Jerry asked.

"The rest is not my story to tell. *He* wishes to speak now. But you will have to listen very carefully because any noise at all brings with it the memory of a great pain. He never allowed himself to utter a single syllable aloud since that day. He doesn't trust that anyone would want to hear the sounds he might make. He cannot even say the word 'father' because it is so loathsome a word to his tiny ears. But you will know of whom he is speaking. He wants to tell what happened next."

Jerry strained to hear, wary, yet fascinated by the tiny, barely audible voice that spoke next.

"When he came for me that night, I didn't make a sound. The pillow felt soft… then hard when he pressed it against my face. But I was afraid to cry out. Crying would make it worse. It always did. I kicked my legs trying to free myself. Then I felt a burning across my knees. He struck me hard. He said I was bad. A very bad boy. And bad boys had to be punished. He reached into the crib and brought the pillow down against my face again. My lips, open and stretched wide against the pillow. Gasping, until I had no breath at all. Finally, I gave up. This is what must happen to bad little boys.

I wanted it to be over. No more pain. No more bad little boy. Mama screamed… but he wouldn't stop. Then, the big, rough hands howled a terrible howl that hurt my ears. The hands fell away to the floor with a thud. In a second… I could breathe again.

I felt myself being lifted. Up… up into my mother's arms. She pressed me tightly against her trembling body. Her nightgown was stained, purple-red, wet and sticky. She told me to close my eyes as she took me from the room. I shut them tight and never wanted to open them again.

The strong hands that threatened me were gone, but I had all but disappeared as well. That's when Jacobellis came to be me."

The cabin in the woods fell silent. All that was heard was the howling winds of the storm raging outside and the rain thrashing against the roof. Jerry sat transfixed, haunted by the image of an infant being suffocated by his own father, then comforted in his mother's bloodied arms. He was anxious to gauge the effect the Little One's painful recitation had had on Popwell, but Popwell's posture revealed little at this point. And who was Jacob Ellis? And how many more would they learn of today?

It was Helen who spoke next. "The Little One has said all he is able to say."

Jerry asked Helen if he could talk to Jacob Ellis, the alter that took over for the Little One. She sighed deeply and replied, "I doubt I could keep him silent now even if I tried. He's been waiting quite impatiently for the Little One to finish. I had to promise him the world to keep him from interrupting. Make him mind you right from the start or he will jabber your head off with stuff and nonsense." Jerry watched as Helen vanished.

"Hola, amigos. Bet you didn't know I could speak Chinese. But I can if I want to," chirped a cheerful voice of a child around five.

"Excuse me?" Jerry replied.

"For what? Did you fart or somethin'? Oh, and hey, did Helen tell you I can make fart noises with my armpits? My sister taught me. She taught me lots of cool stuff if I promised to stay out of her room." Jerry found himself stifling a laugh. "I can hold my breath under water for an hour and twenty-seven minutes. Can you? Did you bring me anything? I really like M&Ms. Not the peanut ones. Just the regular ones. Do you have any?"

Jerry shook his head, "'Fraid not. Sorry."

"Maybe you could go get some and come back?" Jacobellis suggested.

Without waiting for a reply, the youngster proceeded to charge through the room, jumping on chairs and spinning in circles, making buzzing noises like an airplane.

"Do you think I could ask you something, Jacob?" Jerry asked.

"It's not Jacob!

"Oh. Sorry. I thought Helen said I was speaking to Jacob."

"My name is Jacobellis! Pretty cool, huh? I made it up myself. Mommy said it was okay with her. She thought Jacobellis was my imaginary friend, but he isn't. He's me. Do you like it?"

"I like it a lot," Jerry said, smiling.

"Daddy says it's a good name for a ballplayer. I'm gonna be a famous ballplayer when I get big."

"Daddy said that?"

"Uh huh. Well, he's not really my dad. He's Sam, mommy's friend. My real dad went away. He lives in a big, giant castle with iron gates, and trolls and sea serpents that breathe fire all the time so I can't ever go there. One day at school, the teacher asked everybody to stand up and tell what their daddies did at work. I didn't have a dad, so I tried to hide under my desk. When I came home, I told Sam I didn't wanna go back to school ever. Sam said if I wanted, we could pretend he was my dad. Then he said I should go back to school and tell everybody my dad was an Astronaut. Pretty neat, huh?"

"Definitely neat," Jerry responded. "It must've been super cool having a dad who could fly into space?"

Jacobellis put his hand on his hip, quite annoyed with Jerry. "You must be a big dumb doo-doo head, mister. Sam didn't go into space. He almost never left the house. We made it up. We made up lots and lots of good stuff together. I told you that before."

"Sorry. I must've forgotten," Jerry offered. "So, you and Daddy Sam were best buds, huh?"

"Yup. Until Mommy started getting sad a lot. Sometimes I'd come home from school and Mommy would be sitting in her chair staring out her window and crying. Sometimes she cried so long and so hard, she even forgot to make supper. So Sam would make us a sandwich or we'd go to McDonalds if we could find any money in Mommy's purse."

"Do you know why she was so sad?"

"Nope. But..." The ebullient Jacobellis drew pensive for a moment. "... I think it was because of me."

"Why would you think that?"

"Cause sometimes Mommy squooshed my face in her hands and looked at me for a real long time and told me she could see '*him*' in my eyes. Then she'd start to cry all over again."

Jacobellis turned away, and in a difficult little whisper, shared his darkest memory. "One day Mommy flew out the window and went far away forever."

"How did that make you feel?" Jerry probed.

Jacobellis held a vacant stare, then, "I didn't feel anything. That's when Timmy became a part of us."

Jerry took a moment before he spoke. "There's someone else I need to talk with, Jacobellis. Someone who really needs to hear what all of you have to tell him. Do you know who that is?" The little boy nodded. "Will you let me speak with him?"

"Maybe, or maybe I'm not ready to leave yet. I hardly never get to play with anyone anymore."

"What if when the rain stops, we go find some crayons and go color down by the lake. Would you like that?"

"No," Jacobellis spat back, sticking out his tongue. "Sam said coloring was sissy stuff for little kids and girls. I'd rather go to the lake and catch some frogs. That would be really cool."

"Okay. Maybe one day soon we can, but only if you let me talk to him first. Deal?"

"Deal," he shouted. Then he closed his eyes, dropped his head and disappeared. A few seconds later, his eyes blinked open, and he stared long and hard at Jerry.

"Do I know you?" he asked, trying to get his bearings.

"My name is Jerry. Jerry Tomkins. I'm a therapist and a friend of Julie's. And you are...?"

The alter walked to the window, opened the shutters and peered out at the windswept, slanted sheets of rain. "I'm Billy. Billy Rubin."

88

"Where am I? What is this place?" Billy asked, taking in his surroundings.

"It's Howard's cabin," Jerry replied. Julie thought I might be able to help you, since I've had some success treating people with D.I.D."

"Yeah? So? Great. What does that have to do with me?"

"Do you know a boy named Jacobellis, or an infant called the Little One?"

"No."

"What about a woman named Helen?"

"Not that it's any of your business... but yeah, I had a foster mom named Helen once, for a month or two, who lived in Cicero. So what?!"

Jerry chose his words carefully. "The Helen I just met isn't your foster mom. She doesn't live in Cicero. She lives inside you, along with a lot of other alters."

"Alters! Jesus, how many times do I have to say it? I'm not a multiple, Popwell is."

"And Popwell is part of you. He's one of the alters you've created to cope with the traumatic events you experienced as a child."

"Bullshit!"

The kitchen door suddenly crashed open. Both men turned with a start and saw Julie's ashen, frightened face. Her slender arms wrapped tightly across her stomach. "I need help," she said, gasping for breath. "It's the baby! Something's wrong. It's too soon, but I think I'm going into labor."

The pale green walls of the ER offered little comfort as Billy paced the waiting room, his hair matted from the rain, clung to his forehead and neck, a pair of dark glasses masked his anxious eyes. An elderly woman in housecoat and slippers sat crying in a row of chairs, dabbing at her eyes with fists of wadded tissues. A teenage boy, wishing to be anywhere else, leaned against the wall spinning the hard, plastic wheels on his skateboard with his index finger. Over and over they whirled against the grating, metal axle until his frazzled mother finally snatched it from his hands. Everyone in this tense, windowless room was on edge with good reason. And so, they paced, prayed or whirled wheels on their skateboards, waiting for someone to come out and reassure them everything was going to be okay.

Hours had passed since Julie was whisked through the white metal doors on a hard silver gurney. So much was happening Billy's head was throbbing. He could barely recall how they even got to the hospital. And then he remembered. It was that guy named Jerry who drove them there in Julie's car. He remembered holding Julie's hand as they sped down the bumpy back roads from the cabin. He remembered how her nails dug into his skin with each new contraction. He remembered the back of Jerry's head and the urge he had to throttle him. Who the hell was this Jerry to fill Julie's head with nonsense about Billy and Popwell? Billy was Billy and Popwell was Popwell, clean and simple. But none of that mattered now. The only thing that did was that Julie and the baby would be all right. They had to be.

He glanced back at the white metal doors, hoping they would open and someone, anyone would come out and tell him something. He walked up to the admittance desk for the sixth time in the past eight minutes to see if he could learn anything new. Each time the soft-spoken woman behind the glass met his inquiry with patience. Each time she repeated virtually the same thing. "I'm sure as soon as the doctors complete their tests, they'll come find you and let you know."

Despite her pleasant manner, Billy felt the anger swell inside him. He hated feeling helpless. He hated being in a hospital. He sank into a waiting room chair and buried his head in his hands. When he looked up, his eye caught a glimpse of Kip Chapman on a T.V. monitor mounted on the far wall. He wasn't particularly surprised, what with the Cubs in the World Series right now. The picture was fuzzy, the audio muted, as a steady stream of tiny text scrolled rapidly across the bottom of the screen.

At first Billy lacked the patience to sit squinting up at the crawl from across the room. Nor did he have much interest in Chapman's take on tonight's game. But when the on-screen image switched from

Chapman's face to a grainy shot of Marvin Rasher's driver's license photo, Billy slowly rose to his feet.

He stepped closer as yet another photo, taken at some kind of psychiatric awards dinner, showed Rasher seated alongside a pretty blonde woman. He stared in disbelief at the closed-caption crawl below –

-- NOTED ILLINOIS PSYCHIATRIST-- DR. MARVIN RASHER AND WIFE, CONNIE -- FOUND DEAD IN MURDER/SUICIDE AT BOSTON HOTEL -- CHICAGO CUB, KIP CHAPMAN QUESTIONED, AND RELEASED --

It all seemed surreal. He couldn't believe Rasher was dead. That he took his own life and that of his wife. And that Kip was somehow mixed up in this tragedy. He stared at the screen hoping for more details, when a young man, who looked no more than fifteen, dressed in lime green hospital scrubs, approached and tapped him on the shoulder.

"Are you Billy?" Billy turned with a start and nodded numbly. "The contractions have stopped and Miss Hatcher is doing just fine," said the boy-doctor with a reassuring smile. "I can take you to see her now, if you'd like."

A deep sense of relief washed over him, but did little to diminish the dark scenarios his worst fears had conjured up. He trailed obediently behind the young doctor, anxious to see for himself that Julie and the baby were indeed out of danger. "Are you sure she's all right?" Billy asked. "What did the tests show?"

"Doctor Meyers will be happy to answer all your questions as soon as she completes her rounds." Billy wanted immediate answers but part of him was relieved to discover this pimple-faced adolescent was not the physician in charge. "Doctor Meyers gave her a mild sedative. She needs her rest. So don't stay too long."

Billy nodded, despite knowing he had no intention of leaving her side until the moment they released her. And he certainly wasn't going to say anything to Julie about Kip, or the Rasher murder/suicide until she was feeling better.

He watched her lying there. So pale and still. Her eyes closed; her body hooked up to several clicking, beeping and humming pieces of equipment. He reached for her hand, consumed with guilt and remorse.

"Is that you, Popwell," she asked, without opening her eyes.

"No. It's Billy. I hope it's okay. But if my being here upsets you, I'll leave."

"It's alright, Billy," she stated, opening her eyes. He looked so miserable she couldn't help feeling sorry for him. "Don't look so worried. The doctor said it was Braxton Hicks, premature false labor. The baby is fine, and so am I. I'm just really tired right now."

He slid the curtain along its metal track, hoping for a little privacy. "This Braxton… whatever…" he began. "Is it my fault?"

"Don't be ridiculous. It's nobody's fault."

"Maybe not, but if I hadn't brought Popwell into your life you wouldn't be out here in the woods right now. You'd be in some top Chicago hospital. Not some third-rate wilderness clinic."

Julie managed a slight smile. "You sound like my mother."

"I don't understand why Popwell made you come up here." Though Julie insisted going to the cabin was her idea, her words did little to alleviate Billy's guilt. "Is there anything I can do for you?" he asked.

She shook her head and closed her eyes. "You could let me get some rest."

Reluctantly, he left the room and tried to remain hopeful. Hopeful Julie might yet find it in her heart to let him back into her life.

Jerry drove back to the cabin to pick up a few personal items Julie had asked for. He was relieved to discover, upon his return, that Julie and the baby were doing well. As he rounded a corner on the Maternity floor, he saw him standing by the nursery window staring through the glass at a host of healthy newborns.

"Have you been in to see Julie yet?" he asked.

"No. Billy needs to be with her, not me. It's not my place." In fact, Popwell admitted, he didn't want to be here at all anymore. He wanted to continue on down the hall but found his feet rooted in place, mesmerized by the peaceful, tiny faces being cooed and fussed over by their excited new parents. He couldn't help but compare the experience to that of the tortured Little One he met in the cabin. How, he wondered could anyone bury those horrible memories for so long? How was that even possible?

"Because we had to," Timmy answered inside his head. "We had to… to survive."

"That's stupid. You're both so stupid," complained Jacobellis. "You just did what you wanted to do. And it wasn't just to forget what happened to that dumb old baby. You forgot all about me too. I hate you.

You stupid doo-doo heads!"

Popwell leaned in against the glass and shut his eyes, trying unsuccessfully to shut out the hurt and angry voices.

"Can you tell me what you're feeling right now?" Jerry asked. Popwell opened his eyes transfixed by the infants squirming in their bassinettes of blue and pink.

"Go ahead, dear boy," Helen gently prodded.

Popwell stared straight ahead. "I don't feel anything, Helen. I can't feel anything," he said aloud.

"Is Helen here?" Jerry asked. Popwell slowly nodded. "Do you see anyone else?"

Popwell gazed into the glass and saw at least a dozen alters staring back, each with their own urgent thoughts and demands.

"How many are there?"

Popwell shook his head. It was overwhelming. They seemed to be everywhere. "I don't know. Each time I look up there are more."

"Who are they? What are they saying?"

"They're old and young, male and female. I can't hear what they're saying because they're all talking at once. I don't know what they want."

"I think what they want is an honest dialogue. Tell them you're ready to hear them out. It will make it easier for Billy to accept all of them once you do."

Helen stood by the nursery entrance cradling the Little One against her chest. She smiled as she held out her hand, beckoning Popwell forward, then gently placed the infant into his arms. Popwell gazed into its tiny frightened eyes.

Jacobellis began tugging insistently on Popwell's sleeve. "Can I hold him, too?" he asked, hopefully. "I really, really want to! Helen never let me see him before."

Jacobellis stood on tiptoes and strained to catch a peek. "Look," he said, brimming with confidence, pointing to the infant. "He's not scared of me. I think he likes me."

A short time later, Billy opened his eyes and looked around the empty hospital lounge. He had no idea how long he'd been there. He glanced at the clock above the admissions desk, surprised to find two hours had passed. He stretched his arms and looked around. His back was stiff, his head was aching. He considered asking the woman behind the desk for an aspirin, but didn't want to call attention to himself, for fear she'd tell him visiting hours were over and he'd have to leave. The rain had let up, so he went outside to clear his head.

The rustle of newly fallen leaves caught in a sudden gust blew across the red brick footpath, swirling in a circle like a playful pup chasing after its tail. Billy looked up. The sky was still black and angry. The late October chill had a subtle way of whispering winter wasn't far behind and time was running short. Julie hadn't asked him to stay, but Billy couldn't bring himself to leave the hospital grounds. He walked as far as a garden bench beneath an old white oak before the clouds opened up again and it began to pour.

He ducked back inside the hospital, hoping if Julie was awake by now, she wouldn't mind if he stopped in just to say goodnight. There was no one in the lobby to stop him, so he headed up to her floor.

Her bed was empty. It had been re-made with crisp new linens. How could that be, he wondered. And where was Julie? She couldn't have just picked herself up and left. Surely, it was too soon for her to be released. He stopped an intern coming off the elevator and asked how he could find out if a patient had been moved to another room.

"Her name is Julie Hatcher. I talked to her a few hours ago. She was doped up on some sedative the doctor gave her, so I know she didn't get up and walk out of here. She was right there," he said, pointing to her room, "and now she's gone. I'm not crazy." Billy took a deep breath. "Well, okay, maybe I am, a little, but I'm also the father of her baby, so I think I have a right to know if she was moved or not."

Billy followed the doctor down to the Nurses' station on the maternity floor, brushing past orderlies and smiling, late-night visitors who offered friendly nods as he hurried by. Noticeably absent were the hushed voices and tense, teary, faces of worried family members and grim looking physicians treating the diseased and the dying on the floors above.

The floor nurses in their bright pastel uniforms were busy passing around a box of chocolate cigars as Billy approached. "My name is Billy Rubin. I'm trying to find Julie Hatcher's room."

The intern stepped up beside him. "We seem to have misplaced her at the moment."

"Care for a cigar?" offered a pretty young nurse with almond colored skin, while a few of her fellow nurses giggled and whispered to one another behind their clipboards.

"Or anything else for that matter, Mr. Rubin," she added, blushing at her bold, unprofessional remark.

"No thank you," Billy replied, gripping the edge of the counter with both hands, watching anxiously as the nurse pulled up Julie's intake file. A small crease formed between her eyebrows when she looked back up at him.

"Ms. Hatcher was taken up to delivery about forty-five minutes ago. I'm sorry, but that's all the information I have right now. I can try paging Dr. Meyers' assistant for you if you'd like."

Billy panicked. "Delivery?" he managed to choke out. "Why? The doctor said it was false labor."

"Looks like the baby had a different opinion. Have a cigar, Mr. Rubin... or should I say, Daddy."

Billy didn't know whether to laugh or cry. "Are you sure the patient was Julie Hatcher?" At Billy's insistence, the nurse re-checked her computer.

A moment later, Billy was on his way up to the delivery waiting room, numbly clutching a chocolate stogie in a vice grip. When asked if he wanted to scrub up and go inside the O.R. to be with Julie when the baby was born, Billy swallowed hard and shook his head. The last thing he wanted was to go into the delivery room and mess things up. Besides, he wasn't even certain Julie wanted him there. Right now, he wasn't certain of anything. It was all happening so fast he hadn't had time to process it yet. But he was about to become a father whether he was ready or not.

He stared at the Mother Goose characters lining the pink and blue waiting room walls, trying to see if he could remember any favorite nursery rhymes from his childhood. His mind was a total blank. What kind of dad was he going to be, he fretted, if he couldn't think of a single one? Not a story, or lullaby – nothing at all. Then he began to smile, realizing he could always learn a lullaby or a nursery rhyme. All a baby really needed was love and he was certain he had plenty of that to give. He had loved this baby from the second he first learned Julie was pregnant. His daughter was his second chance, a fresh start for all three of them. The only thing he had to do right now, as he caught a glimpse of his reflection, was to wash his face and run a comb through his unruly mane. It was important that he look presentable when he met his daughter for the very first time.

A short time later, Dr. Meyers, still in her scrubs, came into the waiting room. Billy jumped up from his seat.

"How's Julie?" he asked, excitedly.

Doctor Meyers considered her words carefully. "Julie is doing as well as could be expected under the circumstances."

"Where is she? Can I see her?"

"They've taken her to post-op. She's resting. You can see her just as soon as they bring her back to her room."

Billy hurriedly gathered up his things. "Okay. Good," he muttered. "Then, I'll go down and wait for her on the maternity floor."

"She's being moved to another floor... there were complications." Billy looked confused. "I'm so very sorry," the doctor continued. "We tried -- but there was nothing we could do to save the baby."

Billy could see her lips moving, but at first heard nothing. Then, very slowly, her words exploded in his brain.

"Julie suffered a severe placental abruption. We did everything we could. I'm afraid the baby was stillborn."

Billy stood outside the door to Julie's room. His face throbbed, his eyes swollen and red. His soul crushed beneath the weight of the unimaginable loss.

An orderly trudged down the hall pushing a cart piled high with dirty linens. Atop the cart was a small radio, headphones attached to his ear. The orderly shook his head in disgust as he hurried past Billy without looking up. "Shit! The sucking Red Sox won again."

Billy leaned back against the wall and sighed. He didn't give a damn who won tonight. With great effort, he willed one foot in front of another and slowly entered Julie's room. As badly in need of comfort as he was, for once in his selfish life he was determined to be there for her.

Her face, drained of color, was turned to the wall. Her eyes were open but she failed to see or hear Billy as he walked up to her bed. He stood silently, sharing her grief, desperate to find something to say. But no words came.

He reached out and lightly touched her shoulder. She turned back to

him. Her sad, vacant stare desperately searched his face, for something...
anything to explain away the nightmare she was going through.

A nurse stood quietly in the hallway just outside Julie's room. She
paused a moment before knocking, out of respect for the young couple's
loss.

"How are we feeling, Miss Hatcher?" she asked, in a sweet,
soothing voice.

Julie sat up slowly, trying to reposition the bed pillows dampened
by her tears. The tenderhearted nurse scurried over to the bed, expertly
plumping and fussing, in an effort to make her patient more comfortable,
all the while knowing it would take far more than a fluffed pillow to ease
the pain she felt.

"Thank you," Julie mumbled weakly, sinking back into the pillows,
trying to keep from crying in front of the nurse.

"Anything else I can do, you let me know." The nurse turned to
Billy, standing by the bed like a battered heavyweight. Still standing –
but barely. "I'm truly sorry for your loss." Billy looked up and nodded,
acknowledging her sympathy. The nurse smiled back warmly. "Would
you like to see her?"

Billy seemed startled by the suggestion. Tears formed in Julie's
eyes. It had seemed insanely cruel for the doctors to make her go through
induced labor and childbirth, knowing full well her baby was already
dead. It was horrible and excruciating to endure, but Julie had insisted on
remaining awake throughout. No drugs. She would be there, fully
conscious when her tiny, 'sleeping angel' entered the world.

Then, following the final, painful push, she found she couldn't bring
herself to look upon the still and silent infant, covered in blood. She
shielded her eyes and sobbed as the nurses whisked the baby from the
delivery room. Almost immediately, she deeply regretted her decision.
She ached to hold her, at least once – if for nothing else than to say hello
and then goodbye. She never dreamed she still might have the chance.

She reached for Billy's hand and looked into his eyes. He nodded.
Their first and only decision as parents was made without a word
exchanged.

The baby was small but perfectly formed. Tufts of golden, wispy
curls encircled her precious face. Her skin was lightly tinged with blue,
translucent and cold to the touch. But she was the most beautiful baby

Julie and Billy had ever seen. The nurse placed the tiny infant, bundled in a pretty pink blanket into Julie's arms. As she held her child, any fear she might have had about this moment, vanished.

"Hello, Katherine," she whispered lovingly.

"Katherine?" Billy asked, surprised she had chosen to name their daughter after his mother. Julie smiled and nodded.

"Hey, Katie girl, it's your dad."

Their visit lasted but a short time. Not nearly long enough to release them from their grief. But, long enough to capture a memory of their daughter that would stay locked inside their hearts for a lifetime.

The moment the nurse left the room, Julie's hands flew up to her face. Her fingers pressed against her eyes, holding back tears until she could stand it no longer. She looked back at Billy and shuddered as the floodgates opened. Then, closed her eyes and tumbled into his arms. "Oh, God, Billy," she wailed, moaning like a wounded animal as she clung to him. He cradled her gently. They rocked slowly back and forth and cried together, as the storm outside pounded hard against the window.

89

They drove in silence through the rain-swollen streets of Billy's long forgotten childhood. Over clogged storm drains and puddles, so deep the water rose halfway up the tires. Then on past the library, and the old brown brick elementary school he attended as a boy, all of which seemed oddly disconnected to his present state of mind, and to the solemn task ahead.

When they motored past the building he grew up in, he barely even recognized it. The trees of his youth were much taller now. The faded yellow awning above the entrance had been replaced with a brilliant green canopy. Gone was the old metal dumpster at the end of the block once used as a marker, signifying an imaginary outfield fence. Any ball hit over the dumpster was considered a home run by the neighborhood kids.

"How much further?" she asked numbly.

"Not far. Just a mile or two up the road."

She nodded, fumbling through her purse for her sunglasses. Despite the constant downpour, she put them on so Katherine wouldn't see her mother's tears. Her fingers trembled in her lap, entwined with tightly twisted tissues. Somehow she would get through today. They both would. They owed it to Katherine.

Earlier that morning, while Billy was in the shower, Julie tugged on the zipper of her best black pantsuit, straining to pull the crisp linen fabric across her sagging stomach muscles. When the zipper split, she sat on the edge of the bed and wept silently, knowing the fresh, soft drape of her skin with its ugly, opaque stretch marks was all that remained to prove she had ever been a mother -- however brief. How she wished she could still feel Katherine growing inside her.

Her thoughts drifted to the carousel in Lincoln Park, to bedtime stories and nursery rhymes, to children's birthday parties and Christmas mornings, and puppies and ponies and clowns. To everything that now would never be.

They decided their daughter would be laid to rest in Chicago, alongside her grandmother. Billy hoped his mother's spirit would guide Katherine to whatever awaited her on the other side; that she would lovingly watch over her until the day Billy and Julie would join them.

Julie waited in the car while Billy went inside the main building to check on the final arrangements. The service would be simple and small, just Billy, Julie, a pastor from the local parish, Frankie and Howard. Julie didn't know how Billy would feel having Howard at the service, but she wanted him there, and Billy didn't protest.

They gathered beside the open grave beneath a canopy shielding them from the steady downpour. Frankie looked up, wondering why the fuck it always rained at funerals, and when if ever, it would clear long enough to get in Game Seven, which by now had been postponed for three long, storm-drenched days. It wasn't that he didn't feel compassion for Billy and Julie's loss. It was more that there was nothing he could say or do that would make things okay for them right now.

Billy took Julie's hand as they braced themselves to let Katherine go. The pastor began softly, acknowledging the tragedy of Katherine's death; of how dearly she was loved and nurtured for nearly nine full months within her mother's womb, and of the countless expectations anticipated and cherished in the hearts of both her parents, grandparent, family and friends; of the joy and peace that surrounded her as she entered God's kingdom; and of God's many blessings and promises.

In the distance, thunder rumbled, prompting the pastor to raise his voice a notch. "God did not promise life on earth would be easy or free from tragedy. His promise is that with His love, we can heal and grow stronger from them. That we must search within ourselves and re-emerge from the darkness that surrounds us, stronger and whole."

The pastor's words triggered something deep within Billy. He had heard those words before from Julie and Dr. Rasher, from Miss Duncan and Frankie and Dr. Edwards, from everyone who ever tried to help him.

Julie placed a single pink rose atop the coffin, then turned away as the tiny, white box was lowered into the ground.

At the end of the service, Frankie gripped Billy's shoulder tightly. "This may not be the time, but I just wanted you to know I smoothed things out with Hargrove. He gets it. I mean, he really does. He's being a fucking prince." Billy had no idea what Frankie was talking about, and at this moment didn't much care. "So, I mean, whenever you're ready, we can make it work. In the meantime, anything you need, Billy," he offered, his voice cracking slightly, overcome with emotions he didn't know he had. "Anything at all, you just let me know… and I'm there."

Howard stepped forward and shook Billy's hand, then brushed back a tear as he offered Julie his condolences. She thanked him for his beautiful flowers, and for helping her through the past few months. Billy watched her smile weakly; gratefully accepting his comfort and embrace.

Julie and Billy remained behind to spend a few private moments by their daughter's graveside. They sat side by side on a nearby stone bench, her head resting lightly against his shoulder.

"What if the pastor's wrong, Billy? What if I can't find the strength to leave her here all alone?"

"She's not alone. She's with God… and her grandmother."

"It's not the same." She wept softly, as she lifted her head from his shoulder. "I'm her mother."

"We can come back tomorrow if you'd like, and the next day…"

Julie shook her head and looked away. "I won't be here tomorrow or the next day. I'm leaving Chicago."

Billy froze. "For how long?"

"I don't know. But, I can't stay here. Everything reminds me of the plans I had for her. It's too hard."

He stared at the grass beneath his feet, nudging a pebble with the tip of his shoe. "Is this because… what Jerry said? You think I'm a multiple?"

"I think… I just need some time."

"What about Howard?"

"What about him?"

"Is he going with you?"

"No. Howard is my friend, Billy. A good friend." Julie reached for Billy's hand. "That's all he's ever been, and all he ever will be."

"Where will you go?"

"Los Angeles. I know it must seem crazy, but I need to be with my mother right now. I hope you understand."

Billy searched her face. "Will you be coming back?"

"I don't know."

Julie's plane was somewhere over Montana by now, high above the storms that continued to hold most of the Midwest in its soggy grip for nearly a week. Billy didn't blame her for wanting to leave. If he could lessen the pain of his miserable life by stepping onto a plane, he would. But no matter where it would take him, he couldn't escape himself.

He stood in the vacant lot across from the Fullerton Station, ankle deep in mud, staring at the ribbons of train track twisting high above his head. He felt completely disconnected, as if everyone else had somewhere to go and someone waiting for them when they got there.

He wandered without purpose as he strolled past Dominick's, packed with women pulling wagons piled high with groceries, scurrying to take advantage of the lull between the storms. For, despite the most recent optimistic forecast, few Chicagoans believed Mother Nature was done with them yet. And they were right.

The winds began to whip and whistle, howling inside his ears. He hugged his jacket tighter as the rain began to tumble. Before long, most of North Clark Street was awash again. He picked up his pace, ducking between store awnings and building overhangs. The sidewalks were all but empty once again. A few intrepid cars attempted to navigate the eddies swirling in the overflowing intersections. Rain trickled from the brim of his cap like a leaky faucet. Despite the downpour, he stood beneath the corner streetlight staring at the entrance to Wrigley Field for the better part of an hour, until he heard someone call out his name.

It seemed to come from somewhere over by the row of empty news vans flanking the ballpark, rusting side by side, idled by the storms. He thought at first it might have been Paul Middleman, from the Trib, recalling he once promised the reporter first dibs on his triumphant return to baseball before everything turned to shit. But Middleman was nowhere to be seen. In fact, there were no reporters at all, nor crowds scrambling for tickets and souvenirs. The public and the Press had camped out for days, impatiently awaiting Game Seven. Eventually they all gave up and returned to their homes and hotel rooms to wait for a sign from God or the Commissioner – whichever came first.

Then he swore he heard it again, a whisper between the claps of thunder. Or perhaps, it was just the wind playing tricks.

The next thing he knew, he was racing back onto Clark Street, waving his arms to flag down an empty bus about to pull away from the curb. He took a seat in the back and pressed his forehead against the window, shivering from the dampness. As the bus meandered through Billy's old neighborhood, timeworn glimpses of the past began popping up like cardboard ducks at a carnival arcade. The closer they came to the block he once lived on, the more rapidly they seemed to appear, unfolding like pages of a cherished scrapbook.

His hand reached up and yanked the bell cord. A moment later, he was standing in front of his old apartment building; only the awning wasn't green like the day he drove by with Julie. Flapping against the wind was the old yellow canvas cloth from years ago.

A gangly group of boys were playing stickball in the street. A ball crashed off the top of the metal dumpster. "C'mon, Jimmy. Come on!" someone shouted, as twelve-year-old Jimmy Anderson dropped his bat, raced around the bases, and headed for home. Only Jimmy died in Afghanistan five years ago.

A foul ball squibbed its way toward Billy, who blocked it with tip of his shoe. "Hey, Mister! Over here," called Winky Foster, the chubby ten-year old, wiping his runny nose with the sleeve of his jacket, who sat behind Billy in Miss Fiderer's fifth grade English class. Billy tossed the ball back to Winky, who ran off to rejoin his friends, oblivious to the bizarre turn of events unfolding.

A sudden jagged dance of lightning ripped through the sky, causing the boys to scramble to safety and Billy to seek shelter beneath the yellow awning. Curious what he might find after all these years, he ventured inside and made his way up to the top floor, to an apartment at the end of the hall. The doorknob turned easily in his hand. The entry foyer smelled of home, of lilac scented pillows and lamb chops and creamed corn cooking on the stove.

He went inside without a single thought to the consequences his uninvited presence might produce. When he entered his childhood bedroom, it looked much smaller than he remembered. Against the far wall, where his cherry wood, 'Star Wars' blanketed bed once stood, was a shiny new baby crib. He crept closer and peered over the railing of the crib. A tiny infant stared silently up at him. He so wanted it to be Katherine, alive and well, but it wasn't. This baby's small red fists were clenched and shaking.

Billy jumped back against the closet door when he heard someone entering the room. The floor beneath his feet began to quake as the stranger's heavy-soled work boots stomped closer to the infant's crib. The man was massive, tall and powerfully built. He looked angry, or drunk, or both. He smelled like Diablo. He didn't seem to notice Billy flattened tight against the closet.

Billy opened his mouth to speak, but nothing came out. With each advancing step, Billy could feel himself disappearing, until there was nothing left of him but his eyes. And, though he desperately wanted to, he couldn't shut them or look away.

The baby began to fuss and cry with frantic, breathless screams as the man's leathery, snake-like hands reached in and grabbed the infant by his tiny spindly arms, then lifted the child in the air and shook him violently, growling and cursing what a bad little boy he was, ranting, he was the Devil's spawn, not his.

Billy watched in horror as the terrified infant was returned to its crib, and a pillow placed over its small face. The man emitted a horrible grunting noise as his rough hands crushed against the blue taffeta, muffling the baby's mournful cries. Billy could feel the oxygen drain from the room. In the doorway stood a young woman, her face badly swollen beneath the mottled, purple blotches covering her cheeks and neck. Her fiery-red hair thrashed about like wild flames as she clawed at the man's arms, desperate to make him stop. "I won't let you kill our son," she screamed. But he pushed her aside with a swift crack of the back of his hand, dropping her to the floor.

Billy shuddered, struggling to will himself back into the room to come to her aid, but as he felt his body slowly returning, a searing pain tore through his chest, his lungs collapsing inside him.

The woman struggled up off the floor; her hands trembling as she lunged at the man, plunging the blade of a kitchen knife deep, tearing into the monster's flesh. Her nightgown was drenched in his blood as she gently reached for the infant and cradled him to her breast. Her voice, barely above a whisper, her lips a scant breath from the baby's tender ears as she offered a lullaby to sooth his frightened soul.

"Blinka lilla stjarna dar, Hur jag under var du ar," she sang softly, as she carried him from the room.

Billy bent forward, gasping for air, then raced from the apartment back out into the hall and charged down the stairwell. When he reached the final landing, he clamped onto the handrail and stopped, overcome with panic.

He turned with a start when he felt a tap on his shoulder. But the stairwell was empty. The image of Miss Duncan on the day he first entered Highwater suddenly formed in his mind. She was seated in her usual chair in Group, her hands folded primly in her lap. She smiled sweetly. "We're all here to help you, Billy. Each and every one of us."

He shook the sweat from his forehead, more and more confused by the past intruding on the present. His heart raced. He sat down in the stairwell and pressed his hand to his chest. He could hear the rhythmic thumping grow louder by the second. But the thumping wasn't coming from inside his chest. He looked back over his shoulder. A baseball was slowly bump-bumping its way down the steps behind him.

"C'mon. What d'ya say?" he heard Huff remark, poking Billy lightly in the chest with the tip of a bat. "Baseball's not the problem, my friend. You are. Why not try being productive while you're here. Be part of the group."

Billy got up and tried to run, but Armand leapt into the doorway, blocking his escape.

"Fellow Titans," Armand snickered. "Meet Billy Rubin. Starting today he's one of us." His hypnotic parlance echoed in Billy's brain. He squeezed his palms against his ears and closed his eyes. When he opened them, he was back upstairs in the apartment. Though only minutes had passed, everything seemed different. The furniture had been replaced or moved. There were bare patches in the carpet, the once vibrant colors of the couch pillows were faded and worn. A great sadness engulfed him, weighing him down, draped across everything within his view. He had no memory of his childhood home being filled with such neglect and despair. In the kitchen, dishes stood haphazardly stacked by the sink unwashed. Unwrapped food lay spoiling on the counter. There was a profound sense of hopelessness everywhere. The kind that deadens one's soul and destroys one's will to attend to the smallest of life's details. Billy knew that feeling all too well.

A hauntingly familiar lullaby drew him to the threshold of the master bedroom. The woman didn't look up when he entered. She sat very still by the window. The blinds were shuttered, the curtains were drawn. Somewhere in the shadows, her fingernails, chewed and broken were coiled around the wooden armrest of the chair, her stare, empty and despondent. Her skin, ashen, her eyes, sunken and drawn. It saddened Billy to see her in such pain. Pain a child could never comprehend, but a grown man who had experienced his own, had little trouble recognizing.

Unable to watch a moment longer, he closed the door. Guilt and self-loathing gripped his soul. There had to be something he could do to help her. He turned back and quietly cracked open her door. She was no longer sitting in the chair. He swung the door wide, and looked about the room. She was gone. A cold draft rushed against his face. The blinds had been raised high. The calico curtains, flapped wildly in the wind. The planter on the edge of the sill had been pushed aside, the window, wide open.

For an instant he felt his heart stop; wrenched by a sudden inescapable clarity. "No! No!" he screamed.

"What is it Billy?" Jerry asked, leaning forward in his chair.

"My... my mother died because of me. She killed herself because I was bad," he sobbed uncontrollably.

"It wasn't because of you. It wasn't your fault. Your mother was terribly confused and desperate to believe it was the only way to put an end to her guilt and suffering."

"Because of me. Because of me!" he cried, dropping his face to his hands, slumped over on the therapist's soft leather couch.

"I want you to listen to me," he said, placing a firm hand on Billy's shoulder. "There was nothing you could do. You were only a child, an extraordinarily intelligent, resourceful little boy who needed to find a way to escape his own pain. Which is exactly what you did."

"How? By going fucking insane? By losing my mind?"

"No. By using your mind to create alternate personalities to take on the string of horrors you couldn't handle alone. These alters you created, they're all still inside you trying to find their way in the world, and with your help they can."

"You want me to believe different parts of me come out whenever they want to, do things I would never do, talk to people I never met and go places I've never been?"

"At times... during your blackouts, but sometimes you've been there with them when they've come out."

"That's crazy. I... I don't buy it. It's all too weird. I'm a psycho and you know it. You just don't want to say it to my face. If you don't have a pill to fix me, this is a waste of time."

Jerry shook his head and leaned forward. "You're not a psycho, Billy. I know it's a difficult thing to accept, but bear with me a minute. I want you to listen to something."

The therapist rewound the tape and pressed play. Helen began her sad tale of the infant's earliest days alone and unwanted in the hospital nursery. When Billy listened to the voice of the Little One, he couldn't believe what he was hearing. He turned to Jerry. "That's *my* memory. How did you do that? How did you know what happened to me before I did?"

Jerry paused the tape. "Because, you told me."

"But I wasn't there when you were talking to... to them," he said, pointing to the tape.

"But you were. You were there the entire time. Just not in the first person."

As the tape continued, Billy heard the therapist engage Helen in conversation once again, followed by the emergence of the high-spirited Jacobellis as he buzzed around the room. He heard Jerry's promise to take the boy frog hunting one day in exchange for the chance to speak with the one person who needed to hear what they all had to tell him.

What came next rattled Billy to the core --

"Do I know you?" the tape revealed, undeniably in Billy's own voice.

"My name is Jerry. Jerry Tomkins. I'm a therapist and a friend of Julie's. And you are...?"

"I'm Billy. Billy Rubin."

As Jerry turned off the recorder, Billy looked up at him. His eyes filled with tears, his body punished beyond exhaustion.

"I'm... I'm a... multiple," he said, his voice shaken and distant.

"It's nothing to be frightened of," Jerry reassured him. "In fact, it's just the opposite. So many of your alters have qualities to be proud of. They're caring, hardworking, intelligent, funny, even gifted. They just need your help to come together and heal."

"How... how can I do that if I don't even know who they are?"

"But you do. You've already met most of them at Highwater."

"At Highwater? I don't understand..."

"Highwater is your creation. It's all in your mind, Billy. Dr. Rasher sent you there so you'd have a safe place to get to know them better. So you could all start playing on the same team."

Billy stared at Jerry in disbelief, "You mean... the Bellevederes? Henry, Barney, Benish, Huff... all of them? They only exist up here?" he asked, pointing to his head.

The therapist nodded, as he leaned back in his chair.

"What about Popwell?"

"Especially Popwell. His job, among other things was to take on the challenge of living with dissociate identity disorder so you wouldn't have to."

"And Armand and the Titans..."

"Yes, and Miss Duncan and the guards. They are *all* different parts of you, as is Timmy and Cal and Helen and Charley.

Billy shuddered at the thought of Charley being part of him. Horrified to imagine how Charley's behavior must have appeared to Julie. "Julie! Oh shit... she must hate me for what I put her through."

"I doubt that," Jerry responded, shaking his head. "As difficult as it was at times, she never gave up on you."

Billy grabbed Jerry's hand. "Then you've got to help me explain it all to her. You've got to help me make her understand -- the things I said. The things I did – it wasn't really me. I swear I'll do anything. Just tell me how I stop being a multiple? How do I get them to leave me alone? Or do I have to stay fucked up like this forever?"

"Of course not. There's no reason to give up on yourself. Or your alters. Once you begin to accept them, you can start to heal. In time, with proper guidance, there's no reason you can't lead a pretty normal life... as normal as life can be for an incredibly gifted, major league ballplayer.

Billy looked confused. "But that's not me. That's Popwell. If you leave out the one game I played with the Royals, Billy Rubin never made it out of the minors."

"Yeah. You did," Jerry stated calmly, as he nudged today's paper across the table. "Go ahead. Have a look."

Billy stared at the headline of the Trib –

'BILLY RUBIN'S RETURN STILL A QUESTION MARK HARGROVE TAPS DUNAWAY TO START GAME SEVEN'

Billy slowly lifted his head. His eyes drifted up to meet Jerry's reaffirming nod.

91

It was like waking from a dream, or being trapped inside a nightmare. Billy couldn't tell which as he approached the entrance to the clubhouse. Before now, the only time he could remember being here was when he came down with Popwell for their tryouts. But this time the locker room was crowded with strangers. These men were his teammates, and yet, aside from Chapman, each was a face he recognized only from watching them play on TV. There wasn't one among them Billy had an actual memory of having met or spoken to before.

When Kip caught sight of him, he walked over and offered his hand. Billy could tell Kip's entanglement in the sordid Rasher scandal had taken its toll. "It's sure good to see ya," Kip said, his voice a bit ragged, his eyes far less innocent, but the sincerity of his handshake came through loud and clear. "Your coming back today sure means a lot to the team. Me and the guys want you to know how awful sorry we were to hear… you know, about… Julie losing the baby."

He was appreciative of Kip's kind words and taken by surprise by the generous outpouring of sympathy that followed from the rest of the team.

Billy looked around. Popwell's locker was nowhere to be found. But, one bearing the name Rubin was located at the far end of the clubhouse. As he tentatively slid his arm through the sleeve of the Cub uniform bearing his name, it felt as if he was stepping inside someone else's skin. He was certain any second someone would catch on and ask him to leave. But no one did. And so he rose from the bench, took a deep breath, and followed his teammates out onto the field.

It was the first clear evening since the deluge began. From the Waveland rooftop by the firehouse, to the Skyboxes on Sheffield, and all the timeworn buildings in between, no one felt closer to Heaven than the frenzied Cub fans. The stately edifices pre-dating the ballpark shook and rattled, straining to contain their joyous, stomping, rooftop madness.

Weddings had been postponed, vacations and non-essential surgeries, cancelled. Kids up way past bedtimes feasted on hot dogs and cotton candy, their gluttony unnoticed by parents too wrapped in their own giddy delirium to care.

Dunaway had been on the mound through seven shutout innings. And although he gave up four runs in the eighth, by the time the inning thundered to a close, the venerable, old green scoreboard proudly heralded, Cubs 9, Red Sox 4, due in large part to Chapman's two, three-run homers. The young ballplayer's extraordinary exploits on the field easily overshadowed any lingering suspicions surrounding his involvement in the recent murder/suicide. Frankly, after today, most Cub fans would likely have forgiven Kip even if he had been the one who pulled the trigger.

It was the last chance for the Red Sox as Dunaway returned to the pitcher's mound to start the ninth. Although he still looked fresh, and was sporting a five run lead, Hargrove watched him like a hawk, as his pitch count was nearing a hundred. Alfonse Tecata was already up, throwing in the bullpen.

Dunaway served up some heat to the Boston lead-off batter. But the scrappy hitter hung in, fouling off twelve straight, before beating out a slow roller up the third base line. The next batter laced a double into the left field corner, and the curtain came down on Dunaway, as Hargrove headed for the hill and pulled the southpaw to a standing ovation.

Tecata bounded in from the bullpen, eager to put the finishing touches on what has been a miraculous season. The capacity crowd was on its feet, pleading for Tecata to shut the Red Sox down. But the first batter he faced ripped a blazing liner up the middle that nearly took the big right-hander's head off. And just like that, the Cub lead was reduced to 9-6, with a runner on first and nobody out.

They still had a three run cushion, so there was no need to panic. But panic swept in like a tidal wave, as Tecata's control deserted him at the worst possible time, walking the next two batters, loading the bases. Suddenly the Red Sox were back in it, with the go ahead run advancing to the plate.

A biting October wind blew through the dugout, but Hargrove was sweating like a steamy August night. He never thought he'd need to use another pitcher beyond Tecata. No one was even warming up in the bullpen. Then he thought about Chandari's psychic visions, and about the one man he'd pinned his Championship hopes on for weeks. That was of course before he had a meltdown in Game Five and went AWOL. Hargrove pulled at an eyebrow, weighing his options. Would he be totally insane to replace Tecata with a mentally unstable loose cannon?

At this point, every available pitcher had one eye on the field and the other trained on the wireless bullpen phone clutched in the pitching coach's hand, waiting for it to ring. Every man but Billy, who closed his eyes and prayed the fate of the World Series would not fall onto his shoulders.

When the bullpen coach took the call and told him to start warming up, Billy stopped praying and rose from the bench like a man heading for the guillotine.

Hargrove strode to the mound hoping a few inspiring words might help Tecata squelch the rally. But despite Hargrove's pep talk, the onslaught continued. The next batter lined a single to right on Tecata's very next pitch. Another two runs came across the plate leaving runners on first and third, still nobody out, and the Cubs barely clinging to a slim one run lead. Hargrove shot out of the dugout like a torpedo, signaled the bullpen, then ripped the ball from Tecata's grasp. The hapless pitcher, his eyes lowered to the ground, slunk back to the dugout amid a chorus of catcalls and boos.

The Red Sox fans came storming back to life, confident, if there was a way for the Cubs to blow it in the end, they would. They began chanting, "The Curse! The Curse!" as they held up their scrappy toy goats and overstuffed wooly black cats.

Beneath the ethereal, third quarter moon, Billy felt the ghosts of Wrigley's past glory days upon him, as he made his way to the pitcher's mound. His heart beat in double-time as Hargrove handed him the ball.

Cub fans screamed their approval, shouting, "BILL...EEE, BILL...EEE... !"

He knew his catcher and everyone in the crowd was expecting him to a throw a knuckleball. He searched his memory, trying to recall anything Popwell tried to teach him back in Highwater's garage. But, it was useless. It just wasn't there.

Determined to stay focused, he decided his best shot would be to see if he could manage a reasonably decent curve ball from his old street ball days, or perhaps he might be able to come up with a solid slider.

The catcher was baffled by Billy's choice of warm up tosses, but was certain whatever the crazy pitcher had up his sleeve was good enough for him.

Billy picked up the rosin bag, and bounced it around in his hand, as the Red Sox power hitting right fielder, Jason Swift, loosened up in the on-deck circle. Sweet Jesus, Billy thought, this guy had the best batting average in the American League. How the hell was he expected to get him out?

Then he remembered what Jerry told him during their session. How it was possible to call on his alters when he needed them; to tap into their strength; to connect with them in something the therapist called co-consciousness. He felt a little foolish attempting something so bizarre in the ninth inning of the World Series, in the middle of Wrigley Field, but he closed his eyes and concentrated on Popwell.

It was jarring when Popwell suddenly appeared inside his head. Billy took a step back, having never experienced the ability to bring someone living inside him into his consciousness at will.

"Is... is this where you take over, and I disappear?" Billy asked, with rising trepidation.

Popwell fixed him with a stoic gaze. "No. I'm done. I don't want to be the one out front anymore. It's your turn. Besides, we both know it's always been Billy Rubin the fans came out to see."

"Me? But I never pitched a real game in my life. This is nuts. There's no way I could do it."

"Sure you can."

"How?"

"By knowing what I can do, you can do."

"You make it sound so easy."

"I didn't say it would be easy. But you and I both know it's time."

Billy shivered. His eyelids fluttered. Then, everything and everyone inside his head went quiet as he stepped back onto the mound. He took a deep, cleansing breath and gazed up at the huge, red, white and blue World Series buntings and banners glistening beneath the stadium lights. His fingers tingled as they tightened around the white leather ball pressed firmly against his palm. Unsure what might happen next. He decided to let fate guide his hand. He dug his nails in below the seams, his pinky slid off to the side, his thumb beneath. He went into the windup, kicked his leg high, and threw --

Billy was astonished as he watched the mesmerizing knuckleball fly from his grip. It taunted the batter with its slow, steady path. The batter swung at empty air as the ball took a wicked turn to the inside corner and dropped into the catcher's mitt.

"STIRRR-IKE ONE," screamed the ump. The crowd erupted, hoping, praying, Billy could put out the fire.

On the following pitch, the batter swung and hit a high pop to third. Finally, an out. A huge sigh of relief from the faithful.

The raucous chanting continued. BILL EEE... BILL EEE. Teeth were chattering, knees were knocking, as the Red Sox cleanup batter stepped in. Billy came set and kicked. Strike one, yelled the umpire. Billy wasted little time delivering his next pitch. Suddenly, the runner on third broke for the plate. The power-hitting slugger crossed up the defense and laid down a bunt. The runner dove head first into home.

Billy raced over and shouted to his teammates to let it roll. All anyone could do now was watch and pray. The crowd held their breath as the ball traveled up the first base line heading straight for the bag. Billy waited, waving his arms, willing the ball to go foul. A few inches from the base, the ball slowed, almost to a stop. The Cub fans groaned... then miraculously, the ball veered off into foul territory. A roar ripped throughout the stadium. One pitch later, the batter was out on strikes.

The fans were on their feet. Two outs, runners at the corners, the Cubs clinging to a tremulous, one run lead. The Red Sox batter ran the count full. He glared defiantly, his shoulders taut, his jaw clenched, as his calloused hands had a stranglehold on the pine tarred bat. Billy came set, and sailed a slow knuckleball toward home.

The batter took a mighty swing. His flubber-like cheeks flapping in its wake.

The crowd roared. The Cubs dugout emptied. The players exploded onto the infield, leaping and shouting as if world peace had been declared. But, who could blame them. No longer the lovable losers, tonight they were heroes and kings. Hargrove's kids rushed to their father's side as the manager, overwhelmed by emotion, dropped to his knees and flung his cap skyward.

It was sheer pandemonium. Grateful, joyous masses of humanity spilled from their seats, converging onto the field, nearly trampling the team they loved so fiercely through a century of crushed hopes. In the process, bases were ripped from the dirt, handfuls of fabled Wrigley Field ivy were swiftly secured as souvenirs. Bottle rockets, worthy of the Bicentennial lit up the night sky, booming like cannons, yet barely audible beneath the spontaneous outburst of song, as literally thousands raised their voices as one; a singular, cathartic expression of unity and pride.

Billy lifted his eyes to the white victory flag proudly fluttering in the wind high above Wrigley. This was the moment of glory he had waited so long for.

But the triumph on this October night did little to offset the unsettling turn his life had taken.

92

The day after the World Series, Billy checked himself into a small mental health facility. He spent the next ninety days in the Intensive Care Dissociative Disorders Unit, learning how to connect with his alters. Unlike the illusory, stately towers of Highwater, The Maurice Redding Psychiatric Care Facility was a series of modest brick buildings with bars on the windows and a laundry list of restricted personal possessions.

At first, the alters were less than enthusiastic about the newly imposed limits on their individual freedoms. In particular, Charley and Armand, who continued to cause trouble with their petty, inter-alter pissing contests, hell bent on asserting their dominance any way they could. They flat-out refused to attend any of the group sessions, and did their level best to undermine Billy and Helen's efforts to work together to forge closer bonds with the younger alters.

Ten days into therapy, Billy took it upon himself to call a summit, if you will, to bring all the alters together at one time. He decided to offer each personality the opportunity to speak their mind freely, uninterrupted for as long as they wished. Billy started things off, addressing them as a group, apologizing for his past denial, and his alienating, and at times, combative behavior toward them, admitting how wrong he was to try and silence them. He told each one how very proud he was of their virtues and accomplishments and how much he believed he could benefit from their wisdom and input if they were willing to work together as a team.

Under the guidance of the institute's Chief of Psychiatry, the alters gradually began to come around, excited at the prospect of finally being acknowledged and appreciated by Billy. Each one flattered by being assigned important roles and specific responsibilities worthy of their talents. As the weeks went by, Billy became more and more comfortable embracing the mantle of leadership.

During his entire ninety-day stay, he had only two visitors. Frankie, who came by every other week to personally assess his client's progress and drop off the latest batch of cards and autograph requests from Billy's growing fan base. And Kip, who came just once to say goodbye.

Billy listened with newfound compassion as his teammate choked back tears when he told him his father died of a sudden heart attack two weeks after the World Series. Despite Frankie's best efforts, Kip made the decision to quit major league baseball and return to Tupelo to coach Little League and help his mother manage the farm. It wasn't just the loss of his father that prompted his decision to leave baseball. He still loved the game, just not the lifestyle, or the intense pressure and attendant public scrutiny that came with playing in the majors.

On Frankie's next visit, Billy was surprised by the agent's rather Zen-like attitude about Kip's decision. Reluctantly, Frankie owned up to being devastated when Kip first announced he was hanging up his cleats. However, as word got around how he had single-handedly championed Billy and Kip's careers, the blow of Kip's departure was sufficiently softened when six of Scott Erikson's top clients jumped ship to sign with the Frank Tortiricci Agency.

Success was sweet, and definitely had its rewards, Frankie noted, as he headed for the parking lot after dropping off another box of balls for Billy to sign and Frankie to hawk on the internet. Before getting into his car, he noticed a note had been left on the windshield of his recently purchased, shiny new Jaguar. He glimpsed at it briefly, then tossed it aside. It didn't concern him in the least that he was illegally parked in the covered handicapped spot out front. Let's face it, there was no way he was going to leave his brand new Jag out where the fucking birds could crap on it. He was through being crapped on by anyone or anything.

Frankie thought about Kip's recent loss, and the warm and loving relationship Chapman had enjoyed with his parents, and wondered if it wasn't too late to turn things around with his own. Who knows? Maybe he should give it one last try.

He glanced at his watch. Right about now his parents would be sitting down to dinner. His mom parked upstairs at the kitchen table, dreaming of a life she never had, and Frank Sr., down in the basement, sprawled across his Barcalounger in front of the TV, balancing a bowl of chili on his lap.

He stared at his cell resting on the soft leather passenger seat beside him, drummed his fingers on the steering wheel for a second or two, and then –

"Nah! What the fuck for!?" he muttered, as he jammed the key in the ignition, and shook off whatever soft-headed idea he may have had in a weaker moment. Frank Tortiricci liked who he was. He no longer needed anyone else's validation, least of all his father's.

A few months later, on a snow-dusted morning in late January, Billy placed fresh flowers on his daughter's grave, now gently tucked beneath a blanket of white. "Hi Katie-girl," he whispered. "I'm sorry I haven't been by to see you in a while, but I've been working real hard to make you proud of your dad."

As he stood amidst the towering, snow-crested trees that shrouded the cemetery grounds, he tried to imagine his beautiful daughter, happy and at peace, playing with the angels, her loving grandmother by her side.

He cast his eyes to his mother's headstone, but an arm's length away. Then reached over and brushed aside the faded, crinkled leaves Autumn left behind, encased within frosted sheets of ice and snow. They reminded him of the muted collages he labored to construct in art therapy class at the clinic.

He knelt down beside his mother's grave, impervious to the dampness seeping into the fabric of his pant legs. Instead, he felt only the warmth of the Bellevederes, and the Titans gathering around him, respectfully bowing their heads. Helen and Miss Duncan brushed back tears as they drew the restless, younger alters close beside them to pay their respects as well.

Billy threw back his shoulders and took in a deep breath. There was so much he wanted his mother to know. That he now understood the pain she struggled with for so many years. That he was finally free to let go of the resentment and anger he held inside for way too long. He wanted her to know he was healing, that the horrors of the past were slowly being put to rest. That there was real hope for a normal future – a future that now held the promise of happiness. In that instant, he could feel his mother's loving arms around him. He could smell the sweet lilac scent of her touch.

"Take care of her, Mom. Watch over little Katherine for me."

When he stood up and turned around, he saw her standing on the cobblestone path behind him.

"I tried to stay away," Julie sighed, with resignation. "But I just couldn't." Her eyes glistened with tears, her lips offering a slight lop-sided smile, as she took off her glove and held out her hand. It felt warm and sure inside his own.

They sat silently, side-by-side on the bench closest to their daughter's grave. After a moment, Julie leaned back and rested her head against the familiar fold between his neck and shoulder.

Billy looked up. A Peregrine falcon was perched on a treetop high above their heads. His eyes followed as it spread its majestic wings and took flight. A feeling of contentment engulfed him. He closed his eyes and listened to the gentle whisper of the lightly falling snow, and for the first time, in a long time, Billy felt whole.

ACKNOWLEDGEMENTS

Thank you to those special friends, family, and colleagues, especially to those who read through early and partial drafts too long ago and dusty to even recall; who, when asked for 'honest opinions,' offered them despite reservations that we might not want to hear them. Thank you to Diane and Jeff for their encouragement and punctuation. A special thank you to Nicole, whose sensitive, tactful, and supremely valuable editorial skills and publishing knowledge managed to keep us moving forward, all the while balancing her own literary career and receiving her PhD throughout the journey. Thank you to our loving sister, Barbara who was among the first to bravely read, comment and encourage us, and who also managed to laugh and cry at all the appropriate places; to Bill who read, and re-read, and agonized along with us over a multitude of large and small details, and title choices that only another author could appreciate.

And thank you to the Hollywood Entertainment Industry in general, within which we worked for over two decades, for showing us how truly liberating creative writing can be without the constraints of show runners, network executives, and budgetary restraints.

www.ingramcontent.com/pod-product-compliance
Lightning Source LLC
Chambersburg PA
CBHW031414240626
47154CB00001B/38